THE SPARK & THE STAR

TESS HUNTER

BOOK ONE OF THE TIMECHARTER TRILOGY

Book Cover by Clint English

Map Illustration by Jamie Whyte

Author Photo by Morgan Busby

Interior Formatting and Family Tree by Tess Hunter

First Edition 2026

theinksters.com

For Mom, Dad, and my Inksters

TUNDRA
MOUNTAINS
STEPPE
TAIGA
SOUTHREACH
POLYMIA
OLD KIROV
LUN RIVER
SOL RIVER
PETROVIA'S ESTATE
IZUMGRAY
EMERALD RIV
NORGAY
TEIGA
VON
URIK
DUR
THE ROTOV ISLES
LAKE LEBGAY 'THE SWAN'
THE BROKEN FORK
SOLVIA RIVER
UGLA RIVER
ORGENIA RIVER
VARGESH RIVER
ANKESH RIVER
UNSEEN BAY
SEEN BAY
NEW KIROV
KIROV RIVER FORTRESS
KIROV RIVER
WYLBURG
WYLORD
SCANDIA
SCANDIAN OCEAN

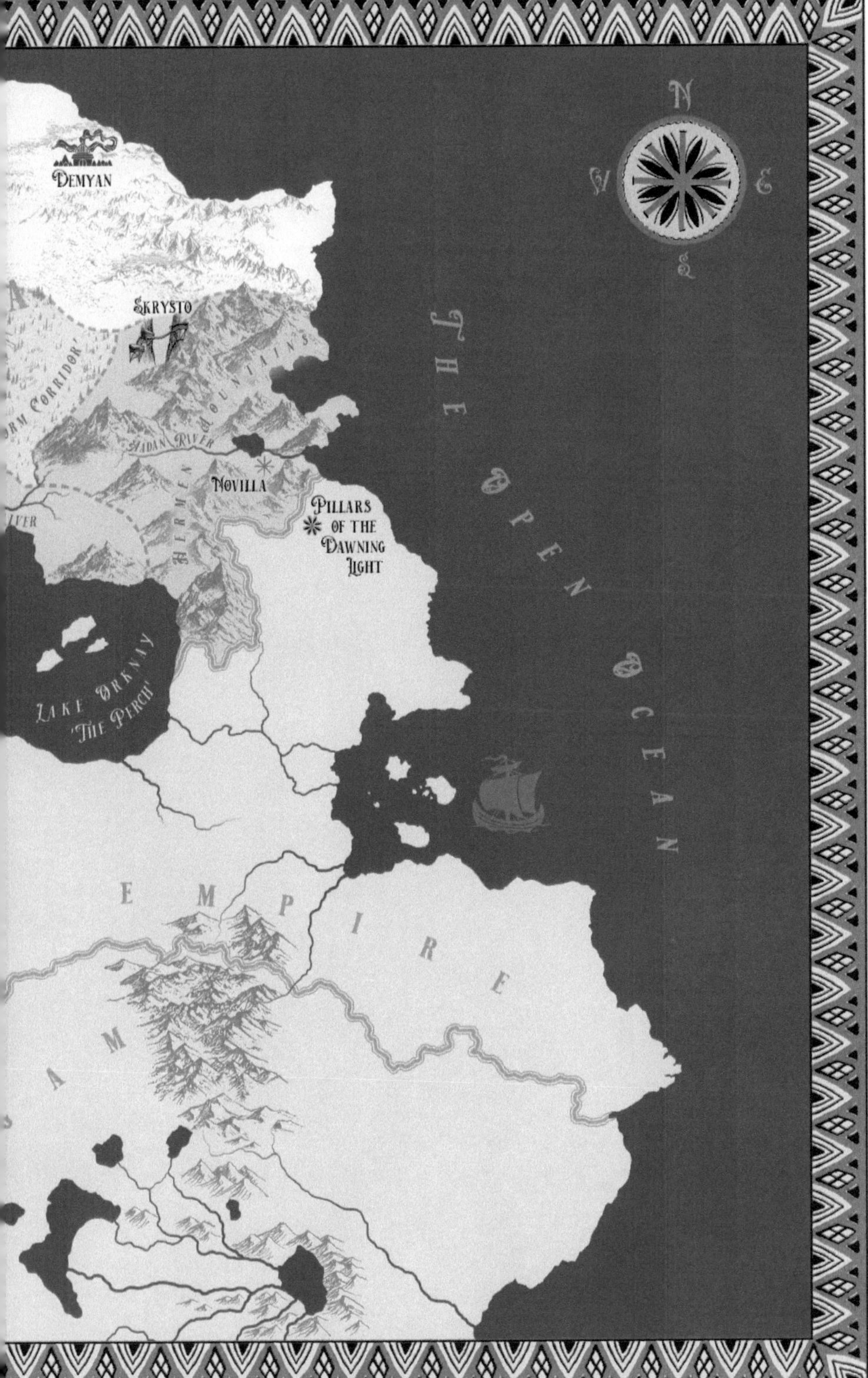
N
W
E
S
Demyan
Skrysto
Storm Corridor
Mountains
Hadan River
Novilla
Hermen
Pillars of the Dawning Light
River
Lake Orknay
'The Perch'
The Open Ocean
Empire

ALKHEMICAL FIRE GRADES

MUNDANE

Bleeds red and can douse an alkhemical flame.

CENTRAL

Bleeds blue. The fire of creation. Neither warm nor burning to touch.

SECRET

Bleeds purple. Primary fire for lab work. Has direction and purpose like a weapon. Can achieve anything Central fire can do.

CELESTIAL

Bleeds silver. Highest grade. Represents the power of divine will. Shines without burning. Colorless and odorless. Can achieve anything Secret and Central fire can do.

ALKHEMICAL FOCUS

SPIRITUAL

Transformation of the soul. Does not strictly require the use of Alkhemical fire.

ARTISTIC

Manipulation of material matter. Requires Central fire.

PROPHETIC

Hypnotherapy, dream therapy, shamanic journeying, astrology, prophecy, charting stars. Requires Central fire.

MEDICINAL

Treats afflictions of the body and mind. Requires Secret fire.

CELESTIAL

The most revered focus. Can transform human abilities, such as increased speed, stamina, strength. Requires Celestial fire.

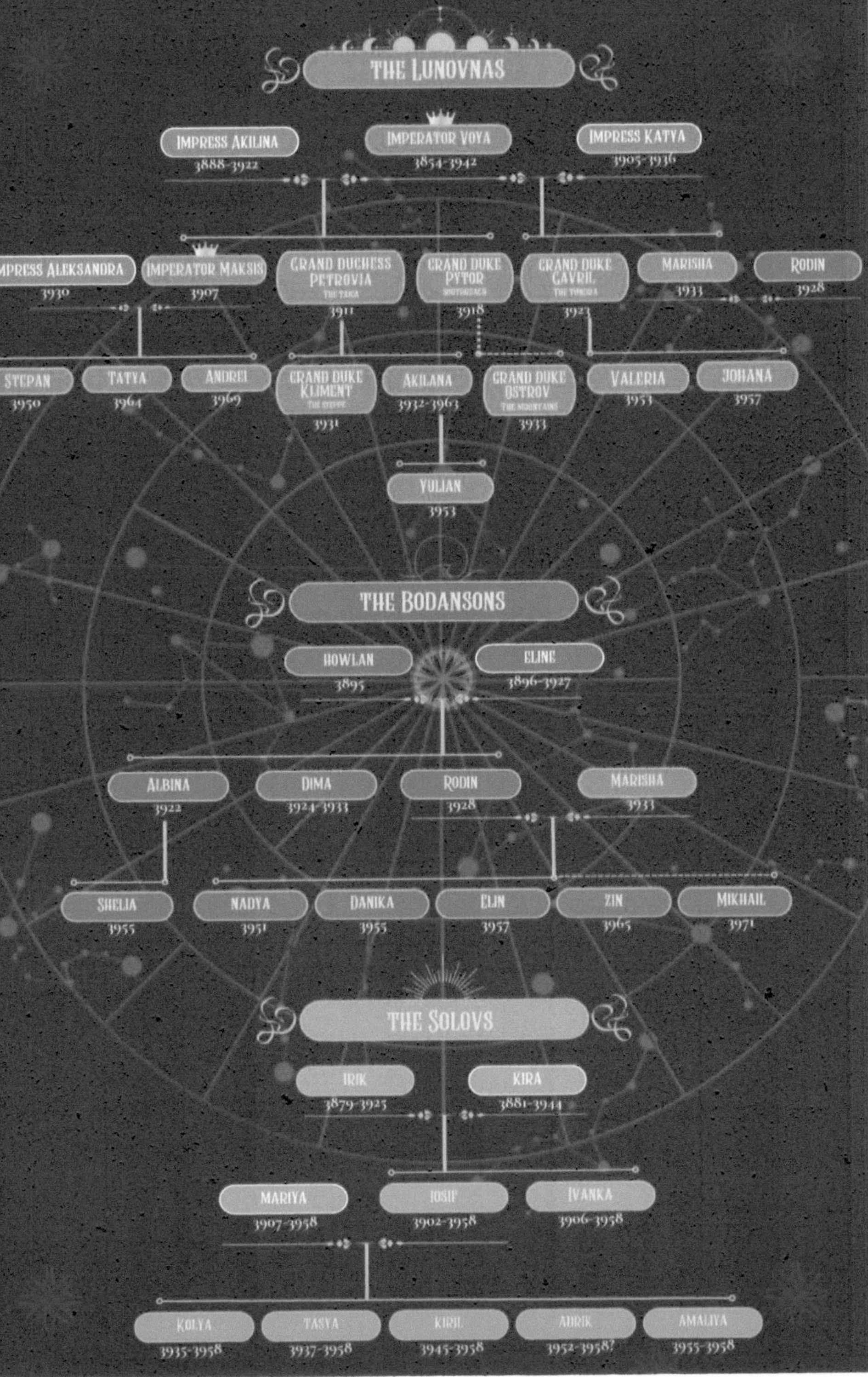
The Lunovnas
Impress Akilina
3888-3922
Imperator Voya
3854-3942
Impress Katya
3905-3936
Mpress Aleksandra
3930
Imperator Maksis
3907
Grand Duchess Petrovia
3911
Grand Duke Pytor
3918
Grand Duke Gavril
The Tundra
3923
Marisha
3933
Rodin
3928
Stepan
3950
Tatya
3964
Andrei
3969
Grand Duke Kliment
3931
Akilana
3932-3963
Grand Duke Ostrov
The Mountains
3933
Valeria
3953
Johana
3957
Yulian
3953
The Bodansons
Howlan
3895
Eline
3896-3927
Albina
3922
Dima
3924-3933
Rodin
3928
Marisha
3933
Shelia
3955
Nadya
3951
Danika
3955
Elin
3957
Zin
3965
Mikhail
3971
The Solovs
Irik
3879-3925
Kira
3881-3944
Mariya
3907-3958
Iosif
3902-3958
Ivanka
3906-3958
Kolya
3935-3958
Tasya
3937-3958
Kiril
3945-3958
Adrik
3952-3958?
Amaliya
3955-3958

Content Warning

This story contains multiple POVs from characters early on in their journey to understanding themselves and the world around them. They are unreliable narrators. They have thoughts and take actions that are ableist. They experience inappropriate sexual relationships and power dynamics, physical abuse, dubious consent, and semi-graphic violence. The author does not condone these behaviors, but strives to depict the often self-sabotaging choices humans can make as imperfect people in an imperfect world.

CONTENTS

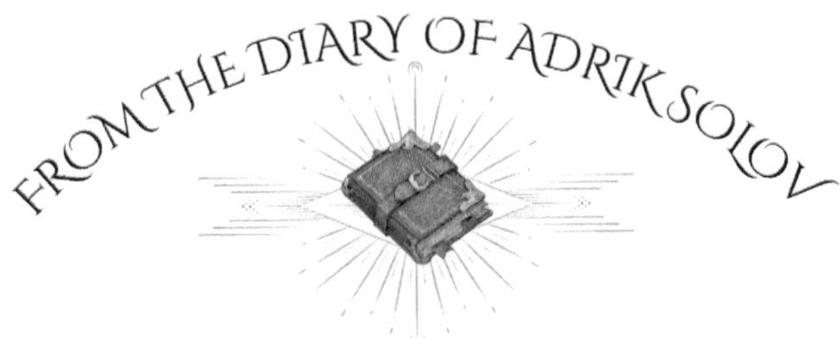

FROM THE DIARY OF ADRIK SOLOV

THE FOURTH DAY OF THE FIRST TENNIGHT OF AUTUMN
YEAR 3974-LUNCYCLE

Remembering is hard — like trying to read a letter after the ink has spilt. Drips and drabs and scattered meaning. But I try. I press my palms to my eyes until they're throbbing, and try.

The room stank of blood. I was a child then, but I knew the stench. I'd seen a pig slaughtered once and this wasn't much different. The squeals, the pops of flesh. The heat. It was no wonder the guard's hand slipped on my throat. As a man grown, I now recognize the war in the guard's eye. Duty or conscience? In the hesitation, I snuck away. The guard carried on.

He'll be an old man now. Retired to the capital, grown fat with his jolly wife. He'll have watched his grandchildren play at his feet, licking salt beef from his fingers. Maybe he's taken time for the theatre and learned to appreciate the ballet. But I do not care.

I do not care about the grandchildren, or the jolly wife, or the guilt. I don't even care about the mercy. When the time comes, the guard will die like Papa — wide-eyed and eager. Like Mama, a rope of red around her throat. Like my brothers, their chests flailing. My sisters — the oldest, Tasya, on a spear; or baby Amaliya crushed beneath a boot.

When the time comes, the guard will die with his masters.

And I will remember every bit of it.

I. AN UNEXPECTED RETURN

The boat appeared on the horizon exactly as Nadya had dreamt it.

True, she had seen Danika's coming in the clear night, the planet of Mercia burning high and bright above — and presently, the sky was a muggy gray, clouds bloated with rain. In the dream, Nadya had worn a thin white shift. Shards of ice pebbled along her face and arms, skin a cage — fragile and dangerous as a layer of frost over a still pond in Wetwinter. Her hair hung limply down her back, nearly transparent in the moonlight; and she clung to the edge of the emerald cliffside, toes curling into the damp grass as if Baba Yaga herself was about to shove her into the solid black waves yawning below.

Currently, however, Nadya stood solid, buffeted against a warm westward wind. Her legs and arms banded in cotton strips. Her usual tunic and apron tied tight around her waist. Hair tucked snugly into a knot at the back of her neck.

But so far as Nadya was concerned, such differences between dreams and reality, Above and Below, mattered little in the turning of the world. There was only one thing that mattered. One thing she knew for certain — her sister was coming home.

The Swansea churned beneath the approaching skiff, as impenetrable to outsiders as steel plate to a dull spear. But Danika was a Kotov, and like all people who lived upon these waters, the tide would bring her in.

Nadya locked her knees, resisting the urge to race down the rocky incline to meet the boat. Mama had called Nadya's errand foolhardy, clucked her tongue and pursed her lips when Nadya told her of the dream that had woken her before dawn. "Don't let that girl disappoint you again, Nedeshda," Mama had said, delicate hands turned brutal as she chopped turnips for the evening stew.

After all, Danika's return was not expected for another thirty days — thirty days of which Nadya would have counted every one. But as the vessel navigated the razor-sharp shore and nestled into its cove, as Danika crested the hilltop and emerged between two prickly bramble hedges, as she joined Nadya at the top of the northernmost peak of the isle they called home, Nadya was grateful to have ignored Mama's naysaying just this once.

A fine mist clung to the hem of Danika's alkhemist's coat. Made of white-fishskin, it shone pearly in the gray light. A leather rucksack dangled from one shoulder, and her hair, a darker blonde to Nadya's light, had been cut to just below her chin. Nadya closed the short distance between them and pressed a kiss to Danika's cheek. She smelled of salt-air and fire.

"I dreamt of your coming," Nadya said.

Danika's face twisted, brow wrinkled. Nadya kissed that too. Just to irritate her.

Whatever Mama or Danika's doubts, Nadya was not swayed. The essence of her dream had been true. Her sister had returned. The only question remaining was why.

Fear bounded in her throat and she scanned Danika with a sharper gaze. "You have returned too soon. Are you ill?"

Danika's face was flushed, but not feverish. She was tall and thin as ever, but not starved. Her gait seemed steady — it would have to be to climb all the way to the isle's peak. There was no obvious cause for alarm, save the blank irritation on her face at Nadya's pestering.

"I am perfectly well," Danika said sharply. "Though stifling hot. Summer is long over, is it not?"

"Tell The Mother. She does not set herself by the Volodyan Calendar."

"If only we could all be so fortunate." There was an ache in Danika's voice. Nadya struggled to find some words of comfort, knowing they would be in vain. There was no stopping the Cycle, and few would suffer its results more keenly.

"You have the Celestial Fire. Some would call that very lucky indeed," Nadya said, taking Danika by the wrist. She ran her thumb along the vein, where a shimmer of a silver-white glowed beneath pale skin. "If you are not ill, why have you come?"

Danika snatched her arm away and started up the gravel path carved between two high rocks. "My instructors sent me back early to finish my final work. It can be done just as well here as from Izumgray."

The narrowness of the lane forced Nadya to keep a step behind. Their turf-house had the finest view on the Von, but the steep climb to and from the shore ensured they paid for it. "How soon will you have to go back?" Nadya queried.

Danika stumbled and caught herself on the outcropping.

"Nika?"

"It is nothing. This coat is ill-suited to the weather. I will have to change into my linens."

"I have never seen you so eager to shed your coat — whatever the weather. Your first Autumn back from Izumgray, Mama had to force you to take it off to sleep."

"I have little need of it on the Isles. I will have no need of it at all soon enough. Why not accept the inevitable?"

Nadya focused on the sharp line of Danika's shoulders. She knew her sister better than anyone, considered it her honor to be the only one among the family who could see past the mask, honed and hard-won as it was. And with as much certainty as Nadya had known Danika would return home early, she knew that Danika was lying now.

Nadya grabbed Danika's shoulder and swung her around. "What has happened? It is not like you to give up before the end."

"What can be done in a year, Nadya?" Danika's voice echoed hollowly. A pair of hawks cawed to each other overhead. They swooped perilously close to the clifftops before darting away again. "What can I do to delay the inevitable? The Suncycle will come, and with it, alkhemy will vanish. Everything I have worked for, everything I hoped to achieve, everything I am... will be gone."

"Alkhemy is *not* all that you are."

Danika stared flatly back at her. None of them knew for sure what a life without alkhemy would look like. It had been twenty-four years since the last Suncycle. Nadya and her siblings had only ever lived under The Mother's moon — the Luncycle — the life *with* alkhemy.

She had heard the stories, of course. The disease, the poverty, the longing for another quarter-century to pass. It affected all of Sivka and the Kotov Isles — even those without the gift of the Alkhemical Flame. Perhaps it affected those most of all. It was a dark time, despite its moniker. Not even Nadya could find a reason to look forward to it and she did not have nearly so much to lose as Danika.

Nadya shifted her hold to the back of Danika's neck. "You will not give up your coat, Danika. Promise me. Not yet."

"There is something I should tell you—"

"It can wait. Your promise cannot."

Danika took in a breath, meeting Nadya's gaze directly for the first time since she had come ashore. Her stormy blue eyes to Nadya's cool clear ones — the sea and the sky, as Papanik called them.

"I promise, Nadya. I will not give up."

Fragrant white blossoms still teemed on the turfhouse roof despite the approaching Autumn. Zin and Mikhail sat crouched in the dooryard around a patch of bare earth, cups in hand, dice scattered in the dirt.

As Nadya pushed through the wattle-gate, its creak caught their attention. Their heads popped up in tandem, eyes widening as Danika emerged into the yard. Zin let out a wordless squeak, Mikhail shouted, "Nika!" and they both ran full-tilt into Danika's middle.

"Oof," Danika grunted. Her rucksack slid off her shoulder onto the grass. She pulled Mikhail into her arms, laying a kiss atop his brown curls. "Zin teaching you to play Liar's Dice already? The pair of you will make great alkhemists."

Zin stared up at Danika adoringly through her dark narrow eyes. The wholesome picture of Nadya's siblings reunited was completed only when the turf-house door flew open and Elin halted on the threshold.

Elin took one look at Danika's shorn locks, and said baldly, "You look like a boy."

Danika's hand fell from where it had been carding through Zin's sleek black hair. "You would know," she said, scowling.

"Difference is, I look like the kind of boy other boys want to fondle," Elin said, fists poised on her broad hips. It was true, her messy braid was a style both the Kotov boys and girls favored. Dirt marred her face, which was rough and briny underneath, as if she had recently stood on the bow of a fast moving vessel and breathed deep the sea air. The effect was not wholly unpleasant, if a little less refined than their Mama preferred.

Less-than-polite greeting concluded, Elin lurched forward and wedged herself between Zin and Mikhail. Danika let out another groan as Elin squeezed her. Elin was only two years Danika's junior, but at least a head shorter, and her face nestled directly into Danika's rather feeble bosom. "We missed you, Nika."

Tears pricked the corners of Nadya's eyes. She, Danika, Elin, Zin and Mikhail — home on the Kotov Isles, together, where they belonged.

"I cannot believe Nadya's dream was right," Elin added with a coarse laugh and Danika shook her head.

"Even lobsters fly once a Cycle."

Zin was the first to abandon Danika in favor of rummaging through the discarded rucksack. A moment later, Elin joined her. Privacy was not a concept the Kotov valued much, even discounting sibling nosiness, but Danika had picked up Sivkan habits in her time at Izumgray and Nadya could see the annoyance on her face.

"Tell me you brought back some spices," Elin said, tossing a bundle of knotgrass carelessly over her shoulder. "Mama is in the kitchen trying to milk flavor out of whitefish without so much as a pinch of salt."

Danika snatched the bag away, but not before Nadya saw Zin slip some small token into the front pocket of her tunic. "At Izumgray, the Sivkans mock Kotov manners," Danika said. "You two make me remember why."

Elin sighed. They made their way into the turfhouse and Nadya smiled to see Danika shove a vial of rosemary into Elin's hand.

Danika's promise to Nadya ate at her all through dinner. She understood that her vow had little to do with her alkhemist coat. It was a promise not to give up. To not relent until the final moments of the Luncycle had ticked away and the last drop of quicksilver in her veins had dulled to mundane. Still, it felt as false as the lie Danika had told Nadya about her unexpected return.

High stakes indeed for someone slurping turnip stew.

Mama's chill gaze watched Danika choke down every morsel. The warm welcome she had received from her siblings had not extended to their matriarch. Their Mama, tall and fine and beautiful, had merely looked at Danika as she came through the door into the turfhouse. That one glance assessed her in an instant, from her whitefishskin coat to her cut hair to her Sivkan boots — so unsuited for the rocky hillsides of the Von — and said simply, "You are home then? The turnips need boiling."

Papanik — Papa's papa, Howlan Bodanson, grandson of Bodan himself — was cheerier in his greeting. He sat at his usual place in the main hall, a rocking chair beside an open fire, silver sparks drifting up toward the vents cut into the raftered ceiling. Another fire crackled at the far end of the hall and a long dining table lay between them. Fragrant mishsmoke and grilled fish mingled in the air.

Danika's stomach rumbled with that particular hunger that only accompanied the end of a long journey.

Papanik rose swiftly for a man of his age, pulling Danika into his chest, smoldering pipe still in hand. He was a bear of a Kotov with a wooden peg leg, and despite Danika's height, she felt swallowed whole inside his arms. She withdrew only with the greatest reluctance. "Where is Papa?" she asked.

"The Imperator has levied another tax," Papanik growled, scratching at his raggedy white beard with the long stem of his pipe. "Your papa has scarcely been home the last two tennights — too busy trying to stave off a revolution."

After the turnip boiling, the family drew to their usual places at the table like alkhemists to the athanor. The threatening storm finally broke as they took their seats. Rain pelted the wattle-and-daub walls, wind gusted through the narrow tunnels in the ceiling, fanning the flames one moment and nearly dousing them the next. But no draft or downpour could put out these fires, for they were ignited from the blood of an alkhemist, and only the blood of a mundane could extinguish them.

Danika took another bitter sip of stew under Mama's keen stare, feeling sure that, somehow, she already knew the secret Danika was so desperate to keep — that she could read Danika's failure all over her face.

"What is the matter, Nika?" Mama said in a sharp, clear voice that made Danika jump. "You do not care for my cooking?"

"It is very good," Danika protested. She sat straighter and gummed another mouthful. Elin snorted beside her.

"Then eat less like a bird and more like a person, if you please."

At the end of the table, Papanik hid a grin behind his spoon. The stew was tepid. In Izumgray, the plates and bowls would be infused to keep the food at the perfect temperature. But the Kotov believed that it was better to be prepared for the long years without alkhemy than to overindulge in the years with it.

A bang sounded as the front door flew open in the next room. The roar of the storm grew louder, then muffled again. The tread of familiar footsteps followed and, a moment later, Papa stepped into the hall.

Rodin Bondanson towered in the doorway, made twice his usual size with his heavy hide coat tied over his kaftan, a switch at his waistbelt. As he scanned the table, his warm brown eyes landed on Danika. He grinned and the eyes wrinkled. He stretched his arms wide. Danika flew from her seat and raced into them. She buried her face in his chestnut beard. He smelled of leather and rain and safety. He clutched her tight and whispered in her ear, "My little Nika. Back where she belongs."

For this, Danika thought, she could almost forego Izumgray entirely.

"Very well. You have seen her before, I think, and no doubt you will again," said Mama. "Sit down and eat."

Danika pulled away, but not before pressing a kiss to Papa's warm cheek.

She resumed her place between Elin and Zin as Papa took the wooden armchair at the end of the table. He smiled convincingly down at his lukewarm meal. With alkhemy or without, the whole of the family knew that Mama could not cook. She had not learned such mundane tasks early in life like most Kotov. But Papa had never concerned himself much with needing a wife who could brew stews and conjure casseroles. He found other qualities in Mama to value.

Though what those qualities were, Danika could not begin to guess.

"I hope there is enough. I seem to have grown an extra stomach on the voyage."

Mama turned her gaze from Danika to Papa, where it softened. "Do not attempt to flatter me in front of the children, Rodin."

"Yes, dearest."

"Nika spelled!" Mikhail exclaimed, spoon banging an uneven rhythm on his plate.

Unsmiling, Mama pinched the boy's cheeks. "Danika, it seems Mikhail is eager to hear more about your time in Sivka." The tension Papa's arrival had broken returned. Mama rarely called Danika's school by its proper name, simply referring to her absence as some long annual sojourn to the north. "We were not expecting you for another three tennights."

"It was very good," Danika answered, refocusing her attention on her stew. Even *it* was better than this line of questioning.

"Very good? Come — do not be so stingy with your tales. Tell us poor, isolated Kotov of the wider world."

You are no Kotov.

The thought flitted across Danika's mind unbidden, and she was grateful she had learned enough self-restraint not to voice it. Babbin would be proud. Still, her eyes lifted to Mama with no small amount of resentment.

There was no denying that Mama had the poised, imperial look of a Sivkan — and there was no ignoring why. Even seated over a rough Kotov table, Marisha Bodanson exuded a grace and elegance that, of her children, only Nadya could match. In fact, put next to each other as they were now, it was impossible to deny the similarities between Mama and her eldest daughter — their high cheekbones, sharp chins, long necks and delicate noses.

It was the last Danika envied the most. Her own nose had been the source of much ridicule during childhood, large and crooked as it was. Mama's ebony hair flowed long and black as the night sky at New Moon. Nadya's, in contrast, shone the palest gold, ever tied in a neat bun at the back of her neck — some halfhearted attempt to conceal its brilliance.

It was just one reason of many that Danika was grateful for her gift, her Fire. Without it, she would be all the more invisible.

"Still nothing to say for yourself?" Mama tsked.

Nadya ducked her head, two pink spots appearing on her cheeks — and Danika was reminded where the real difference between her older sister and Mama lay. They were both starkly beautiful, but Mama possessed none of Nadya's kindness to soften the edges.

"What news from the Telga?" Mama turned to Papa instead, who seemed as reluctant to share his secrets as Danika. He glanced anxiously at Papanik. In the distraction, Zin slid a piece of parchment across the table to Elin.

"I heard a troubling rumor out of Old Kirov," said Papa. "I would like to go to the Vienper tomorrow to see if I can dispel it. Perhaps Danika could join me? She knows that isle better than most."

He looked in her direction. Danika was only too happy to offer her agreement. She feared what other uses Mama would find for her otherwise. "Of course, Papa."

"Danika spelled!" Mikhail squawked again. Elin slipped the note under the table to Nadya before Danika could get a look.

Mama's lips pursed. "What rumor is this? What has the Imperator done now?" Like all of them, Mama understood that news from the capital city of Old Kirov truly meant news from Imperator Maksis Lunovna.

"We will discuss it later," said Papa. "I would rather hear of Danika's adventures."

She would have glared at him for turning the attention back on her, but her stomach was too busy twisting itself in knots to muster any expression at all. "I— Adventures? I would not call them—"

Nadya looked down at her lap and gasped. Her wide gaze returned to Danika, who raised an eyebrow. Nadya gave a tiny shake of her head and tucked the note into the folds of her apron.

"Danika spelled! Danika spelled!"

Mama slammed her spoon down. "Mikhail — what *are* you saying?"

"Danika—" Mikhail swallowed and forced himself to sound out the word in painful, earnest clarity. "Danika ex-spelled."

There was a moment's silence. Then—

"You were expelled?" Papa said slowly.

Danika found her expression then, and it was rage.

"Elin!" She turned on her nearest sister, who somehow managed to look both ashamed and proud.

"I didn't tell them!"

"*Them*?" Danika shouted, eyes flicking around the table to Zin and Nadya's guilty faces.

"I meant him — *him*!" said Elin. Then, seeing it was hopeless — "Oh, what does it matter? Zin stole the letter from your bag. She showed it to me. And I—"

"And you decided to spread the word?" Danika whipped to her other side where Zin slunk low on her bench. Danika knew on some level that her anger would be better directed at the thief, but Zin did not speak, so she could hardly be blamed for spreading gossip.

"I was explaining it to her! Then Mikhail overheard. You know he follows her everywhere," Elin reasoned. "And it didn't seem right for only Nadya not to know..."

Zin disappeared entirely under the table. Danika looked to Nadya and found confirmation in her sister's sky-blue eyes. The chain of betrayal seemed to stop there, and for a moment there was only the crackle of the fire and the sound of Mikhail gumming his spoon.

Then Danika launched herself at Elin.

Knocked her off the bench and tackled her onto the packed earth floor. She landed with a satisfying "oof," but it was not enough. Danika snatched her tin plate off the table and reared back to hit Elin over her stupid head in the Kotov way — but strong arms encircled her, dragging her backward.

Danika kicked and writhed and wriggled free of Papa's grasp just as Elin regained her feet. Elin rushed forward to exact her own revenge, but Papa lunged between them, hands outstretched.

"Enough!" he barked. It was a rare thing indeed for Papa to raise his voice under the turf. The resulting silence was like an ice bath thrown into a steaming cauldron. "I will not have bloodshed in these halls! I will have answers or you will both stay out in the rain until you come to an accord. Elin — apologize to your sister."

Elin's jaw dropped. "Me? Apologize to *her?* But she is the one who—"

"You betrayed Danika's trust. There is no deeper wound between siblings. Make it right."

"Sorry," Elin muttered churlishly.

Danika did not think that a sufficient show of remorse, but knew better than to ask for more. She would exact her price later. Papa turned next to Danika.

"Now you will answer for what you have kept hidden," he said, and it was the betrayal in his voice that cut Danika deepest. "Is what Mikhail says true?"

Danika's heart pounded, shame cloyed sticky in her throat, gums too tacky to speak. Everyone had come to their feet in the chaos — everyone but Papanik, who still sat eating his whitefish with single-minded intensity, as if this was all some sort of dinner theatre put on for his amusement.

"It is true," Danika finally answered.

Papa's arms fell to his sides. She expected his first question to be obvious — *why?* But he surprised her with an amendment. "Why did you lie?"

"I did not lie. I just did not tell the whole—"

"I do not know what they teach you in Sivka, Nika, but on the Kotov Isles that is a lie by another name. Explain yourself."

"I am sorry, Papa. I did not know how."

"I say again — why? Have we ever made you to feel like your alkhemy is the biggest part of you?"

"No." She had done that to herself.

"And have we ever pressured you into your studies? Into going to Izumgray in the first place?"

"No." If anything, it had been the opposite. Papa had never expressed his direct opposition, but Mama had. And only Nadya had ever voiced her support. Despite all they knew about her ambitions, her past, her *need* for alkhemy, they had never offered one word of encouragement.

"I did not want to be the first Kotov to go to Izumgray and fail."

There was nothing anyone could say. No argument to be brokered. It was simply an unbearable truth that had come to pass.

Eventually, Papanik laid down his fork. He looked directly at Danika from across the long table. "Any school that does not want our Little Nika is not worthy of the name."

A flush crept up her neck. "Thank you, Papanik."

Slowly, Zin crawled out from her hiding place. Mama returned Mikhail to the bench and Papa waved a hand. "Everyone sit. The turnips are getting cold."

After dinner, Nadya attended to the Oratorium with Mama. She did not always do so — she was not sure that she held to the practices of the Cyclican religion as Mama did.

As far as Nadya knew, their household was one of the few on the Kotov Isles that even had an Oratorium. Cyclican Celebrants rarely journeyed this far from Sivka for worship and if they did, most Kotov would not attend such services. They preferred a more natural form of worship, spurning idols or officiants, and instead finding peace in the Divine Spark at the root of all things — in nature, at the intersection of the world Above and the world Below.

But the thin vein in Mama's temple was pulsing wildly and Nadya knew it would only be calmed by a few moments knelt before the altar.

It sat in a darkened corner of the entry hall, lit by the Alkhemical Flame of a single candle. In a year's time, that candle would go out, and it would not light again for another twenty-five years. As Mama bowed her head, Nadya felt Danika's eyes on them from the bedloft overhead. Between Mama and Danika, Nadya did not know who to comfort first. But she would focus on Mama for now. Danika would follow.

She stared ahead at the central figure on the small table of the altar. A hemaphroditic Thoth, hewn from pale granite, wielding a moon-tipped spear and sun-adorned sheath. To the right and left of the Thoth figure perched two smaller idols carved from the same rock — a moon-decorated Mother, Lunovna; and a sun-bedecked Father, Solovich. Lastly, on the table by the candle, sat a small book with a cover so green it was almost black. Most households, both on the Kotov Isles and in Sivka, possessed a copy of the Velvet Book, but few were so fine as this one. It was one of the only relics of Mama's old life that she had chosen to share with her children.

After a suitable amount of time in silent prayer, Mama raised her head and opened her eyes. "As Above," she said.

"So Below," Nadya finished.

She climbed the ladder to the bedloft to find Zin already asleep. Danika, unsurprisingly, was not.

"Is she angry with me?" she asked as Nadya slipped beneath the linen sheet.

The stars had begun to break through the cloud cover. A circular shaft of moonlight pierced the warbled glass of a small skylight above the bed, illuminating Zin sprawled out on her stomach atop the blankets between them. The air was unseasonably hot and muggy, even with the storm breaking outside, and Zin had stripped off her nightgown. Her bare bottom shone like twin moons in the dim light.

"I do not think so," Nadya answered eventually. "She did not say anything."

"She never does. Not to me." Danika leaned back against a stack of pillows, knees bent, fiddling with something in her lap. She reminded Nadya of Zin, slouched under the table to avoid a scolding. Often it was easy to forget that Danika — with all her knowledge of alkhemy and the wider world — was Nadya's junior. But at times like these, the gap seemed to stretch well beyond a mere four years.

"What of you and Taito?" Danika whispered into the dark, clearly eager to change the subject. "Has he made you an offer yet?"

"If he has made one, he has made a dozen." Him and many others.

"And will you put him out of his misery?"

"I may accept him soon, yes. But whether that is the end of misery or the start of it, I do not know."

"Oh, Nedeshda," Danika sighed — as ever, reserving Nadya's true name for only the most trivial matters. She raised Nadya's knuckles to her lips and planted a kiss there. "He will be the happiest of men to have you for a wife. How could he not be? The great beauty of the Von."

Nadya only wondered if she would feel as blissful. "What is that in your hand?"

"Nothing." Danika's fist closed on a folded piece of paper.

"More lies, Nika?"

Her face flushed purple in the moonlight. "It is a note. From Babbin."

Babbin was the Mad Old Alkhemist who lived off the eastern shore. She was something of a legend — feared, revered, and scorned in equal measure. The Kotov visited her only when they had no other choice, desperate for a potion to cure some ailment or flourish a dying crop. As was so often the case, Danika had proved the exception. She had sought Babbin out at a young age — first out of cruel necessity, then out of curiosity — for Babbin was the only person on the Isles who could match her sister for alkhemical skill and, in many ways, exceed it.

"What does she want?"

"She asks me to visit." But there was some strangeness in Danika's voice. Nadya studied her profile — the familiar bump in her nose, the heavy, ever-furrowed brow, caught in some deep thought. It was a face more familiar to Nadya than her own, so many nights they had spent in this loft, whispering secrets only the moon and stars could hear. "I suspect she knows the reason I was expelled."

Zin's even snores peaked into a snort. It astounded Nadya that a creature so silent by day could make such loud exclamations in sleep. "Do you want to tell me?"

"No. Not yet. I am sorry."

Nadya squelched her disappointment. Whatever the truth was, it would not change things between them. If Danika needed time to come to terms with this, Nadya could grant it, and then, after Danika had confessed her secret, talk her out of her self-pity.

Zin flipped onto her back, stretching out a sticky hand, and gripped the skirt of Nadya's nightgown. Danika's smile faded. "I wish you could have joined me at Izumgray. Perhaps you could have saved me from myself."

Nadya reached across Zin for Danika's hand, still curled tightly around her note. "I would not have wanted Izumgray for myself, but I would have gone for you if I could."

It had been one of the saddest days in Nadya's memory when Danika left — she, twelve years of age; Nadya sixteen. They had bid farewell on the shores of the Von as Zin wept silently into Nadya's neck. Zin had only just come to them that Spring, during the Aadan's Day festival — barely more than a toddler, paddling a canoe across the Quicksilver River and pleading, silently, always silently, for asylum.

But Zin had proved difficult. Sullen and mistrustful, eating by herself in the byre, stealing anything small enough to fit in her pocket. Only Danika had been able to break through that quiet shell. In a few short seasons, Zin marked Danika as her favorite. Nadya could not begrudge Zin her loyalty as she felt much the same. And it was clear that Zin also would have gone with Danika to Izumgray if she could.

Nadya, however, was not gifted with Danika or Zin's ambition. She had no great desire to leave and explore new lands. She loved her home and her people. The salt-air of the Kotov Isles was the breath in her body. But if Danika had gone where Nadya could follow, she would have.

As was the way of things, all of Mama's natural-born children had inherited her Alkhemical Fire in varying degrees. But Danika alone possessed the silver glow of the Celestial Fire — the highest grade an alkhemist could hope for. Nadya was born with the weakest Fire — the Central Fire — a blue blood that only distinguished itself from mundane when cut. A mundane's blood would toxify in the air, turn a blazing red. Nadya's, at least, remained blue.

It was not enough. Izumgray did not take blue bloods.

Time would tell Zin's own Fire grade — if she possessed it at all. For girls, the Alkhemical Fire showed itself at their first bleeding. For boys, it came later, with the first hint of stubble on the chin. At best estimate, Zin had seen nine or ten years. If her blood came early, her Fire grade would be revealed. But time was not on her side.

For when the Suncycle dawned one year from now, they would all bleed red.

2. CAPTIVES ON THE VIENPER

The morning dawned too warm for fishskin. But Danika had made Nadya a promise, and she would not turn her back on it so soon. Thus, it was with her alkhemist coat stretched tight across her shoulders that Danika knelt in the dooryard, favorite short-blade in hand.

The first time she had returned home from Izumgray, the grasses of the Von crunched dry and brittle beneath her boots. Now, six days into Autumn, they flowered. Thistles of white and gold and palest purple. Danika cut the stem of the brightest bulb — *Knautia arvensis* — and raised it high against the blood-orange glare of the sunrise, twisting its bud between her fingertips. A pop of perfect violet in a sea of craggy rock.

She drew back the flap of her coat. Six silk bags lined the interior. The treasures inside contained the fruits of her foraging — bottles of dew, clippings of antelope fur, bushcat feathers, and flora of every variety she could scavenge from the moment she had left Izumgray to the instant she had arrived on the Von. She tucked the purple bud into the third satchel and stowed the dagger in one of the sheaths dangling from her waistbelt. The tools of an alkhemist's trade were best kept close at hand — or so her instructors at Izumgray had taught her.

Her gaze drifted to the right lining, to the dozens of narrow pockets loaded down with thin glass vials. The weight of them would have dragged heavy on her coattails if not for the elixir she had imbued into the glass to make the vials lighter than air.

Each stoppered tube contained the product of seven years hard labor at Izumgray. Seven years, sweating over fires, deciphering ancient script by alkhemical candlelight; seven years, enduring the whispers and jeers of her fellow apprentices as the only Kotov to ever grace Izumgray's sacred halls; seven years, proving herself to teachers she could have outbrewed on her worst day. Danika suffered it all, and gladly, for the chance to prove herself, to learn her art. To be the best.

And when she had returned home to the Kotov Isles each year — languishing in the salty shores of the Swansea, counting down the nights until her return to Sivka — she had endured the mutterings of her own people as well.

Did she think herself too good to study alkhemy in the old way, as every Kotov had done before her? Did she think the Sivkans could teach her better? Her siblings had elected to stay on the Isles, despite also possessing the Fire. Why did Danika think herself so special?

Babbin would say it was greed. Mama would call it stubborn pride. Nadya, ever the adoring older sister, would only think the best of her.

But the truth of it was that Danika *needed* alkhemy. It had been her salvation since she was a child, clinging to Mama's skirts as they knocked at Babbin's door, seeking answers only an alkhemist could provide — and Danika could not give it up.

To others, it might seem that her desperation had ballooned into ambition, arrogance. But they did not know the whole truth of it. They did not know what awaited her just 349 days from now. And if they themselves were in her position, she did not doubt that they too would cling to alkhemy with the same bare-knuckled grasp. And if that drive — that arrogance — led to success, it would be worth it.

It would all be worth it....

Everywhere Nadya went, the topic of conversation seemed to focus on one of two subjects — Imperator Maksis' decision to tax the Kotov and Danika's expulsion.

Of the former, the Kotov position was universal outrage. Papa had been away as often as he had been at home, sailing daily to the other four Isles in the hopes of staying all-out revolution. He was determined that with a little time and level-headedness, Imperator Maksis could be reasoned with. But Kotov were not known for their skills in diplomacy. Kotov were known for one thing — waging war.

As for Danika's situation, Nadya felt certain that not even Elin could be held responsible for leaking the news of their sister's dismissal from Izumgray to the whole of the Von, but it had leaked out nonetheless. And since Danika's acceptance into Izumgray had always been of interest to the Kotov, both for good and for ill, Nadya supposed it was only to be expected that news of her expulsion would be equally fascinating.

What she did not anticipate was the malice behind the whispers.

"I always knew no good would come of it," Selja Waterson was saying to Anut Barren at the brewhouse the day after the two strangers had been welcomed into their home.

Taito had asked Nadya to meet him at Bodan's Brews just after his shift ended so that she might accompany him back to the turfhouse for supper. Nadya supposed he really must love her if he was willing to brave Mama's table. But as she crossed the threshold into the smoky bar, the harsh words from the nearest table waylaid her.

"Kotov should not spend so much time away from the sea. Especially for such mysticism," Anut replied.

Nadya ducked behind a pillar near the entryway. Perhaps she could wait out the conversation. When it inevitably turned to the Imperator and his taxes, she would emerge — avoid any unnecessary awkwardness.

"It was only to be expected. It was trouble when she went there and it will be trouble now she is back — heed my words."

"What makes you say so?"

Selja Waterson leaned in and said in a dark whisper, "Look at the stock she sprouted from. Rodin's lineage is prestigious enough, but Marisha... That marriage should never have been. She is the cause of this trouble. She and her ilk. Three children from her womb — one was bound to go wrong."

Outrage spurred Nadya's steps. She stepped out from behind her pillar — awkwardness be damned — but before she could utter so much as a cutting threat, Taito rounded the bar and shoved Selja clean out of her chair.

Selja landed flat on her back, vodka spilling across her broad chest. The sharp smell of it cut through the haze of mishsmoke and pipe tobacco.

"Oy!" Selja shouted, red-faced. But as she started to heave herself up, her beady gaze fixed on Nadya, then Taito, then Nadya again. If possible, she went even redder as she realized precisely what had been overheard and by whom.

"You will retract your words and repent to Nadya's family or I will meet you in the ring," Taito growled.

Nadya placed a staying hand on his arm. Selja was a known fighter. Taito was a barman, like his mother and father before him. He had done his training as all Kotov did, but he had never seen true combat. There was little doubt who would win in such a challenge.

Perhaps it was the prospect of facing Nadya's papa in the ring that truly frightened Selja. Or maybe she felt genuine regret for her words. Nadya hoped so. Regardless, Selja shifted to one knee.

"Forgive me Nedeshda Bodanson. My words were not the loyalty of a Kotov. Name the price of my penance."

Nadya forced a smile. "Your apology is enough, Selja Waterson. We will speak no more of it."

"Your gentle heart does you credit."

The anger from the confrontation lingered on Taito's face as they made the climb from the village to the turfhouse. It was not an expression she had seen on him often. She always thought of Taito as a tender spirit, like herself. But now, he swatted at the swarms of mosquitos flocking over the damp hills like the kind of Kotov who kicked his dog after too much to drink.

Much like Zin and Mikhail, Taito Eletski had come to the Isles from Sivkan shores on an Aadan's Day over ten years ago. Unlike Zin and Mikhail, Taito had arrived with his mama and papa whole and healthy beside him.

On the misnomered "Day," any Sivkan vassals who had paid their debts to their masters could flee to the Kotov Isles during two tennights — once in Spring and once in Autumn. To many in Sivka, the vassals were little better than slaves. But to the Kotov, the vassals who fled to the Isles twice a year on each Aadan's Day represented a chance to replenish the numbers of those who had fallen in battle. The Kotov adopted the vassals as their own — free people, equal upon the sea, beholden to no master.

Desperate to prove themselves, the Eletskis wasted no time in doing what they were best at — making liquor. The purity of the vodka that sprang from their still made them many friends on the Von. The family was offered the previously defunct brewhouse within a tennight.

The Eletski home expanded over the years. Taito's parents added two more children to their number, and soon every one of them had earned a reputation for good humor. Though perhaps it was the effect of the vodka that made them seem so — no one could be cheerful all the time.

Nadya studied his frowning face — so much like Zin with his black hair and dark, narrow eyes. His skin was darker than Zin's — a healthy gold that never seemed to fade no matter how much time he spent in the brewhouse. She squeezed his hand, hoping to draw him from his reverie. "What is troubling you, Taito?"

He traded his grimace for a grin as gracefully as he poured a glass. "You know me well," he said. "If you had not been there... Selja would not have apologized."

"And?"

"And I would have had to face her in the ring."

Nadya rested a hand on his arm. "You would have done admirably."

"Admirably, maybe. But I would not have won."

Taito stopped her just outside the gate into the dooryard. "A woman such as you, Nadya... You deserve someone who would win."

Something squirmed low in her ribcage. She forced herself to ignore it and cupped Taito's face between her hands. "I do not need a man who fights others. I need only a man who will fight for me."

His expression softened and he pressed a firm, but quick, kiss to her lips. It left something to be desired. But she supposed that now, just before they were due to supper with her family, was not the moment. She just hoped that he would, eventually, find one...and soon.

Papanik often said that if the Von was the rock, the Vienper was the pebble.

"You think Hurkan will see you?" she asked Papa through panting breaths. They walked at a brisk trot, the flat terrain of the Vienper quickening their pace. A stitch pinged in Danika's side — Izumgray had made her soft. But at least the short boat ride to the neighboring isle of the Vienper had been made all the swifter thanks to a tincture poured over the oars.

"Hurkan holds a grudge longer than The Mother has held a spear." Papa's lips twitched behind his brown beard. "But he does love to talk."

"What is this new tax that Imperator Maksis wants to levy?" she said, taking particular effort to keep her voice steady.

"The prizes of our raids. He is demanding a cut of all Kotov spoils."

Danika stumbled, certain she must have heard wrong. "But he cannot," she said with blind certainty. Five years at Izumgray had taught her there were few immutable facts in the world, but Kotov independence was one of them. "It is against the treaty laid down in the Velvet Book. The Kotov only fight for Sivka on the condition that all Kotov may keep their plunder, maintain their independence, honor Aadan's Day in the old way, and *pay no taxes*."

Papa's lips thinned into a narrow line. "I fear that many of our privileges are coming to an end. The Imperator does not think the Kotov as valuable as he once did. He has not needed to call on us for true war since the last Suncycle."

Danika bristled. "Not a true war, no. But who does he think will keep his shores safe from the Jinmen if not us?"

Papa merely shrugged.

Vienper Village was restless with talk. Uncles grouped together around their pipes, speaking in low, mutinous voices. Aunties gathered about their washing, eyes wrinkled with doubt. The young folk had taken a different route — congregating in the yard to run at each other with shields and wooden sabers, their collisions cracking through the gossip like thunder.

As they made entry, Danika's eye was drawn to the largest and most famous building on the Kotov Isles — the Folktan. The Folktan was unique in that its roof was not a roof at all, but two longships turned upside down and crossed at the middle. Reed and turf patched the walls and a tendril of fragrant mishsmoke emanated from one of the stemposts turned chimney.

"Rodin!" A dark man with protruding ears approached, tossing a small canvas sachet from hand to hand. "I hope you did not come just to hear Hurkan grumble."

Papa chuckled dryly. "Someone must. If I leave it too long, he will have all five Isles called to oars." He placed a hand on Danika's shoulder. "Tangier, have you met my daughter?"

"Ah, yes — the alkhemist!" He offered his sachet. Danika looked inside and saw that it was filled with pumpkin seeds. She took one and crunched it between her back teeth. Tangier grinned approvingly. "You are the one who goes to Izumgray?"

Danika did not know how to reply. Yes, she *had* gone to Izumgray. But to say she would not return — out loud, in front of Papa and a perfect stranger? If she thought she had made her peace with her fate, Tangier's simple question was a sharp reminder to the contrary. By The Mother's mercy, Papa changed the subject.

"Is Hurkan inside?" he asked, chin jerking toward the Folktan. As he did, Danika caught sight of a familiar figure lurking in the shadow of the Folktan's bow. The figure stepped into the sunlight briefly enough for Danika to glimpse his tan face — the quirk of his head, the press of a finger against his lips. A thrill of intrigue shot up her spine and she looked at Papa to see if he had noticed.

"Ack. Fool that he is." Tangier's friendly smile twisted into a scowl. She understood his disapproval. In peacetime, there were no leaders among the Kotov. They were a free people, equal upon the sea. And while Hurkan had been the Vienper's Chieftain during the last skirmish — just as Papa had been the Von's — that did not give him the right to house in the Folktan. That was a sacred place, meant only for meetings of all the Isles.

"You mean to convince him to pay his taxes?" Tangier's voice was very neutral. As was Papa's answer.

"I mean to steady his saber. We must consider before we take drastic steps. The Imperator's papa was a loyal friend to the Kotov."

Tangier made a humming noise that did not quite pass for agreement. Danika could see what he was thinking. Every Kotov knew Papa. He had a proud lineage, going all the way back to Bodan himself. And every Kotov knew *of* Mama. She had a proud lineage too — but hers was Sivkan.

"I wish you luck."

Papa nodded. "As Above."

"So Below." Tangier sauntered off, crunching his seeds.

"Well?" said Papa. "Will you be joining me? Or will you be rushing off to join Lukin in some scheme?" A smirk played beneath his beard — Papa *had* spotted the figure by the Folktan. She should not be surprised. Papa was a renowned warrior, as well as a politician — if the Kotov could claim such a thing — and he could never have achieved such a reputation without a skill for observation. Fortunately, it was a skill he had passed onto her.

"I suspect he is here paying a visit to his Mama," said Danika.

Papa raised a skeptical eyebrow. "Is that what you suspect? I have my doubts."

So did Danika. Lukin did not visit his mama unless forced by dire circumstance or his own papa's gentle prodding.

"Meet back at the boat at dayfade. And whatever it is you are doing — remember, I am here to stop a war, not start one."

"Yes, Papa."

Lukin awaited her at the gate leading out of the village. His hazel eyes were squinted as if he could not believe the sight of her. He had grown since she had last seen him, if that were possible. Lukin was one of the few boys on the Isles that stood taller than Danika. Though, she reminded herself, he was not a boy anymore. No more than she was a girl. Nineteen and grown, the pair of them, and, much like the blooming grasses of the Von, Lukin's amber skin still clung to its summer tan.

"You cut your hair," he said. His tone was accusatory, as if she had whipped his favorite dog instead of taken a blade to her unremarkable muddy locks.

Danika's fingers skimmed the ends where it brushed her shoulders. "It was easier to keep out of the fires."

He scowled. After all, Lukin's chestnut mane was longer than hers now, and he spent many an evening bent over the blacksmith's bellows without fear of ignition.

"What are you doing here?" she asked. "Not visiting your mama?"

Lukin's scowl deepened at the suggestion. "No. I spoke to Elin. She told me about what happened — about Izumgray."

A fizzle of righteous fury zipped over her skin like the brush of a flame. Elin was the laziest Kotov on the Isles — never waking with the dawn, never climbing from her bed a moment earlier than she had to — unless it came to the urgent need to spread gossip. Then she could always be relied upon. "She should not have told you about that."

"Why? Would you not have told me yourself?"

"I— I am sure I would have." In truth, Danika did not know if she would have confessed her shame to Lukin. There were so many other secrets she had kept from him — what was one more? But Elin had taken that choice from Danika and, with the same certainty that she knew the patterns of the tides of the Swansea, she knew Lukin. She knew that he would try to fix it.

"Come with me," he said, setting off down the easterly path out of the village. His mama lived on the west shore.

"What are you taking me to see?"

It was amazing what a simple smile could do to transform Lukin's face. "It is not a what. It is a who."

He brought Danika to a hut half a mile from the village. Its stone walls clung precariously to the cliff face. A well-brewed tincture was likely all that kept it from falling into the sea. Danika thanked The Mother that the Suncycle was still 349 days away. Still with that strange hint of a smile, Lukin guided her inside.

The wind slammed the door shut behind them, plunging the small hut into blackness. There was no windows or light to see by, so Danika did what came naturally to her after so many years at Izumgray — she pushed up the sleeves of her coat.

Her skin was pale — in daylight, the white glow of the Celestial Fire was invisible to the naked eye. But in darkness, the veins in her forearms glowed like silver rivers, offering an illumination only the Suncycle could squash. It was not enough light for Danika to see much beyond Lukin's ghostly silhouette. But she was able to watch him strike a match against the rock wall and carry the red flame to a lantern by the door. The flame caught and grew, Danika's skin faded back to normality, and the subject of Lukin's excitement was revealed.

Two men were trussed and chained to the wall, arms dangling above their heads. Each had a gag tied around his mouth. They were dirty and bruised. Danika turned to Lukin, bewildered.

"I found you a hostage." He grinned — sharp canines flashing a little maniacally. "Two of them, actually. We can present them to your papa and join the Host."

Danika rocked back on her heels. She had been back in the Kotov Isles for less than a day — knowledge of her expulsion from Izumgray had barely begun to spread — and already Lukin had commandeered a boat, attacked two foreigners, claimed them, bound them, and brought them to shore. For her. So that she could join the faction of Kotov warriors feared the world over — so that they could join the Host together. Slowly, she turned away from Lukin to take stock of his gift.

The captive on the left was around Papa's age. He had the rust colored skin of a Jinmen, a full head of black hair, black eyes, and an impressive mustache. He did not have Papa's muscles, but he also had not let himself go soft like so many other men his age. Even bound, there was a lithe danger to his frame. His clothes were foreign. And rich. He wore a black silk tunic with matching trousers and a red velvet cape that draped from shoulder to hip. It was adorned with a golden pin. Danika could spot gold a mile away — any alkhemist could. But the strangeness was not just in the metal, but in the subject — a sun with a dozen sheaths for rays.

She shifted her gaze to the man on the right.

He was the most beautiful person Danika had ever seen.

Everything about him was golden — his hair, curled at the edges, cut short in the Sivkan style; his smooth, white skin; his slight, muscular build; his eyes, especially. Much like the sun pinned on the other man's chest, they shimmered with precious knowledge. This man, though he could not have been much older than Danika, had seen worlds. Worlds, and war, and women. No person could hold himself like that — proud and strong, even while trussed like an elk at Windwinter — without having known and pleased a woman. Danika wondered what it would feel like to be taken by such a man.

She noted that his right pointer finger was missing and hoped that Lukin was not to blame. Men often found it hard to forgive loss of limb.

A gag hid his mouth. Danika wanted it gone. She needed to see the rest of him — his lips, his smile. She knelt and pulled the short-blade from her waistbelt, as if he were nothing but another specimen for her to forage. He did not flinch as she approached. She snipped his muzzle. His grin was everything she imagined despite being somewhat crooked. That was good, Danika decided. She could not trust perfection.

"You're an alkhemist." His voice was like warm honey, deep and confident as the rest of him.

"And you are?"

"Your prisoner." He flashed that lopsided smile again, eyebrow quirked. "For the moment."

She looked to Lukin. If he had his way, the hostages would be sold back to their native country or put to work as the newest Kotov citizen. As much as Danika liked the idea of this handsome man joining the Kotov people, the prospect of selling him for ransom was much less welcome. To make no mention of the fact that there was no possibility of Danika ever joining the Host...

She got to her feet and ushered Lukin to the far corner of the hut. She pitched her voice low, but she was sure it still carried to their captives. "This was a kind gesture, Lukin, but I cannot accept it."

"Why not?" His eyes blazed. "If the alkhemists will not have you, then join us. Join me. Come back to your people." He paused, hands twitching at his sides as if they longed to reach for her, but then settling on his hips instead. "This is your chance to do something else, Danika. To be more. Do it now — before the Suncycle. Do it on your own terms."

Danika could not fathom Lukin's belief that *not* being an alkhemist was somehow being *more*. But that was beside the point. He was offering her a new life among their people, at his side. This was what came of not telling Lukin *all* her secrets — with a little honesty, she could have prevented him from doing something so gallant and so wrong. He did not realize that this new life he offered her was as impossible as the one she was leaving behind. But now was not the time to try and explain why.

Danika stood over their would-be hostages. The beautiful one smiled idly, eyes twinkling up at her like molten metal. She would have found his smugness insulting if it was not so attractive. She had known men and boys like him at Izumgray and they rarely disappointed.

"Your names?"

He hesitated a moment too long — clearly thinking of a pseudonym — then said, "Adrien."

"And him?" She jerked her chin at the other.

"That's Avdotya. But you can call him Dunya. I always do."

Avdotya growled again, but this time, his ire was directed at 'Adrien.'

"We should find out his tribe," Danika said to Lukin. Avdotya was not a Jinmenese name, but perhaps his moniker was as false as Adrien's. She knelt again and cut Avdotya's gag. Without it, his lips curled into a sneer. The disdain in his black eyes was pitiless. It reminded her of the look Adept Porchik would give her when she completed a potion supposedly too advanced for her years.

"What is your tribe, Jin?" snarled Lukin.

Avdotya sniffed. "I have no tribe. I'm Sivkan. We're here on a matter of diplomacy. I demand you release us and take us to the leader of your people."

Danika laughed. "You are no diplomat if you think the Kotov have anything so simple as a leader."

Avdotya's eyes narrowed, flicking down to her exposed forearms. "And what would an alkhemist know of such things?"

Danika shoved the gag back in his mouth.

"We seek Hurkan Odanson of the Vienper," said Adrien. "We've heard that he's the most likely to be sympathetic to our cause."

"Sympathetic is not a word I would use to describe Hurkan," Danika climbed to her feet. "And he has no liking of Jin."

"No-a-in!" Avdotya said in muffled outrage.

"How did you come to be here?" she asked Adrien.

"Boat," he said. Danika glared. His grin widened. "We came by way of Polvia. We were sailing into port after a truly harrowing journey when your friend here—" He nodded to Lukin, who clenched his fists. "—came aboard."

The fine clothes, the fake name, the sunburst pin, the route through Polvia... It was fast becoming clear these men held more value than as simple hostages for the Host. If Danika could contrive a good enough reason, perhaps Lukin would let her decide the hostages' fate.

"I'm afraid he made quick work of us," Adrien continued. Beside her, Lukin puffed out his chest. "I made the mistake of leaving Dunya on watch. I was having a lovely dream about a redhead I met in Scandia. I think her name was—" Avdotya kicked Adrien with one of his shiny black boots. Adrien gave a little shake of his head. "The name doesn't matter. But we're not foreigners." He paused. "Actually, in truth, we *are* foreigners. In a way. I haven't lived in Sivka for over a decade, but—"

"I do not need your life story," Danika snapped. She hoped he would not be so chatty when they were alone. But in all his ramblings, he had finally offered her a solution... "You are Sivkan? Both of you?"

"Yes."

"Very well. Then you can come with me."

Surprisingly, Adrien did not leap at her offer. "As your hostages?" he said, watching her carefully.

"No. As allies. My mother is Sivkan. We do not prey on our own."

Adrien's face broke into a genuine smile — it was just as tempting as the one filled with bravado. Lukin, however, had settled into one of his meanest scowls. "Danika, what are you—"

"It is no good, Lukin." She reached into her coat for an unlocking tincture. "I thank you for trying, but no." Lukin's intentions had been true, but not even joining the Kotov Host would be her salvation. So far as Danika was concerned, she had 349 days left to live. Perhaps this beautiful, golden-haired boy would help her do it to the fullest.

She made short work of the chains. When they were free, Adrien stood, rubbing his wrists. Danika was pleased to find that while he was not taller than her, he was not much shorter either.

"Thank you for your help, Danika."

She had never liked the sound of her name so much. She liked too that he was observant enough to catch it, despite her never offering an introduction.

Avdotya sulked in bitter silence. There would clearly be no gratitude from him.

"Forgive Dunya," said Adrien. "He's not the best at making friends."

"Fortunately for you, you do not seem to share that problem."

They returned to the boat precisely at dayfade. A storm was forming to the west and Danika knew Papa would not want to delay. When he saw that their numbers had doubled, he simply raised his eyebrows.

"These are new friends of ours," Danika said by way of explanation.

She looked over at her companions. Of the three of them, only Adrien could be described as looking anything close to friendly. Both Lukin and Avdotya stood grim-faced, stormier than the clouds forming off the Dural.

"They need shelter and a place to stay."

Luckily, Papa was not the sort to ask questions. He took in the strangers with a look — it was a fearsome look, not one to be crossed — and waved them into the boat.

Danika and Lukin worked the oars furiously to beat the storm. The current swelled and sank by drastic turns. The wind whipped at their hair, stealing Danika's breath. Adrien sat across from them, staring out at the choppy waters with a vacant smile.

"Would it surprise you to learn that I don't know how to swim?" he asked, then stretched his arms over his head, leaned back against the stern post, and fell into a deep sleep.

3. THE MAD OLD ALKHEMIST

The little alkhemist and her father steered them ably across the waters of Lake Lebgay. Even Avdotya could admit, this was no small feat. The Swansea was a lake so massive, so powerful and strange in its peculiarities, that no Sivkan dared to call it one. Its size and avian shape had earned it the misnomer and it was only truly navigable by those it was home to.

Their party docked at a secluded pebble beach with such little incident that Avdotya seethed. He'd paid good silver to that oaf from Gam to guide them safely to the Vienper, and at the first sign of weather, they'd run aground, leading them right into the hands of that barbarian. Fortunately, their idiotic oarsman had drowned in the siege. Unfortunately, he'd taken their ingots with him.

The alkhemist's house wasn't much more than a hillock, indistinguishable from the grassy knolls bleached inky blue in the moonlight. The inside was slightly more civilized than one would expect from an outward glance. Few introductions were made. Instead, they were shoved onto a bench and forced to choke back a barely edible meal of salty mussels on a bed of soggy greens. Only the overloud clamor of chewing, slurping and scraping forks broke the silence.

But when even that died away and the half-full plates were cleared, the quiet settled deeper still. Avdotya's stomach couldn't be the only one still rumbling. Just because the alkhemist's family hadn't bound, beaten and eaten them yet, didn't mean they wouldn't, and the whips and sabers dangling from the rafters didn't exactly bid welcome. Nor did the old man at the head of the long table with eyes like two dark coals spat out from the fire.

Adrik — or "Adrien" as he had so dubbed himself to the alkhemist (at least not all of Avdotya's lessons on discretion had gone to waste) — twitched beside Avdotya, leg bouncing in time with his own restlessness. It was a habit from childhood Avdotya had tried, and failed, to correct. If it didn't stop soon, he would have to take it out on the whipping boy — always assuming they saw the whipping boy again.

Adrik sucked in a breath and Avdotya grit his teeth, bracing himself for what came next. He considered jabbing the fool with his elbow — it would not do to break the custom of their hosts, not so long as they remained off the menu — but refrained. It would make a nice change to hear someone else reprimand the boy for once.

"We'd like to thank you for welcoming—"

"Silence!" boomed the old man. "Talking is tomorrow's work."

This was Adrik's third warning. One more and they would doubtless be gagged again — an experience Avdotya was not eager to repeat while the corners of his mouth still chafed. He rubbed a hand over his mustache. In the absence of their captor, who'd broken off from the party the moment they made landfall, Avdotya cast his glare in the little alkhemist's direction.

She perched on the edge of one of the bedclosets lining either side of the hall, hunched over a book. She pretended to be absorbed in her task, making notes and scanning the pages with careless abandon, but every so often, her dark blue eyes would lift to fix on Adrik.

Avdotya had seen that look before. The hope, the longing. The ignorant belief that she alone would be the one to tame the handsome young stranger from far flung shores. Often, the girls succeeded. For a night. Then they vanished, forgotten among Adrik's long list of conquests. The girl could hope, but hope was all it would be. She was too plain for Adrik's tastes. Still, Avdotya could use the girl's infatuation as and when it was needed. Just as he would file away his other observations...

The short legs of the dining table — their hosts lacked regular access to lumber. Ornately crafted sabers hanging over the doorways — the family had a proud military history. An Oratorium by the front door — practicing Cyclicans in a land of agnostics. The unspoken tension emanating between the little alkhemist and the older woman Avdotya assumed to be her mama — a conflict to be exploited?

It was a large family. There were many children. He would not bother to know them all yet. Doubtless this group observed the Kotov tradition of adoption, but there was no telling if they treated their adoptees as their own flesh and blood or as vassals in all but name. They *had* all been served the same foul, fishy meal — but that could hardly be considered a kindness.

The youngest girl in the pack stood out particularly. She had tried to steal the last ingot in Avdotya's pocket as they'd taken their seats. When her mama scolded her, she'd bowed her head in the Gam way. Her features were Gam too, dark narrow eyes and long black hair, but Avdotya knew better than to assume. He himself was so often mistaken for a Jinmen — as today's exploits had proved.

There was much to reconcile. Avdotya had feared all their plans would come to naught on the shoals of the Vienper, but perhaps this family would suit their cause just as well.

His gaze cut to the pretty young woman seated next to the alkhemist, stitching a lavender bud onto a linen napkin. Clearly a blood relation. The pair shared something similar around the mouth, but the sister had inherited all the beauty the alkhemist lacked. Even by the harsh shadows of the silver firelight, it was obvious. She had high cheekbones, light blue eyes, and brilliant blonde hair.

And Avdotya was not the only one who had noticed.

A clock chimed on the wall, louder than the toll of a dozen Polvian funeral bells. The old man stood up at their cue.

"We will speak tomorrow," he said. "Now — bed."

Adrik opened his mouth to argue. Avdotya pinched his arm. Adrik might have thought the evening pointless, but Avdotya knew better. This was one Kotov custom he could come to appreciate — he had learned far more in the silence than with words.

Adrik woke gasping — red screams and bloody agony chasing each other in circles around his mind. He shook off the horror with the routine of long practice and ground himself in the little Kotov home fate had landed him in.

He glanced around the hall where dust motes floated idly in the still morning light and quiet settled deep in the warm air. He and Avdotya had spent the night in a pair of unclaimed bedclosets in the main hall. Adrik was grateful their hosts seemed to have so much room to spare — he and Dunya had shared a bedroll many times on their journeys, but it was never a comfortable experience for either of them. Avdotya usually woke with a black eye courtesy of Adrik's nightmares and the resulting bruises to Adrik's shins took days to fade.

After he and Dunya had stripped down to undershirt, trousers and boots — always boots — Adrik had slipped between the linen sheets, which smelled faintly of lavender, and watched as Danika's papa retreated to his own rest.

Adrik noticed that Rodin left the sliding door to his bedcloset ajar, and that the saber that had hung over the doorway on their arrival had vanished. Meanwhile, the one Danika called "Papanik" fell into a loud, snoring sleep in a rocking chair by the fire — a switch gripped tight in his fist.

Adrik didn't blame them. A man was duty-bound to protect his family.

The sudden pressure on his bladder broke Adrik's musings and he slipped off the bed platform onto the earthen floor. The old man was gone from his rocking chair, but a silver fire still danced at both ends of the hall, kept alive — no doubt — by the blood of the alkhemist.

A small skylight provided the only illumination in the next room. The deep breathing of more sleeping bodies drifted down from a loft overhead. Interestingly, an Oratorium sat beneath it. Dunya had warned Adrik that the Kotov didn't ascribe to any particular religion, let alone the Sivkan one. But with this symbol of Cyclican worship before him, Adrik wondered if The Father had guided their oars to friendly shores after all.

Two doors led off the entry hall to his left and his right, but Adrik couldn't remember which he had entered from the night before. He took a chance on the left. As he turned the handle, he expected to stumble out onto a grassy knoll, where he could then hunt out an appealing bush or stone wall. Instead, he crossed into a room the likes of which he'd only seen in the grandest Polvian palaces.

"A latrine?"

His words echoed back at him, for this was no mere outhouse, but a cavernous expanse nearly as big as the main hall. Two long benches hugged the walls on either side, each with five round holes carved into the seat — enough for the whole family to be pissing at once. Adrik heard a faint trickle of water and suspected a gravity spring ran beneath the benches to send the waste off from the house. He shook his head in astonishment and mounted the nearest hole with relish.

Some time later, the door flew open.

Danika marched inside and headed directly for the basin across from the door. She didn't seem to notice him. Adrik froze where he sat, pants down around his ankles, wondering why Avdotya hadn't ever thought to teach him the proper behavior for *this* custom.

He squeezed his knees together and was about to clear his throat to announce his presence, when—

"Do not let me disturb you." Danika caught his eye in the mirror above the bowl. She wore a white shift with a wool cape draped over her shoulders. For the first time in many seasons, he felt himself blush.

"Apologies," he said, suddenly at a loss for what to do with his hands. "I should have locked the door."

"There is no lock. What would be the point?"

True enough. He doubted the ten toilets had been built in one open room for privacy's sake. He averted his gaze from hers and noticed a silver flame flickering in her cupped hand.

"Impressive."

"I will tell Papa you think so. He built it as a wedding gift for Mama. It is the only attached latrine in the whole of the Kotov Isles."

Adrik's lips twitched. "I meant the flame."

"Oh." Her hand clenched, snuffing the pretty spark.

He used her moment of distraction to stand, turn his back and yank his trousers up. He spoke to her over his shoulder as he fumbled with the ties. "Your mama is an alkhemist?"

"Of course."

There was a note of disdain in her voice. To be fair, it *had* been a stupid question. Anyone who was an alkhemist had a mama who was also an alkhemist. "But your papa is mundane?"

"Yes."

Adrik rubbed his jaw. He thought last night that he'd charmed her... Maybe he'd hit a nerve? Adrik had never met anyone with the highest grade of the Celestial Flame who had only one alkhemist parent. But then again, in Polvia, one wasn't likely to meet any alkhemists at all, and even if you did, they weren't likely to admit it.

"What about your siblings?"

"Nadya and Elin have the Fire. Lesser grades. And yours?"

Adrik tensed. Dunya would not want him to give away too much. Best to ignore the question altogether. "What about the little boy? Mikhail?"

"He is too young to know yet. You did not ask about Zin."

Adrik assumed "Zin" was the little Gam-looking girl. "Well, she's adopted, isn't she?"

It seemed to take Danika a moment to place the word. "Oh. Yes. But so is Mikhail."

Avdotya had also warned him that the Kotov didn't set much stock in bloodlines.

Danika bent over to retrieve a tray from the shelf beneath the basin — a set of ten vials lined neatly in a rack. She plucked the seventh vial from the row, uncorked it, and swallowed it in one. He resisted the urge to ask about the vials and said instead, “Is Zin from Gam?”

“We do not know.” She replaced the vial next to another empty one. There were three full vials left — one for each remaining day of the tennight. She returned the rack to its shelf, dried her hands on a towel and turned to face him.

“You don’t know if she’s from Gam? How can that be?”

Danika shrugged. “She has not told us. Where is your family from?”

“I told you.” He could hear the tension in his own voice. “I’m Sivkan.”

“You said that, yes. But Sivka is a big country. The biggest, in fact.”

Adrik didn’t reply. Danika shuffled to the nearest hole in the opposite bench and began to lift her skirts—

“Wait! What are you doing?”

“I am not Sivkan.” She raised a pointed brow. “And I have places to be.”

Adrik’s momentary panic at the sight of a young lady about to piss in front of him was drowned out by his curiosity. “Where do you have to be?”

Danika sighed and dropped her skirt. “You ask a lot of questions, but you do not answer them.”

“Can I come with you? Wherever you’re going?”

He shifted from one foot to the other, the sudden need to be free of the cramped little house pushing at the edges of his ribs like a bag of grain bursting at its own seams. He needed to explore this new foreign shore. He needed open sky overhead and fresh air in his lungs more than he needed strong drink after a hard day, or a willing woman after strong drink. He felt he might die if she gave him anything other than unequivocal agreement.

“You may come on one condition...,” she said.

“Name it.”

“You let me piss in peace.”

Danika led Adrik out of the latrine and into the dooryard while the rest of the house still slept.

"Children!"

Or so she thought.

The boom of Papanik's voice scared a flock of gulls from their perch on the roof. Adrik flinched violently. Papanik grinned at them from where he crouched behind the closest hedge. "Going to see the old nut?"

The note summoning Danika to Babbin's house had been tucked beneath her pillow the first night after her return from Izumgray. Danika could not begin to fathom how such a feat had been achieved. It read simply: *You cannot hide from me, Little Nika.* She doubted that Babbin expected her to visit with a foreign stranger in tow — but hopefully Adrien's presence would prove a useful distraction for the Mad Old Alkhemist.

"We will be back by dayfade," Danika said, squinting out over the cliffs. It was still early, the ground covered in a low mist.

"See that you are. Your mama was fearsome having to make supper without you last night."

Danika worked not to purse her lips. Mama was always fearsome about something. Still, she nodded. There was not much she could deny Papanik. "As Above," she said.

"So Below."

It was not until they had passed through the wattle-gate and left the grassy roof of the turfhouse behind them that Adrien spoke again. "What was that about? Why was he crouched behind that hedge?"

"Papanik does not care for the latrine."

As they made their way down the cliffs, it occurred to Danika that two buffers between her and Babbin might prove even more effective than one, so she led Adrien into the dooryard of the blacksmith's house.

The dwelling was a simple hillock like most turfhouses on the Von, except for a thatched awning that sprouted off the far end accompanied by a tall stone chimney. Lukin's papa stood at the forge beneath the awning. The painful scent of molten metal permeated the air.

"I hope you have come with my brine," Dondar greeted as he worked a half-formed saber over the coals.

"I have." Danika reached into the right side of her coat for the correct vial. Before leaving Izumgray, she had prepared a number of basic solutions the Kotov always seemed in need of. A last great brew, she had told herself.

Dondar pulled the saber from the embers and placed its glowing tip onto the anvil. When it was settled, Danika offered him the solution. He took it with a bow of his sweaty bald head. His face was nearly as red as the sword. "My thanks."

"You could make the brine yourself," Danika wheedled. "It is a simple matter." *A boring matter.* "It does not even require the Alkhemical Flame—"

"I leave such things to the experts. I will stick to my horseshoes."

Should she protest? Warn him that she meant to give up her fires altogether? Or had he already guessed? And so what if he had? Elin would have spread the news of her expulsion to all five Kotov Isles by now. It was no matter. She was used to Kotov judgement.

The door to the turfhouse opened with a creak then, stymying her dark thoughts as Lukin emerged. He had barely crossed the threshold when another figure spilled out behind him.

Shelia — Danika's cousin — beamed toothily, one hand on Lukin's broad chest. As she caught sight of Danika, the cheerful expression on her face crushed like salt before the pestle. "Oh," she said. "You have returned."

"I have missed you too, cousin," Danika answered dryly.

Cousins they may have been, but Danika and Shelia had never warmed to one another. Shelia was the daughter of Papa's sister, and looked more like her own papa than a Bodanson. She had a long horse-like face with wide-set eyes. A flat mole sat above the left corner of her lip like a thumbprint dipped in ink.

"You are back early." Shelia could not have sounded less pleased for the surprise. "How was your journey?"

"The tide brought me in," said Danika, repeating the old Kotov mantra.

"And you brought a friend home with you?" Shelia's vacant gaze slipped between Lukin and Adrien with relish. "Is he from Izumgray? He is clearly Sivkan."

"Indeed. Who is this handsome stranger?" said Dondar. "It was rude of me not to ask."

Danika shook her head. "It was my rudeness not to introduce him. He is not from Izumgray. We were...acquainted only last night. Lukin introduced us, in fact."

"Did he?" The surprise on Dondar's face was shadowed by the storm cloud on Lukin's. Clearly, he did not care for Danika's version of events. Shelia looked least pleased of all.

Adrien bowed shortly to Dondar, then Shelia. "I am Adrien. As Above."

"So Below." Dondar nodded, but his brow was furrowed. Danika knew why. Adrien had not provided his patronymic, nor even his family name. Strange, for a Sivkan. He had seemed so eager to introduce himself last night...

"Is he staying under your turf?" Lukin spoke like Adrien was not there, hazel eyes fixed on Danika.

"Yes."

"Sleeping in the hall?"

"Yes..." She did not understand his tone.

"Forgive my boy," Dondar said. "He clearly has not taken his Basic today."

Lukin ignored his papa. "Where are you taking him now?"

"To Babbin's. I was wondering if you might want to join—"

"Yes." He abandoned Shelia beneath the gable.

"That old crone? What need do you have of her? Are you ill?" Shelia squeaked, scanning Lukin like a mother hen counting her chicks.

"Alkhemical matters," said Danika. "Lukin promised to help me. I am sure you would not care for the details."

Shelia bristled, arms tightening across her chest. "I am sure I would not. Very well then. I will see you soon, Lukin?"

Lukin nodded and Shelia slouched off — looking much grimmer than she had at the start. As the gate clattered behind her, Danika, Lukin and Adrien found themselves under Dondar's keen stare.

"What?" said Lukin.

Dondar chuckled. "I am reminded of the tale of the stud and the mares."

Lukin pursed his lips. "What of it?"

"The stud ended up with two hoof prints. One on his head and the other on his—"

Lukin ushered them away before Dondar could finish.

The "Mad Old Alkhemist," as Danika's papanik had called her, lived off the western shore of the Von. Her hut rose from the mossy earth in a stout cylinder, topped with a roof domed and turfed. To Adrik, the black stone walls looked charred, as if the very mortar had been imbued with the woman's dark arts. Thick smoke puffed from the chimney and a black goat with only one ear grazed on the patchy lawn out front.

Danika led Adrik and Lukin inside without hesitation — though Lukin still paused anxiously in the doorway. As they descended the steps into the single, sunken room, a damp heat embraced them, like slipping beneath the water of a warm bath. But then an unrelenting stench knocked Adrik backwards. He let out a noise of disgust as Lukin began to cough.

"You will get used to the smell," Danika said without sympathy.

Adrik gripped his nose tightly. "What is it? It stinks like rotten eggs."

"Rotten eggs," she answered, peering coolly into a barrel of gurgling black liquid at the base of the stairs with an air of professional curiosity. "Among other things."

There wasn't much room to maneuver in the strange room. Four workbenches circled the perimeter, piled high with wooden casks, earthenware jars and an array of colored glass bottles. Batches of henna and dogwood hung from the ceiling like earth turned upside down. Hooks lined the curved walls where glass retorts, beakers, cylinders, flasks and funnels dangled in varying shapes and sizes.

Adrik's trepidation rose. This was a place both holy and exotic, off-putting and thrilling. Like a siren song to a sailor, the fire in the furnace at the center of the room drew Adrik, Lukin and Danika closer with its promise of warmth. But what they found on the furnace shelf wasn't a cauldron or flask of some new and dangerous brew, but—

"Bread?" said Lukin, astonished.

What untold powers did it contain? It looked harmless, but Adrik knew appearances could be deceiving. Half entranced, he reached toward it with four aching fingers—

A wrinkled hand slapped him back.

"No touch!"

Pale blue, almost-white eyes flashed before him. Adrik stumbled back, but the old woman's visage pressed ever closer like some bodiless specter. Danika caught Adrik firmly by the shoulders before he crashed into a rickety table overloaded with glass vials.

"Sourdough. Harder than most elixirs. Do not breathe on it too much." The woman's croaky voice spoke in short, declarative sentences. Jowls and wrinkles flattened the curves of the her face. She wore a ragged black cloak and a hat that looked something like an upside-down bird's nest. Adrik barely had time to process her words before she was lunging again — this time at Lukin.

The bird's nest perched precariously atop her head wobbled as she squeezed him tight around his middle. The sticks at the top of the nest grazed his chin and he stared at Danika, eyes wide with alarm.

"Babbin?" Danika queried lazily — she seemed to be getting great enjoyment out of Lukin's predicament. Adrik couldn't deny he felt the same. Lukin *had* taken him and Avdotya hostage, after all.

"Shush — I am listening."After several long moments wherein Danika let Babbin listen — to what, exactly, Adrik was not sure — Babbin stepped back and declared, "He is a good boy."

Lukin went pink. Not a very intimidating quality in a Kotov warrior. "Er—thank you?" he said. Adrik rolled his eyes.

"Adrien, this is Babbin," Danika said then, turning the woman's white-eyed gaze back on him. "Babbin, meet Adrien."

"Adrien — pah!"

Adrik braced himself. Anyone who wore a bird's nest atop their head was likely a few eggs short of a dozen. She lunged forward again and grabbed him around the waist, giving his chest a hard sniff.

"Pah! Still a child."

Adrik squirmed out of her arms, heat rising to his own cheeks in the wake of Lukin's smug grin. "I am no child."

"A child who is no child is an infant." Babbin turned her steely gaze on Danika. "So, my Little Nika...You have been expelled from Izumgray."

Danika shot a furtive look in Adrik's direction. He wondered if these kind of proclamations were why people avoided Babbin and called her names — ritual humiliation seemed to be a key part of her process.

"Yes," Danika acknowledged tightly. "I was expelled."

Adrik schooled his surprise. He knew, after all, that his rescuer was an alkhemist. And he knew that Izumgray was Sivka's elite institution for studying alkhemy. What Avdotya had failed to convey in all his teachings, though, was that Izumgray even accepted Kotov students, let alone expelled them.

Adrik noted that Lukin didn't seem shocked by the news, and recalled his pleas with Danika the night before to use Adrik and Avdotya as a means to join the Kotov Host. Had their capture all been some sort of ploy to soothe the ego of a rejected alkhemist? Adrik might have been impressed by the lengths Lukin had gone to in this elaborate mating ritual if it hadn't come at Adrik's own expense.

"You will tell me why," said Babbin.

"You know why."

"You will tell me anyway."

Danika crossed her arms and leaned on a table piled high with several varieties of burnt bread. She pulled a chunk from one of the loaves and chewed, clearly stalling for time. Adrik found himself curious as to her answer. Lukin stared at

Danika equally intently. Between mouthfuls she said, "I attempted to make a Philosopher's Stone."

A thrill, not unlike the feeling that came from felling an enemy, shot through Adrik.

Danika had attempted to make a Philosopher's Stone?

Beside him, Lukin let out an affronted sort of growl. Adrik supposed he could understand the concern — there was a reason the making of a Philosopher's Stone was forbidden by law.

Its discovery and subsequent replications had buoyed the population…for a while. It had cured incurable illnesses, endowed the penniless, extended lifespans, and — most impressively of all — continued to work even through the Suncycle. Its power had spread across the globe like blown glass. But, as Avdotya always said, pressed too hard, and any glass will shatter. The shards of that Stone still cut today.

For her part, Babbin did not look the least bit alarmed. "And?" she prompted. "What else?"

"I used another's method to do it."

"Used? Pah!"

Danika swallowed. "Stole, then. If you can steal from the dead."

"The only thing that *can* be stolen is ideas. And ideas live forever. I do not care that you tried to make the Stone, Little Nika. Any true alkhemist will feel its call, whatever the Imperator's laws. And you will feel it most of all, given your troubles." Danika flinched, casting another swift glance in Adrik and Lukin's direction. "I care that you did not do it honestly. What have I always taught you?"

"You cannot transform a thing without first understanding it," Danika replied, the words sounding rote on her tongue.

"And how can you understand a thing that you stole? That is not yours?"

Danika seemingly had no answer for that. She stood, withering under Babbin's silent judgment, until she raised her chin and gave an audible sniff. "Your bread is about to burn."

"Pah!" Babbin scrambled to retrieve the sourdough with a pair of flask tongs. She set it amongst the dozen other burnt loaves and knocked on the steaming bottom. "Still good."

"Is this my punishment then?" Danika scanned the stacks of bread lazily. "Am I to revert to baking? I may as well. I will need some profession come the Suncycle."

"I will not have your pity parade in my home," Babbin snapped. "You will start at the beginning. You will remember who you are, what an alkhemist is. Begin with starcharting."

"Starcharting?" Danika scoffed. "Starcharting is for blue bloods — artisans and prophets. My sister enjoys starcharting!"

"I will not hear your silly Izumgray talk. Blood is blood. Alkhemy is alkhemy. As Above—"

"So Below," Danika parroted.

"Very good. You will translate the tablet. You will do your starcharts every night."

"But why? What will it matter if I learn your lessons if in a year—"

"What you learn in that year will carry you through the Suncycle. Do not doubt it. Or me." Babbin grasped Danika's hands in her wrinkly ones. "I know why you did what you did. I do not blame you for the attempt. But you will never succeed until you accept who you are."

Something passed between Babbin and Danika then, the significance of which was lost on Adrik. But it did allow another thought to take root in his mind — these isles were as strange to him as any of the distant shores he and Dunya had traveled, even though the Kotov were his own people — Sivkan by all technicality. And yet Adrik knew next to nothing of their ways. Nothing at all of alkhemy, per Dunya's insistence. It was an error in Avdotya's teaching as far as Adrik was concerned. An error he intended to remedy as quickly as possible.

"The cycles are a balance, Little Nika, not a curse," said Babbin. "If you do not have what you need now to complete your work, you will find it in the mundane. Then, when your Fire returns—"

"Twenty-five years from now!" Danika shouted, hands curled into fists.

“Power shifts in the cycles.” Babbin’s gaze did not drift from Danika, but Adrik felt her blank eyes boring through him all the same. “You will see that soon enough. It is the way of things — like the Spark and the Star.”

Babbin released her hold, waddling to the bench piled high with bread. She pressed the still-steaming sourdough into Lukin’s fumbling hands and patted his cheek. “Take this. You deserve something warm.” Babbin turned back to Danika. “Now go. Do not come back without my starcharts.”

4. A TALE MOST TRAGIC

Adrien was quiet on the walk back. Lukin was decidedly not, even as he clung to his loaf like a child with a favorite doll. “You risked too much, Danika!” he shouted as they crested the first hill toward home. "A foolish amount. Why would you do it?”

Danika stared at him, surprised at the force of Lukin’s reaction. She thought back to Babbin’s words. *‘You will never succeed until you accept who you are.’* But wasn’t acceptance just another form of failure? She could never make peace with herself until she had done everything in her ability to avoid the fate that awaited her. But to explain that reasoning to Lukin was futile — not when he still did not know the whole story and certainly not when he was in such a rage.

“You know why, Lukin! The Stone works through the Suncycle!”

“So that is what this is about? You do not want to give up your alkhemy?” He spit the last word like a curse. “You are simply too stubborn to give in to the Cycle as every alkhemist has done since the moment The Mother cut herself by the Quicksilver River and bled silver?”

"When you put it that way, you make me sound mad," she quipped. But Lukin was not amused.

"Are you not? Is that not the reason you risked your own life? For a bit of rock?"

Danika swallowed her outrage at anyone calling the Philosopher's Stone 'a bit of rock.' He knew as well as any what the Philosopher's Stone could do. The fact that its discovery had nearly brought about the ruin of all Sivka seemed trivial in comparison to the Stone's gifts.

"I did not risk my life. My freedom, perhaps..." She shook her head. "But even Imperator Maksis does not execute for such a crime. Exile would have been my punishment."

"Oh, only exile, she says. Just a lifetime in a frozen tundra!" Over Lukin's shoulder, she saw Adrien stifle a laugh. But then Lukin closed the gap between them, forcing her attention back on him, his eyes blazing like coals at the bottom of the athanor. "Is that the reason you did it? To keep your power?"

Irritation prickled at her lungs like stinging nettles. Did he not see that some risk was necessary to achieve greatness? And if greatness was not her only reason for pursuing this course...that was none of his concern. She was certainly not about to confess her real motives — not after facing this derision.

"So what if it is?" she said, chin jutted high.

He reared back, the fire in his eyes doused as quickly as it had sparked. When he spoke again, it was with hollow disappointment. "Then I think it is time you stopped visiting that old crone and doused your fires. It is time to accept your life amongst us mundane."

His words stung. They should not have — she had told herself a thousand times that she must do exactly as he suggested when she returned to the Isles. But perhaps she was as mad as he accused, because now that someone else had demanded she do the very thing she had planned, she found she did not want to do it at all.

"You are asking me to give up who I am, Lukin. It cannot be done so easily for something so much...less."

He fell back a step. "I see. I did not realize you thought so little of your own people."

"That is not what I meant."

"I think I will walk the rest of the way alone. I know such *mundane* tasks are beneath you."

"Lukin—"

He made it halfway to the top of the hill before he turned to look back at her. His words were no less potent for being thinned by wind and distance. "I am not the one making you give up who you are, Nika. The Cycle is doing that."

She and Adrien stood in awkward silence until Lukin vanished over the ridge. The sun had dimmed, pregnant clouds bobbing over a gray horizon, air thick with the threat of rain — a perfect evening for brewing outdoors if she could only summon the will. But Danika found much of her ambition dimmed, especially now that this handsome stranger had born witness to so much of her embarrassment.

As Danika began to follow in Lukin's long shadow, Adrien picked up a reed along the path. He whacked at the passing banks on either side. For all his apparent distraction, she could feel his attention on her in her periphery. "Avdotya told me that there is at least one Stone still in existence. That Imperator Maksis has it." Adrien spat the Imperator's name with particular venom.

Danika stepped back to watch the mesmerizing shift of the muscles in his arm and back as he swung his stick. "He does... By law, any citizen of Sivka can petition for use of the Imperator's Stone. But the number of successful petitioners dwindles every year. I have not heard of any being granted in half a decade."

"Typical," Adrien scoffed. "But there must be more Stones somewhere if their existence was enough to cause so much chaos—"

"Chaos is an understatement. When the Suncycle came and the Stones continued to work, people were elated. For a time. But then the economy collapsed. There was mass starvation. The division between those who had Stones and those who did not turned violent. Riots broke out in the streets. Still, people were desperate to acquire Stones wherever they could — no one was ready to let the possibility of endless riches, a long life, and a miracle cure to any ill, out of their grasp."

The breath evaporated suddenly from Danika's lungs. She found she could not voice another word. She did not realize she had stopped walking until Adrien turned back to look at her only to find her several paces behind. He closed the gap between them in two long strides, brow furrowed, "Danika? Are you alright?"

She gave herself a shake. Forced herself to focus on the gleam of Adrien's eyes, which had turned pale yellow in the reflection of the gray skies overhead. "Avdotya taught you about Maksis' Stone, but not what happened to the others?"

"Avdotya doesn't care for alkhemy. Or my questions about it."

"Not long after the Suncycle and the economic collapse, it was decided the Stones should be destroyed," she explained. "This was back when the alkhemist Lunovna Imperators ruled together with the mundane Solov Imperators." Danika expected Adrien's eyes to glaze over — he seemed the sort more suited for action than history lessons — but to her surprise, he looked more enthralled by her words than ever before. "When Impress Lizabeta Lunovna took the Lunar Crown upon the death of her father, Lizabeta's co-ruler, Impress Tatiana Solov, used the distraction of the coronation to her advantage. In secret, Tatiana Solov reclaimed the Philosopher's Stones. She burned every recipe, blocked all imports from other nations, and executed every maker of the Philosopher's Stone she could find.

"The Solov Impress destroyed what Stones she could and then went into hiding. She knew that such action would not be without cost, but had decided it was best for her people. Then Impress Lizabeta Lunovna found Tatiana Solov and executed her for her crimes. It is said that they agreed together to ban the making of any more Stones before the ax fell."

Adrien's lips thinned into a grim line. She had never seen him look so serious. "Then where did Maksis get his?"

"That is less certain," Danika continued up the path, Adrien nipping at her heels like an eager pup. It was not an unpleasant feeling. "We do not know whether Tatiana and Lizabeta purposefully kept a few Stones hidden in case they had need of them or if Tatiana simply missed some in her purge. Regardless, by 3500-Luncycle, the Imperator at the time admitted that some unknown number of Stones still remained in their possession. If yet another Stone came into being... If people knew of it — it would upset the balance beyond measure."

The thought caused an uncomfortable squirming in her gut. She recalled the fury in Lukin's face and wondered if he had not been so out of line after all. But it was some consolation that Adrien seemed nearly as fascinated by the Stones as Danika was herself.

They continued in silence for a moment or two before Adrien was at her with yet more questions. "What did you give to the smithy earlier?"

"Brine. It is for cooling iron."

"But you offered to show him how to make it? Isn't he mundane?"

"Yes. But that does not matter for that particular solution. Anyone can make it. It is not so much alkhemy as—"

"Chemistry," Adrien declared with relish. "Science."

Danika paused. That word had been forbidden for as long as she could remember. A law laid down in the Velvet Book by Imperator Maksis' father — Imperator Voya Lunovna — the very man who had imprisoned the last generation of the Solov family for dabbling in such "dangerous mundane arts."

"You should teach him how to make the brine for himself," Adrien said. "We will all need to fend for ourselves come the Suncycle."

His words were like sour milk in her stomach. After all, in 348 days, when the Luncycle ended and all things alkhemical ceased to exist, she would have plenty of time to make brines. There would be nothing better to do.

"Is Lukin courting you?"

Danika tripped over a log placed inconveniently in the pathway.

Adrien caught her. His grip was firm. She could feel the hot pressure of all nine of his fingertips on her waist, the long line of his chest pressing against her back. She looked over her shoulder and as he grinned at her, her face warmed. "I'll take that as a yes."

"What?" Danika tried and failed to pull out of his arms, but there was nowhere to go with the log ahead of her and Adrien — suddenly so large — behind. "No, of course not."

"Is that such a strange question?" His breath ghosted over the shell of her ear, sending a shiver down her spine. "Do your people not court?"

"We do, yes."

"But not you?"

"I do not concern myself with such matters." Did she not? Was she not very concerned with one particular matter at this very moment? But her mouth had run off without her, even as she held herself stiffly in his embrace. "I have been from home for a long time. And my work—"

Adrien laughed and released her to wave a hand. The sudden return of air to her lungs was like being freed from a cage she had no desire to break open. "I get it," he laughed. "You're very busy and important."

"That is not—"

"Danika, I need to ask you something." She forced herself to turn and face him. The sight of him, curls wild and expression cracked open, earnest as a child before New Year's feast, was no less arresting than the heady feeling of his strong arms holding her close. Something in her chest began to ache.

"Yes?"

"Will you teach me alkhemy?"

Danika stared at him. A tiny raindrop struck her forehead. "But you are—"

"Mundane, yes."

"Then you know that I cannot—"

"I know. I know that I can't ever do alkhemy the way you can. I understand that. But I want to learn anyway." He smiled that beautiful smile, so bold and naive and full of possibility — and the fear that had frozen around her heart during their visit with Babbin, thawed slightly. "Will you teach me? It might even help you figure out the Philosopher's Stone! Avdotya always told me the Kotov don't care much for Sivkan laws, but unlike Lukin, I think you risked just the right amount. So why not risk a little more?"

The arrogance of what he asked was nothing short of astounding. Only an alkhemist could wield the powers of the Alkhemical Flame. But if he, a mundane, believed he could summon alkhemy during a Luncycle with naught but his own stubbornness at his disposal, then who could doubt that Danika — the most talented student to grace Izumgray's halls in a generation — could master the Philosopher's Stone, and bring alkhemy with her into the Suncycle?

In asking her to do the impossible, Adrien had ignited in her a belief that her own mission was, in fact, probable.

"You might be as mad as I am," said Danika.

His grin widened. "Is that a yes?"

As if she would ever tell him anything else.

"Why are you here, Adrien?"

"I told you. I wanted to come with you—"

"No. Why are you *here*? On the Von? On the Kotov Isles?"

The humor slid from his face. His gaze skirted away. "Avdotya said I was to wait... He wants to explain—"

"You mean to overthrow the Imperator."

His mouth fell open. "Why do you say that?" Once again answering a question with a question.

Danika could just see the long line of the turfhouse roof peeking over the hill. The smell of roast fish overpowered the hint of rain and she shivered in the chill breeze. "You have come from Polvia — the Imperator's enemy nation. Your knowledge of alkhemy and Sivkan history is somehow both impressive and sorely lacking. You are clearly trained for combat, yet you bring a strategist with you to treatise with the Kotov — we who are renowned for our skill in battle and little else, we whose loyalty to the Imperator has been known to wax and wane with the phases of the moon. You both claim to be Sivkan, and yet Avdotya wears a sunburst crest on his breast... The crest of the Solovs. The Solovs, who are long buried — thanks to Imperator Maksis."

She could see the war in his eyes. The teetering between his desire and his better judgment, like two metals of opposite attraction, fighting each other and binding together with equal force.

"You do not have to tell me now," Danika said. His shoulders slumped in relief, and she brushed past him to open the gate into the yard. "You will tell us tonight. These things are better done with vodka."

"It was nearly Tasya's birthday, or so Avdotya tells me." Adrien stood over the silver fire at the end of the hall, ghostly shadows skipping over his face and a tin cup of the strongest Eletski vodka clutched in the four fingers of his right hand.

The rest of the family had gathered around him by unspoken agreement. It was strange for Nadya to see the whole lot of them together under the turf on an Autumn evening when there was still a harvest to manage, herds to tend, and shallows warm enough to swim in. Tales like this were best saved for the depths of Whitewinter, when there was nothing better to do but listen to snow pelt the frozen roof and watch ice form on the windowpanes.

But, as in so many other ways, Adrien had proved the exception.

"The twenty-first birthday is an important occasion for Sivkans. It's when we choose our patronymic," he said, staring into the depths of his cup. "You see, none of us children ever knew a life outside the palace walls. Our mama and papa had been imprisoned on their wedding night. For nearly 30 years, each of us was born into a gilded cage. I was only six — I didn't know the life I was missing. But Tasya? And my eldest brother, Kolya? They were grown. They were old enough to read books, study paintings, understand what real life could be and know they would never have it.

"Mama was the one who made it all bearable. She taught Tasya everything she knew — music, sewing, dance. And when Mama ran out of things to teach, she learned more. She filled Tasya's head with literature and history, math and science."

Adrien took a deep breath, looking up from his cup to meet each of their eyes in turn. Nadya thought he lingered over her the longest, but when he uttered the word 'science,' it was to Danika that he turned. "My sister was likely the most educated woman in all Sivka, though no one would ever know it. Mama gave Tasya a purpose outside the longing to break free. So we knew that, come her majority, she would name herself after mama. After Mariya. Her full name, by the time the night was done, would be Tasya Mariyavna Solov."

Solov. But if his sister was a Solov, then...

Nadya gasped. She was not the only one. Mama's cup slipped from her fingers. Papa reached out to take her hand. Adrien's eyes flickered up to meet Nadya's before he carried on.

"There wasn't any doubt about the Solov," said Adrien. "Whatever her affinity for Mama — Tasya was still the daughter of an Imperator."

The air in the room shifted. The story had changed. This was not what any of them, save perhaps Danika, had expected when they gave shelter to two strangers from the south. Adrien — if that really was his name, and it was becoming abundantly clear it was not — was part of a long dynasty begun some two thousand years ago, and ended by one man. Nadya thought back to another tale. The first story in the Velvet Book. One she had heard so many times she could recite it by heart:

The Mother and Father had been cast out of their kingdom, left to wander the land for a new home.

They struggled across a vast expanse of nothingness in search of shelter, to no avail. Then a great storm blew in, so cold it cut through blanket and fur and skin until Mother and Father clutched each other blue and frozen abreast an icy lake.

As they shivered beneath the moonlight, beside a fire that would not light, Father saw with fresh eyes. Where his veins ran a dull blue, Mother's glowed white in the darkness.

Driven by Thoth's voice in the form of a whispering wind, Father handed Mother a blade. She split herself over the deadened fire, and as her silver blood dropped over the branches, the fire caught to a blazing white.

Lives saved by the spark of the Alkhemical Flame, they marched on to Sivka.

And since that time, The Mother and Father's descendants had ruled their new nation together. Eventually, The Mother's descendants — the Lunovnas — claimed the Luncycle, ruling every quarter century when alkhemy took hold.

And when the Luncycle faded and Suncycle began, The Father's children — the Solovs — took their place. So it had gone for generations — Lunovnas and Solovs.

Until Imperator Voya Lunovna. Voya had broken the pattern established two dozen generations before. He imprisoned the Solov family and he, a Lunovna, reigned during a Suncycle. And Sivka did not crumble. The world did not end.

But Adrik's had.

The name came to Nadya slowly, dredged up from a distant memory of Mama teaching her to read from the Velvet Book. The book contained many diagrams of family ties — even the Solov family. And there had always been rumors, whispers that one boy had survived The Slaughter...

Adrik.

They had unknowingly given refuge to the lost child of Iosif Solov — the Imperator's greatest enemy.

The options now before them were stark. They would have to declare, in the harshest terms, for one side or the other. Just as Lukin had entrapped Adrik, Adrik had bound their destiny to his. Nadya resented that he had thrust this choice upon them with so little thought for the consequences.

Adrik did not wait long for them to get their bearings. It seemed that now he had begun his story, he could no sooner stop himself from the telling than he could stop it coming to pass.

"Mama, Kiril, little Amaliya and I were hold up in the Blue Room, planning the menu for the party. Maksis had restricted most delicacies — there wouldn't be any champagne for the toast." Adrik flashed a dark grin. "But over the years, we'd learned to make do with what we were given. And the cooks were kind — they always snuck me extra sweets.

"I remember little Amaliya bouncing on Mama's knee. She had the most brilliant head of red hair." Adrik stared at Mikhail — the only one of them not entranced by Adrik's story. He sat splay-legged on the ground between Mama's feet, gumming a wooden spoon. "Kiril's hair was a little lighter..." He paused, still watching Mikhail, then shook his head and returned to his tale.

"Kiril was only a few years older than me. A nine-year-old, a six-year-old, and a three-year-old — needless to say, we weren't much help with the arrangements. Mama talked over our heads to the cook, trying to decide between pheasant or pork. I made a face at Amaliya. She stuck out her tongue. The tip looked like a little red raspberry and I wanted to ask Mama if we could have berries at the party — but before I could, the guards stormed in.

"There were four of them. More than I'd ever seen in one room. I suppose they wanted one for each of us." Adrik's face darkened. "I can't imagine why they thought a baby posed such a threat." It was as if he thought he, a six-year-old, had posed greater. "I didn't know the guards. They'd never stood watch on us before. Two of them yanked Mama out of her seat. Mama pushed Amaliya into my arms. The third grabbed Kiril around the middle. And one — one shoved me and Amaliya down the hall. I followed another guard down a dozen staircases, until we were deep in the bowels of the palace. I'd never been there. You'd think — a young boy, trapped in a palace all his life — the courtyard would be the first place he'd go exploring." He frowned. "But I never did."

His expression cleared. He continued on in his detached voice. "Another four guards arrived with Tasya, Kolya and Papa. The courtyard was small. Too small to hold a dozen, let alone twenty. Papa was the biggest man I ever knew and he had to tuck his elbows to fit. I tried to catch his eye. I knew if I did, if I could see the strength in his eyes, it would make me braver. But it was like he didn't recognize me. He was too focused on the guards. I know now they were Lun-Protektorate — elite servants loyal only to the Imperator. Papa's papa must have had his own Sun-Protekorate when he was in power. But obviously they weren't very good at their jobs, for us to end up there.

"Papa argued with one of them. The leader, I suppose. 'You must speak with the Imperator,' he said. 'We've done nothing. Twenty-nine years we've been here. We've done nothing.' But the guard didn't listen. He pulled his sword and felled Mama with a single slash across her throat. The screams started. It was a cacophony. Like nothing I'd ever heard. I spent my entire life trapped with these seven people, but I couldn't distinguish one cry from another. All I could think was that I had to protect Amaliya. Somehow, she slipped from my arms.

"She was sitting on the floor, in a pool of blood, face red from screaming." His gaze flicked to Mikhail again. "I ducked down and crawled to her. Kolya stared back at me, but there was no one left in his eyes. His chest was a gaping chasm and Tasya's fingers were curled in his ribcage. Tasya knelt, but only because the spear kept her upright. I crawled the last few inches to Amaliya. My fingers had just reached her bare toes when the boot came down on her skull.

"I curled into a ball. There was sick on my shirt. Papa was on his knees too, but there was no spear keeping him up. He'd fallen there at the first strike and hadn't moved since. I finally caught his eye. It didn't make me any braver. Finally, a guard hauled me up by my throat. My head cracked against the stone wall."

Adrik stopped, staring hard into the fire, as if he could discern the truth in the shape of the silver flames. "I don't know what made him stop. I don't care. He released me, and I ran. I'm ashamed to admit I didn't turn back until I was at the door. I watched as they finished Papa. I could swear I saw Kiril—"

"Adrik."

It was the first Avdotya had spoken all night. He gave a sharp shake of his head and Adrik copied the gesture like a little boy playing a game of mimic. "I was about to go back for them when Avdotya grabbed me—"

All eyes turned to Avdotya. He had taken a vodka pail like everyone else, but his cup sat untouched on the table. He did not meet their eyes, staring instead at Adrik. "We fled out the tunnels and took the first sledge to Polvia."

"I owe you my life."

Avdotya waved a hand. "You'll return the favor."

Nadya had heard many tales around this fire. Tales of war and danger and heartbreak. Tales as true as this one, spoken in the whispering black of winter. But even by this unseasonably muggy heat, with fruit flies nibbling at her ankles, no tale had ever struck such a chill in her heart. It was a long time before anyone spoke or even moved.

Finally, Papa rose. He put a gentle hand on Adrik's shoulder and Nadya saw Adrik fight the instinct to flinch away.

"You have shared a harrowing tale with us," Papa said, cup raised high. "We honor it."

"It is one the Imperator would argue," said Papanik. He had not raised his cup.

Adrik bristled. "I am sure he would."

"We do not doubt you," said Papa firmly. "Everyone knows what Imperator Maksis did to the Solovs. The why of it may be much argued, but that is not my concern. There was even rumor that a son escaped—"

"Was there?" said Elin, voice obscene in its eagerness.

Papa ignored her, focussed on Adrik. "I can guess what you mean to do—"

Adrik did not hesitate. "I mean to avenge my family. I mean to take back my crown. I mean to—"

"Kill my brother." Mama's voice was cold, her face cryptic.

"Your relation to the Imperator is the reason we did not come to the Von first," Avdotya said. "We thought—"

"You thought the Vienper would be more sympathetic to your cause," Mama said. She tucked a length of black hair behind her ear. "And so they will be. But I have no great love for my brother. He is not my family. This is my family. I would not have you put them in danger."

But whatever Mama's wish, Adrik had disrupted their fragile peace. The contentment that had so long cocooned Nadya's world was about to burst. Not Mama, nor Thoth, nor The Mother herself could stop it.

"It must be put to a vote," said Papa. "I will call the Folktan. There you can speak your story and the Kotov will make their choice."

Adrik looked to Avdotya, who nodded. A vote was risky. The Kotov were unpredictable. They liked a fight, but not quite so much as they liked to refuse a Sivkan. The Kotov decision may have been uncertain, but as Nadya looked to Danika, to the light in her sea-blue eyes, one thing was clear — she suffered no doubts. Danika had made her choice. And it was Adrik.

5. THE FIRST FOLKTAN

"My apologies," said Dondar as he shifted backward onto Danika's foot. She waved a hand and inched to the left, but only slightly. The Folktan was so packed with people there was hardly room for breathing. She bumped shoulders with Lukin and he skewered her with such a glower, she immediately wished she had stayed beneath Dondar's heel.

"I am surprised you and your papa came," Danika said to him in as low a voice as she could manage in the overcrowded room.

The Folktan stretched several fathoms wide and another thirty long, but still was not space enough to house all the Kotov. Gaining entry entailed a combination of unspoken rank and how willing one was to throw elbows. Most would stand out in the yard, waiting for word to trickle out. As daughter of the former Prime Chieftain, Danika had no trouble securing her place. Lukin's papa, though — he was just a blacksmith.

"They *were* my captives," Lukin growled. Danika blinked. She had almost forgotten. She had thought to claim Adrik as her own personal discovery, but in truth, Lukin *had* got their first.

"So they were." She did not bother to point out that they were hers now. That was clear by the way Avdotya and Adrik stood in the center of the hall, consulting with Papa.

"What are they after?" Lukin said, a hint of curiosity breeching his sullen tone.

"I could not say."

"You mean you will not say."

Danika ignored Lukin's bitterness and focused instead on the Folknik wandering the room, hide sandals scraping the packed-earth floor. He spoke aloud the law of the Kotov as he did before every Folktan, but no one bothered to listen, not even Danika. Kotov justice was not determined by any law, but by instinct and truth.

An exceptionally tall Urik chose that moment to stand in front of Danika, blocking her view of the small clearing in the center of the room. If the ridiculous length of his saber was anything to judge by, he was not the sort to be reasoned with. She grit her teeth and turned to Lukin. "If you get us up front, I will tell you why we are here."

Lukin flashed a dark grin, took Danika by the hand, and charged.

Excuses or pardons would have shown weakness and Danika refused to miss a moment of Adrik's victory. Her victory. Today, as with most days on the Kotov Isles, politeness took second place to pride.

With one strategically stomped foot, Lukin secured them a spot at the front of the circle formed around Adrik and Avdotya. They would not miss so much as a whisper here. Danika was still reveling in her victory when she spotted Nadya. Her sister had not had to fight to secure pride of place — she stood between Mama and her would-be betrothed, Taito, who clung white-knuckled to her hand as if he feared she would try to escape if he loosened his grip. When Nadya caught Danika's eye, she shrugged apologetically. The perks of being Mama's favorite.

"I've done what you asked, Nika. A fish caught is a bargain made — tell me what you know."

She turned her gaze to Lukin. She had relished keeping her secret earlier, but now found herself all too eager to spill it, even despite their argument over the Stone. So much had happened since then. Lukin's concerns were mere trivialities to her now. Danika lowered her voice — though there was little point in the cacophony of a thousand jabbering, restless Kotov — and said, "They wish to overthrow the Imperator."

Lukin's eyes went wide, then narrow. "And I saw a lobster at the top of Mount Ironwood."

Danika bristled. She did not like to be called a liar, especially by Lukin. She crossed her arms. "You will see."

Avdotya chose that moment to step forward. The Folktan was slow to quiet and Avdotya did not hurry them. He paced the perimeter of the circle, running a thumb over his carefully groomed mustache, until finally, only the crackling of torches and shifting of bodies remained.

"I am not here to speak to you of my accomplishments. Nor even of his," Avdotya said, nodding his head toward Adrik, who stood at the rear of the circle with Mama, Papa, and Nadya. "I am here to speak of *your* destiny, *your* accomplishments."

If Adrik was nervous to be sitting in judgment of thousands of Kotov, he did not look it. His hand with the missing finger curled on the pommel of a sword Lukin had begrudgingly returned to him just days ago at Danika's request. She stared at the stub where his right pointer finger should have been — had no one thought to reattach the severed limb? There were plenty of potions for such procedures...

Avdotya stopped circling, black eyes staring intently into the crowd. His own sunburst pin was back in place, fastened prominently over his sash. Did anyone recognize it for what it was? If they did not, they would soon. "You — who have lived on these little islands ever since The Mother shed her blood by the Quicksilver River. You — who have hidden yourselves away from Sivka, Polvia, Jinmen and Gam." Disquiet murmured through the hall. The Kotov did not hide. "You — who claim to tame tides that do not exist and have the audacity to call your lake a sea."

There were more than murmurs now. Furious tension bristled through the room and the circle around Avdotya seemed to shrink. Danika seethed. What was he doing? Did he mean to ruin Adrik's chances?

"You have lived by your own rules, built your own own customs, and answered to no one but yourselves." A few nods met this. But Avdotya quickly ruined what traction he had gained — "Or so you would claim."

Hard silence met these words. Avdotya languished in it.

"The truth of the Kotov legacy is not quite so straight forward." He paced to the opposite side of the circle. As the crowd's fury ratcheted, so, seemingly, did Avdotya's. "The truth is that you spent centuries squandering your talents on petty border wars, fighting over waters none but you sought to hold. You hired yourselves out to any passing nation and in doing so you built a reputation as feckless," the word was like the sting of a lash, "wanton," a second strike, "and barbaric," the final hit.

"Your greatest triumph came the day your greatest hero, your bravest warrior, bedded an Impress. Bodan took Yuliya to the bedcloset and in so doing accomplished the first bit of Kotov diplomacy in the history of your race. Allied with Sivka, you were unbeatable. Feared by all, bathed in fortune, you became the Impress' greatest regiment. But it could not last forever. Your greed and lack of forethought got the better of you."

Like a carrion over his prey, Avdotya honed in. If he had not held the Kotov so enraptured, he would have been in a fight for his life. But despite their rage and disdain, they listened on. Perhaps they would kill him after.

"Impress Yuliya died. And Bodan died. And then what did you have? Nothing but enemies on every front — all of them claiming to be your ally. For all your talk of independence and equality, you crumbled without a leader. You turned on each other. You splintered. Your greatest war was not with the Jinmen or the Gam, but with each other." Avdotya feigned a laugh, shaking his head. "Oh, certainly you claimed to fight for separate nations, separate ideals. Some of you went to Polvia, some of you remained with Sivka, but all of you were weaker for it."

The fury siphoned off. The crackle of silence shifted into doubt. Many an Auntie and Uncle had fought in the civil wars. Papanik had lost his sister. Papa, a brother. The pain of its memory was fresh. And Avdotya promised answers.

"The war resolved as they always do. Your Polvian masters turned out not to be as benevolent as you hoped. The Sivkans offered aid that could not be ignored. You took the gifts of the new Imperator to end a war of your own making and in doing so, you tied a noose around your necks and handed Maksis the rope.

"You call yourselves Kotov. You carry the Kotov legacy and history and language. You practice your own religion and rituals. You live far from the Imperator and his problems. In return, he offers protection you have no need of; luxuries you are too lazy to make for yourselves; and on Aadan's Day, twice a year, you add to your population through the gift of his fleeing vassals. But *you* must protect his border. *You* must fight his wars. You must give him the best of yourselves. And now...you must pay taxes?"

Avdotya's words landed with the precision of an alkhemical arrow. There were mutters in the crowd again, but they were ones of agreement and righteous outrage. Neighbor whispered to neighbor and more than a few hands tightened on their sabers.

Avdotya stopped in the center of the circle, hands on his hips. "You call yourself Kotov. But there is no denying — you are Sivkan. Sivkan in all but name."

There were shouts of dissent — "No, we are Kotov!"

Another yell, "The tide will bring us in!"

But even more stood silent, contemplative.

"In all your fighting, your squabbles and tantrums, your broken loyalties and feeble alliances, one fact has remained true — you are the greatest warriors the world has ever known."

Silence reigned. Avdotya had said the one thing all Kotov knew with the certainty of the Cycles. And true it must have been for a man as disdainful and cruel as him to say it.

"You make armies twice your size tremble in their boots. Jinmenese and Gam, Frexlanders and Scandians — they have one villain in their hearth stories — and it is you."

Cheers of agreement, stomping of boots. Danika cast an eye to Papa. He held a fist over his mouth, eyes shimmering darkly. Mama had taken Nadya's hand in a vice.

"My name is Avdotya Rostislav. I served under the True Imperator Iosif Irikovich Solov. It was my greatest honor to advise him and my greatest sorrow to lose him. There is only one man who could take his place. Only one man who I could serve in penance, and deign to ask the Kotov to hear. I give you a man escaped from the clutches of the Imposter, raised in secret and security, and bred for one purpose. Son of the True Imperator, and the only man living worthy of your respect — Adrik Iosifvich Solov — rightful heir to the Sivkan throne."

Avdotya slithered back and Adrik stepped forward.

Head bowed, he rubbed the back of his neck in a careful pantomime of humility. He smiled bashfully up at the stunned crowd. "I doubt there is anything I could say that would live up to the man Avdotya just described, but there is no doubt in my mind, he has understated you.

"You know what the Imperator is. Better than I, you know his half-truths and broken promises. And you know as well as I do what it's like to live under Maksis' boot. But no one knows as well as I do how it feels to have his guard's hand around your throat as your mother bleeds out on the gravel.

"I won't ask you to serve me. I won't bargain away your rights until you have no choice but to cling to your customs like a shield. If you join me, I will be the one who is indebted. I will tell stories of the Kotov salvation — the partners who helped me dethrone a dictator."

Adrik's golden gaze melted through the Folktan. He focused firmly on each Von, Vienper, Urik, Telga and Dural he passed. He seemed to meet everyone's eye but hers.

"I am no fool. I know the risk I ask you to take. A year from now, the world as we know it will change. The alkhemy the Imperator has relied on for so long will be nothing but smoke and memory. Without intervention, we will live another

25 years yearning for the next. In a country of 10 million, only 500,000 are alkhemists. Do you think their status will wane during the Suncycle? I don't. I suspect they will burrow further into Maksis' embrace as the rest of us shiver out in the cold. I suspect Maksis will withhold progress and aid so that your gratitude will be all the more potent when he can give you the potions to cure all your ills. But would you waste 25 years? Would you spend your best days waiting for better?"

Finally, they locked eyes. Danika stared back at him, fingertips crackling with unspent fire.

"I would have you live your life," he said on a whisper, as if his words were meant for her and her alone, and, foolishly, she found herself blinking back tears. "I would have you join me."

Adrik turned to Papa. Only a Kotov could call a vote.

Papa licked his lips, then, ever so slowly, stepped into the circle beside Adrik. "I, Rodin, son of Howlan, citizen of the Von, call a vote. Will the Kotov join Adrik, son of Iosif, in battle against Imperator Maksis? Cast your stones."

Mama and Nadya drug two stools into the center of the circle. Each bore a bowl — one of white marble representing 'Yay,' the other black granite representing 'Nay.' As Mama and Nadya retreated, there was a great rush forward.

Not every citizen was present to cast their vote, but any above the age of sixteen had a stone to represent them. Men and women, young and old, pressed ahead to drop their rocks into the bowl. As the clank and clatter filled the room, Danika noticed most of them had the broad, bullish look of the Vienper.

The Vienper had begun the conflict Avdotya had not dared to mention by name. One hundred and forty-three years ago, they had broken with Sivka and Bodan to wage war against their fellow Kotov on behalf of Polvia. They had been making up for it ever since. But there was no doubt how they would cast their vote now — not when there was a chance to best an Imperator.

Danika rose up on tip-toe as Hurkan came forward. If the Vienper elected their leaders by brawn, there was no question why Hurkan had served as their last Chieftain. His bulbous nose flared in triumph as he met Papa's eye. Danika had never in her life rooted for the Vienper's bloodthirstiness, but today she could not help but celebrate as Hurkan dropped his over-large rock into the white marble bowl.

With Hurkan's vote cast, the Durals scurried forward. It was a tale as old as the Flame itself — where Vienper went, Dural rushed to follow. Moments later, the Dural cleared.

The 'Nay' bowl was all but empty. So likely was her triumph that Danika threw a grin to Lukin.

No Von had yet to vote, Danika included. No Kotov was required to vote with their isle, every Kotov's choice was their own, but the rule of mob was powerful. And Papa even more so.

He stepped into the clearing. His brow wrinkled and his gaze turned inward. The choice for many would be his alone. That was the thing about Papa — he did not need to boast his lineage as Adrik and Avdotya had done. Papa was the son of Howlan, yes. But more importantly, he was the great-grandson of Bodan.

Papa ran a calloused thumb over the flat gray stone. He had to make a show of consideration, it was his duty as former Prime Chieftain, but Danika was so sure of what his verdict would be that it took a long moment to register the gasps.

It had to have been a trick of her eyes. He could not have— He would not— But he had.

Papa had voted 'Nay.'

Danika stood numb as hundreds of Vons, Telgas and Uriks filed past her to add their stones to Papa's. She could not bring herself to even look at Adrik, nor bother to cast her vote. Some distant awareness registered Mama adding a stone to the marble bowl, but what did her approval matter? It was over. Papa had decided, and Danika's fate was sealed alongside Adrik's.

The votes were cast. They had failed.

Avdotya wanted to leave right away. Where exactly he hoped to be going, Adrik wasn't sure. They'd taken a great risk revealing their identities to the Kotov. To move on to find the next, second-best army in Sivka seemed foolhardy at best. Luckily, Rodin had offered his home for as long as they had need. Adrik's pride wouldn't allow them to stay much longer, but he couldn't resist the invitation to the Aadan's Day festival. And just because the Kotov as a people had renounced Adrik's cause, didn't mean all hope was lost. In fact, there was one Kotov in particular that Adrik was sure he could still claim for an ally...

"We were fools to think the Kotov could be reasoned with. Their motives have always been selfish. What benefit do they reap from us?" Avdotya paced the dooryard in front of the turfhouse for the tenth time in the last three days. For a man usually so collected, his voice was inappropriately loud. Avdotya did not handle disappointment well. And this was disappointment of the highest order. Years of planning gone with the cast of a single stone.

"If we succeed, we offer—"

"Yes! Should we *succeed*! That is the point. To realize it would require forethought — a trait these people clearly lack."

"Dunya—"

"And for his wife to even join our cause! But for him to back away? It is unfathomable."

Adrik balled his hands into fists. Did Avdotya really think he wanted this more than Adrik? That he pined for Maksis' downfall more deeply? No other man living could claim that mantle. The difference was, Adrik had no intention of giving up. He'd seen too many setbacks on this path to let this one finish him.

But there was no reasoning with Dunya when he got like this. Best to leave him to his fuming. Adrik was late for a lesson with his alkhemist.

As if on cue, Danika barged out of the turfhouse, hauling a pair of heavy-looking grain sacks, brows knitted in a scowl. The door slammed behind her as she rounded the corner and marched toward the back of the house. Adrik ran after her.

"Boy!" Avdotya called. "Where are you going? I am not done—"

Adrik waved a hand over his shoulder and let Avdotya's cries disappear into the wind. He followed Danika down the narrow path between the turfhouse and the cliffside behind it. The only person who seemed more outraged by the result of the Folktan than Dunya was Danika. The little alkhemist had taken to storming around the house, avoiding conversation with everyone but her beautiful sister.

"Running away?" Adrik called. She did not squeal or jump as a mainlander maiden might, but spun around, ready for attack. Adrik held up his hands innocently. "I thought we had a lesson planned?"

She did not smile at his flirting. She did not smile much at all. It was one of the things he liked about her. "Mama asked me to store these in the byre." She hefted up the heavy sacks. If she were anyone else, he would have offered to carry them for her.

"Is there not a door into the byre in the kitchen?"

"Yes," she said, and scowled. He waited for her to explain. She huffed out a breath. "But Papa is in there."

"Ah." He dropped his hands and hooked his thumbs into his leather belt. "You shouldn't worry, I'll find a way to defeat the Imperator without the Kotov. Perhaps Frexland, or Gam—"

"I am certain you will," she snapped, and stomped off. He jogged after her again. She had a very long stride.

"Does that anger you? I thought you wanted—"

"I wanted to be part of it!" she shouted, kicking in the door to the byre.

He followed her into the darkened barn. It smelled of hay and old animal droppings. The narrow shaft of light from the doorway lit her furious face. She threw the sacks down and a cloud of dust plumed in its wake.

"You still can be," he offered. "And what about our lessons?"

She glared at him. "What is the point? You will be leaving soon on your great quest. You do not need me or my false teachings."

He wondered how best to appease her. Somehow he didn't think his usual tactic of flowers or jewels would do the trick. "I could send for you once I—"

"Please. Do not make promises you will not keep."

He couldn't muster any offense — she wasn't wrong. He wandered over to the nearest stall and pretended to test the gate. "Perhaps it's for the best. It could take half a year to secure another army. Then there are funds, weapons. We hoped to take on the Imperator before the end of the Luncycle, strike when he least expected, but with things as they stand now, the Suncycle may dawn before we find the field. And you're an alkhemist — without your abilities—"

The blow came hard and swift to his shoulder blades. He fell forward onto the swinging gate. Scrambling for balance, he turned round to a fist soaring at his nose. He ducked, and, on instinct, shoved. Danika crashed backward into an empty trough. She collapsed inside it, wedged there, legs kicking in the air like a baby. Adrik burst out laughing.

"Get me out!"

He clung to the gate, heaving breathlessly. She continued to writhe, thrashing side to side in a futile attempt to escape.

"Get me out! Get me out now!"

A strange note in her voice forced Adrik to look up through streaming eyes. Her face had paled, knuckles white on the trough's sides as she struggled to get free. Her eyes were blown wide. But it wasn't fury — it was panic.

He launched forward. She gripped his four-fingered hand in a vice as he hauled her up and out. She released him at once and fell to her knees in the dirt. All the laughter left him at once.

"Nika—"

"Do not," she spat, still panting. "Do not...pity me." Her hands curled around a fistful of hay.

He did the only thing he could think of, and knelt down before her. "What is it? You can tell me."

She squeezed her eyes shut and shook her head once. "If you think me worthless now—"

His hand fell over hers. "I could never think you worthless."

She finally met his eyes. He could see her deciding — whether or not to trust him, whether or not to hit him again. She chewed the words in her mouth before she finally spat them out, "I have— I have the Swimming Sickness."

Adrik felt his hand try to pull away from her. He didn't let it. Still, he had to ask...

"When did you—"

"Nine years ago. You need not fear." She smiled bitterly. He tightened his grip in apology. "There is a pond a short walk north. We played there often as children. The Kotov never bothered with purifying tinctures. It was not a problem until..."

"None of your siblings...?"

Terror blanched across her face. "No, thank The Mother. Only me."

He looked down at her legs and away again. She still caught it.

"I take an elixir. It keeps my muscles from decaying." Her hand twitched beneath his. "It is no cure. When the Luncycle ends—"

"Will you be able to walk?"

Her eyes cut away. "I do not know," she said. But he knew she was lying.

"So you want to join me while you can still fight?"

"It is not only that..." She met his gaze again. It was reluctant. "You said it yourself. Maksis has a Philosopher's Stone."

Adrik pulled away. He sat back on one knee and looked at her with clear eyes. Dunya was always telling him to never underestimate self-interest. One of these days, he would remember it.

"You want to steal Maksis' Stone for yourself? What happened to Babbin's high-minded ideals about understanding a thing before you change it?"

"I can worry about ideals once I am able to walk."

Adrik tried to think what Dunya would say. Self-interest was rampant, yes. But if it aligned with his own....

"Then it's a shame your papa voted 'Nay,' isn't it?"

6. AADAN'S DAY

The crispness of Autumn finally took root the following tennight, hardening the earth beneath their boots and dulling the grass to shades of yellow. Nadya and Mama had spent the afternoon pulling winter coats from the shed, beating the dust from furs and wools on a line behind the turfhouse, brown clouds pluming before a blazing sun.

Nadya took an armful of fleece jackets off the line and set off around the house, where squeals and shouts of laughter led her to the dooryard. She found Danika leaning against a hedge, watching as Zin, Mikhail and Taito's youngest sister, Manet, circled a kneeling Adrik.

"Have mercy, I beg you!" Adrik cried out, hands upheld. Zin, Mikhail, and Taito's little sister Manet bore down on him with wooden swords.

"Kotov show no mercy!" Manet shouted, jabbing the tip of her blade into Adrik's chest.

"How long has this been going on?" Nadya asked, joining Danika at the hedge.

"Too long. He was supposed to be in my laboratory at suncrest."

"Let me join your host!" Adrik pled with his captors. "There is no one more loyal or faithful than me!"

Nadya smiled. "I cannot decide who is more the child in this game."

"I can," said Danika darkly. But for all the disapproval in her voice, Nadya did not miss the glimmer of amusement in her sister's eyes.

"What skills do you have?" Manet asked, raising her training sword to perch just beneath Adrik's chiseled chin.

"I can paint."

"No painting!" Mikhail shouted.

"Do you need a cook? I can cook."

Manet scoffed. "Only those who cannot fight cook."

"Fighting — we want fighting!" said Mikhail, waving his sword with such reckless abandon Adrik had to duck to avoid a bruising.

"Oh! You want a fighter?" Adrik said in mock surprise. "Well, I suppose I could become an alkhemist..."

Manet let out an exhausted sigh. "You are a mundane! You cannot be an alkhemist."

"But Danika is going to teach me!"

Nadya looked to Danika, who avoided her gaze.

"You cannot *teach* alkhemy," said Manet. "Everyone knows that."

"I don't know it," said Adrik. "I bet I could be a great alkhemist."

"Danika is ours!" Mikhail stomped his foot.

Zin emphasized Mikhail's point by slapping the broad of her sword across Adrik's shoulders. He let out a high-pitched yelp.

"It is true!" Danika called out. "The salt of the Swansea runs in my veins."

As if these words had been some secret cue, all three of the children cast down their swords and tackled Adrik to the ground. Beneath the rabble, he cried out, "Betrayer!"

Nadya pressed a hand to her mouth to muffle her laughter. Even Danika could not hide her grin. Focused as they were on the wholesale slaughter taking place on the yard before them, Nadya did not notice Taito's approach until he captured her hand in his.

She jumped away.

"Nedeshda?" he said, a flicker of hurt in his voice.

"Taito! You startled me. I am sorry."

"We had planned to meet today, did we not?" His brow wrinkled.

"Yes, of course. It slipped my mind."

"I see."

"But we may go now." Nadya passed the coats to Danika. "Will you give these to the children?" Danika nodded and Nadya turned back to Taito. "Remind me — we are visiting your parents?"

Taito's lips thinned. "Perhaps eventually. But not yet. I wanted to take you to the lagoon, remember?"

"Ah, yes. The lagoon..."

The lagoon was not a lagoon so much as a small pond filled with algae where Taito liked to catch frogs. It was one fascination of his that Nadya could not find it in herself to share, no matter how much she tried.

"There's a lagoon on the Von?"

They turned to find Adrik emerged from his battle, a bit worse for wear. His golden curls were in disarray, his fine Sivkan coat had a tear in the shoulder, and the knees of his camel-colored trousers were marred with dirt. Adrik seemed neither to notice nor care. He staggered forward, Zin dangling from one leg and Mikhail from the other, paying no mind to his clingers-on. Manet followed behind, all three training swords pointed at Adrik's back.

"It is a secret spot," said Taito with a forced smile. "Known only to the Kotov."

Which Adrik most surely was not.

"You have recovered from your time in the wars so soon?" Nadya asked him, hoping to smooth over Taito's uncharacteristic display of rudeness.

"Barely. This is why Avdotya says to never trust an alkhemist." Adrik glared at Danika, who smirked.

Taito's hand gripped Nadya's elbow and tugged. "I am afraid we really must be going."

"Of course." Adrik bowed his head. "Don't let me keep you."

"Toads wait for no man," Danika muttered. Nadya glared back at her.

"I am sorry I forgot our meeting," Nadya said as they stepped off the road into the brush.

"I am sorry I took offense." Taito paused to brush a kiss against her knuckles. "I admit, I am rather nervous."

"Nervous? I have never known you to balk before a toad."

"Not about the toads."

Twilight was dawning and the buzz of mosquitos had been replaced by the rhythmic humming of crickets. The air, which had been pleasantly crisp in the afternoon, turned chilly with the setting of the sun. Nadya shivered and wished she had taken one of the jackets for herself.

As they reached the lagoon, fireflies and starlight provided dim illumination. Taito bent to pull the coverstone off a hole he had dug near the water's edge. It was here that he kept his nets and baskets and a lantern to see by. He struck a bit of alkoal against the rock and soon had them bathed in the silvery glow of an alkhemical flame.

As he settled the lantern by their feet, Nadya expected him to reach for his nets, but instead he remained kneeling and pulled a simple iron band from his pocket. He held it up to Nadya.

"Nedeshda, I have loved you from the moment I landed on Von Beach and you offered me a heel of potato bread and a gallon of warm cider. I never dared hope that you would choose me over all the men on the Isles who have adored you as I have. But I hope now that I have done what those others could not. I hope I haven proven to you that none will cherish you, nor take care of you, as I wish to do. Nedeshda Bodanson — will you be my bride?"

Unlike Babbin's stone hut, Danika's workshop was built of alkhemically-infused birch — impenetrable to the destructive fires that could so easily ignite in an alkhemist's lab. It was one of the few wooden structures on the Von and it had doubtless cost Papa a shiny sivnik to import all the materials. Danika had never been brave enough to ask exactly how much it had cost him, and she knew Papa would have been insulted if she had.

Also unlike Babbin's hut, Danika's lab was orderly. Every crucible, retort, flask and stirring rod had its proper place. Her manuscripts were neatly organized and her jars of fertilizer, marble chips, and saltpeter carefully labeled. But for all its tidiness, a thin layer of dust coated every surface. A stale must hung thick in the air, and the athanor sat cold and dark.

"Take a seat," said Danika, pointing to one of the stools beside the high work table.

Adrik did as asked, canvassing every corner of her little sanctuary. She rarely allowed visitors into her lab. Even Nadya and Lukin had barely crossed the threshold in the years since its construction. It felt uncomfortably like opening the windows to her soul.

"So, Adept Danika. Where do we start?" Adrik sat primly, hands folded over the tabletop, a perfect imitation of the perfect student she was sure he was not.

She was suddenly, viscerally reminded that Adrik knew her secret. Her shame. It was like having an open wound where her heart should be to see Adrik walking around, laughing with her siblings and tossing Mikhail over his shoulder — all while he carried her truth inside him.

Every time she looked at him, the wound gaped wider still, exposed to any disease or malice eager to creep in. Adrik had offered her a life of escape, an opportunity to prove herself, and a chance at salvation. The Philosopher's Stone. But all of it had been thwarted by her own papa — the man she admired most in the world. For this alone, Danika had taken to her and Adrik's lessons with particular relish.

"At the beginning, I suspect. You said to me before that Avdotya does not care for alkhemy?"

Adrik chuckled drily. "No, alkhemy is not a tool on which Avdotya likes to rely. And spending the last few years in Polvia means I didn't see much of it even when his back was turned."

Polvia had been both ally and enemy to the Kotov so often it was difficult to keep track of the latest political turnings. But one thing was for certain — their neighbors to the south had chosen to solve the Philosopher's Stone problem by banning alkhemy in its entirety. For that alone, they were a nemesis of Imperator Maksis.

Danika took up position on the opposite side of the workbench. "Very well. The beginning. Alkhemy is the art of transformation. By focusing on the single Divine Spark in all things, the alkhemist hopes to reveal the essence of a substance and guide its growth to a natural state of perfection."

Adrik's interest fell away. His shoulders slumped and his palms flattened on the table. "Is this going to be a lecture? I was really hoping to see some explosions."

Danika arched a brow.

"But theory is good too," he said, hands raised. "Carry on."

"There are three fundamental tenants. First, that the material world — our world, the Below — is not the only reality. A hidden reality exists that determines our very existence — the Above. The Below is simply a shadow of that higher reality that cannot be grasped by the mundane senses. Only the highest faculties of the human mind and soul can perceive it.

"Second, the basic duality of the material versus immaterial realities is mirrored within us. Our material body is subject to physical realities; but our soul and spirit is not subject to such loss and decay. Instead, it carries the essence of who we are. This divine energy at the heart of everything is known as the Quintessence."

Adrik seemed to be following, or at least was too afraid to interrupt, so she carried on.

"The final tenant is that all human beings possess the capacity to perceive these separate levels of reality, both in themselves and in nature. But in the Below, we are taught to ignore the subtle clues to our greater reality. The perception and application of this ultimate truth is the goal of human beings, the purpose of our existence, and the purpose of alkhemy.

"This philosophy holds, to varying degrees, in most religions practiced in Sivka today."

He flashed a grin. "That I actually knew."

"In the Kotov practice, we believe that there are as many paths to enlightenment as there are people in the world. But at Izumgray, we study a more...regimented method."

Adrik sat up a bit straighter.

"Alkhemists are born from an alkhemist mama. So it has been since The Mother first cut herself by the Quicksilver River. As an alkhemist boy or girl becomes a man or woman, their blood begins to change, and when the change is complete, it can then be ignited to create a flame upon which alkhemical transformations can be brewed. But not all alkhemists are created equal. There are three grades of alkhemical fire — Central, Secret, and Celestial — each distinguished by the color of the blood in the alkhemist's veins.

"Central Fire is the first grade and bleeds blue. It is the fire of creation — tenacious, digesting, maturing, neither warm nor burning to the touch. It is used in Artistic and Prophetic transformations."

"And what are those — Artistic and Prophetic?"

"Artistic Alkhemists can manipulate material matter — they can make armor unbreakable, craft weapons of flame or frost, weave clothes that are never too hot or too cold, turn plates that keep food at the perfect temperature." Danika waved a hand around the room. "Build walls that cannot burn or break."

"Nice," said Adrik in a low voice.

"There are some artisans, of course, who do not use their skills for such practical matters, but instead devote themselves solely to art — paintings that move, tapestries that glitter, sketches that jump off the page."

"I can tell from your tone that doesn't impress you."

"It serves little purpose that I can see."

"And Prophetic Alkhemy?"

Danika sighed. "That is a realm of even less purpose. It is the only focus which does not even require a flame to brew by. It is a skill in which my sister, Nadya, likes to dabble. Hypnotherapy, shamanic journeying, reading signs in nature and the stars..."

"And do they teach these things at Izumgray?"

"They do.... But they do not teach anyone with the Central Fire. At Izumgray, one must possess the Secret Fire at minimum in order to study. Those with the Secret Fire or Celestial Fire can then choose what specialities are within their ability."

"So what does the Secret Fire do?"

"The Secret Fire bleeds purple. It is the primary fire for lab work. It has direction and purpose, much like a weapon, and anyone with the Secret Fire can do anything an alkhemist with the Central Fire could accomplish, but they can also practice Medicinal Alkhemy."

"I think I can guess what that does."

"Yes, you probably can. Medicinal Alkhemists can do healing of all kinds, mending wounds and illnesses, far beyond what a mundane healer could accomplish. Noted Medicinal Alkhemists have given us The Wife's Relief — the potion which makes childbirth largely safe and pain-free during the Luncycle."

"And, of course, the Second Relief," he said slyly.

Danika pursed her lips. Of course he knew the potion for birth control. "Why am I not surprised you know so little of alkhemy but know of the Second Relief?"

"Dunya may despise alkhemy, but he dislikes surprises even more."

Danika's insides squirmed at the thought. She gave herself a shake and forced her focus back on the brew that was bubbling.

"Lastly, there is the Celestial Fire. The highest grade of Alkhemical Fire, it bleeds silver and burns a brilliant white. It is smokeless and odorless and creates an everlasting flame that can only be doused by the blood of a mundane. Some say it represents the power of divine will."

"And that's what you have."

"Yes."

"So what can you do with all that divine will?" His smile turned dangerous. "Besides light up a room just by standing in it?"

The back of her neck went hot and she forced herself not to balk from the intensity of his stare. "Celestial Alkhemists can create potions and tinctures that no other grade can manage."

He leaned forward, a greedy gleam in his eye. "Such as?"

"Potions that can make a person breathe fire or give them the strength of twenty men. Skin that turns to shielding; improved speed, stamina, lightness or buoyancy. It can keep lakes from freezing in the winter, sterilize rivers for drinking water, make dead soil fertile, keep food fresh. Then, of course, there is the realm of poison....

"In truth, a Celestial Alkhemist is limited only by their imagination."

There was a moment of silence. Then he said, "It's no wonder you fear the Suncycle."

Danika balked. "I do not fear—"

He looked at her. Her jaw clicked shut.

"Is there anything alkhemy can't do?"

"No alkhemist has yet been able to make something invisible. Animals are impervious to our practices. Ingesting multiple mixes at once must be done very carefully, if at all. A bad combination can result in painful death, illness or insanity. Mundanes can use alkhemical weapons or objects, and be healed by an alkhemist, but abilities such as fire-breathing or skin-shielding can only work for alkhemists."

"So far," he said, a challenge in his voice that Danika could not resist.

"So far," she agreed.

Adrien let out a sigh and clapped his hands onto his thighs. "That was quite the lesson, Little Nika. I've got plenty to keep secret from Dunya now."

"Why did you want to learn it? No matter how much theory I tell you, you will never be able to make an Alkhemical Flame—"

"Tut, tut. What were you just saying about an alkhemist only being limited by their imagination? Now, show me something that goes 'boom.'"

Three nights they feasted and waited, feasted and waited.

"These things cannot be hurried," Papanik said on the fourth day. But there was uncertainty in his eyes.

Long wooden trestle tables scattered the village yard, wedged between alleys and balanced over embankments. Nadya's lavender bags hung from the gables above the doors and the smell of grilled fish drifted over the fires, making Danika's mouth water.

Aadan's Day celebrations marked the end of the Autumn harvest and one of two tennights in the whole year where vassals were free to leave their masters' estates for a new life. A life with the Kotov. Ordinarily, it was one of Danika's favorite times of the year.

But this year was not like the others.

For one, they had strangers under their turf. One stranger who became less strange every day. Like the pull of the sun on the moon, Danika found she could not ignore Adrik's summons. Each time he called her to her lab, she followed willingly, soon finding her athanor lit and her extractor condensing despite all her previous resolve to staunch her fires.

Lessons passed on the differences between the Greater Circulation and the Lesser Circulation; the animal and mineral kingdoms; the best means to collect and prepare plants; the elegant process of maceration, circulation and extraction — all made new to her through his eyes.

And so Danika found herself setting and rising in his shadow, and not minding the cold one bit.

Adrik had promised a life of escape, an opportunity to prove herself, and a chance at salvation. The Philosopher's Stone. But all of it had been thwarted by her own papa — the man she thought she admired most in the world. For that alone, Danika had taken to a different kind of flask.

On the fourth night of Aadan's Day feasting, as she and Lukin shared a bench shaded by a lone plum tree, passing the vodka between them, Taito called for attention. Danika and Lukin exchanged a look. Taito was not what one would call a public speaker.

"Nadya and I wish to make an announcement." His voice quavered as he stood up from the table he shared with Nadya and his family. He rested a hand on Nadya's shoulder, smiling softly at her in the bold blue of twilight. As Nadya reached up to squeeze Taito's hand, Danika's breath hitched. "Nedeshda Bodanson and I have agreed to be married."

A chorus of cheering met this pronouncement. Nadya dropped Taito's hand and found Danika's gaze across the vast expanse of the village yard. She smiled uncertainly. Danika forced herself to unfreeze, to release a breath, to grin back.

She had always known this day would come. Nadya was too beautiful to remain only Danika's forever. The selfish impulse to keep her close, the resentment that Nadya had not told her first, was overpowered by the joy in Taito's face. He would worship Nadya as she deserved, that much was certain. And if Nadya had accepted his proposal over so many others, there must have been good reason.

Danika left her bench and took her sister in a warm embrace.

"You are not angry with me?" Nadya whispered in Danika's ear. "Taito swore me to secrecy."

"Hush. I am not angry." Danika pressed a kiss to her sister's forehead. "Only sad to lose you so soon."

Nadya tucked a strand of hair behind Danika's ear. "You will be my sister much longer than I will be his wife. Nothing can change that."

Danika laughed. "Wait here. I will bring us a drink to toast with."

But when she left Bodan's Brews, a cup in each hand, it was Papa who awaited her.

"I must bring these drinks to Nadya." She attempted to duck around him. He stepped into her path. He was a broad man, and agile despite his years. Danika spotted Adrik over his shoulder, gripping Taito in what looked like a punishing handshake.

Papa pinned her with a look. "You will talk to me, Nika. I will not have this silent punishment any longer. We will speak the truth as Kotov do."

"The truth?" Danika's anger spiked sharp and eager. She skewered him with a cutting look of her own. "The truth is that you have disappointed me."

"You must understand—"

"You are the great-grandson of Bodan. You are not supposed to be a coward."

He reared back, then set his mouth in a firm line. "You are the great-great-granddaughter of Bodan. You are not supposed to be so blind."

"Even Mama voted—"

"Mama has her own reasons for despising Maksis." He grabbed her by the shoulders, eyes imploring. "Hear me, Danika. I will not sacrifice my family to avenge someone else's."

She shook him off. "Then you are not the Kotov I thought you to be."

Two more nights came and went with nary a dinghy on the shore. And with every passing day, the chill of Autumn seeped deeper into Danika's bones.

"The cast says they will come," said Nadya. Her palm was full of broken bits of sea rock and lakeshells. She tossed them over a white cloth spread out on the tabletop. Danika knew the shapes they landed in were meaningless, but Nadya would not hear it — even if her 'prophecies' were wrong three times as often as they were right. "They will come in great numbers. Too great to house."

But still the horizon remained empty.

Finally, on the tenth and last night of the Aadan's Day festival, a smallboat floated into shore. Adrik and Avdotya slipped quietly into the baker's hut as a familiar figure stomped up from the beach.

"Antonia," said Papa as the Norgay merchant stripped a piece of fish from the grill. Vast layers of furs and leathers cocooned Antonia's usually petite form. "What brings you to the Von?"

"I have news." The woman grimaced, dark eyes glimmering in her black face. Officially, Antonia was a traveling candle merchant based out of Norgay. But during the Luncycle, her occupation was akin to selling ice in Whitewinter. And so she put her skills to work as a guide, helping travelers and fleeing vassals cross the great expanse of Sivka. As a result, she often traded in something far more valuable than spices or furs — rumor.

She dove into a satchel slung over her shoulder and extracted a battered scroll. She handed it to Papa, who unfurled it. Most of the Von had gathered on the first nights of the would-be celebration, but after so many days without a single vassal, many had given up the waiting to return to their hearths. Those who remained pressed in close as Papa read.

His gaze traveled up and down the parchment several times before he spoke. Then he rolled the scroll tight and lifted his eyes to the gathered. They lingered on Danika.

"By order of Imperator Maksis, Aadan's Day has been dissolved. No vassal may flee their master, and none but a natural-born citizen of the Swansea may call themselves Kotov."

The eruption was immediate. Feet stomped over the hardened footpaths, fists pounded the tables. A few ran off to spread the word and gather more in their fury. But Danika sat frozen, waiting for Papa to decide.

There was a small hiccup of noise beside her, and Danika looked to find Mikhail curled onto Nadya's lap. She saw her own fear reflected in Nadya's sky-blue eyes. Mikhail had come to them in the arms of a fleeing vassal four years ago.

His mama had trekked long and hard from a Sivkan dukedom to reach the Kotov Isles. Danika still remembered the sight of her on Von Beach, knees quaking, a curly-haired baby strapped to her chest. And when they took her to the turfhouse, fed her and bathed her, the lash marks marring the woman's back had told Danika all she needed to know about the civility of Sivkan nobles. The woman had not lasted half a tennight under their turf before perishing to an infection not even alkhemy could cure.

Mikhail's mother may not have survived the journey, but their brother had.

Danika ran her fingers through his soft curls. Adrik and Avdotya emerged from the baker's hut. Papa handed the scroll to Avdotya, who passed it off to Adrik without looking at it.

"What does this mean?" Elin said, looking to Papa for answers.

Danika could see the worry in Papa's face, but there was something else there too. Her heart began to pound. He granted her the smallest nod and she sprang to her feet. Those who remained in the yard looked from Papa to her. She heaved in a breath, hand still poised in Mikhail's curls and said, "I Danika, daughter of Rodin, citizen of the Von, call a vote."

The Folknik did not even need to count the stones so unanimous was the verdict. Five thousand of them descended on the Vienper to raise their voices. And when Danika dropped her stone into the white marble bowl, Papa's was swift to follow.

The Kotov were going to war.

7. THE TURNING OF THE TIDE

The Kotov might have lost their vassals, but men of another kind were pouring into the Von. Adrik watched the longboats pull into harbor, pride swelling in his chest. The hardest part was done — they'd secured their allies and their army. All that was left now was war. And as far as Adrik was concerned, war was far easier than treaties and votes and politics.

The Kotov handed people off the boats onto the shore with only a hint of suspicion marring their faces. The men and women stumbling onto dry land looked less certain. There were some warriors among them, but many more bore heavy packs bowed over their narrow shoulders, loaded down with the tools of their trade — the tools of their science.

Avdotya watched the proceedings with a scowl. Adrik couldn't begin to guess why aside from compulsive grumpiness. This was Dunya's victory more than anyone's, but Adrik suspected his advisor wouldn't be happy until they stood in the throne room at The Palace at Old Kirov.

"Finally," Dunya snarled, dark eyes narrowed on the last boat of a dozen. "Took him long enough."

Yulian, with his mop of vibrant red hair and soldier's girth, was easy to spot amongst the feeble-boned scientists. He shoved a middle-aged man with a gray goatee aside in his haste to jump from the boat, landing shin-deep in the water and trudging the rest of the shoreline into Adrik's arms.

Adrik hauled Yulian close. "I thought you drowned in the Swansea."

"It wasn't for lack of trying," said Yulian. "I've decided that a boat with too many brains is heavier than one with too many backs."

Across the beach, Adrik spotted Lukin. He and Danika were hauling crates off the boats. Adrik wondered if Danika's curiosity would get the better of her and if she would crack one of the crates open before he had a chance to explain its contents.

"So — you found us an army?"

Adrik gave his friend a vicious grin. "The best in Sivka."

Yulian's blue eyes flicked to Avdotya, who watched them with pursed lips. "Matters look promising," Dunya admitted grudgingly. "But they are not yet settled."

"You know Dunya — always looking on the sunside. We've taken Maksis' greatest warriors and secured them for ourselves. What more could you ask for?"

"Secured is a strong word, boy. You speak as if battle will commence at dawn, but there is still much to reason before that time. Patience."

It was Avdotya's favorite mantra and Adrik had never been less keen to hear it. Not when victory was waiting just off shore.

"Enough chatter." Avdotya's voice dropped, became almost affectionate. "Where is Renata?"

Yulian rolled his eyes, then turned to shore where the goateed man, a chemist if Adrik remembered right, lurched up the beach. He had an iron birdcage in his arms.

Avdotya swept forward. "I told you to trust him to no one but yourself! How long has he been locked away?" He wrenched the cage from the man's arms.

"He kept taking the fish from the water. It was this cage or our bellies," said Yulian.

Dunya gently set the cage on a driftwood log and opened the hatch. A large raven fluttered out to settle on his shoulder. The bird, Renata, had a speckled white head and chest with black feathers circling its tail and neck like a noose.

Adrik glared as Dunya reached into his front pocket for a bit of raw carrion. He fed it to Renata, who thanked his master with a caw. The affection in Avdotya's eyes was nauseating. Many times in Adrik's youth, he'd wished the bird dead, though he'd never gotten up the nerve to make the attempt. Yet.

"Many Kotov have volunteered to take in the scientists," said Adrik, dragging his gaze from the pampered pigeon. "There's room for you at Rodin's house. Nedeshda is here to escort us."

Adrik scoured the beach for Rodin's eldest. He'd left the fair maiden shortly after their arrival — swarmed as she was by well-wishers for her engagement. He found her on the far side of the beach, pressed between a massive boulder and Taito Eletski. The fawning masses had dispersed and only her besotted betrothed remained, staring soppily into her fine blue eyes.

Yulian let out a low whistle. "That is our host? She seems much occupied, Adrik."

"So she does," Adrik grunted.

"Put your eyes back in your head and show Yulian to the turfhouse," said Avdotya. "You know the way well enough yourself."

"Won't you join us, Dunya?"

"Someone must see to your scientists. Now, go. And stay out of trouble." His dark gaze narrowed on Yulian, who winked at Avdotya in reply.

Adrik and Yulian talked all the way to the village, ripping news from each other like dogs fighting over scraps of meat. After Adrik finished relating his and Avdotya's harrowing journey, Yulian launched into his own tale. Apparently, the crossing from Polvia through the Jinmen Empire had been treacherous — they'd had to pay off two farriers to not reveal their course to the Sultan of Orgenia. The price had taken most of their provisions and they'd spent the rest of the voyage living off sundried fish scrap. But Yulian admitted the longer route was worth avoiding the Sikvan border — and Maksis.

"The scientists were stronger than I expected," he said. "Warriors — we're used to living on a pittance. But men of books and letters and learning? I expected the moans to signal the Sultan long before his farriers."

"But they surprised you?"

"I heard less complaints from them than from our own men. I suspect they learned hard living in exile."

They passed beneath the wattle-gate into the village. Vestiges of the Aadan's Day celebration still lingered in the yard. Nadya's lavender satchels had dried up since the Second Folktan. She'd spent her nights preparing fresh ones for the impending wedding.

"A life on the run from Maksis isn't easy," said Adrik.

His words slowed Yulian's step. He felt Yulian's eyes on him and fixed his own gaze on a merchant selling mussels out of a rolling cart. Yulian shoved his shoulder into Adrik's. "So what of the Kotov women? I've heard wondrous, terrifying tales." His cheeks dimpled beneath his amber stubble as he looked over a full-bodied young woman with jet-black hair in the next yard. She wielded a large ax and brought it down deftly, splitting a log with an almighty crack.

"I'm ashamed to admit I've yet to sample the local fare."

Yulian mock-gasped. "You? How can it be? Not even the pretty blonde by the water?"

"Her least of all. Dunya would have my bollocks in a sling." At Yulian's questioning look, he explained, "She is Rodin's eldest."

"Ah."

Most of the scientists had made it to the village and were being sorted into lodging by grim-faced Aunties. There was a flicker of unease in some of the scientists' eyes — they were, after all, on a remote island, surrounded by the fearsome and mysterious Kotov. But Yulian was right — there was courage there too.

"Perhaps a less forbidden fruit, then?" Yulian said, gaze returning to the wood-chopper. Adrik considered. He'd never had a woman with arms larger than his...

He grinned at Yulian and made for the gate.

The rumors of Danika's role in the Second Folktan spread through the Isles like Celestial Fire. Keenly aware of the approaching vote for Prime Chieftain and her potential to undermine Papa's authority further, Danika left the gossip mongers and their new allies on the shore and made her way to Babbin's — and another fruitless conversation.

"When Adrik takes the throne he means to rule for all people — alkhemists and mundane alike," Danika explained for the dozenth time, pacing in front of the athanor as Babbin hunched over a work bench, distilling a solution of nitrate between two beakers.

"Just as Maksis does now."

Danika stomped her foot. "Even I know Maksis rules for alkhemists alone."

"And so? I thought life was not worth living without your alkhemy?"

"Of course I oppose it! I am not a monster. Everyone will suffer under Maksis when the Luncycle ends. So long as he continues to stall scientific progress and hoard the Stone—"

"So we come to it at last."

"Babbin—"

"Pah! You may be able to fool your Papa, and your siblings, and even that little princeling," Babbin turned to fix Danika with her pale stare, "but you do not fool me. You speak of a world where science and alkhemy live together, but your reasons are far more selfish, Little Nika."

Heat crept from Danika's fingers to her toes. But was it anger or shame? She balled her hands into fists and steadied her voice. "And what is so wrong with finding the Stone? The Imperator has kept it to himself long enough. If I have it, I will put its powers to use in myself. With my alkhemy, with my legs, there is so much good I can do for the Kotov *and* Sivka. And perhaps seeing the finished product will help me recreate—"

"If you have to steal the Stone to possess it, then you do not deserve it."

Purple sparks popped over the flask on the table. Danika could smell a hint of bilberry and fennel — *Tatiana's Sight*. A curative for blindness.

"I see we will not agree on this."

"We will not."

"But what of my other argument? The ideals you think me too selfish to champion? I know you believe in a better world."

"I do. I just do not think it exists in this one." Babbin turned her back on Danika to make a note in one of her journals.

"Adrik has three dozen exiled scientists coming to his aid. Among his handful of alkhemists, I am the best trained. Even I can agree I am not enough. Not to start a revolution." Danika closed in, hovering over Babbin and her table of scattered journals and recipes. "We leave in just over a tennight. Come with us."

"You know my answer, Little Nika. This is my place. Come back to me when you find yours."

A fading pink sun guided Danika's footsteps home. It was late to set, especially as Autumn was slowly giving way to Graywinter and a chill air nipped at her skin. She would need to douse her alkhemist coat in a warming tincture soon — time was slipping away too quickly...

Two-hundred-and-eighty-five days...

Panic surged bitter and pungent in her throat just as a hand landed hard on her shoulder.

It was only thanks to her distraction that she did not break its owner's nose.

"You do not do much to dissuade the Kotov stereotype," Avdotya said from the puddle she had thrown him in.

"You do not make me wish to," Danika spat — but still with a twinge of guilt. Somehow, she had set herself against Avdotya the moment they met. But perhaps she had been too hasty. For whatever reason, this man was Adrik's confidant. He must have something to redeem him...

Avdotya wiped his scraped and muddy hands against his silk pants and Danika reached out her own. After only a moment's hesitation, Avdotya took it. She hoisted him to his feet, dropping his hand as quickly as she had offered it. They stared at each other in the frigid dusk for several long moments. He had come to her, after all. If he had something to say, Danika would not hurry him to it.

He sniffed and looked to his left. A giant spotted raven took flight from the nearest bramble hedge and landed on his shoulder. Danika's resolve to silence was broken. "A pied raven?" she said. "Where in the Tundra did you find him?"

"There was a time when an Imperator's advisor could not be refused." The bird nipped affectionately at Avdotya's mustache. "I believe I owe you an apology."

Danika was too mesmerized by the bird to immediately comprehend Avdotya's words. When she finally did, she said dumbly, "I do not understand."

"You have done much to help Adrik's cause. Perhaps more than anyone, excusing myself." His black eyes fixed on Danika, assessing, but not so dismissive as they once were. "It's time we recognize that we are on the same side."

The notion made her uneasy. But fresh from Babbin's rejection, there was little choice. She needed powerful friends if she was going to win Adrik's war.

"I agree."

Avdotya smiled. It was a strange, brittle thing. With it, she could almost see the handsomeness behind the calculation. "Wonderful. In which case, I will venture to tell you that our work isn't done yet. Our alliance with the Kotov is strong to be sure, but I feel there's one way to make it stronger."

"And that is?"

"Marriage."

Wind gusted down the emerald cliffside, pushing at Danika's back, urging her toward Avdotya. She locked her knees against its force. "Marriage?"

"Indeed, yes. After all, it's how your mama came to be with your papa, was it not? She was a gift to the Kotov from the Imperator. It seems only right to keep this tradition when we have flouted so many others. And think of this — the first union between a mundane Solov and an alkhemist Lunovna in history? What a symbol of unity that would be."

"I see." She felt as if she had swallowed a mouthful of sand.

"I am sure you do. Think on it. I know Adrik will."

Danika did think about it. As she laid beneath the furs that night with Nadya on the far side and Zin curled around her, she pictured a life she had never before envisioned — that of a wife.

It did not come easily at first pondering. It never had. When Nadya and Elin and Cousin Shelia had splashed in the waters of the Swansea as children, veils over their faces, taking turns as officiant, groom, and bride, Danika had sat apart with Lukin, forging makeshift bows and wooden sabers, glaring waspishly at her kin, hoping their childish games would soon be over so they could turn to the real task of preparing for imaginary battle.

In the end, their games had become reality far sooner than Danika's. Nadya had already announced her betrothal to Taito — Mama had begun airing out the bridal linens. Shelia would get Lukin to the altar soon enough if she had her way. And now Avdotya had the temerity to suggest that she, Danika, could be wed to Adrik Iosifvich Solov...?

What would it even look like?

She did not bother dwelling on the wedding — the trappings of ceremony and tradition — it was the marriage that interested Danika. She doubted it would be the same domestic scene promised to her with a Kotov spouse. She and Adrik would not settle into a turfhouse down the road. They would not be distracted by cleaning and washing and mundane drills with the Host as Danika and Nadya waddled around with swollen bellies, providing the next line of Kotov warriors.

No. A marriage to Adrik would look nothing like that.

A marriage to Adrik would be a partnership in power. Together, they would challenge Maksis on the battlefield and in the halls of the nobles. Danika could see it clearly — he the able warrior, she the even more apt politician. Her, brewing potions and tonics for his warriors. Him, worshipping at her feet every night.

There would still be children, of course. He was an Imperator after all. And she would be his Impress. They would need an heir. Possibly two or three. And while the idea of more mouths to feed did little to make her heart race, the thought of what it took to get them most certainly did.

She had felt it three nights ago on Von Beach as they bent over a brew bubbling on an open fire.

"*The Key* is a tincture of moonwort," Danika had explained, raising her voice over the crashing waves. "It can only be brewed by the light of the full moon and will open any iron lock."

His golden eyes gleamed silver in the water's reflection. "And here I thought you just wanted to get me out under the stars..."

"If I had wanted to do that, there are better ways than the promise of a tincture."

The smooth sound of his laugh had reverberated low in her ribcage. She forced herself to focus. Just as a watched brew never bubbled, an untended fire was sure to scorch. She pulled a dagger from her waistbelt.

Adrik stared warily. "Is this a coup before I've been crowned? Should I call for my guards? Oh wait, I don't have any."

She pursed her lips. "You have nothing to fear from me on that front."

"Oh good. If I ever do, be sure to let me know."

She took the blade and sliced it across the tip of her finger. "Now you."

Eyebrows raised, Adrik did not hesitate, nor — for once — ask any questions. She cradled the four fingers of his right hand in her five, lingering over the fine lines of his palm, the smooth whiteness marred by the pink calluses from a pommel.

She sliced the blade across the pad of his thumb, then pressed her bloodied finger to his. "The blood of a mundane and the blood of an alkhemist must meld together over the flame." She led him over to the cauldron, positioned their clasped hands over the tincture. "One drop will do."

He squeezed their hands and a single pinkish drop fell into the mixture, turning it from inky blackness to the same glowing white as the moon above.

How easy it would have been to pull him to her, to press her chest against his, to snake her hands through his golden curls. How willingly she would have gone had he thrown her down, shed her white coat, taken her in the sands by the light of her alkhemical fire.

Danika slunk further into the blankets and let the thought follow into her dreams.

Avdotya thrummed with accomplishment. He had placed the seed in the little alkhemist's ear, and with a few more of Adrik's charming smiles, there was no doubt it would bloom. The thought steadied him. He'd been at loose ends since arriving on the Kotov Isles. None of his usual tactics of diplomacy seemed to work on these people. He shouldn't have been surprised — barbarians rarely wrote sonnets. But it stung more than he liked to admit when it had been the little alkhemist, and not his powers of persuasion, that had secured the Kotov vote in their favor.

The question of how and why the vote came to pass could be debated by the historians. Avdotya was more concerned with fixing the present than how he would be remembered in the future. And presently, he feared for the depth of Kotov loyalty.

He didn't think the Kotov would back away from their promise so soon — it was later that worried him. When they could no longer lurk in the shadows, secure from Maksis's wrath, but were put on the battlefield, face-to-face with his army of alkhemists; when they were no longer quiet usurpers, muttering into their flasks, but targets for Maksis's vengeance — that was when the promises made in the Folktan could fall to dim memory. History had proven as much.

Hence, a marriage. Oaths taken would be much harder to forget with a ring on the finger or a baby in the belly. The only way to ensure Rodin's loyalty was to tie his fate to Adrik's. Adrik's family would be his, and they would succeed and thrive, or fail and perish, with their Imperator.

Avdotya left the turfhouse early the next morning. The sky was still black as he descended the steep path into the village and the last thing he expected to find on his morning sojourn was a tousled Adrik sneaking out of the nearest dooryard, one hand still working at his fly.

Avdotya lingered in the shadows as Adrik eased the gate closed behind him, lowering the latch with careful quietude. He let out an accomplished sigh — that of a boy thinking he'd gotten away with some malevolent prank — then turned slowly round.

"Dunya!" he yelled when found Avdotya standing mere inches before him. "What are you— I was just—" Guilt swathed his face. But it was not the guilt of true remorse. It rarely was. He was only sorry to have been caught.

"Did I not warn you?"

"You did. I'm sorry. I couldn't help—"

"You could. That is the problem. You succumb to your own weakness. You always have. Your papa would never—"

"My papa didn't have the chance," Adrik muttered.

Avdotya seized Adrik by the jaw. "What did you say? What did you just say to me about the man who died to see you on the throne? Our situation is tenuous in the extreme. And you would ruin it all for the sake of your satisfaction?" He punctuated each question with a shake. He could barely stand to look at the brat. What if Rodin had seen? What if word spread though the village? Rodin was an honorable man. He would not marry his daughter to a scoundrel. Even if that scoundrel would be Imperator.

"I'm sorry, Dunya—"

"Do not bother with platitudes. You may not be sorry now, but you will be soon. Where is Yulian?"

Avdotya bestowed his punishment in the byre behind the turfhouse. Most of Rodin's ilk were at the docks shoring up the fleet, or in the village canning food for the coming march. Over the years, Yulian had learned to stifle his screams when the occasion called for it. On other occasions, it did Adrik good to hear.

Avdotya wiped the belt on a rag hanging beside the stable door. Yulian clung to the gate, knuckles white on the rail.

"Have you learned your lesson?" he said to Adrik, who, as always, held tightly to Yulian's forearm. It was unorthodox, to allow them that connection, but Avdotya felt it more effective than distant observation. If Adrik could not take the blows himself, he could at least feel their impact.

"I have, Dunya. I swear it."

He had sworn it more times than Avdotya could count. But somehow Yulian always ended up with his chest against the stable door. The lines of years marred his back beneath the fresh welts, proof of Adrik's lie. But now wasn't the time to doubt. Now was the time to strike.

"You realize what you've risked?"

"I do."

Avdotya grabbed Adrik by the collar. "It's not just your legacy you threaten, boy. With your foolishness, everything your family sacrificed would be for naught."

Real remorse sparked in Adrik's eyes. "I know. I won't fail you again."

"Good." He stepped back. "Then you will do what I ask without question."

"What— what do you ask?"

How quickly contrition morphed into hesitation, defiance.

"That you take some responsibility in securing this alliance," said Avdotya. "It's past time. And people are more likely to follow a married man."

"Marriage?" Adrik squawked. "To who?"

Avdotya glared — Adrik was feigning stupidity. "You will secure your place in Rodin's family and soon. I won't give them time to doubt before we set sail."

Yulian gently shifted off the gate, curled in on his own pain. He watched Adrik curiously, sweat lingering on his brow. This was not Avdotya's first attempt to secure alliance through marriage, but before now, the boy had proven too stubborn to yield. Adrik looked to Yulian, who gave the smallest shrug — then winced.

Adrik heaved in a long breath. "Very well. I'll do it."

Avdotya could see the bargain forming in Adrik's eye, and waited.

"But I get to choose the girl."

In the end, Adrik's choice made no difference to Avdotya. He pulled Rodin aside that night, as the others filed into their beds. "A word, Prime Chieftain?" The title was appropriate now. Rodin had been elected over Hurkan by the narrowest margin.

"How may I help you, Avdotya?" Rodin tipped his empty cup. "More vodka perhaps? I am sure your pail is dry by now."

Avdotya's cup was full to the brim, which Rodin knew very well.

"I have a more serious matter to discuss. It is my duty and honor to convey a message from Adrik Iosifvich."

The humor vanished from Rodin's eyes. "What is this message?"

"He wishes to marry one of your daughters."

Rodin did not look surprised. He did look reluctant. The sort of man facing an unavoidable task, like a tooth-pulling or bone-setting. "Which one?"

"Your eldest. Nedeshda. Nadya, as she is better known."

8. A SEASIDE PROMISE

Papa said it was her choice, but he delivered the news like a man offering a burial shroud. Mama chewed at the inside of her cheek and snapped a bed sheet over the drying line.

"Do not rush to a decision," Papa said softly, brushing a calloused thumb over Nadya's cheek, then turned and left them to their washing.

Nadya stared blindly at the shift crumpled in her hands. She would have to wash it again... already it was wrinkling beneath her grasp.

There were many reasons to say no.... Taito, for one. Though, much as it pained her, Taito was also a compelling reason to say yes. Then there was the question of whether or not she even liked the man. She had not taken much time to ponder the possibility, so obvious was it that Danika—

"Danika," she said aloud. Danika had set her sights on Adrik from the start. How could she possibly—

"Do not trouble yourself about Danika," Mama said, voice as hard as her jaw. "That girl does not know what she wants." She clipped the last pillowcase onto the line, then let out a sigh, all the rigidity in her posture dissolving in an instant. She met Nadya's eyes over the linens flapping like spent sails in the wind. "Decide this for yourself, Nedeshda. It is your life and no one else's."

The door to the hall was barred — Danika's first clue something was amiss. She could count on one hand the number of times that door had been shut in her life — and on every occasion, when it opened again, the world as she knew it had changed.

She could hear Papa and Avdotya's muffled voices, but not well enough to make out the words. She scurried around the outside of the turfhouse and back into the kitchen, where Mama was chopping turnips for supper. Again.

"What is going on?" She nodded to the door leading into the hall — it too was barred.

Mama faltered briefly in her chopping. "Negotiations."

"For?" Danika had thought everything settled in their alliance with Adrik. And if it was not, as the Kotov who had called the Folktan, she would hope to be included.

But perhaps these were negotiations of another kind? Perhaps this was the moment? Perhaps Avdotya had approached Papa.... Her heart hammered. Even now, Adrik could be—

"Adrik wishes to marry Nadya."

Danika caught herself on the nearby table. For a moment, she thought her legs had been taken from her too soon. "Nadya?" she said, voice distant even to her own ears. "But I thought..."

"Yes? You thought?" Mama's voice was even colder than usual. She shifted from the turnips to the carrots. Each slice its own violence. "You thought the age of trading women like fish at the stall was over? You thought your Papa immune to such archaic notions?"

Danika had never thought any of those things. But Mama did not seem to be talking to her. She flicked her long black hair over her shoulder and tossed the vegetable refuse into the barrel.

"You were a fool."

Danika doubted Mama knew how right she was. "I must go," she said numbly. "Papanik asked me to tend to the goats."

Mama finally stopped in her work to look up. "I need you here. The kitchen work has tripled since that boy and his friends arrived."

But Danika was already at the door. Mama may have called for her, but Danika did not hear it. She could not hear anything over the ringing in her ears. Her feet led her out of the yard, past the goats, down the steep slope to Lukin's house.

He was sitting in his own yard with Cousin Shelia — a person she had never been less eager to see.

Fortunately, Lukin took one look at Danika, turned to Shelia, said, "I must go," and left her sitting, alone and outraged, in the field.

They trod up and down the rocky inclines and grassy valleys of the Von for miles in silence. She felt his gaze bruising at her flesh, but ignored it until she was certain she could speak without a quaver in her voice. By the time that moment came, they were perched at the top of the stairway leading down into the village. The very spot where, not so long ago, they had fought over the past, the future, and the Philosopher's Stone.

"Adrik has asked Nadya to marry him."

She could not bring herself to look at Lukin to see his reaction. If she did, the chance was too high he would look in her face and see her own.

"Did she say yes?"

"I... do not know." It had never occurred to her that Nadya would say anything else.

"Then it will not happen," Lukin said with certainty. "She has Taito."

That was true.... A dim flicker of hope began to grow in Danika's chest. But a voice in her head reminded her that many a betrothal had ended before the altar.

As if sensing this argument, Lukin added, "Nadya would not betray you in that way."

"Betray me? It would not be a betrayal! I hardly—"

Lukin stared at her and her protests died on her lips.

"Are you alright?"

She could not believe he could ask it so baldly. "Of course. There is nothing to—"

He interrupted again. This time, pulling her into his arms.

She froze. She could not recall a time she and Lukin had hugged...ever. She fought the instinct to resist. When, after a long moment, he had still not released her, she gave in. She relaxed into his sturdy embrace, breathed in the molten metal and sea air, and let herself be held.

Nadya found Adrik at the Dianara riverhead, crouched beneath a large acacia tree. Few trees could survive the winds off the Swansea, but this one sprung proudly from the top of the Von's highest peak. Its trunk hunched like an old woman, picking wildflowers in the grass below. A seedpod fluttered down from the treetop and nestled in the roots of Adrik's golden curls.

He was not so intimidating like this — alone and without his ego.

"Mamanik used to say that trees were people once who became too rooted in the ground."

Adrik sprang to his feet and turned to face her. He transformed before her eyes, back into that smug creature full of want and swagger. "Nadya, I'm glad to see you—"

"Only my family may call me that. You may call me Nedeshda."

His confidence dimmed slightly. "Nedeshda then. Either is beautiful."

Nadya pursed her lips. She marched to the riverbank, careful not to look at him directly, though she could feel his attention on her like a tick over goatflesh.

"The trees were stubborn and could not face change when it came," she said.

"Is that a message to me or you?"

She looked at him. There was a teasing tilt to his lips. "Mamanik said also that the Swansea was once a barren canyon — until The Father died and The Mother filled it with her salty tears." Nadya paused. "She must have loved him deeply to cry so much over his loss."

"Er — yes. I suppose so." He looked every bit the Sivkan lost at sea.

Nadya chewed her tongue, working up the courage to voice the thing he had not been brave enough to ask her directly. "You wish to marry me?"

"I do."

"Perhaps you might have spoken to me first. I am sure one conversation would change your mind."

He shuffled closer, slowly breaching the distance between them — as if she were some fawn who might startle back to the woods. When she did not, he reached out to tuck a flyaway hair behind her ear. The seedpod was still stuck in his. "I doubt anything you could say would change my mind."

But they would never know for sure.

Nadya had met a dozen men like him in her life. Men who wanted her before they even knew her. In her youth, some had fooled her. Far fewer after she learned to recognize them. The tricksters had held her in their arms, worshipful until she became more than a pretty flower, blooming into a person with thoughts and will. Then they left her to the wind.

Nadya tossed her fur shawl to the ground and reached back to undo the ties at her apron. She threw it on top of the fur and kicked off her shoes. Her stockings went next.

"What are you doing?" Adrik's voice pitched high and choked as Nadya worked at the laces of her dress.

"I will know what I am getting before I make you my groom." She watched his eyes follow the course of her fingers.

"But— We can't," he sputtered. Pink flooded in his cheeks. "It isn't proper."

Taito had been shy at first, too. Too much so, even now. But she had taught him her ways as best she could, and if she was expected to give up all that training and tenderness, she would not do it without knowing she had something better to work with.

"So you may crawl into Janna Hillyard's bed, but I may not taste my future husband in a field?"

He went even pinker. "It's not— It's not about the *location*! She wasn't a wife. You are. You deserve—"

"I deserve fidelity. I doubt I will have that. So let us be certain that when we are together, it is something we both can stomach. Now — take off your pants."

He did not move. Nadya sighed and shed the rest of her shift. It fell neatly at her feet. She looked up to find Adrik trying to look anywhere else. Trying, and failing. His eyes settled on her as a chill breeze dusted the grass. Her nipples tightened. She heard him swallow as his shock faded and his lust surged. He threw his belt to the ground and lunged forward.

As his lips caught hers, Nadya thought perhaps there was something here worth fighting for after all.

Danika did not have to face Nadya again until the morning. Lukin had invited her to sup with him and his papa and she had jumped at the invitation. She lingered over her meal so long Dondar was forced to offer her a bed for the night, which she gladly accepted.

By dawn, she felt just barely strong enough to face the walk home.

She climbed the frosted hillside to the turfhouse, steeling herself for what was to come. There was no doubt in her mind who Nadya would choose. It had become clear to her as she slept. Obvious, even. The match with Taito was ill-fated from the start. He would never have been enough for Nadya — the most beautiful girl on the Isles could not settle for the son of a brewer.

It was so much easier to picture Nadya at Adrik's side than it had been to imagine herself as an Impress. Nadya would stand beside him — *could* stand beside him — a crown atop her head, whole and healthy. Nadya was the prize, the one who belonged at center stage, the one who could bear Adrik's children and care for his people and do it all with an effortless grace and kindness that Danika could never have managed.

As for Adrik... More than likely, Nadya had always been his choice. Avdotya had merely assumed, what with the bond Danika and Adrik had formed, that Danika would be the one. Avdotya clearly was not so wise as he believed.

No, Danika's place was at Adrik's other side — in the shadows, in a chair.

"Nika!" Nadya rushed toward Danika from the turfhouse, still in her night shift, a fur wrapped around her shoulders. Dark circles lingered under her eyes. "Where have you been?"

"I stayed the night at Lukin's. I am afraid we were deep in our cups." The lie fell off her tongue easily.

"You have heard?" Nadya took Danika's hands in her own. "About Adrik's—"

"Yes." The correct thing would have been to congratulate her sister. But despite her newfound resolve, Danika's mouth could not form the words.

"I told Taito last night."

For the first time since Mama so elegantly broke the news, Danika felt sorry for someone other than herself. She squeezed Nadya's hands. "Taito...of course. How did he take it?"

Nadya bit her lip. "Not well."

Danika nodded. The morning frost stung her cheeks. She rubbed her damp face against her shoulder. "So you have decided then?"

"Not— Not without your blessing."

Danika tried to pull her hand away, but Nadya clung on tighter. "You do not need my blessing."

"No, but I want it. I will not go through with it if you say so. I know that you cared for him—"

"I lusted for him. Nothing more."

"Danika—"

"It is true. He was a welcome distraction, that is all." She forced a smile to her lips. Nadya's eyes shone with tears. She shifted her grip to Danika's shoulders and drug her into a rough embrace. As Danika tucked her chin into the crook of her sister's long neck, she noticed a seedpod nestled in the back of Nadya's hair.

"I tried to tell them you were the better choice," Nadya whispered in her ear.

Danika shook her head. "I am no bride. I am an alkhemist."

"Only for you would I deign to sleep in a barn." A muscle pinged in the back of Avdotya's neck. He sat up on the makeshift bed of hay as a pair of warm hands settled over his shoulders.

"You need a little rustic in your life," said Yulian, thumbs shifting expertly over muscle and bone. Avdotya craned to one side, guiding Yulian to the right spot. "Keeps you from succumbing to your age."

Avdotya growled and slapped the spot Yulian continued to miss. Yulian chuckled softly in his ear, fingers dancing further away. "Do not think you fooled me," said Avdotya. "You encouraged Adrik to bed that village wench, didn't you?"

Yulian's hands stilled briefly. It was all the answer Avdotya needed.

"Did you mean to ruin our chances?" he hissed.

"Of course not. I want Adrik on the throne more than anyone."

"Then why?"

The hands faltered and Avdotya turned. Yulian sighed, bare chest rising and falling carefully. He looked luminous on his knees, naked and unabashed in the center of the cold barn. Morning sun crept through the slatted roof, turning his red hair gold and casting stripes of shadow and light over his scarred chest.

"I could see he needed some relief," he answered with a shrug.

Avdotya watched him toy with the edges of a frayed horseblanket. "Or you did."

Yulian looked away.

"I don't ordinarily mind your little games. But see if you can't restrain Adrik, and yourself, until the wedding, hm?"

Yulian's blue eyes went wide. "Wedding? It's settled then?"

Avdotya made a noise of assent and began the slow process of getting to his feet. Rustic adventure or no, his joints couldn't take these hard floors. He had to stop allowing Yulian's youthful exuberance to convince him otherwise. "It soon will be. Our boy will finally become a man."

"If you think matrimony can do that. I'm not surprised you never married."

Avdotya dressed swiftly. He had agreed to meet Rodin in the main hall of the turfhouse to work out the details of the pending nuptials. Avdotya was sadly lacking in knowledge of Kotov bridal custom. It would be a bit like crossing the Swansea without an oar.

He strode to the birdcage hanging from a bracket on the wall. The door stood open and Renata rested peaceably inside. Avdotya stroked a finger down the bird's black chest. Its eyes fluttered open.

"You never wake me so gently," Yulian muttered.

Avdotya patted his own shoulder. The bird burst into flight and settled lightly on his new perch. "*You* are not nearly so obedient."

"Your daughter will have wealth beyond imagining. Palaces, gowns, jewels."

"My daughter cares little for such things."

"Think of the honor then. Life as an Impress will grant her unimagined power."

"Always assuming she lives that long," Rodin said, staring hard at Adrik, as if the boy had already got her killed.

Avdotya grit his teeth. Adrik vibrated beside him, hands clasped on his knees, knuckles gone white from biting his tongue. His restraint wouldn't last much longer.

"I understand a dowry is traditional in Sivka— " started Rodin.

"It's not so untraditional here, either," countered Avdotya. "Did you not receive a dowry when you married your wife?"

Rodin's eyes flashed. "Yes. A generous one. My wife's brother is the Imperator."

"As is your daughter's future husband."

"It is a long time between now and the coronation," said Rodin. "The risk in our alliance is high enough without making my daughter his wife. Do you really think Maksis will spare her just because she is his niece?"

"Of course not," Adrik snapped. It was the first time he had spoken since presenting the letter of intent. That letter now sat open on the table between them and Rodin. Avdotya's fingers itched to reach out and snatch it — futile as that gesture might be.

"If I am caught, she will be too," said Adrik, lips drawn as white as his knuckles. "Maksis shows no mercy."

Rodin nodded, gaze considering. Adrik was slowly earning his future in-laws trust, but he was doing little for their coffers. The Kotov might live simply, but Avdotya knew they saved plentifully. Raids and pillages were their lifeblood, their spoils the gift of the Imperator. The Kotov were among the richest citizens in Sivka. And this one in particular, Bodan's heir, even more so.

"Then you see my concern," Rodin continued. "You wish to take my Nadya into untold dangers, take myself and my people to fight your battles. You leave our shores undefended, our hearths untended. And now you say I owe you?"

Avdotya breathed in long and deep through his nose. Unfortunately, the action earned him a whiff of something overripe and pickled coming from the kitchen. Perhaps it has been Maksis' little joke to saddle the Bodansons with such a cook as Marisha. Still, Rodin's logic could not be argued. And he was right about one thing — Kotov warriors exceeded any dowry.

"Very well then. What about a bride price? What do you feel is fair compensation for the loss of your dear daughter?"

This was indelicate phrasing. Rodin gripped the whip-pommel at his hip and Avdotya scrambled to correct.

"Perhaps a dower? A promised sum should Adrik be killed and Nadya survives?"

Surprisingly, it was not Rodin that snapped at that proposal, but Adrik.

"Enough!" he shouted, flying to his feet. "I won't listen to any more of this. My wife isn't some ingot to be weighed out divided up among the men. She is mine to be protected. Give him whatever he wants — but leave me out of it."

"Adrik—"

The boy stomped out of the hall in an uncanny reenactment of his childish tantrums of yore. Avdotya turned to Rodin. "Forgive him. His passions sometimes get the best of him."

"*He* has nothing to regret." Rodin pulled the letter out of Avdotya's reach. "He has shown me his intentions. They strike me as more honorable than yours."

Avdotya bit sharply at his own tongue. "I will speak with him. And return with a solution."

"See that you do."

He found Adrik pacing the yard, sword drawn with no target to swing at. Avdotya approached cautiously, having learned long ago not to underestimate Adrik when he had a weapon in hand.

"Stow your sword, my boy."

Adrik spun, but did not stay his sword. If anything, his grip tightened. "These negotiations are disgusting."

"I understand you find them distasteful, but they are necessary in order to—"

"What's it to be — ten-thousand selniks should I die, but she lives? Does the manner of death affect the price? Double for a beheading? Triple for a draw-and-quarter? How much for both of us, assuming anyone is left to collect?"

Adrik swung and planted the sword in a bramble hedge tucked between the turfhouse and the alkhemist's lab. He leaned over his slain enemy, panting hard. "And what if our positions reverse? What if it's *her* that dies, and *I* must—" He was too choked to finish. He buried his hands in his hair and crouched, elbows balanced on his knees. Avdotya inched closer. When he settled his hand on the boy's back, the flinch was barely perceptible.

Avdotya kept his voice soft, "I will take care of this. You go. Clear your head." He squeezed Adrik's shoulder. "I only do what is best for you."

Adrik's hand came up to clasp Avdotya's. "I know. Thank you, Dunya."

"Be gone. I will give Rodin the stars if you ask it."

Adrik straightened. His eyes shone as they met Avdotya's. "She's worth it."

He watched Adrik head off a winding path far from the village. He didn't know what the boy hoped to find, but with any lucky he'd return a man ready to bear a crown.

As for his bride — the choice had surprised Avdotya, there was no denying that. He'd thought Adrik's bond with the little alkhemist too firm to break. But, in the end, his first instinct had proved true... Beauty always won out.

Avdotya turned back toward the turfhouse. Nedeshda was the better choice. She was not so headstrong as her younger sister and her charms would be an effective tool against the weak. A tool Avdotya was only too happy to wield.

Rodin could have the stars *and* the moon if Adrik wished it. Just so long as Adrik kept the sun for himself.

The day of the wedding, Nadya left the turfhouse just before dawn. Danika lay awake, staring up at the raftered ceiling, awaiting her return. The sun had risen fully by the time the door creaked open again and Nadya entered, hair damp, skin scrubbed clean, glowing from oils Danika herself provided to the bathhouse in the village. But for all Nadya's luminescence, her expression was inscrutable.

Soon Nadya and Mama's muffled voices drifted out of the hall. Danika wondered what they were talking of. What sort of wisdom would Mama give on the morning of her daughter's wedding? Danika doubted she would ever find out.

She was given the honor of dusting the rose powder over Nadya's cheeks. Mama stripped Nadya of her shift. It was Kotov tradition for the bride and groom to eschew any undergarments. Nadya stood naked in the hall, serene as Mama draped the wedding gown over her shoulders. The dress itself shimmered like the surface of the Swansea — the palest blue Danika had ever seen. Layer upon layer of nearly translucent chiffon cascaded down Nadya like rain on a mountaintop. Long fitted sleeves gave way to an open back. It did not cinch at the waist, but flowed across her chest and hips with every movement. It was the kind of thing reserved for royalty — Maksis' last gift to Mama before he sent her to the Kotov and never saw her again.

Mama stared at her eldest daughter, pale in the morning light, and managed the barest smile. "You should wear your hair down," she said.

Danika pulled the combs from Nadya's blonde curls. Her sister usually kept her hair pinned up, out of the way of her daily chores, and showing her long neck to best advantage. But it suited her now, flowing gently down her bare back.

Zin shuffled up next, clutching a delicate crown formed from the branches of an acacia tree and a spruce. The spruce branch Danika had gifted from her collection of Sivkan flora; the acacia was snipped from the tree at the top of Mount Ironside — a symbolic merging of the two lands.

As Elin placed it on Nadya's head, Danika wondered how soon it would be before the silver and gold Sky Crown took its place.

Danika moved to seal the powder jar, but Nadya caught her hand, blue eyes blazing. "This will not change anything between us, Nika. He will be my husband, but you were my sister first."

The familiar sentiment — spoken not so long ago about another man — felt hollow.

"I will ready the cart," said Danika.

She found Adrik pacing outside in the dooryard. His uniform was not nearly as elaborate as she had expected. Someone had clearly advised him against any formal Sivkan attire. Instead, he wore the traditional Kotov groom-suit — cream linen trousers and a white tunic.

For her part, Danika had donned her best dress — blue embroidered damask beneath a coat trimmed in rabbit fur and a matching fur cap atop her head.

Adrik stilled when he saw her.

"What are you doing here?" she asked, marching past him toward the barn. "You are supposed to be in the village."

"She hasn't changed her mind then?"

The note of panic in Adrik's voice forced Danika to look at him directly for the first time since he made his fateful choice. She found him to be unnecessarily sweaty for such a cold morning.

"Of course not," she said. "Your contracts saw to that."

She marched on. Adrik caught her by a shoulder. "You think that's the only reason she agreed?"

Danika suppressed the urge to lie, to confirm his worst fears, to doom Nadya's marriage before it started with just a few cutting words.

"No. Despite what you all may wish, Nadya is a Kotov. She would not do anything she did not wish to."

Adrik let out a sigh of relief. He even managed a grin. "Good."

She tried to step around him, but he cut her off, blocking her path to escape. She did all she could to avoid him, even as the warmth of his body drew her in.

"I wanted to thank you, Danika. Without you rescuing us, bringing us here, calling the Second Folktan — none of this would be happening. It seems I owe all my future happiness to you."

She could not stand the sincerity in his voice. She wrenched her shoulder free of his grip. "I am glad to be of service."

Whistles and cheers filled the village yard as the pink and teal cart trundled into view. It careened down the steep hill with Mama and Nadya bouncing in the back. Danika thought the sight most undignified, but it did nothing to dim Adrik's smile.

Every Von on the isle — and a few non-Vons — had packed tightly around the fighting ring. They perched on fence posts and drooped over railings. Adrik and Papanik stood at the center, awaiting the bride's arrival, while Danika and Lukin lingered outside the gate.

The cart, pulled by two fine mares, stopped at Danika's feet with a great creaking lurch. Papanik raised a large bell overhead and clanged it until some semblance of quiet settled over the crowd. Then he threw down the bell, took Adrik's wrist and held it skyward.

"This young Sikvan means to take our Kotov daughter for a bride!"

Roars of mock-disapproval met these words.

"But no man, Sivkan or otherwise, can take a wife without proving his mettle!" Cheers resounded. "And who better to serve the bride than a sister?"

Danika entered the paddock to the chorus of stomping feet and calls of "Dan-i-ka! Dan-i-ka!"

One of the voices she recognized as Elin's. It was nice to know that despite their many differences, Elin would always support Danika over a suitor seeking their sister's hand.

A training spear and shield awaited her inside the gate. She armed herself swiftly. It had been some time since she had squared off in this ring, since she battled without the aid of alkhemy in her pocket, but, as for all Kotov, the rhythm of battle came to her as naturally as breathing. It felt good, in fact, to use her body now — and for this purpose — while she still could.

Danika tightened the shield strap over her forearm and turned to face her opponent. Adrik looked characteristically smug. She did not find it so charming anymore. Papanik strode between them, waving his arms, playing to the crowd.

"The victorious shall claim the bride. Let battle begin at the toll of the bell!"

Across the yard, Danika spotted Yulian and Avdotya standing where the groom's family would usually take pride of place. Adrik was bantering with the crowd, gesturing them louder. He turned his back on her to speak to Yulian, and the bell rang out.

Danika clocked him over the head.

Adrik stumbled into the fence and she tucked her shield into defensive position. The crowd roared in shock and delight as Adrik staggered to face her. He looked at her in confusion and she struck out with the spear, nicking him on the calves. He tripped but did not hit the ground, catching himself on a gate post.

"Nika?" he said, breathless, and still a little amused.

She flew out with the spear again, but Adrik dodged, the humor sliding from his face like wet mud. He squared his shoulders and, for the first time, met her as an opponent — but he did not scare her. He flung out his spear; Danika hopped it easily. Adrik was a warrior to be sure, but like most Sivkans, his weapon was the blade. She could read his every movement with the spear.

Danika dodged left, then right, plowing into his side with the face of her shield. He staggered again, but launched back just as quickly. His foot caught her behind the ankle and landed her on her back. Her air escaped her in her shock.

Adrik took a knee, hand extended, consternation plain. "What are you doing, Danika? This isn't meant to be—"

She did not let him finish. She whipped out her spear and locked it behind his neck. She had not flipped anyone in years, but it worked just as well as it had in training. As Adrik was flung onto his back, she knelt on his chest and slid her spear free. He was a wall of panting heat beneath her. She reveled in the angry tilt of his mouth. There was much she could accomplish in this position.

"Danika—"

She threw herself off him and regained her footing. As Adrik climbed to his, her focus slipped. She caught Papa's gaze in the crowd. The minute shake of his head.

Blood pounded in Danika's ears. She could not bring herself to look at Nadya, poised high in the painted cart. Sense slowly began to return.

This was Nadya's day. The victor was already decided.

Adrik stood and glared at Danika, sweat plastering his hair to his forehead. He had lost his patience with her games. And just in time too.

He launched forward, gestures still as clear to her as Fool's Gold, and rammed his shield to hers. The impact would have knocked her off her feet even if she had not allowed it. She fell onto her back again — pinned at the end of Adrik's spear.

He stared at her, brow raised, and Danika lifted a hand in defeat.

"I yield," she said.

The bell clanged. The crowd roared. Kotov poured into the enclosure to lift Adrik onto their shoulders. Danika watched from the dirt as Yulian slapped Adrik on his tight behind, as Avdotya ruffled his curls. She was still watching when Lukin came over to offer her a hand up.

Danika looked past the crowd to Nadya, who still sat high on the cart bench, hands clasped in Mama's. Mama stared witheringly at Danika. Nadya granted her a small, sympathetic smile.

Papanik clanged the bell once more. The crowd turned to face Danika — waiting for the final words of approval.

"The Sivkan is worthy," Danika yelled out, voice wobbling only a little. "March him to the water."

The men, Yulian first among them, carried Adrik in a procession. It was not the harbor to which they journeyed, nor even Von Beach, but to the secluded Dianara Rivermouth, tucked between two high cliffs. The bridal cart could not fit through the passage, so Papa hoisted Mama and Nadya out of the buggy and onto the frosted grass.

Danika kicked her shoes off into a pile of boots beside the cart, then followed a trickling stream to a beach pebbled by white rock.

Nadya's hand trembled slightly in Danika's, so she squeezed some warmth into it.

The skies overhead had turned dark, the very air smelling of rain. Avdotya hooked Adrik's arm in his and, together, she and Avdotya led Nadya and Adrik into the sea.

The water was warm for such a cold day — relic of a long Autumn quickly fading to Graywinter. They stopped when the waves lapped at their knees. Avdotya released Adrik first, stepping back into the shoals between the beach and the betrothed. Danika's fingers were slower to release.

Wind roared between the cliffs, catapulting Nadya's hair into a wild torrent around her face. Danika tried to tuck Nadya's hair back behind her ears, but it was no use. Nadya laughed softly, shaking her head. Her eyes shone — the sea and the sky. Danika pressed a kiss to Nadya's warm cheek, and let go.

As the waves crashed and the river tumbled out, Adrik's plain white tunic and Nadya's fine blue gown became translucent in the spraying waters, nothing but a clinging veil between them and their naked forms. Tossed in the wind, purified by the sea, bare to each other — as they had been at birth — making vows of eternal devotion.

They stared deeply into each other's eyes, sparing not a glance for the gathering on the shore or for Papanik, who spoke Thoth's words over them.

"In taking a husband to bare or a wife to bed, there first must be truth," Papanik raised his voice, barely audible over the crying of the wind. "Truthfulness that will speak out of every word and action. There must be a love for mankind that knows no passion, a readiness to gladly share one's possessions, and a willingness to put the needs of your chosen above personal desires.

"Those who have done this will meet on the same plane. They will have climbed the mountaintop together. Theirs is the mastership over the world Below. They can see what those in the valley cannot. They are that which is essential. And that which is essential cannot be destroyed by Fire."

Papanik pulled a single candle from his cloak and clasped Nadya and Adrik's hands around it. Danika waded back into the depths to cut herself over the wick, then lit the flame with a snap of the flint rings nestled over her thumb and middle finger. The light burned bright and white and everlasting, even as the water writhed around them.

"How do you come to this place?" Papanik said.

"I, Nedeshda, come here, to the mouth of the River Dianara, at the place where the Isles meet the Swansea, of my own free will. I come to be married to Adrik Iosifvich Solov."

"I, Adrik, come to this place, on the Isle of the Von, in the land and sea of the Kotov Isles, of my own free will. I come to be married to Nedeshda Bodanson."

"Each of you will be Imperator and Impress of your own domain," said Papanik — traditional words for every bride and groom that never rang more true than for two souls intending to rule over all domains — not just their own.

"As man and wife your joys will be doubled and your sorrows halved as each trouble and triumph is shared between you," Papanik raised his hands. "Say the words."

"You, Adrik, will be my husband for as long you shall have me and as long as I will allow."

"And you, Nedeshda, will be my wife for long as you shall have me and as long as I allow."

Danika hid a twisted smile in her collar, thinking back to just days ago when Nadya had reviewed the vows.

Every moment of the ceremony had been negotiated to make for a perfect blending of Kotov and Sivkan, alkhemist and mundane — a ceremony that would satisfy their subjects, solidify their union to the Sivkan nobles, and (most importantly) make Mama happy.

Up to that point, Nadya had not insisted on much, but she had insisted on this.

"I will not vow to wed until death," she had said, hands on her hips as she glared down at Adrik.

Danika had rarely seen her sister angry. It was a sight to behold, and even Adrik was cowed by it, withering in his chair in front of the fire.

"This is the Sivkan way," Avdotya scoffed. "What use is a wedding without a union promised for eternity?"

"What use is a wedding without a bride?" Nadya snapped back. "I will not be bound in such a vow. We will do this in the Kotov way. I will choose you and you will choose me. We will earn each other. That must be enough."

And if it was not, one of them only had to speak three words three times to end it — *"We have broken."*

Adrik knew what Nadya was demanding. She wanted a Kotov wedding, yes. But even more, she wanted assurance of a Kotov divorce — an assurance that was not promised to Sivkan brides.

Adrik had sat in thought for some time. He did not quite meet her eye as he nodded. "It's enough."

Avdotya lurched forward. "Adrik, don't be silly! You can't succumb to such barbaric customs. You are going to be an *Imperator—*"

"It's enough!" Adrik turned a soft gaze back on Nadya. "We'll do this whatever way my wife wants."

Now, on the banks of the Swansea, Papanik smiled and said, "Together, you are crowned husband and wife. Offer your vow to the sea and seal your promise with a kiss."

Adrik did not hesitate. He tossed the candle, the flame of which still burned, into the depths of the Swansea and caught Nadya around the shoulders. He kissed her long and deep, and the crashing of the waves was at last drowned out by cheers.

9. FAREWELL TO THE KOTOV ISLES

The toasting and feasting and drink went on for two more days. Farms stood forgotten and the beds sagged with the weight of thick heads. Nadya and Adrik took to the barn, remade with an extra-wide cot and strings of dried lavender hanging from every stable post.

On the third and final evening of the celebrations, Danika, Elin and Lukin sat at the end of one of a dozen trestle tables scattering the dooryard outside the turfhouse, smoking a strange vine gifted from Bolonclan of the Telga. It left a pungent cloud of charred cumin overhead. The Bolonclan had liberated it from a Jinmen port on their last raid and sang praises about its effects.

Elin clearly agreed, rolling back and forth in her seat like a rowoman in high seas. If Danika were still not so angry with Babbin, she would have brought some to the old nut. Not only to break down its compounds for future works — but because Babbin would certainly love to smoke it.

Danika reclined across a long wooden bench that she had claimed entirely for herself, relishing in the comforting warmth that settled over her with every puff.

Lukin sat still and stiff beside her, knuckles white as he clung to the edge of the tabletop.

"Marriage is like the ebb of the sea, would you not say, Nika?" Elin had been talking, mostly to herself, since sunset. Long, rambling metaphors that lost the point before they found it. "As one wave comes in, another follows, and the beach is there to meet it."

"Is the beach the groom or the bride?" Danika asked.

Elin shook her head furiously, almost tumbling out of her seat. "No, no, Nika! You do not understand at all."

"You are right. I do not."

"The couple is the beach. The waves are... The tide is..."

Danika took a long inhale and muttered, "The tide will bring us in."

"Exactly!" Elin clapped her hands and fell onto the grass.

"I thought Kotov could hold their vodka better," said a dark voice. Danika lifted her eyes from her sister's crumpled form to Avdotya. Lukin growled at him — truly growled. Like a bear.

Danika thought these rich words for a man who never emptied his cup. "It is more than liquor that tempts her," she said.

"I see." Avdotya took Elin's now vacant seat and raised an eyebrow at the pipe in Danika's hand. "I'm pleased to discover you aren't so susceptible."

"I do not know why you should care." Danika's tone was churlish, but what did it matter? Avdotya had nothing over her anymore. He had proven his fallibility with how badly he had misjudged Adrik. Perhaps she had spoken these thoughts aloud because Avdotya's next words were —

"You and I were both surprised by Adrik's choice."

Danika glared at him. This was not a topic she wished to speak on with anyone, let alone Avdotya Rostislav. But he ignored her, gaze shifting to the clearing where Adrik and Nadya were dancing merrily to the tune of Papanik's stringed lute.

"I think, in time, it will prove the right one."

"I am sure it will," Danika said with all the confidence she could muster — she owed her sister that much.

"You and I are better suited for other matters. Ones not so easily bound by rings."

Danika hid her surprise in a puff of smoke. "You and I?"

"Adrik told me he wants you in a position of importance when we begin our march. No one could argue your skills are valuable — at least until the Luncycle ends. Your influence has been helpful thus far. I'd be a fool to discard you now."

She narrowed her eyes at the mustached-man, watched his bird waddle down his shoulder to peck at the crumbs on the table. "I was not aware it was your choice to discard me or not."

Avdotya smirked, bowing his head in acquiescence. "Perhaps not. Adrik is fond of you. But matters of strategy will remain under my purview. We could be allies, if nothing else?"

Danika had thought they already were. But if she said anything else now, she would surely make an enemy. "I will go where you advise."

Avdotya looked satisfied. He swung his legs over the bench to make his departure just as a familiar figure pushed through the gate into the yard. Antonia pulled a wagon behind her, loaded down by a large wooden crate the size of a baby goat. Danika hoped it was not a goat. Adrik and Nadya had already received three and Danika feared the smell would follow them all the way to Sivka.

"More gifts for the happy couple," cried Antonia. She brought the wagon to a halt in the center of the dooryard and undid the straps securing the crate to the wagon. Papanik ceased his tune and Adrik and Nadya arrived hand-in-hand to open their latest gift.

As the contents were revealed, Nadya gasped — the hand once intwined in Adrik's covering her mouth. Adrik stared inside, face as set and blank as a capstone.

Danika and Avdotya rose to their feet as one. When she saw what rested inside the box, she bit down hard on her tongue to keep from gagging.

It was a pair of human heads.

Perfectly preserved, eyes shut so neatly they could have been sleeping if not for the fact they were missing their bodies. They were of middling age. The man had salt-and-pepper hair shorn to his ears, a formidable mustache, and — even in death — a worried tilt to his brow. The woman boasted an elaborate bun, a stray blonde curl framing her high cheeks. A pair of jeweled earrings dangled past where her neck ended, nearly lost in the bed of hay beneath her. The shade of her lips was more blood than rouge.

A note rested between them —

No parent should miss their child's wedding.

The festivities came to a swift end. Abandoned flagons and empty plates scattered the yard. Only the family, Avdotya, and Yulian remained, and though Adrik stood fiercely at her side, Nadya found it hard to reach for him as she had in the last days. The flush of wedded bliss had lowered Nadya's inhibitions, but the reality of the Imperator's gift reminded her how little she knew the man with whom she now shared a name, a bed, and a future.

"They were alkhemically preserved," Danika said in a low voice.

The crate sat on a table, its lid refastened, but their party had shifted into the inky shadow of the turfhouse, far from the imagined stench. Danika's face was nearly indiscernible in the night, but her sea-blue eyes gleamed with reflected moonlight, and Nadya knew they were fixed on the crate.

"Though why he would keep them..."

Danika was wise to many matters Nadya would never understand, so these flashes of naiveté always surprised her. The desire to hold Adrik close pulsed in her again, but she resisted. She took the safer path of resting her palm on his shoulder. His skin jumped beneath her hand."We should set them to sea," Nadya said. "Put them to rest."

"Sivkans do not set their dead to sea," Avdotya sniped, though Nadya heard far more defensiveness than anger in his voice.

"Whatever your custom then. It is only right."

Adrik turned slightly toward her. His profile was striking against the cold indigo sky. He did not meet her eye, but nodded. "Your customs are mine now. What would you do?"

Her fingers flexed into the hard muscle of his back. She had not expected life with a Sivkan to be so accommodating. Even before the wedding, she had begun packing away the pieces of her old life. Like clothes from childhood, she folded those parts of herself she deemed undesirable delicately inside her mind, tucking each ill-fitting habit into the dark drawers of youth. But perhaps this too was merely the flush of wedded bliss; and though she was touched by his gesture, she could not come to depend on it.

"The Kotov practice is a float at dawn—"

"Might it not wait a few more dawns?" said Avdotya between barred teeth. "I would like our little alkhemist to take a closer look. Perhaps there's more meaning hidden in Maksis' message."

Surprisingly, her sister brooked no argument. Danika's curiosity had always run toward the macabre.

"It is not polite to make the dead wait," said Nadya, and Adrik's mouth twitched in agreement.

"They have been dead sixteen years," said Avdotya. "I doubt another day will do more harm."

As the others returned to the house, Nadya and Adrik made for the barn. They slid into the bed on opposite sides as they had the last two nights. The mattress was a soft cotton sack stuffed with goose down. Their blankets were even finer — one of Mama's cream silks from her palace days, and Papa's best white mink. These gifts were meant to be taken into Nadya and Adrik's own home, but it would likely be many moons before they saw anything so stable as a bedcloset.

In four days, they would begin their march. The tents would be foreign, the land more so, but at least the silks beneath them, above them, entwined among them, would carry reminders of home.

Nadya tucked herself under Adrik's chin, the skin of his bare chest hot beneath her cheek. He had less body hair than any man she had ever lain with, but she enjoyed toying with the fine blond curls he did possess. She scraped her nails through their thin foliage, waiting for his squirm of protest, but it did not come. There was nothing teasing in this night.

"Adrik?"

"Hm?"

"Do you remember them well?" She settled her hand over his stomach. If she could not look into his eyes, she could at least feel the rise and fall of his breath. "Your mama and papa?"

He was silent for so long, she wondered if he had fallen asleep, but then her whole body heaved with the force of his inhale and he said on the release, "It's hard to remember much beyond the blood."

Nadya squeezed her eyes shut. He had painted such a vivid picture that night, it had haunted her dreams many evenings since. But she imagined her own nightmares paled in comparison to his.

Perhaps she should offer him solace in her body.... They had found enough excuses before now. After their first meeting by the river, they had rarely let a day pass without finding their way back to each other. He was a fast learner — and what he lacked in chest hair, he made up for in stamina. No one had ever brought her to the edge so often and so powerfully. And what natural skill he brought to the bed, what she had not needed to teach him, but what he taught *her* instead still bore much contemplation.

She slid her hand down the taut planes of his torso, but he caught her just shy of her goal.

"I remember my siblings better." There was eagerness in his voice. A question of how much she would bear to hear — weighed against how deeply he needed to tell it. Nadya doubted Avdotya had ever encouraged much discussion of painful memories.

"That is the way with siblings," she said. "They stick in your mind even when you would rather forget."

He huffed a laugh. "My little sister, especially. She was a terrible wailer when she was young. I avoided her best I could because of that. But one night when Papa and Mama were away—" His chest hitched and Nadya looked up into his face. A short line had appeared between his brows. "I took her out of the crib mid-wail. I think I meant to strangle her, but the minute I held her, she quieted down." He smiled softly. "Little Amaliya — she was mine in a minute."

"She knew a fellow whiner when she saw one," Nadya teased. He only looked offended until he caught her grin.

"Married three days and already she knows all my faults."

"Oh, I doubt that is the only one."

She watched the smile fade from his eyes as they dropped to her lips. He ran a thumb over the curve of her mouth and a shiver spiraled down her spine. The mood in the air began to shift, but she was too curious to let it just yet. She tucked herself back into his chest. "You said siblings? Who else do you remember?"

His four-fingered hand caressed up and down her upper arm. "Kiril."

"Your older brother?"

"By a few years." He fell silent again. Nadya waited. "I've often wondered if I wasn't the only one who could have escaped.... Dunya says it's wishful thinking. He had the palest red hair you'd ever seen. It almost didn't deserve to be called red at all. Even in all that blood—" His chest went still and Nadya waited for his heart to continue beating. "I remember meeting his eyes in the middle of it. It was after the guard had dropped me, as I was fleeing toward Avdotya. Everyone else was gone, glassy-eyed and unrecognizable, but him, Nedeshda — "

Nadya pulled out of his arms once again. She had not quite mastered his expressions yet, but what she saw stole her breath. "What was it, Adrik?"

"He was alive. He was seeing me. He was alive. I know it." But the tremble of his voice was far from certain.

"Avdotya would not have left him behind if he was," she said, wishing suddenly she had not pursued this line of questioning.

"I know that." The vulnerability on his face shuttered itself into quiet fury. "Dunya's told me a hundred times. But I also know what I saw."

"I believe you, my lo—" The endearment was on the tip of her tongue, but she swallowed it back. "I believe you."

Adrik relaxed, everything in him giving away beneath her — all with that simple affirmation. He shook his head, a rueful smile on his face. "It's probably nothing. A dream. It was all so confused. Dunya tells me Kiril didn't have red hair at all, says that he was blond like Mama. But still—"

"A thing does not have to be real to be true." She smoothed the worry from his brows. "We should sleep now, if we can." He nodded into her caress and they shifted onto their sides. Nadya enjoyed being tucked beside him. It reminded her of cold nights with her sisters in the loft.

"Adrik?"

"Hm?"

"You may call me Nadya. If you like."

She felt the hot press of his lips on the back of her neck. "Nadya."

Adrik laid his papa and mama to rest at the riverhead beneath the acacia tree. Nadya said the waters would spill onto the beach where they'd wed, and Maksis was right about one thing — no parents should miss their child's wedding. After, Nadya headed for the village to continue packing and organizing the scientists. Adrik ventured south, back towards home.

He whispered the word into the chilly afternoon air, "Home."

It tasted strange on his tongue. Sivka was his home — a home he scarcely remembered, and yet to be realized, but it had been his goal for as long as Avdotya had told him so. When Adrik took Maksis' place in Old Kirov, he had every intention of learning the word's whole meaning for himself.

He guessed it felt something like this... The warmth in his chest at the sight of a turfhouse swamped by vibrant emerald hills, the tingle of excitement at the smell of burnt fish, the rumble of familiar voices in the yard. The Bodanson house might not be Sivka, but it would do for now.

"There were no other messages in the crate that I could discern," Danika's voice drifted out of the open laboratory door into the yard. He wondered who else she had invited into her sanctum and squashed a surge of jealousy. "I studied the heads, as well." Adrik moved nearer, trying to banish the image of his parents' faces peering up from Danika's table. "There was no alkhemical substance in use save for a preservation tincture."

"Very well," said Avdotya, and Adrik startled. Danika and Dunya were the last two he expected to be conferring — and so peaceably. Then Dunya said, "I suppose we must take your word for it," in his snidest voice and Adrik's world righted.

"Unless you know another alkhemist who studied seven years at Izumgray," said Rodin firmly. The picture in Adrik's mind became clearer. This was no secret conference between nemeses, but a meeting of the minds. Best he join them.

Adrik entered without knocking and was greeted without ceremony. "Adrik," said Dunya with a nod, "I was just making sure Maksis had no more surprises in store for us."

"I'm glad to hear it, since Danika gave me their remains this morning."

Avdotya glared at Danika. She must have left that part out of her retelling. She crossed her arms and met his stare cooly. "There was nothing left to discover."

Dunya opened his mouth to argue, but Rodin cut him off. "The larger problem is that we no longer work in secret."

"Indeed," said Dunya, running a finger over his mustache. "We couldn't hide from Maksis forever. But I would have preferred if our alliance with the Kotov had been kept quiet a little longer."

"He may know I'm wed, but he might not know the bride—"

"He knows," said Avdotya. "And even if he doesn't, we must always assume the worst."

"If you are implying that a Kotov told him—" Danika said, eyes blazing.

"I'm not implying it. I'm stating it," said Dunya. "Don't take offense, little alkhemist. A man may be trusted alone, but men as a group cannot. Not even the Kotov are exempt from this truth."

Danika turned to her papa for support, but he gave none, saying instead, "War is upon us now. The only way is forward. You have a plan?"

Rodin looked to Adrik, but after he looked to Avdotya. Adrik answered before Dunya proved Rodin's assumption correct. "Maksis may know what we're planning, but he won't have called his troops to muster. Not when there's still a chance he could strike from the shadows."

Dunya nodded. "He's right. Maksis would prefer to take care of Adrik quietly, without ever worrying the nobility, or inspiring the vassals to rebellion. If we move quickly, we may still catch him off guard."

"You have a spot in mind?" asked Rodin.

"New Kirov," Dunya answered swiftly.

Avdotya had been planning this coup for as long as Adrik could remember. Some children fell asleep to stories of heroic captains and mighty nomads roaming the Steppe, Adrik went to bed with tales of battle lines and alliances dancing in his dreams.

"As the former capitol of the Solov reign, New Kirov has been in disrepair since The Slaughter," Avdotya said. "The vassals there are the most overworked and least compensated for their trouble. If we can make it through the Norgay Pass to bank in Southreach undetected, we can move south, collecting vassals and supplies along the way. Winter will be slower to reach the southern steps and, should we take the Kirov River Fortress, we'll have direct access to Polvia."

"What has Polvia to do with it?" Asked Danika.

Dunya cast her a disdainful look. "How do you think we got here, child? Polvia has given us shelter and aid since the day I fled with Adrik from The Palace at New Kirov. They've been generous with their silver, and promise to continue that support. But they won't give men until we've secured the river and hold New Kirov."

Rodin nodded, eyes glazed in some distant thought. "Kirov River leads straight to the Polvian capital. If their support is as firm as you say, it would be an unlimited supply route." But he sounded skeptical.

"Their support *is* firm," Dunya insisted.

"And what do they want in exchange for it?" pressed Rodin.

Avdotya bristled. "Merely a partnership that's been too long neglected. The Lunovna practice of isolation has borne us nothing but trouble and backward thinking. We are the largest country in the world, yet the most inconsequential on the world stage. A laughing stock. Adrik will bring Sivka into the future."

"I do not care for campaign promises. I wish to know that I am not putting a Polvian puppet on the throne."

Adrik flushed. "I'm no puppet — Polvian or otherwise." He held Rodin's gaze, but his father-in-law showed no fear. Nor even any respect. It was atrocious behavior for a soldier, let alone a relative. Adrik's hands clenched into fists. Avdotya edged forward, ready to step between them if it came to blows.

"I do not think we should go to New Kirov."

All eyes turned to Danika. She stood, unabashed, next to her athanor. Did she mean to shock them into supplication? If so, it worked.

Avdotya scoffed, shaking his head. "A fine jest, little alkhemist. But I know you don't presume to tell *me* how to wage war."

"You think you can take New Kirov with only four thousand men? Maksis' army—"

"At full strength could exceed a hundred thousand," said Avdotya smoothly. "But he won't be at full strength. Not if we act quickly. And not if we divert his vassals."

"Among the Kotov, I have only a handful of alkhemists at my disposal, of which, I am the best trained." Danika shook her head. "I know you think I am not enough. *I* know I am not enough. You could never triumph over an alkhemical army even if it were half Maksis' numbers."

Adrik looked imploringly at Avdotya, who stared pointedly in the opposite direction. "Dunya—"

"No," Avdotya snapped, avoiding Adrik's gaze. "It's only of value as a secret."

"It won't be a secret forever," Adrik argued. "You said yourself — men can't be trusted, and the scientists are men." When Dunya refused to yield, Adrik went on, "Our allies are only as powerful as we make them."

Danika's brews gurgled cheerfully as Avdotya came to a decision. Just as the one in the athanor shifted from shimmering pink to milky white, Avdotya nodded. Relieved, Adrik turned to Rodin and Danika, "Follow me."

He had them wait in the dooryard as he raced to the barn. He'd hidden it underneath the mattress after Maksis' "gift" and a sleepless night staring at the darkened barn roof, trying to rid himself of the blood flashing behind his eyes.

When Adrik offered his prized possession to Danika, she examined it with narrowed eyes, like it was one of her potions and she could list its ingredients just by looking.

"What is it?" Rodin asked.

Adrik hoisted the weapon onto his shoulder and took aim at an empty flagon on one of the trestle tables.

Danika gasped. "No! How did you get one?"

Adrik grinned. "Care to assist?"

He nodded to the short string dangling from the flint. Slowly, Danika came forward. With the practice of years, she dug a nail into her palm, cracked the two flint rings on her fingertips together, and lit the celestial fire. Adrik had never tried the weapon with alkhemical flame before, but he found himself excited to see the result.

"Step back," he said. He retook his aim, waited for the telltale click of the chamber, then squeezed the trigger.

The flagon exploded in a crack of flying metal. Imagined or not, the kickback felt fiercer than usual. Adrik thought he heard a scream and the shattering of glass inside the turfhouse. Rodin stumbled back with a whispered, "By The Mother." Danika looked fevered with excitement.

"How did you do it?" she said, staring at the weapon with fanatic interest.

Rodin's eyes were fixed on the spot the flagon had been. "Is it alkhemy?"

Adrik shook his head. "No. It's—"

"Science," Danika whispered. Adrik grinned. It was no small victory to impress *this* Kotov.

"So you see, we will not need your alkhemical tricks," Avdotya said, not quite smiling, but smug all the same. Danika's look of amazement soured. "They've been making them in Frexland since the last Suncycle. This is what I mean by Sivka's isolationist policies doing it ill. Adrik's father's father acquired the first schematics. When Imperator Voya found out what the Solovs had in store—"

"He imprisoned them," said Rodin. "Voya always claimed he put the Solovs into exile because they threatened the safety of Sivka."

Avdotya smirked. "The power of an Imperator — any claim is truth when the head that spouts it wears the crown."

"Then why The Slaughter?" said Rodin. "The borders were sealed, the plans destroyed. Why not just keep the Solovs imprisoned?"

"I suspect Maksis had become uneasy by reports of foreign warfare. Frexland's expansion continued even into the Luncycle once they implemented guns in their armies."

"Guns?" said Danika.

"That's what they're called," said Adrik. "Generally, anyway."

"But progress can't be staunched forever," said Avdotya. "Only delayed."

They descended into silence. Adrik spotted a mop of curls peeking out over one of the high windows in the turfhouse — Mikhail. Zin must have hoisted him up to spy. Adrik waved and watched him drop back inside the house.

"I still do not think we should go to New Kirov," said Danika.

If it'd been Adrik talking like this, Yulian would already be up against the barn.

"I've been planning this for decades, little alkhemist!" Avdotya snapped. "Since before you were born. You mean to say you know better?"

Danika held out a hand — still bright with white flame — to her Papa. Rodin sighed, but dug out a dagger to slice his own finger. The red droplets dampened the fire, and Danika settled both hands on her hips. "I suggest that you have been so long in your plans, you cannot see your own potential."

"Danika—" Warning filled Rodin's voice, but she ignored it.

"Your weapons are powerful. But have you ever considered how much more powerful they could be *with* alkhemy?"

Avdotya seemed too stunned to answer. Adrik's blood began to thrum with excitement. Was she suggesting...?

"I imagine when you began your plans, you did not think you would have an alkhemist for an ally. I am offering you an advantage you never dreamed of."

Avdotya stared down at his shiny black boots. But was he pondering her offer or resolving his position?

"The guns are impressive," Danika continued. "Miraculous, even. They will change the world as we know it come the Suncycle. But here, now...alkhemy still reigns. And Maksis can do almost as much with an alkhemical arrow as you can with a gun. But with an alkhemical..." She looked to Adrik, seemingly searching for the word.

"Bullet," he supplied.

"An alkhemical bullet..." There was a dangerous tilt to her smile. "We could ignite all Sivka."

Finally, Avdotya looked up. "What do you suggest?"

Danika paused, apparently considering her words for the first time. Her stormy eyes shifted to Adrik. "Do you intend to give up the throne come the next Luncycle?"

Avdotya scoffed, but Adrik squared his shoulders. "Of course not."

"Then I suggest you consider a future where science and alkhemy exist together."

Avdotya stared at Danika for a long time, arms crossed tightly over his narrow chest, so still even his stupid bird seemed to have frozen. Then he said, "You wish to go to Izumgray."

Rodin's head snapped toward his daughter, who nodded. "I do."

"Izumgray is a hub of Lunovna worship," said Avdotya.

"Not entirely. I am one person. I cannot supply an army. But at Izumgray — I know who to go to. I know what to take."

Avdotya ran a finger over his mustache. He was considering it. "Izumgray is Maksis' outpost — filled with his spies. We would be begging him to strike us down before we even begin. To make no mention of the symbolic gesture — there is no greater font of alkhemical knowledge than Izumgray. "

"Precisely," Danika said, a gleam of vengeance in her eye Adrik recognized all too well. "So think what a grand gesture it will be when we take it for ourselves."

Mikhail was too young to understand. To him, Danika was just leaving for another stint at Izumgray. But Zin...

Zin clung to Danika with a familiar desperation. She would not whisper pleas, but Danika heard them all the same. *Take me with you. Do not forget me. Do not let the fighting end until I get my chance.* Danika had said the same things to Papa every time he took to oar and left them standing on the beach.

So while Nadya left their siblings with empty platitudes of, "Do not be sad," and "We will be back before the New Year," Danika gripped Zin by the shoulders and said, "I will write you about every moment. Nothing spared." The sorrow in Zin's eyes dimmed slightly. Danika did mimic Nadya's final platitude. "Take care of Papanik."

Mama could take care of herself. She stood beneath the gable, arms crossed tight over her chest, pale and strangely young-looking in the gray dawn. They had spent the previous evening in silence, preparing for the long journey ahead. Danika was grateful for the custom — it meant she and Mama did not have to spare awkward words. Danika took a small step forward — better to face them now than never — but was caught up in the arms of the old bear instead. She buried her nose in Papanik's white mane and breathed deep the scent of tobacco and dried fish. For the first time that morning, she felt her resolve waver.

"Will I be good enough, Papanik?" she whispered. "Can I do everything I hope?"

Papanik growled and jerked out of her arms. "You dare ask me such questions?" His right eye squinted, then he shook his head and his wrinkles softened.

"Ah, Little Nika. You are a daughter of Bodan. And more than that—" His smile crinkled both eyes. "You are mine."

Danika threw her arms tight around him again before she did something as foolish as cry. Further down the yard, Dondar held Lukin in a tight embrace. Lukin towered over his papa, clutching Dondar's bald head in one of his broad hands. Danika wondered what was worse — having an entire family to miss in all their peculiarities, or having to place all that homesickness and longing onto just one person. Mama came forward next. Her arms did not uncross.

"You will look after Nadya?" she said, more an order than a question.

"Yes, Mama."

"Good." She nodded sharply and started toward her favorite daughter, but stopped short. "Be safe," she said, then walked away before Danika could reply.

The last farewell was Mama's to Papa. It was not an unfamiliar scene. Danika had witnessed it a dozen times in her youth, but it never failed to break her in two. Mama gripped Papa by the collar, her bony hands bleached white. Papa buried his gloves in Mama's thick dark hair and bowed his forehead against hers. They murmured words no one dared to try and overhear. It reminded Danika of the way the Cyclicans at Izumgray would pray — though their postures had never showed such reverence.

Papa kissed her. Mama pulled away first, as she always did. And Papa led the march down the cliffside, as he always did. Only now, Danika marched with him.

Their boats waited in the harbor. The guns had been loaded out of their crates and distributed, not a one without a musket strapped to their back — Danika included. She, Nadya, Lukin and Papa took one ship; while Adrik, Elin, Yulian and Avdotya took another. Danika could see her own discomfort reflected on her sister's face, and gripped her by the hand. "It is the safest thing. Should one boat capsize—"

"I know," said Nadya, but she clutched Danika's hand all the tighter as Adrik grinned to them across the water. Nadya pulled her gaze away and stared off at the horizon. A wistful look crossed her face as Lukin pulled up the anchor.

"I have never left the Isles," she said softly.

"It is not so different. Most places are just like others, only with different dressing."

"I fear I will not know the way home."

"You know what Papanik says."

"The tide will bring us in."

Danika squeezed her hand. "And so will I. You will not lose your way so long as I am with you."

As they pushed off, Danika looked up at the high cliffs, memorizing the jagged lines and low valleys as she had each time she left for Izumgray. She spotted a diminutive form standing beside a domed hut — her bird's nest hat stood firm in the wind. And as the figure shrank bit by bit, Danika peeled her fingers from Nadya's and waved Babbin farewell.

10. OLD FRIENDS AND NEW PLACES

They made their camp at the base of the Quicksilver Mountain in the heart of the Taiga. Their tents and fires sat beneath a sheer rock face, shielded by a dense canopy of pine, spruce and fir trees, far from Izumgray's view.

Still, Avdotya felt the presence of the alkhemists like a predator pack looming over unsuspecting prey. They would not be able to delay the journey to Izumgray much longer. It had been three tennights to cross the frosted grasses of the Steppe, trudge through the snow-packed forests of the Taiga, and root out a campsite that could be hidden from Maksis' sight. The trek was made faster and more comfortable thanks to the little alkhemist's brews speeding their steps, warming their boots and coats, and thawing the several feet of snow in their path, but Avdotya would have preferred a long ride in an uncomfortable saddle to taking a potion from that silver-veined hand each morning. He took some comfort in the knowledge that soon they'd be back to conducting matters on his terms — making alliances with nobles and vassals, securing mounts and more men for the fight. The alkhemist may have taken the lead out of the starting gate, but Avdotya would be the one to finish the race.

Dunya left his tent just after breaklight, pulling his furs high around his neck against the bitter cold. Another foot of snow had fallen over the treetops in the night, piling at the tent mouths, unable to collapse the tinctured-roofs or douse the alkhemical fires. The smell of bitter air, evergreens and open flame brought back memories of decades past, when he would trudge through snow as high as his knees in the gray light of dawn to The Palace at New Kirov to attend an exiled Imperator — an Imperator he'd foolishly placed all his hopes on.

Avdotya hoped he was wiser, as well as older, now. He'd bred Adrik to be a ruler of his own making and no amount of pretty Kotov girls would change that. But as Adrik's council gathered in the Imperator's tent — the largest and finest of the few dozen scattered between the towering timbers — Avdotya couldn't help but wish that Rodin had produced a few more men for the cause — and one or two less daughters.

Nedeshda snaked her arms across Adrik's shoulders. He sat playing a round of Pasha with Yulian. "Adrik, darling, finish that later?" Nadya's hands snuck lower down Adrik's chest and she brushed her lips against his ear. "We have visitors."

Adrik looked up from his game and noticed for the first time Avdotya, Rodin, the little alkhemist and her burly shadow — the one whose name Avdotya could never remember... Lodan? Linken? Adrik caught Nadya's hand and pressed a kiss to the palm, then got to his feet with a weary sigh. Avdotya chewed his tongue. If the boy thought an interrupted game an inconvenience...

"What are we here to talk about today?" said Adrik, still clinging to his bride like a lovesick pup. "Have we finally agreed to depart for Izumgray?"

"No," Avdotya said at the same time Danika said, "Yes."

Adrik smirked. "So long as we're all in agreement."

"We should secure mounts and allies before we commence this foolhardy raid," said Avdotya.

"It is not a raid," Danika sniped. "It is a covert undermining."

The alkhemist wore a fitted fur over her ostentatious white coat, its high collar brushing just below her sharp chin. The brownish fur blended seamlessly with her muddy blonde hair. She'd insisted that all soldiers be outfitted with the best hides, boots and armor silvniks could buy, claiming her tinctures could "only improve that which already exists." Translated into mundane, Avdotya gathered that an alkhemically doused fur would always be warmer than an infused cotton.

"I have already written to my contact at Izumgray," she said. "He seems eager to hear what we have to say."

Avdotya grit his teeth. "And what exactly did you tell this *contact*?"

"Nothing that would give away Adrik's identity. I know firsthand that this person is no friend of Maksis. He has spoken to me often of the rights of non-alkhemists and an intellectual revolution."

"And where did he speak of this? In the classroom? Or somewhere more intimate?"

Her ruddy face flushed. Her burly bodyguard lurched toward Avdotya, arms crossed over his broad chest. "Hold your tongue before I cut it out."

Avdotya melted his aggression into a smile. "Do excuse me. I was simply trying to ascertain the trustworthiness of a potential new ally. I see now that reason matters little when we have so many... *feelings* flying about."

"Avdotya..." Adrik sighed the name. As if *he* thought *Avdotya* the one in need of a scolding. "Can we please focus? I'd like to get back to my game — I nearly had Yulian beat."

"Doubtful," said Yulian.

"Of course, Imperator." Avdotya bowed to Adrik, who rolled his eyes. Avdotya turned back to the alkhemist and mustered his most simpering voice. "Dare I ask who this contact is? Or will doing so incite your guard dog?"

Danika's shadow growled.

"He is a professor," she said. "An esteemed one." Avdotya waited for more. Danika sighed. "He is also the Imperator's Timekeeper. He manages the Volodyan calendar." Avdotya found himself involuntarily impressed — clearly the alkhemist had a taste for powerful men. "I am merely suggesting that we have no need of mounts and men until I have what I need to properly equip them."

"You can make brews for the horses, as well?" Adrik said, eyes aglow.

The alkhemist's gaze stuttered on the spot where her sister's arm wound through Adrik's. "No amount of sage or silver will make animals take to alkhemy," she said. "But it is still best to gather horses once our brewers can focus on the more...dramatic potions."

Adrik's brows raised, his attention finally engaged. "Such as?"

"Weapons imbued with unbreakable elixirs, flaming and frosted tinctures, incendiary ammo, poisoned blades. Armor that's never too hot or too cold, boots that never wear. Food made to last beyond its mark, a bite which can fill a belly. If we can recruit a medicinal alkhemist, casualties on the field will be cut in half." She paused, clearly relishing the putty Adrik had become in her hand. "And I have not even reached my specialty..."

Adrik dropped Nadya's palm, drawn to the alkhemist like a mundane to a Flame. "Which is?"

"I can make you warriors. Men who rarely tire, whose skin is armor itself. Speed unmatched and courage unrivaled. They will never have to fear pain in battle. Their arm will carry the punch of a catapult. Their legs can kick a boulder over a castle wall. The possibilities are—"

"Endless," Adrik breathed. Avdotya nearly advised them to seek out a private tent. It was unseemly — acting this way in front of Adrik's wife, Danika's sister.

Even more bizarre was the two of them working together, a melding of the minds. Avdotya had never seen Adrik respect a woman for anything other than her beauty. He'd expected the wedding to put paid to their little bond, but it seemed it would survive the recent awkwardness. Perhaps it was a nearer thing than he'd realized.... If Avdotya had nudged Adrik in Danika's direction, might he have chosen the little alkhemist after all? Perhaps Avdotya had made a mistake. A wife was a much duller threat as time wore on and boredom set in. But a calculating advisor? He himself had proven the longevity in that role.

"You forget that Maksis will have a dozen brews for every one you craft," Avdotya said. "What good are these tricks when the enemy has the same?"

"They give us a chance," Adrik answered before the alkhemist could. "Without Danika, we wouldn't even have that. We're camped with Izumgray at our door, Dunya. It's done. No more doubting."

Avdotya tasted sour rage on his tongue, but swallowed it back. "As you say, Imperator."

He ticked another mark in his mental ledger against Rodin's daughters... Danika Bondanson may not have much to offer in the way of beauty or charm. But she had found the one thing even more valuable to trade in than sex — power.

There was a certain satisfaction in returning to the place that had rejected Danika so brutally with the future Imperator of Sivka in tow — even as freezing rain slicked the steep and jagged ridge, encasing the blankets of snow along the mountainside in sheets of glass. Danika had refused all pleas to aid their climb with brews. Supplies were at a worrisome low after their long journey from the Kotov Isles and it was better to save what little they possessed if they were forced to make a hasty exit.

Also, there was something to be said for enduring the struggle to the top.

"Is this not a school of magic and mysticism?" Elin moaned, clutching a stitch in her side. "Should there not be an easier way to get there?"

"That would defeat the purpose," said Danika, hiding a grin.

Lukin caught her eye. Even he was breathing heavily. "I am eager to see the place you disappear to every year," he said softly.

"It feels like a betrayal to lead you all here." She snuck a glance at Adrik, who led the party at a relentless pace, surefooted even when he slipped.

Lukin looked offended. "A betrayal?"

"I do not speak of you, specifically. Izumgray is a sacred place. Outsiders are rarely admitted. And only alkhemists with the brightest flame are allowed to attend."

"Then why did they make you leave?"

He meant it as a compliment, but it stung all the same.

"Danika — what is this?" Adrik's voice called over the next outcropping.

Danika abandoned Lukin in her haste to reach Adrik, hoisting herself up by her hands and feet until she summited the last bit of craggy, frozen rock. A long, narrow path emerged on the horizon — at the end of which sat Izumgray.

Barely distinguishable from the gray stone surrounding it, the only thing that differentiated the school of alkhemy from the cold and steely mountaintop was the unnatural curvature of its spires. Like the bulwarks on a longship, the towers stood solid, unwavering in their resolve to hide away the school's secrets and majesty. A beacon for only those who were seaworthy. Once, Danika had been at its helm — until her shipmates threw her overboard.

The problem that had drawn Adrik's ire was the deep, gaping chasm at the center of the bridge leading to their destination.

Adrik stood on the precipice, where the foundation gave way to blackness, the tips of his boots perched over the long fall. He rocked forward, peering into the dark abyss. Danika resisted the urge to seize him by his cloak and drag him back from the edge.

"Washed out in a storm?" he posited. "It's not the season for it."

"It was no storm."

"It must have happened after you left," said Lukin behind her. He, Elin, and Papa had finally joined them.

"No," said Danika again. "It is always here."

She joined Adrik at the ledge. Warmth emanated off of him, like the steam off a cauldron, a protective barrier against the freezing mist. Their shoulders brushed and he stared down at her, a small wrinkle between his brows. She bit back a smile and pulled her favorite dagger from her belt. His jaw clicked shut as she sliced the short blade across her palm.

"What are you—"

"I will have to take you across myself." She reached out to Adrik, blood dripping on the snow between them. "Take my hand."

He hesitated only a moment, looking back at Papa. But it was not Papa who disapproved; it was Lukin who had steam puffing out his ears. He had old fashioned ideas about fidelity ever since his mother left for the Vienper and another man. But what impropriety could there be in this? Adrik was married to her sister. He was practically her brother now, though the thought turned her stomach even as it occurred.

Danika repeated that mantra as they stepped off the edge of the cliff together… and landed onto solid rock.

The bridge had appeared whole and unyielding beneath their boots. Adrik let out a *whoof* that reverberated down his arm and into her palm, which pulsed hard with the effort to stem the blood oozing between them. "Was it here this whole time?"

"It was for those who knew how to see it."

"Now you're talking like that mad old crone." Amusement danced behind his eyes. Rain plastered his golden curls to his forehead and she resisted the impulse to comb her fingers through it.

"That mad old crone taught me everything I know."

"I thought that was what this place was for?"

"I learned a few things here, too."

She pulled her sticky hand from his and turned back to retrieve the others — but Lukin was already stepping forward. "Lukin, no!"

His foot sank through the seemingly solid stone like water. He overbalanced in the effort to stop the free fall. Papa lurched forward, caught him around the chest and hauled him back to safe ground. Lukin bucked against Papa's hold, hands clenched into fists. "I can see the path before me!"

"Do not trust your eyes!" she snapped, hurrying back to him. She was not so foolish as to try to run — it was still a narrow bridge, and the fall on either side was all too real. When she reached Lukin, she held out her hand again. "It is not *what* you see, but who you are *with* that matters."

He glared at her palm smeared red. She wondered if he could see the imprint of Adrik's hand there as she could. If he did, he overcame it, caught her in a firm grip, and allowed her to lead him across the ravine.

Adrik had slipped out of bed in the blackest part of night, before the moon had even lowered in the sky. Nadya ached for him. Particularly on such a cold morning, she found herself longing for the warmth of his bare skin and strong limbs entangled in her own.

He and Danika had left her for Izumgray. As such, Nadya expected to spend a long, lonely day in camp, worrying until they returned. But she had only just drug herself out of bed and donned her doeskin robe when Avdotya entered the tent without ceremony.

"Make yourself ready," he said. "We leave at once."

"Ready? For what?"

"For duty. You're an Impress, remember? It's not all lounging in bed surrounded by furs — not until you are with child, anyway. There's work to be done and you are an emissary of the crown."

Nadya dressed quickly and as best she could with so little practical understanding of where they were going. She dared not ask for further details lest it incite another lecture. Her mink fur stole and high collar were cut for fashion more than function, and a woolen half-cape draped her shoulders, stopping just shy of the buckle at her waist. Matching bands filigreed with roses cinched the sleeves of her dress to her forearms. It was an outfit not exactly fit for an Impress, but thanks to many fine wedding gifts — and a good portion of Mama's closet — it did give her a passable impression as a Sivkan noble.

A driver and sledge with three horses saddled abreast awaited her at the edge of the encampment. They were the only three horses in their possession, much to Avdotya's chagrin. Yulian hefted Nadya up and into the back seat. Avdotya already occupied the front.

"Perhaps now you will tell me where we are going?" she said, settling a fur over her lap.

"Alkhemists will not decide this war, whatever your sister thinks."

"Who will decide it then?" she asked without a trace of malice. He narrowed his eyes as if to try to find some hint of it anyway.

"The same people who build our cities, pave our roads, and keep our homes, Impress — vassals." Avdotya turned to the driver. "Take us to—"

"Ho! Wait just a minute." Yulian heaved himself onto the bottom step. "Budge over, oh wise one." Nadya bit her lip as Yulian plopped down very near Avdotya, who had been seated in the center of his long bench. Curling his lip, Avdotya scooted down to allow Yulian more room.

"You didn't think to leave without any protection, did you?" he said with a smug grin he must have learned from Adrik — or perhaps Adrik had learned from him.

"We have nothing to fear from vassals," said Avdotya, grip tightening on his black walking stick. A silver finial in the shape of a raven's head topped the cane and Nadya wondered if he had it made especially to look like Renata.

"Forgive me for not being so optimistic. Besides, you have the Impress with you. We can't take any risks with her welfare," Yulian said with a wink. "Even now, she may be carrying the future Imperator in her belly. Isn't that right, Nedeshda?"

"I thank you for your concern, Yulian," she said, summoning the patience she usually only reserved for her siblings. "I pray every day to The Mother that you are right. Though my dreams tell me it will be an Impress I give to Adrik first."

They settled into silence as the sledge lurched forward, cutting through the snow like a scythe through wheat. Nadya turned her gaze outward — to the land that would be hers and Adrik's kingdom should this mission succeed. Danika's advice to her as they had prepared to leave the Kotov Isles had rung true in some ways and so very false in others. *'It is not so different,'* her sister had said. *'Most places are just like others, only with different dressing,'*

But for a woman who had never sailed beyond the boundary of the Kotov Isles, Nadya found much to marvel at.

For one, she had never looked out at a horizon without a sea upon it. In that way, the Steppe, with its wide open sky and endless swaths of untamed land, had felt like a cage. With nowhere to sail, how could she flee? She had dreamed each night of long walks on an endless earth that offered no glimpse of rain. But it was not until they reached the ridge marking the border between the Steppe and the Taiga that Nadya fully marked her sister a liar.

It was like peering off the edge of a cliff into a different world. The timberline stretched as far as the eye could see. Heights and widths and quantities of trees Nadya had never imagined, as endless and mysterious as the Swansea. She had thought of the acacia tree she and Adrik first made love beneath. If Mamanik was right and trees were people who became too rooted in their ways, then there must have been many a stubborn soul in Sivka.

Nadya clenched her hands in her furs as she stared into the wooded depths, yawning out on either side of her like a monster's maw. They sped along a road cut just wide enough for the sledge, greens and blacks and browns whipping past in a gullet that threatened to swallow them whole.

Adrik had explained that sledge was the only way to travel in these parts. Fortunately, the dense forest broke the wind and the snow in their path lay evenly before them like thick icing on a New Year's cake. Adrik had told her that in some places of Sivka, such as the Tundra, snow could drift higher than the tallest wave in a hurricane, devouring rooflines and fences and even trees. He spoke of all matters Sivkan with such authority that she often forgot he had not crossed its borders since he was a child.

The cold whipped at her cheeks as the sledge flew faster down the lane. Nerves and excitement fizzed inside her like a bottle of spirits uncorked. Avdotya's invitation to join him on this mysterious journey pleased her. She had begun to reconcile her role as Adrik's wife as merely ornamental — not all that different from the part she would have played for Taito. But there was no denying that Adrik was a greater man than Taito, a man destined to live a bigger life. Which made her life greater too, in a way. She would serve as Adrik's support, his confidant — the place he could lean when he felt weak, without judgement or fear of reproach. She would guide him in the gentle way that all wives guide their husbands, raising their children in the spirit of light and goodness, Thoth willing, and make him a man worthy of the Sky Crown.

That would be a life well lived. Even if she was the only one who ever knew the depth of her contribution.

It was nearly midday by the time Avdotya called the driver to a halt. To Nadya's untrained eye, their destination seemed no different than their journey.

Avdotya stopped them on a stretch of barren road, lined on either side by high conifers. The smell of piney woods was as pungent as the Swansea.

"We will stop here and walk the rest of the way," he said. "It would look suspicious for anyone in a sledge to be visiting this place." Avdotya stared at her, a hard glint in his eye, as if expecting her to waver at the prospect of a hike.

"Lead the way, Master Dunya."

They trudged through the snow and timber for two miles before they came to a gravel path swept clean of snow. Another mile up that road put them in view of a village surrounded by a high log fence. Such ominous fortifications did not bode a warm welcome, but when they moved closer, Nadya was surprised to find the gate ajar and unmanned.

Yulian grinned at her confusion. "You know what they say — fields for the Luncycle, fences for the Suncycle."

As they entered the village proper, Nadya found comfort in the familiar for the first time since crossing the border into Sivka. Though the trappings and architecture had a distinct Sivkan flavor, the bustle of village life reminded her so keenly of the Kotov Isles that she could taste the salt air on her tongue. Log homes towered on strange wooden stilts, and the people wore more furs than linens or wools; but the pub, blacksmith and tannery sat together in a neat row just as they had on the Von. Dozens of steeply peaked roofs rose across the flat clearing — the better to shed their snow, she realized.

This village had been carved flat from the earth, cleared of trees and hills and all that made it beautiful — and perhaps that was where the similarities ended, for she could not imagine the Kotov wiping away the work of nature so blankly, no matter how convenient.

Avdotya marched them down another path without delay. He seemed familiar with the road, not lingering to take in the sights, though, like Adrik, he could not have seen such a place for many years.

Much of the snow had been cleared away here, too. Shoved to the sides of the path in muddy piles that would only mount the longer Whitewinter dragged on. Nadya disliked the practice. She would have rather trudged through snowpack than abandon the sparkling beauty of a white frost.

Avdotya's relentless pace brought them to a hut indistinguishable from the rest. They climbed a dozen slippery steps to a high porch and Avdotya knocked lightly on the front door. This meeting, whatever it was and whoever it was with, was clearly prearranged.

Nadya could not hear any stirring from within. She began to worry that another of Avdotya's plans had come to naught, when the door swung open and a silent figure, cast in shadow, ushered them across the threshold.

Once her eyes adjusted to the darkness, Nadya was shocked to find a large family inside the hut. A mama with a baby on her hip stirred a clear broth over a hearth. Two older children sat at a table, chopping potatoes. A little boy, Nadya guessed to be around five years old, coughed beneath a thin blanket on the lone mattress in the corner. A young man with dark coloring and darker eyes — possibly of an age with Nadya herself — sat at the bedside of his younger brother, smoothing a hand over the boy's fevered forehead. The last child, a red-headed little girl, tugged at Nadya's skirts, staring up at her with hollow blue eyes.

The silent figure that had ushered them inside stepped into the light of a single candle guttering on the table. He was a weedy man with a hooked nose and a patchy brown beard rimmed with gray. He did not look happy to see them. He did not invite them to sit, nor offer them a loaf of salt bread as Adrik had assured her was the Sivkan custom.

With no windows, the only other illumination was by the flame of a silver fire — clearly struck by the single brick of black alkoal smoldering in the grate.

"I never thought to see you here again, Dunya," the man said in a gravelly voice.

"I promised to return, didn't I?"

The man grunted and sat in one of two wooden chairs nestled in front of the hearth. Avdotya took the other.

The Mama dropped her ladle and managed a dim smile for Nadya and Yulian. "Will you be needing breakfast? I don't know how long you've journeyed..."

Nadya heard the reluctance in the woman's voice. She was not eager to spread her thin broth even thinner. All of the family, even the darling little girl at Nadya's hem, had too many angles to their bones, too deep hollows in their cheeks. Yulian's gaze was fixated on the doting older brother and sickly boy in the bed.

"Thank you for the offer, but no," she said. "We did not journey far and we had a large meal before we left."

The woman nodded, relief plain on her face. "Be seated then. I'll fetch the vodka."

Nadya regretted her lie as the woman poured deep. In truth, she had not had time to eat before Avdotya ushered her into the sledge, and the thought of a morning dram on an empty stomach left her queasy. Still, it would be rude to decline what little hospitality these people could offer.

As soon as Nadya sat, the little girl climbed into her lap.

"Misha, no—"

"I do not mind," Nadya said to the Mama. The girl tucked easily against her, like a pair of nesting dolls. "She reminds me of my little brother. I miss him terribly. We had to leave him—"

"Do not go giving away all our secrets, Nedeshda," Avdotya said sharply. He turned his black gaze to the papa, who was staring darkly into the fire as if doing so would render Avdotya invisible. If such a trick existed, Nadya was sure Danika would have found it by now.

"Josef and I have much to discuss." Avdotya's eyes dropped to the little girl in Nadya's lap. "Such as how to abolish vassaldom once and for all."

Once Danika had brought Lukin, Elin and Papa safely across the bridge to Izumgray, she stared up at the building that served as the only other home she had ever known. Ice swirled around the tower roofs and snow dust rose from the rocky base like morning mist off the Swansea. Adrik made to mount the steps to the entrance.

"No, Adrik. Not that way."

He threw up his hands. "Perhaps you should lead the party then? If I'm not to be trusted to find the door?"

"Earnest said he would bring us in through a side entrance." She had not told Adrik this part — she feared it would bruise his ego.

"You mean we're to be smuggled in like thieves in the night? I thought we were here to find allies in the war against Maksis! I am the future Imperator of Sivka! How can I make allies by sneaking in the back door?"

Clearly, her instincts were sound.

She moved close, until barely an inch separated them. To the others, it probably looked like she was offering him some secret council. In truth, she merely hoped to shield them from an undignified tantrum.

"You forget where you are. Izumgray is the ultimate symbol of Lunovna power. Loyalty to Maksis runs deep here."

"Then why did you convince me—"

"Because that loyalty is not as deep or as strong as Maksis believes. And whether you like it or not, you will need alkhemy to do this thing."

He pouted his lips in a frightening imitation of Mikhail when he wanted more sweets. "Aren't you enough?"

"If only. Now come. Earnest will be waiting."

But it was not her old mentor who greeted them at the base of the east tower, clad in a white doeskin cloak.

"Shura Agrifnovna," said Danika with ill-disguised disdain. "What are you doing here?"

"Earnest sent me to greet you," the young woman answered with a condescending grin. Even now, despite the coterie of armored men at her side, Shura looked at Danika as a minder looks at a child. It reminded her vividly of Avdotya.

"Someone has to do Earnest's bidding now that you are no longer here," she said, head high, curly black hair bound into a bun at the top of her head. Her dark skin and black eyes gleamed, as flawless as her imperious demeanor. She and

Danika were of an age, but Shura had the manners and bearing of a true Sivkan, and never failed to remind Danika that she did not — that she was merely a simple Kotov, paddling in waters too deep to tread.

"Why don't you and your...*friends* follow me." Shura's gaze passed over the group, lingering on Adrik with a certain suspicion — and Lukin with a certain appreciation.

She led them to a side door at the base of the northeast tower, barred by a heavy chain that Shura's cut palm unlocked. They followed her up a spiraling staircase, Danika wishing alkhemy gave her the power to stare a flame into the hem of Shura's white robe. Her clothes were immaculate in comparison to Danika's — perfectly fitted, pressed and unstained. Danika, meanwhile, had been living hard on the road for nearly a season. Mud splattered the skirt of her fishskin coat and clashed with her coonskin mittens and hat.

She patted the ends of her damp and stringy hair — it had grown an inch or more since Autumn, now just past her shoulders. Sweat pooled beneath her hat and it occurred to Danika for the first time that this was not the most flattering ensemble with which to greet, and persuade, a former...friend. Nadya may have been able to pull off the windswept look, but Danika certainly could not.

She drew back her shoulders and tried to dismiss the thought. Earnest had never been turned by the prettiest girl in the room — that was evidenced by their relationship in the first place. Danika would just have to rely on her other qualities.

The top of the tower housed Earnest's private quarters — a place only Danika could once claim access. But as Shura pushed through the door, giving it a habitual shove when it stuck on the frame, Danika was forced to contemplate in what other ways Shura had replaced her.

Her musings cut short, however. Danika had barely crossed the threshold into Earnest's rooms when she was greeted with a smiling face and the press of lips against her own.

Clearly, Earnest had missed her.

II. THE IMPERATOR'S TIMEKEEPER

Earnest held Danika's chin between his forefinger and thumb and seemed in no hurry to end the kiss, even with a squadron of hulking warriors standing watch. Earnest was an affectionate man, had always been so. When he finally broke away, Danika took a quick step back, heat creeping up her neck.

There were no rules against such indulgences at Izumgray. Technically, the school did not operate in the rigid structure of teacher and student. All alkhemists were considered students and teachers in different stages on their journey. And though the Izumgray motto of "health, humility, patience and chastity" was spoken before every breakfast, the chastity portion of the vow had never been taken particularly seriously. There were even rumors that such a stipulation was added after too many alkhemists found themselves in need of the Second Relief and other remedying potions.

It was all she could do not to wipe the heat of him from her lips as she snuck a glance at the others. Papa bore the same stern expression he wore whenever Howlan tried to propose another war with the Jinmen. Elin looked more disgusted than disapproving. Lukin was running his thumb over the blade of his ax with unnecessary relish. Adrik, of all of them, grinned in some parable of admiration. Danika tried not to let that deflate her.

"Danika Bodanson — we have missed you here at Izumgray," said Earnest, expression as wide and open as the broken bridge to Izumgray. A Sivkan in his early forties, his reddish blonde hair was cut short and his customary beard was shorn beneath gray eyes that seemed to sparkle with the promise of his next grand idea.

He stood amongst all the trappings of nobility and title that life as Maksis' Timekeeper afforded. Scarlet curtains and the finest specimens of alkhemical art bedecked the high stone walls. There was the three-dimensional painting of the Qabalistic Tree of Life, a moving depiction of the Above and Below, ciphers of Hermetic geometry — alkhemy made manifest. Two plush velvet couches and overstuffed chairs sat upon a large woven Jinmen rug in front of a massive fireplace, the chimney of which towered up through another three stories. Only a handful of Adepts could lay claim to an entire tower of Izumgray's halls and these particular rooms boasted a parlor, bedroom, washroom, private laboratory and observatory.

Danika recalled the observatory with its brass telescopes, large compasses and clear vistas that seemed to stretch beyond the furthest boundary of Sivka into the very stars themselves. She had cared little for the mysteries said to lurk in the skies at the time, but ever since she had taken up her own starcharts at Babbin's insistence, sketching with single-minded purpose into the small hours of the night, Danika found herself all too eager to attempt the task with proper tools.

"Things are not nearly so interesting here in Izumgray without you sneaking around trying to make Philosopher's Stones," said Earnest.

"Making *what*?" Papa boomed.

Danika's shoulders shrank. Was it the fact that she had lied to him about why she had been expelled that ignited his fury? Or was it that he knew precisely why she would try something so risky?

"Forgive me," said Earnest. "Introductions have not been properly made. I am Earnest Mishevich Andosky — an Adept here at Izumgray and the Imperator's Timekeeper. I worked with Danika closely while she studied with us. What is your name, sir?"

Papa took a deep breath through his nose, slowly unclenching the grip on the pommel of his whip. "I am Rodin Bodanson of the Von." When this seemed to make little impression on Earnest, Papa added, "I am Danika's papa."

Earnest blanched, but just as quickly, covered it with a wide smile. He extended his hand in greeting. Papa eyed it with disdain. A Kotov would never approach a stranger with a bare hand. In Sivka, it was common courtesy to welcome a guest warmly, but on the Isles, such pleasantries were saved for when trust had been earned. What Papa failed to realize was that the Sivkans were no more trusting than the Kotov — they just hid their suspicion beneath a thin veneer of pleasantry.

"You must be a proud father indeed," said Earnest, dropping his hand. "I have rarely seen a student with such natural talent pass through Izumgray's halls." Shura scoffed from a shadowy corner. If Earnest heard it, he ignored that too. "If only my colleagues weren't so afraid of progress, perhaps she'd have shared her talents with us a little longer."

"You would like that," muttered Lukin.

Danika closed her eyes. "And this is Lukin — a very old, very *protective* friend of the family." She introduced Elin next and saved Adrik for last. "This is Adrien. He is an ambassador from Polvia. He seeks Izumgray's wisdom as to what can be done about the Imperator."

Earnest's expression turned serious, though the twinkle in his eye did not fade altogether. "Ah. Then you come to the right place. I have had many a thought about Imperator Maksis and his rule."

"Then perhaps it is time to break out our cups?" Adrik suggested with the same swagger he had used to win Danika, Nadya, and even Mama.

She and Adrik settled on one of Earnest's plush sofas, a full cup of Sivka's finest in hand. Danika watched Lukin's expression as he took his first sip, eyes widening with an approval he quickly tried to mask. Not even Taito's home-brew could match Sivkan vodka.

Beside the light of a silver fire burning brilliantly in the hearth, Danika, Adrik and Earnest wheedled at familiar topics — the inequality between the few precious alkhemists and the much greater mundane, the treatment of the vassals, the petition system for a Philosopher's Stone that no one had seen proof of in a decade — causes that she and Earnest had often ruminated on in the mussed sheets of his fourposter bed.

"Sivka cannot continue to cut itself off from the rest of the world," said Adrik. "Technology is evolving in Polvia and in many other countries. There is progress to be made through industry, chemistry...science."

Earnest's eyes lit with a different kind of gleam — something altogether more greedy. "Science, you say?"

Adrik nodded. He balanced his elbows on his knees, cup gripped between two hands, the clear liquid shimmering only a sip or two below the brim. "I was told you had an interest in such things."

"As the Imperator's Timekeeper, I've been given the great honor of maintaining the Volodyan Calendar," said Earnest. "As you can imagine, there are few greater responsibilities in Sivka than understanding, and predicting, the Cycles."

Adrik nodded. "An important job, no doubt. But I imagine it's one that has little to do with alkhemy?"

Earnest's eyes narrowed. Danika could feel his suspicion growing. No doubt he had only one guess as to who had bestowed a mundane with such forbidden alkhemical knowledge.

"It's not alkhemy, per say. But some would say charting the movement of the stars isn't so far removed from it," said Earnest.

"That I leave to the experts." Adrik chuckled and took another short sip. "One thing's for certain... The Luncycle won't last much longer. Do you really think Maksis' grip on Sivka is so strong we can survive another 25 years of the poverty and ruin that will ensue once alkhemy has gone?"

"I remember the last Suncycle all too well," said Earnest with a grimace. "Our vassals perished by the dozens as their homes froze without the reinforcement of a tincture, as their fires smoked and doused without alkoal, as crops withered on the vine."

"What if they didn't need the Alkhemical Flame to live as people? What if all men and women could live with dignity?" Adrik perched on the edge of the sofa, knees mere inches from Earnest's. "What if we could achieve as much with science and chemistry as we ever could with alkhemy? And what if we did it all with a mundane on the throne?"

Earnest's gray eyes turned steely. "What you suggest is treason."

"It would be." Adrik flashed another grin. "But I'm from Polvia."

Earnest leaned back with a sigh. His empty flagon dangled from his fingertips. "How would you achieve this? Maksis will never cede the throne willingly."

Adrik looked to Danika. It was a look she had seen him give Avdotya many times — one that brokered respect, that posed a question, that asked permission. Swallowing the lump in her throat, Danika nodded, hoping against all evidence to the contrary that he would use some caution.

Adrik's gaze slid back to Earnest. "Maksis' way isn't the only way. The Lunovna way isn' the only way. Others ruled not so long ago — those whose blood ran as mundane as the next man's."

There was a long pause. Earnest bounced his cup by the handle as he considered. "You speak as if the Solov name is forbidden, my Polvian friend. It's not forbidden. It's worthless."

Adrik did not hit him — Danika supposed she had to be grateful for that. But the fury that flashed across his face was as good as a strike. And it confirmed something to Earnest.

"What did you say your name was again?"

Adrik hesitated too long. Then Danika made the mistake of answering for him. "Adrien. Adrien Tysowski, Master of Trade in Polvia."

"Yes, that is a mouthful. I'd forget it myself if I were you."

If the first pause had been long, the second was interminable. No one seemed to breathe for fear of breaking the silence.

"Who are you really?"

Adrik sat up straight. If it would not have usurped his authority, Danika would have slapped her hand over his mouth. “I am Adrik Iosifvich Solov, rightful heir to the Sivkan throne and the Sky Crown.”

Earnest did not twitch at this pronouncement. The air stilled around them, pregnant with possibility. Earnest watched Adrik with an unblinking eye. “So you are not so bad with names after all. And what do you want with me?”

Danika took her chance before Adrik could ruin it. “It is not just you, Earnest. It is the others here as well. You know the ones. We have spoken so often of this moment, of a just and true society where mundane and alkhemist could live as equals. Where alkhemy could extend beyond its bounds, into the mundane. There are others that believe in this. Convince them to join us. Give us the supplies we need to be rid of Maksis for good.”

“So it’s a revolution you propose then?”

“You proposed it first.”

“I did, didn’t I?” Earnest stood. He crossed to the drink cart and poured himself another measure. He took a sip, his back to them as he considered. “But that’s what you never understood, Danika. To speak of revolution requires only forethought. To act on it...that needs a different strength entirely."

As if triggered by Earnest’s words, the door flew open with an almighty crash and Maksis’ guards burst in.

“What can you possibly hope to gain from me alone?” Josef said to Avdotya.

Josef sat before the fire, skating a curved knife over a pipe. With each stripe of his blade, a delicate curl floated to the floor.

“From you alone, perhaps not much,” said Avdotya, cradling his untouched cup between his hands like a precious jewel. Did he fear the drink? Did he fear what he would do under its influence? If so, he showed his weakness. Any Sivkan host would notice such a slight. Like the Kotov, the Sivkans did not trust a man who did not drink deep. But perhaps his reasons were not so sinister... Perhaps it was simply that Avdotya was too busy in his schemes to stop for a simple thing like thirst.

He leaned forward, black eyes flecked with silver stars in the reflection of the alkoal flame. Adrik had told Nadya that he hoped to replace alkoal with something called a 'match.' It sounded like feeble competition to Nadya, but Adrik insisted that the innovation could be produced at a fraction of the cost of alkoal and was a welcome alternative to freezing come the Suncycle.

"Technically anyone can use alkoal," Adrik had said — a scheming look in his eye not dissimilar to Avdotya's now. "But how many can make them? How limited is the product? How expensive? It's a luxury under Maksis' control, Nadya. Under my rule — it would be no more special than a bundle of wheat."

His words had given her pause, then hope. Perhaps she had not married a man driven solely by ambition and revenge. Perhaps she had married someone good, as well.

"You alone can't accomplish much," Avdotya said to Josef. "But together?"

"I know your choice to come here — to me — was no accident, Dunya."

It was the second time Josef had uttered Avdotya's familiar name — the only person to ever do so in Nadya's presence save Adrik. And Avdotya, hardly an outdoorsman or tracker, had known the path through the woods to the village, and then through the village to this hut, blindly, even after years on the run in foreign lands. But, Nadya reminded herself, she could no sooner forget the way home than she could forget to breathe. As the Kotov always said — *the tide will bring us in.*

"We are the largest contingent of vassals on any property — some two thousand strong," Josef continued. His gaze flickered to his oldest son in the corner, who had turned away from nursing. He watched his papa with a lowered gaze, dark hair falling into his eyes, grip tight on the sick boy's ankle — too thin beneath a feeble blanket. It reminded Nadya of herself, of so many conversations she had born witness to, knowing that their result could change her own life forever.

"But two thousand won't topple an Imperator," Josef said. "Even if I could get them all to agree on who that Imperator should be."

"You underestimate yourself. It may start with two thousand, but think how quickly word of that unification would spread among the other vassals," Avdotya argued. "An uprising on the land of Maksis' most loyal sister? The largest contingent of slaves—"

"Vassals, Dunya," Josef snapped. "You would do well to remember the distinction."

"You would do well to forget it. Which should be easily done as there's little to distinguish you."

The young man let out a laugh, bitter in its agreement.

"Emir," Joseph snapped at him.

Yulian cleared his throat. His gaze also followed Emir, who now hung his head between hunched shoulders. The mama and children at the table had gone rather pink, chopping their potatoes with renewed force. The little girl in Nadya's lap gummed the edge of Nadya's coat. But Avdotya and Josef were ignorant to their effect, locked in a private battle of wills.

It was Josef who broke the stalemate, speaking low and slow. "Your feelings are strong on this. I don't doubt your intentions, Dunya. I don't even suggest there are others a stone's throw from this house that wouldn't agree—"

"Well then—"

"But if you really mean to do what you suggest... If you really mean a revolution — a vassals' uprising—"

"A *people's* uprising," Avdotya corrected.

"Then you had best remember that there are just as many proud of that moniker as there are who would spurn it — even while fighting your boy's war."

Avdotya leaned back in his chair. For a moment, Nadya thought he might actually take a drink, but he only rolled the goblet between his palms. "Very well then. Let's do away with the semantics. Will you join us? You're the head of this leaderless faction. If you were to back us, others would listen. And if they followed, imagine how many more would be brave enough to unite."

"You paint a pretty picture," said Josef, resuming his work on the pipe. "But we won't risk everything on a dream. Your boy—"

"He is not my boy. He is the son of Iosif, rightful heir to the Sky Crown," Avdotya growled. "And his time is coming."

This hefty title did not impress Josef. "Whatever he is — he hasn't proven himself. He's nothing but a name born of a memory some sixteen years dead. Come back to us when he does something in the present. Come back to us when you have a chance."

Adrik's body responded to the attack like it was expected, like it was a long-standing appointment on the calendar — as familiar as a birthday or the passing of a new year. The bitter irony that the man responsible for such timekeeping was also the person responsible for this treachery wasn't lost on him. As Adrik surged to his feet and unsheathed his sword, he saw Earnest and Shura flee the room. The familiar sting of betrayal was nothing to the surge of hot battle blood simmering inside him.

These guards were Lun-Protektorate. These were the guards that had killed his family. And now they were coming for his new one.

His wife's father — dancing with a dagger in hand. His wife's sisters — Elin leaping bodily onto a man's back, Danika reaching into her white alkhemist's coat. He hoped she had enough potions for this particular problem. If she didn't... Would Nadya ever forgive him?

Adrik blinded himself to those thoughts. They wouldn't serve him here. Nor would they serve anyone else. Instead he focused on the rage, and the bloodlust, and the guard in easiest reach of his sword.

There were only six of them, but he couldn't discount the possibility that the other six lay in wait just outside the door. He would have to finish them all. And wouldn't that be a fitting start to his reign?

Adrik parried and thrust against his opponent, clashing steel and strength against that haunting silver armor and blank face. The warrior left his right side open and Adrik struck. He slashed his blade across the Protektorate's shoulder — and didn't even leave a mark.

No puckering of flesh, no satisfying splatter of blood. His sword deflected off the armor like a pebble skimming the flat surface of a lake. For the first time, the man's face came into sharp focus. His full black Sikvan beard. His overgrown eyebrows, cheeks rusty from too much drink, a thin grin on his fat lips.

Of course Maskis' Protektorate would use alkhemy.

Adrik roared and lunged forward again, heedless of the facts before him. Hopeless or not, he would still die swinging.

Delighted, no doubt, to see this usurper humiliate himself, the guard's smile widened — then froze. A cloud of white smoke puffed up from his feet. For two breaths, maybe three, he pushed through it like a fly trudging through molasses, then succumbed to stillness. Adrik reared back and plunged his sword through the man's heart.

The fragility of human flesh and bone had never felt so satisfying. As Adrik pulled the sword back out, the guard didn't collapse to his knees as Adrik would have liked, but stayed suspended in his clouded prison. Adrik swung round to face his next attacker and found himself caught in another kind of trap — another one of Danika's making.

When Adrik had been studying at the University at Frexland, he'd attended a performance of dancers — a ballet, Yulian called it. He'd said it was nothing to the Sivkan Ballet he'd seen with his mama in the city of Old Kirov before he'd come into Avdotya's employ. Still, Adrik had found it magnificent. An artful kind of battle-making with steps both elegant and furious....

Danika put those dancers to shame. Glass phials fell from her fingertips like raindrops, spilling at the feet of the Lun-Protektorate and shattering into explosions of wildest deformity. She seemed to have more hands than The Father gave her, dipping into the inside lining of her white coat and coming out with a dozen new kinds of destruction. One female guard fell flat on her face, legs tangled into a single malleable braid. One man's head ballooned to the size of a molten red wagon wheel.

Two guards were coming at Lukin from either side as he swung wildly with his ax. Danika dropped a vial at his feet and his ax swelled — seemingly no heavier for it — and in a graceful arc, Lukin cleaved one man in two and gutted another.

So entrancing was this sight, so rich were its possibilities, that Adrik failed to consider that the other side was just as equipped. Not until something that could only have come from a bottle flipped Adrik onto his back. The wind left his lungs as the floor rose to meet him. A face hovered over him, gray and sallow and steeped in alkhemy.

Distantly, he heard Danika cry out, "Adrik!"

As the ghostly figure pulled a blade from a sheath bound to his forearm, Adrik wondered why Danika hadn't given their clothes the same protection as the Protektorate's armor, but then remembered her words as they'd set off in the black hours before a freezing dawn: "The cold is a greater threat to you than anyone at Izumgray."

If he survived this, Adrik would have to account for her naivety in future.

The blade, when it struck, was so quick and light and painless that for a moment he thought one of Danika's potions saved him after all — that she'd thrown up some invisible barrier between him and Maksis' reaper.

But then blood began to bead in a shallow arc over his heart, frothing over his wool tunic, not enough to kill on its own — just enough to scar into a pretty crescent moon. But the toothless smile in the guard's pale lips was that of a victor. This wasn't an invasion, nor a full-on assault on the halls of Izumgray. This was their true mission. One nick of one poisoned blade was all that was needed to end Adrik's insurgency before it even began. Venom and acid raced through his veins with every beat of his treacherous heart. The reaper vanished as quickly as he came and, though Danika soon replaced him, it was not her face Adrik saw as the world faded to black, but the sky-blue eyes of her sister, welcoming him home....

12. THE LONG TENNIGHT

Josef would not be moved. No matter how Avdotya raged and cajoled and promised, Josef insisted that Adrik had not earned their loyalty, and Nadya could hardly fault his reasoning. In the end, he offered Avdotya another pour of vodka, knowing his cup was still full, and Avdotya threw it on the fire. Josef's wife escorted them out after that.

The ride back to camp passed in stoney silence. Avdotya brooded, staring into the darkening, twilit forest. Yulian seemed equal parts repelled and enthralled by the man's mood. He sat with one leg pressed firmly against Avdotya's, but flinched every time Avdotya so much as twitched.

Nadya took it upon herself to dissipate the tension. "Perhaps Josef is right. We must accumulate more allies. Once we have those—"

"And who do you propose we recruit, Impress?" Avdotya's voice dripped with disdain. Yulian began strangling his own wrist in his lap. "How are we expected to garner the allegiance of dukes and duchesses when vassals won't even join our cause?" He turned back to the shadows of the forest, muttering darkly. "Though what they fear to lose is a mystery to me. What freedoms they have left are being carved away by Maksis with each passing day. And the nobility of the realm — they won't want to risk their castles, or their potions, or their slaves — excuse me, *vassals*."

"Perhaps you do not need someone who has something to lose, but rather someone who has something to gain."

"They've everything to gain!" Avdotya burst out, inciting Yulian into a full-body spasm. "I propose to raise them out of their shackles and into true citizenry! Who else could make such an improvement on their lives?"

"Yes, but they have been so long without improvement, in so dismal of circumstances, with such little hope for advancement, that what you suggest must be as unlikely to them as the tale of Babba Yagga." Avdotya stared at her, eyes narrowed, but he did not interrupt, which Nadya took to mean she should continue. "They do not know how to hope for better because they can scarcely imagine it. What we need is someone who has lived a life doing nothing but wanting more. Who, perhaps, do you think fits that description?"

There was a pause. Nadya thought she detected a note of admiration in it. When her answer finally came, it was not uttered from Avdotya's lips, as she had expected, but Yulian's.

"Grand Duke Kliment," he said. Then, with a wry grin, added, "My dear sweet uncle."

"Your uncle?" Nadya gaped.

"Indeed." Yulian's smile twisted wryly. "You don't think Avdotya would bring just anyone into Adrik's service, do you?"

Certainly not. Nadya was quickly learning that Avdotya never wasted his time on anything or anyone that did not benefit his plans in some way.

But if Yulian was related to Kliment, who was in turn related to Maksis, then that meant... "Does this make us cousins?"

Yulian barked a laugh. "I suppose it does. Something to consider if Avdotya ever tries to marry *me* to one of Rodin's daughters."

Avdotya only growled, pointer finger smoothing over his mustache as he considered the possibility of all this new idea could offer. As son of Grand Duchess Petrovia, ruler of the Taiga, Grand Duke Kliment had quite literally lingered in his mama's much grander shadow his entire adult life. Petrovia's vast forests towered over Kliment in his grassy Steppe, whispering a promise of promotion that never came. He was not a man known for his manners or kindness or loyalty — but, as Avdotya pointed out, that did not make him useless.

They arrived back at camp just as the afternoon sky muddled into a beaming indigo, stars creeping in at the edges of the night's horizon. Lukin and Elin huddled at the entrance and the sight of their hunched shoulders lodged a shard of ice into her heart. As the sledge drew nearer, torchlight cast their faces into sharper relief — serious and shadowed. Their arms were crossed and they were conferring with Taito, of all men. No one had been more surprised than Nadya when Taito had volunteered to man the cooktent in Adrik's war. But perhaps it had little to do with any lingering feeling for Nadya. Perhaps he simply refused to be left behind. Nadya understood the impulse. As ever, his eyes followed her, and the look in them was grim.

"They shouldn't be back yet," Avdotya said in a low voice.

The sledge stopped with the soft crunch of snow and Nadya bounded from it without waiting for assistance. She did not stop for Elin's shouts, nor Taito's grasping hands. She raced past the sentries and made her way to the heart of the encampment. Papa was there to greet her.

"Where are they?" she panted.

He nodded toward the tent which served as Danika's laboratory, mouth a thin line. Nadya could not bring herself to ask. All she knew was that one or both of the people she most feared to lose in the world was inside, writhing under an alkhemist's tender mercies. Was there one she hoped for more than the other? The answer squirmed uncomfortably in her belly. It did not warrant looking at now. Not when they needed her.

She took a deep breath and pulled back the tent flap. Before Nadya could even cross the threshold, Danika stood before of her, grip painful on her shoulders.

As quickly as one relief came, a more certain dread replaced it. "What has happened?"

"It was a trap. I am sorry, Nadya—"

"Is he—" Nadya wrenched from her sister's grasp to find Adrik lying unconscious and gray beneath a dim candlelight. The infinitesimal rise and fall of his bare chest was as subtle as a leaf floating on the surface of a still pond. He looked well enough, whole and not hideously maimed — save for a cut in the shape of a crescent moon over his heart. "What—"

"It was a poisoned blade." The fear in Danika's voice tightened Nadya's own throat. She turned to her sister, who was even paler than Adrik. "I do not think I can save him."

"It is *Agathodaemon*," Danika explained some time later. "The deadliest of all contact poisons. No one has ever found a cure for it."

Danika sat on a stool at Adrik's bedside, cleaning the wound with infinite care — though if it was really as bad as she claimed, Nadya could not help but wonder why she bothered.

Damp heat clogged the small tent, stoked by cauldrons and beakers simmering across three different flames. Nadya and Danika had shed their furs. Sweat beaded along their brows and upper lips. Nadya sat at the end of Adrik's bed, hands clutched around his bare feet. A thready pulse beat through his arch into her palm and she would not yield it for anything, not until the precious little warmth in his skin had gone.

"But surely — with all of your potions—" She nodded to the tables overflowing with vials and kettles, bundled herbs and shimmering liquid — secrets unfathomable for one as powerless as Nadya.

Danika's lips twisted. "Unfortunately Maksis and the Lun-Protektorate have all the potions and tools that I possess. More, really, seeing as we went to Izumgray to acquire supplies."

Papa, Avdotya, and Yulian hovered silently in the entryway, almost identical in their hunched shoulders and clenched fists. They did not seem to know what to say. Perhaps only a wife could stomach such a conversation.

"Then what is the point of it?" Nadya snapped. "If we cannot fight the Fire with Fire? Why did we go to Izumgray and not New Kirov as Avdotya suggested?" Danika's guilty silence was not reassuring. Nadya clutched Adrik's foot harder, hoping the pain would force him from his sleep. He did not flinch. "It cannot happen this way. I dreamt it. I dreamt a daughter."

Again, no one answered her. Perhaps they were all thinking of the very future that frightened her most of all — that she carried his child even now. That she no longer needed Adrik for the task. One hand drifted to her belly. But she was certain no other life beat beneath her flesh. If he died now — what had it all been for?

She looked up to find Danika watching her, studying Nadya's gesture.

"I will keep trying, Nadya," she said. "I will not fail you."

It was a promise Danika came to regret. She had never denied her sister anything, but she feared she would fail Nadya in this.

The others drifted out, first Papa, then Yulian, and, eventually, Avdotya. His reluctance to leave Adrik's side redeemed Danika's opinion of him slightly. But like all of them, he knew that no amount of agonizing at a deathbed would stay the inevitable. He had contingencies to implement, plans to make, steps to take.

Danika, meanwhile, had hearts to break — her own chief among them.

She began with nettle and thistle. The simplest antidotes in an alkhemist's arsenal. Danika knew it would not work against the *Agathodaemon*, but it was the foundation on which she could build. She hoped.

Copper came next — a basic combination of combustion and sulfur. When that failed, she tried a slower burn and an infusion of orpiment, then as the Blue Vitriol solidified and liquidized into useless ether, she turned to the power of Mercia's Quicksilver. The seventh combination showed promise — transforming into a fine white powder and healing the cut on Adrik's chest to a faint scar, but managing little else.

Nadya assisted where she could, slept when she could not. She never laid down, merely curled in a chair at the foot of Adrik's bed like a loyal pet, head bobbing on her chest, fingers curled around his ankle.

How could Danika have been so foolish as to trust Earnest? What if it all ended here, in this room, with her mistake?

Danika did not sleep. There was, at least, a potion for that. The double doses would cost her dearly when she finally gave up this hopeless venture, but she had resolved herself — she would not stop until Nadya told her to.

On the third day, Danika concocted something new — a healing tincture combined with *Fly Paper Potion* — a brew used in battle to slow the enemy's charge. One minute, a man could be rushing at you with the force of a stampeding herd, the next he would be frozen in invisible cloud.

This brew, at least, slowed the poison.

But four days after that, she was no closer to a cure. Adrik was not dead, but he was not alive either. And the *Frozen Clock* — as she had so named it — would not last forever. Nor would her supplies. Her personal stores of the rarest ingredients had been largely intact before they had left for Izumgray. It was good alkhemical practice to never let your options dwindle, but options were not enough to mount a war, and now Danika began to fear that she would not have enough to save one man, let alone slay thousands.

Eventually, not even potions could keep her upright. Draped over her workbench, head pooled in her arms, her eyes drooped. Like Adrik, she was not awake, but she was also not asleep. It was in that half-dreamful state that it came to her. The answer.

It was a dangerous combination of lead, tin, and a drop of the same poison which had done the damage. Danika first had to brew the *Agathodaemon*. That alone was no simple task. She barked orders at Nadya, who had become a surprisingly apt assistant — if too inclined toward the mystical.

"This came to you in a dream? Perhaps you were journeying. Perhaps Thoth planted it—"

"It was not a vision, Nadya," Danika snapped. If anything had brought the answer to her, it was more likely to be a combination of sleeplessness and an overdose of sustaining brews — not a message from Thoth. "Now, please, tend to the Athanor."

She muttered the steps to herself, trusting Nadya to follow along without question.

> *Bring the Athanor to a low heat. Distill the sulfide and arsenopyrite. Take all that has not been distilled and place in a clean flask. Re-destill at higher heat. The distillate should then be distilled again. This is to be performed seven times from the first distillation. Add Mercury, Salt and lime. Stir continuously at a simmer until the gray, dead metal awakes the tiny spark of its own resurrection. Distill again through an extractor. Let cool for one turn of the moon.*

She dropped the mixture past Adrik's cracked lips at dawn the next day. The black liquid was thick and unpretty, but Babbin's voice whispered in her ear — *"Dull lead and gleaming gold are but the same being at different stages of growth, Little Nika."*

Only Nadya stood watch. Danika could not bear to raise the hopes of the others. Word had reached their tent that some two hundred men had already deserted. Undoubtedly, one more failed attempt would send the rest back across the Steppe.

Nadya took up position in her usual place at the foot of the bed. Danika sat at the head. They waited in silence, hardly daring to breathe....

Adrik let in a shuddering breath.

But his exhale never came, his eyelids never flickered, and his gray pallor turned grayer.

"Nika..." Nadya's voice rang like the distant toll of a worn bell. Her sister stared into Adrik's face, knuckles white on the tips of his once golden toes, but there was no more hope in her eyes.

"Nadya... I am so sor—"

The tent flap opened and ushered in a blast of cold air. Lukin's head shoved through, his coonskin cap askew, cheeks as flushed and feverish as Adrik's had once been — back when there was still a fever to fight, a will to live.

"Danika — there is someone here for you. The girl. From Izumgray."

Danika blinked at him. She could not fathom whom he meant. Her eyes itched. Her limbs were numb. Her brain was full of white noise — nothing but the chattering sound of waves crashing over the pebbles at Von Beach.

"Now, Nika!"

She had no choice but to follow. She could think of no reason not to.

Emerging from the confines of the tent roused her. She blinked in the pale light of frozen morning. The pungent fog of the tent was replaced by the crisp smell of snow and evergreen. Stripes of softest pink brushed the white sky between the treetops. A Taigan thrush sang overhead, rustling branches and dropping great icy globs to the earth. Her mind became ever so slightly clearer. She turned to Lukin.

"What did you say?" Her voice cracked. "Who is here?"

"Just follow me." He put a steadying hand on her elbow.

Their footsteps crunched over the snow as he led her through camp. Distantly, she noted the gaps amongst the trees and the blank patches of melted snowcover where tents used to be. The men who remained seemed half-alive themselves, huddled around their silver fires, eyes vacant and resentful as she passed.

Signs of hope appeared at the entrance. Just past the sentries standing guard, three sledges bowed with the weight of their contents. Some two dozen alkhemists — identifiable by their white and purple coats — stood patiently as Adrik's corporals patted them down.

There was Flora Rusinovna from Adept Molski's class — she had always excelled at medicinal alkhemy, but was pitiful at starcharting. Wilifred Ciskarvich with his white-blonde hair, pale eyebrows and spotted complexion — he had tried to kiss Danika in an empty corridor, but she had spurned him, having just sealed her relationship with Earnest. Markus Drilewich and Irja Felkowski, Sondra Pierzovna and Aleksy Miznik. And perhaps most shockingly of all... Shura Agrifnovna.

Danika stepped numbly out of Lukin's grasp. "Shura? What— what are you doing here? What is this?"

Shura's chin jutted out the way it always did when she knew an answer Danika did not. "I know Earnest proved a disappointment to you — to us both. But your cause is true. I didn't escape vassaldom to become an alkhemical slave for Maksis."

Danika could not comprehend it. The world had reformed into a dream, hazy and implausible — nothing more surreal than the notion of Shura coming to the rescue. Perhaps it was the cold. She had not donned a coat or furs before Lukin dragged her outside.

Slowly, the smugness slid from Shura's face, shifting into the more familiar visage of flared nostrils and annoyance. She sighed, threw up her arms, and said, "We are here to help."

Elation came swift and heady. All of Danika's sins washed away in a single moment of redemption. But the triumph was followed too swiftly by bitter disappointment.

"You are too late. Adrik is— He will not—" The finality of the word 'death' could not spring from her lips. "His time is coming," she said instead.

"Oh, Danika." Shura's chin titled even higher. "Despite what you may think, you don't know everything there is to know about alkhemy. And I've brought something that may help—"Shura pulled a familiar silver blade from the inside of her white coat — crusted with Adrik's blood. "Foolish of you to leave it behind."

The faintest flicker of hope ignited in Danika's chest.

Perhaps the problem lay in her recreation of the poison.... After all, the best alkhemists were known to add innocuous ingredients to an otherwise familiar potion in order to prevent counter-brews. And an alkhemist within Maksis' Lun-Protektorate would certainly be a master of the craft. But now that she had the actual blade with the true poison—

"Danika!" Elin raced up, face as white and panicked as her voice. "Come quick — Nadya needs you."

"Nadya? Why?"

"It is Adrik. He is dead."

13. A FUNERAL FIT FOR AN IMPERATOR

Danika herself brought the burial shroud into the tent. Five hundred men watched, their faces set, their fates sealed. Perhaps they understood, as Danika did, that with or without a living leader, Maksis would show no mercy. And if they did not understand that yet, they soon would.

At midday, envoys wound through the camp, summoning the troops to the Imperator's tent. Danika, Nadya and Elin stood shoulder to shoulder outside the closed canvas. Behind that thin wall of fabric, Adrik lay beneath a clean white linen. Nadya swayed and Danika and Elin squeezed in closer on either side.

The last of the remaining forces assembled — a quarter less than what they had before Adrik took ill. There had been no snow for over a day and the air stung colder for it, the sky low and gray and fat with wanting. Papa stepped onto an overturned carton, which just a day ago had been packed full of several dozen sheets of mercury, tin, copper, silver, gold, iron, and lead; jars of ammonia, sulphate, and sodium biborate; bundles of knotgrass, willow, ivy, and hemlock — all promising a revolution that may never come.

"The Imperator is dead," Papa called out.

These simple words crashed through the crowd like the sling of a trebuchet. Those who had not yet heard, and those who had hoped it only rumor, let out cries. Others whispered their shock, heads bowed. Avdotya stood in Papa's shadow as he had stood in Adrik's, watching the reaction with a finger circling his black mustache.

"Adrik, son of Iosif, was a true child of Sivka," Papa continued in his clear, calm voice. "He served his people as best he was allowed from the moment he was born to the moment he escaped his gilded cage. For years, when any other would have fled, Adrik fought to return to his people. Fought to reclaim his throne, fought to overthrow Maksis' yoke, and for a tennight, fought the poison Maksis' assassins hid in their blades. Adrik has succumbed, but our fight is not over."

The faces of grief rose, twisted. Those who had turned to anger shifted into even more bitter hostility. Danika could read their thoughts as clearly as her own — *surely Rodin was not suggesting...*

"We must fight on in his name," Papa called to the stunned gathering. "And we must fight on — not only for Adrik, but for ourselves."

The silence gave way to a low rumbling. Papa's voice rose accordingly. "We, my friends, have spurred a rebellion. Whether it will succeed or not, we have brought a fight to Maksis' door, and he will not forget it. He will not forget and he will not forgive those who rose against him." The grumbling settled into still fear. "If we are to face his wrath, is it not better to do so for a cause than for an executioner's fee?"

Pride surged in Danika's chest at her father's words. Pride and resolve. She thought the others had begun to feel it too, but then a deep voice called from the crowd —

"What is the point with no one to lead?"

More shouts joined the first. "Maksis does not know my face."

"Better to flee than to die for nothing!"

Papa had lost them. At the edges, men and women started to scatter. Their last hope had failed —

The warmth at Danika's shoulder gave way to biting air and for a moment, she feared her sister had fainted. But Nadya had joined Papa on the crate. Her crisp voice rent the air: "Hold!"

Those nearest the makeshift dais turned back, but those at the rear continued to filter away.

"Your Impress is speaking," she shouted, and all but a few followed her voice like she was the battle master and they were mere children in her training ring.

For the first time, Nadya looked not like the wife of an Imperator, but an Impress in her own right. A wife in mourning, she wore no jewelry. But she did not need the crown to command. She stood nearly as tall as Papa. A freezing wind tried to yield her, but she was unbroken, unbent, solid. The same woman who had stood in the waters of the Swansea, at the mouth of the River Dianara, speaking her vows to Adrik into the wind and waves, now uttered a new kind of oath.

"If you will not fight for the memory of your Imperator," she said, "fight for the future of his child."

Danika thought of the stories of the fiercest warriors — of Bodan and Tatiana Solov, and Lunovna herself, calling her people to flee to the Undiscovered North with the stolen Emerald Tablet in her grasp.

Nadya's hand drifted low on her belly. "Fight for the next generation. Your children. My child." Her pale hands curved over her stomach. "The Sivka that could be and the Impress that will rule it."

In the end, only a dozen packed their bags and headed back the way they came. The others prepared for battle. After the speeches, Danika tucked herself behind the officers' tent at the eastern edge of the encampment and heaved. A pile of sick pooled at her feet and another was soon to join it. A hand fell on her shoulder mid-gag.

She spun, expecting to find Nadya or Lukin or even Papa. Instead, a stranger with reddish hair and light blue eyes greeted her. He had a vacant expression. A scar marred his hairline, cutting a cowlick at the front of his head just between the eyebrows. He could not seem to meet her eye — but perhaps that was because he realized what he interrupted.

"Excuse me — I'm looking for someone. The guard said I should come to you."

Danika swallowed bile and wiped her mouth on the back of her hand. The man could not have been much older than her, but his head shrank into his shoulders like a child caught stealing a sweet.

"Can you— Could you help me?" He stared at the vomit in the dirt. Danika looked anywhere else for fear of a resurgence.

"Who are you looking for?"

This simple question shrunk him further. "I— I'm looking for— for *him*."

Her patience was wearing thin. One of the guards had clearly gotten fed up with this person, assumed him to be one of the newcomer alkhemists, and pawned him off on Danika. "Who is *him*?" The camp was bustling with activity in the wake of Nadya's call to arms. Sergeants were barking drill orders in the yard. Cookmages scurried to and fro with slabs of boar balanced on spits. Alkhemists were losing their lunch at the perimeter....

"*Him*. Adrik."

Danika narrowed her gaze. "Who are you? Are you a messenger? What do you want with the Imperator?"

"I am Kiren."

Danika waited for more, but no more came. "Kiren...?"

He simply blinked at her.

"What is your patronymic? Your family name? Where are you from?"

"I'm from New Kirov, originally. I think." He shook his head. "I work as a tanner sometimes, when Mama hasn't taken us away."

Through the irrelevant detail Danika discerned one useful clue — a vassal. One unlikely to be delivering a message from a duke or duchess eager to join their fledgling cause and, therefore, of little use.

She considered dismissing him altogether, sending him off to the camp cook or the kettlemage. Whatever he wanted, it was not worth her notice at such a time as this. Not when she had a battle to plan and an unborn — and likely non-existent — Impress to fight for....

"Adrik is dead," she croaked. Kiren's body went rigid. His eyes danced madly. She began to suspect the boy was defective. "Come — I'll have the kettlemage fill your belly, then you can be on your way."

She placed a guiding hand on his shoulder and ushered him up the tent rows toward the center of camp. A large fire burned outside the large cook's tent, which overflowed with trestle tables and benches, flagons of vodka and wine. The sultry scent of venison wafted out of the opening as a soldier emerged with a bowl of gamey stew. "Ask for Taito Eletski. He will take care of you. Good day."

Danika managed a few steps down the snowpacked path when the childlike voice stopped her again.

"Adrik is not dead."

She looked back at him. He seemed more sure of these words than he had been of anything that came before.

"I am afraid he is." The words were like tar in her throat. "Struck down by a poisoned blade. He succumbed just last night."

Kiren said nothing, but a wrinkle appeared beneath his scar. Danika took a step toward him, drawn in despite herself. If he really was as addled as he seemed, Nadya would chastise her for abandoning him—

"Danika!" Shura stood outside the newly erected alkhemist's tent, lips pursed, foot tapping. "We need to discuss provisions. Unless you've found a better dinner companion?" Her dark eyes flickered to Kiren. "Replaced Earnest already, have you?" She smiled viciously and disappeared back inside the tent.

Danika growled. Her gratitude to Shura for her miraculous arrival had already begun to stretch thin. "Goodbye, Kiren," she said to the dazed boy, resolving to spare no more thought for wayfaring strangers.

Second in size only to the cook's tent, the alkhemist's tent looked less like a temporary holding and more like the laboratories at Izumgray. Shura's alkhemists and Adrik's scientists rubbed elbows with a tension that ranged from budding to battle-making. A dozen workbenches were piled high with retorts and crucibles, silver and violet fires burned by the dozen. They were efficient, at least — work would need to commence quickly if they were to incite a war.

"We'll need bedrolls and separate sleeping quarters," Shura said to Danika as soon as she crossed the threshold.

"All that can be arranged. How have they taken the news?"

"Better than some of your scientists. The alkhemists didn't join this cause for a man, but for a promise. If I can convince them that such a pledge will carry on without your Imperator..."

Danika turned her attention from the apparatuses to the people. One glance confirmed the truth in Shura's words. The scientists, so strong and enduring after their long sailing to the Kotov Isles, had lost much of their fight. They dogged the heels of the alkhemists like pups. Danika recognized only two of the alkhemists present — Ulovi Drikovich of Southreach and Antonia Scarborough of the Steppe. Neither she knew very well. But then, she had not spent much time at Izumgray making friends.

"And what promise is it that they cling to?"

"A future," said Shura, staring at Danika with a frankness she found difficult to mirror. "You truly don't know what connects them?"

Danika bristled under Shura's scrutiny. "I was a very focused student."

"That's one way of putting it." Shura sighed, taking Danika by the elbow and leading her into a secluded corner where several flasks digested into Vegetable Stones. "As you know, our abilities occur rarely and are only in The Mother's gift. All too often those who come to Izumgray are, like *you*," she added pointedly, "from noble and established families."

Danika's jaw tensed, outraged at the suggestion. She had hardly been treated as one from a 'noble and established family.' She had been Kotov — little more than a barbarian to the civilized Sivkan. Sensing this impending rebuttal, Shura railed over her.

"On the rare occasion that an alkhemist comes to Izumgray from the home of a merchant, they're rarely given their due. Can you imagine, then, what it was like to be an alkhemist coming from the hovel of a vassal village?"

Her jaw loosened. She looked at Ulovi and Antonia with new eyes. In an instant, their years at Izumgray came into sharper focus — the shabby patchwork of frayed tunics and thinning trousers, the flinches at the slightest reprimand, the pack mentality she had never been able to breach.

If an alkhemist thrived on her observations of nature, did Danika fail for her ignorance of man? A question for Babbin.

"Just like the rest of the world, not all alkhemists are created equal," said Shura. "Perhaps your sister's child can change that."

Danika's stomach rolled. The weight of the promises they had made to vassal and Kotov, alkhemist, and scientist alike descended on her like grave dirt. All of it pinned on the notion of a child she had seen no evidence of.

"Danika. May I speak with you?"

Nadya looked ghostly in the silver and violet glow of the alkhemists' fires. Her hands were clenched tightly in front of her, as if they did not know what to do when they were not wrapped around Adrik's arm. Danika bid farewell to Shura, but found herself no more enthusiastic for her sister's company. Not when she knew what Nadya would ask of her next.

They walked along the edge of the camp in silence. True night had fallen and there was no more sign of Kiren. Danika hoped he had got something to eat. He had looked even frailer than Nadya did now, trudging wearily through the high snow, nose red as a cranberry nipped with frost.

"Do you think we can win?" Nadya whispered into the cold.

Danika thought before she answered. "It is unlikely. But if we do... It will go down in the Velvet Book as the cleverest campaign there ever was."

"I would rather be alive than in the history books."

Danika could think of nothing worse. "It is too late for that. You secured your place in history the moment you married Adrik. What remains to be seen is who will be the victor that writes the stories."

The crunch of snow beneath their boots kept them company for several long moments before Nadya heaved a breath and said on the exhale, "If we fail or succeed — there will need to be a child."

Danika stumbled on the path and recalled a similar moment on the Kotov Isles when Adrik had been the one to catch her. "Oh." *A child.* "You do not believe there is one now?"

"No."

Danika tried to reason it through. If they failed in battle, and were taken by the enemy's troops, they would all be killed long before anyone started to question Nadya's girth. Regardless, Nadya would be the first to face Maksis' ire, especially if word reached him that she was carrying a potential heir to the throne. The possibility froze Danika's resolve to be clever and history-making.

A light snow began to fall, drifting over the camp fires, transmuting into streaking stars. A cosmic universe brought to life over every flame. Babbin's voice rang in her head once again — *"Patience, Little Nika."*

But that was the Kotov way. In Sivka, they had elixirs for such problems.

"I can brew you something," Danika offered. "It is not always effective..."

Nadya's eyes gleamed. "It will be if you make it."

That Nadya still had such faith in her abilities, even after everything...

Her earlier vision sprang forth again — their party defeated on the field of battle — Nadya first to the chopping block. "There are tests, Nadya. Tests that Maksis could perform that could reveal the truth. If we are captured and it is proved you are *not* with child—"

Nadya surprised Danika with a laugh. Though it was a laugh Danika had never heard from her before — cold and sharp. "You are usually much more pragmatic, Nika. Do I need remind *you* of the depths of Maksis' rage? His depravity? I see his mama's face every night before I close my eyes — her head sat in a bed of hay."

"That was different—"

"How?" Nadya's eyes turned sharp. They were still the sky, but night had fallen in them. "Did she not marry the man she loves — an Imperator — as I did? Did she not bear his children, as I hope desperately to do?"

"Yes, but you are Maksis' niece—"

"Indeed. I am his own family, which will make the betrayal sting all the more keenly." She drew in a breath, the tight line of her shoulders relaxing, resolving. "The Solov Slaughter was a political move by an Imperator over a decade younger and less mad. The Solovs were quiet and contented prisoners when Maksis put them to the hilt. They were killed on the mere whisper of a revolution — we have started one in full. And I will not pretend to be ignorant of my role in it."

Nor could Danika be ignorant of hers. If Nadya ended up on a pyre or chopping block, Danika would be the one who put her there — all for the selfish desperation spurred by a young man's smile.

"Nor will I lead men to battle on a lie."

"There will be no lie," Danika said. "I will make sure of it."

The battle met on the eastern bank of the Sol River on a crisp, clear night. If Danika's plan proved sound, it would not be a complete disaster. Noble sacrifice was all well and good, but history did not look as kindly on stupidity.

The walled fortress of Old Kirov glimmered tantalizingly on the horizon, marked only by the silver lights of the city surrounding it. The capitol city was strategically secured on four fronts — the mountains to the north, the Sol River to the east, the Lun River to the west, and in the narrow 'V' where the two rivers met on the banks of the Swansea — Grand Duchess Petrovia's Estate.

As men were more easily defied than nature, it was here that they decided to strike.

Petrovia was Maksis' eldest sibling, a woman in her mid-70s, whose power was rivaled only by her brother's. She had held the Taiga for longer than Maksis had held the throne and ruled it with an iron will. With its abundance of lumber, fertile ground, and hundreds of thousands of vassals, the Taiga was the most coveted Principality a Grand Duke or Duchess could hope to possess. As such, Petrovia was not only a powerful ally to Maksis, but — if she were not so loyal — a potential threat.

It was why she not only had to be eliminated, but replaced.

The idea had been Avdotya's. It was a good one, Danika had to admit, inspired by some mysterious visit he had taken with Nadya the day she and Adrik left on the disastrous mission to Izumgray.

"Petrovia has but one living child," Avdotya had said in a low voice outside the Imperator's tent five nights ago. It was a small council this time — made up only of herself, Avdotya and Papa. It was the one time they had all come to quick agreement, which was fortunate given that Adrik was not there to mediate them.

"His name is Grand Duke Kliment. He rules the Steppe now, but he's always viewed the Taiga as his birthright. Unfortunately for him, his mama isn't interested in death or retirement. He himself is past middle-age, and I'm told he grows...impatient. Fortunately for us, I've someone in my charge who could make a friendly entreaty to Kliment when the time comes."

"And who is this person?" Danika queried.

"Yulian. He's Kliment's nephew. The son of Kliment's dearly departed sister."

Danika looked to Papa to see if he was equally stunned by this family connection, but his beard merely twitched. "You do seem to have many friends in high places, Avdotya."

"I'm fortunate in that way, yes," Avdotya said with a wicked grin. "If we can prove to Kliment that his mama is fallible and offer him her seat, we will have a loyal ally indeed."

"A greedy ally does not make a loyal one," said Papa.

"It does if you pay him enough."

Not a cloud lingered in the sky as they came to the battlefield in the dark of night. They charged down the hillside into the river valley, bayonets pointed and cloaks weighed down with vial after vial of the best concoctions Danika, Shura, and their band of alkhemists could muster in a tennight.

Papa led the frontline with the strongest of the Kotov Host. Danika, Elin and Lukin rallied the second wave. No amount of pleading from Nadya could stop Danika from joining the fight. She was a Kotov and an alkhemist, and this was the destiny Adrik had promised. Thoth only knew how long she would be able to pursue it. A small part of her could not help but think it would be nobler to die like this, with the acrid stench of gunfire and poultice pluming around her, than to wither away, bound to a sickbed or a wheelchair as the promise of the cycles — and her mother's own selfish stubbornness — came to pass.

She would still take Adrik's hope over the Suncycle's certainty any day.

Avdotya had finally got his wish, paying handsomely for five-hundred mounts from the nomads that roamed the Steppe. Now, he sat on horseback at the rear of the battlefield, directing the men from the hilltop. Rules of combat dictated that anyone clothed in scarlet was to be spared the blade or bow, but it was something of a moot point as no arrow could possibly stretch across the valley to reach him.

But a bullet could.

The first shot cracked the air with such finality that Danika imagined it piercing Maksis' heart. After all, hadn't it been the mere whisper of such weapons that Maksis used to justify his slaughter of the Solov family? Danika hoped the irony was not lost on him.

When the bullet met its target not just with a piercing wound, but with the blue flame of an alkhemist's explosion, Danika savored the sight of fiery revenge.

Panicked shouts tittered across the field like cicadas in twilight. It took Petrovia's troops some time to recover their wits from the first volley. But they had plenty of alkhemical weapons of their own — albeit not shot from the end of a muzzle.

Their own line warbled at the return fire, soon colliding into close combat. The snow at their feet turned from clean white to the black and red of smoke and blood. The gun-bearers lingered in the first and third waves, told to save their alkhemically-infused ammunition for Avdotya's signal. This was Danika's least favorite part of the plan.

She herself did not wield a gun — a potion drunk just after dusk had gifted her with an aim long and perfect, allowing her to toss her vials with the precision of any arrow. And toss she did.

Third pocket, top row — *Bertram's Boils* — dropped at the feet of a Junior Lieutenant, who broke out into pulsing purple hives and abandoned his sword in the agony.

Sixth row, fourth pocket — *Waking Nightmares* — launched down the helm of a cavalryman, who bellowed in fear of a foe only he could see. He fell off his horse and writhed on the ground, batting at an invisible swarm.

Second pocket, bottom row — *Crystal Eyes* — Danika threw the pink vial at the feet of a junior sergeant bedecked in Taigan green. It hit his boot and bounced off without shattering. She caught it on the rebound, popped the cork, reached for a vial of powdered hemlock in her left coat lining, added a pinch, recorked and threw again.

This time, the vial pierced the barrier, shattering in a brilliant display of pink sparks, which drifted up into the sergeant's eyes. He blinked, and in that instant, his eyes crystalized from muddy green to red rubies.

As he clawed at the place where his eyes should have been, a Kotov warrior buried a saber into his chest. After he fell, the Kotov stooped to collect the gemstones.

A canon boomed in the distance and Danika broke her concentration to watch the effect. The cannonball crashed into a clump of Taigan soldiers, felling a handful. That could have been the end of it, but then there was a great cracking sound. A shudder reverberated all the way into her calves and a hundred men vanished into earth as a sinkhole swallowed them whole.

"Nika!"

Elin's voice. Danika spun to find Lukin and Elin up to their knees in black sludge. Four men bore down on them. Should she get Lukin and Elin out or stop their attackers? The indecision paralyzed her for a moment, until Lukin yelled, "Danika! Stop thinking so much!"

She reached into the fifth row, seventh pocket and threw a pale blue concoction into the sludge. As it shattered, the sludge roiled like a great wave, then slurped into the ground and solidified into a lake of pure ice. The four attackers slipped and crashed, but so did Lukin and Elin. Elin slid into the feet of a captain of the regulars, who reached into his vest pocket.

Danika realized too late — he was an alkhemist.

The man withdrew a virulent green flask shaped like a flat disk. Her heart seized — it looked caustic enough to penetrate Elin's armor. Danika pulled her last *Fly Paper Potion* from her coat, uncorked it and lobbed it into the air between Elin and the disk falling toward her chest. A stream of white cloud emanated in its wake and Danika held her breath to see whether the disk or the river of white would reach Elin first — whether a potion designed to stop a man in his tracks would freeze such a small object in its free-fall....

The stream caught the disk, held it in mid-air. Elin let out a cry of triumph and leapt to her feet.

The fool.

Danika saw the widening of Elin's eyes, the realization that came a moment too late. Elin was now the fly caught in the paper. The captain grinned, bright white teeth pointed savagely. Danika pictured him plunging his fangs into the tender flesh at Elin's neck. There were maybe a handful of vials left at Danika's disposal. She grabbed the topmost one and aimed into the air. She tossed a marble a second after it and gloried in the collision.

With a crack of poison thunder, a green cloud appeared above the captain's head. A second later, acid rain fell in a torrent, drowning the man in a downpour of peeling flesh and burning armor. He screamed as his body became an acid prison with no escape.

But Elin had no escape either.

The *Fly Paper Potion* may have been thick enough to hold the captain's vial, but apparently it was still porous enough to let the drizzle of venom strike Elin's face in slow motion.

"Elin!" Lukin called as he realized Danika's mistake. He had managed to keep his feet thanks to the *Light as a Feather* tincture she had dosed him with that morning. He flayed one of the other three attackers with the sharp strike of his ax, but still had two more to contend with. He could not save Elin, but Danika still could.

She raced the twenty feet that separated her from her sister, sorting through her mental inventory. Moonwort would not do. She was out of Black Ivy. Cinnabar perhaps... Or Lead Monoxide. She would need to undo the *Acid Storm* first, free Elin from the *Fly Paper*, then get her to a medicinal alkhemist before the poison ate into bone.

It was a difficult formula to judge with Elin's screams rattling in her ears.

She flung *Clear Skies* into the storm and let the acid dissolve its glass chamber. The storm disappeared in a pop of indigo, then she retrieved a quickening dram, added a dash of ground aluminum and hurled it at Elin's feet.

A moment later, Elin collapsed as the *Fly Paper* dissolved. She was too pained to scream. Her face dripped like the melted wax of a candle.

I can fix it later, Danika told herself and rustled in her pocket for the very concoction that had slowed Adrik's poison for a time. It would be enough for Elin too, she was sure. At least until they got her off the field. She splashed the *Frozen Clock* over Elin's prone form and tried not to think of it as a corpse.

Across the field, the battle was beginning to turn. The lack of colorful explosions meant the gunmen had reached the end of their supply. Petrovia's army took notice and surged forward. Lukin felled his second attacker, slicing the back of his knee like a tree trunk. Danika finished the last attacker with a perfect toss of her spear. Lukin raced back to her and Elin.

"We must get her to a medicinal alkhemist," Danika said, hooking one arm under Elin's right armpit while Lukin took the left.

They made it only a few yards before they were forced to drop Elin and resume battle, her unconscious form prone between them.

After Lukin dispatched another Taigan with a crack over the head and Danika turned two enemies on each other with a gaseous tincture tucked up her sleeve, their eyes met over Elin's body. Together, they looked back at the hillside where Avdotya and the medical tent awaited in relative safety. It seemed an impossible distance away, through a writhing mass of soldiers clad in steel, hide, and leather armor — hiding Thoth only knew what kind of alkhemical weapons beneath them. Lukin said, unnecessarily, "Do it now."

Danika nodded, reached into the right breast pocket of her vest and pulled out a magenta vial — the only color she had not yet seen on the field of battle. She broke it at her own feet. A streak of pink and gold shot a hundred feet into the air — a signal not even Avdotya could miss.

She shielded her eyes to try and make out his figure on the hillside. The sun had begun to rise behind him, casting a clear light over the snow and blood and horse tracks. Avdotya shifted on his steed, then disappeared behind the ridge. The crunch of enemy footfalls sounded behind her and Danika distantly registered Lukin's shout of warning, but she could not turn away. She trusted Lukin to watch her back while she watched the horizon and waited.

It was an eternity before the horn blasted across the valley and a new figure emerged on the ridgeline, the sun at his tail in a five-fingered burst of yellow rays.

He was still weak. She could see it by his grip on the reigns, the stiff line of his shoulders. His silhouette swayed in the golden glow. The horn sounded again, and across the field of battle, Kotov, Polvian, Sivkan and Taigan stayed their weapons where they could, turning as one toward the shining beacon on the hill.

Cast in Solov's own light, returned from The Slaughter, reborn from the grave, not once, but twice — word of it would spread across all Sivka, turning Adrik Iosifvich Solov from myth into a living god.

"Adrik Iosifvich!"

"Imperator!"

"Solov!"

Cries rent the air, louder even than the horn, as Adrik steered his horse down the hill. More and more called out as he moved into the battlefield, born by the flaxen light of The Father's rising sun. The silver and green forms of Maksis' greatest defenders retreated from his rays like stars fleeing the dawn.

"He is reborn!"

"Resurrection!"

"Imperator Adrik!"

Another horn sounded, this time from the west, and what remained of Petrovia's army raced back across the river.

14. KLIMENT VICTORIOUS

They camped the army on the beach outside Petrovia's estate, where the Sol and the Lun let out into the Swansea. From here, they could control both channels, take reinforcements from Polvia, and staunch any supplies coming into the city.

All in all, Adrik thought it worth playing dead.

"They *could* resupply from the north," Avdotya pointed out, standing beneath the vaulted ceiling in Petrovia's great hall.

The lapping of the waves on the shore outside drifted in through the shattered windows. As Petrovia's army had fled to Old Kirov, they'd smashed every bit of glass on the estate and surrounding grounds in one final, petty act of rebellion.

"It is unlikely," said Rodin. "It would take half a season for any of Maksis' allies to scale those mountains. Still, we should send scouts to the northern border of Old Kirov — see if we can prevent Maksis from seeking aid a little longer."

"How long do we expect their supplies to last?" Danika asked, pacing in front of the enormous stone hearth. A silver fire of her own making blazed behind her, but Adrik couldn't feel much of its warmth. He hadn't been able to shake the chill in his bones since he woke in a frigid tent a tennight ago with Danika's ruddy face grinning maniacally above him.

Everyone else had bathed and changed after the fight, but Danika still had the stench and smear of battle on her. Adrik recognized the bloodthirstiness, wished he could share in it, but riding a horse up and down a hill had been exhausting for all that it wasn't the thrilling heroics he'd hoped for in his first official battle with Maksis.

Danika's plan to fake his death had seemed mad at first — why risk alienating what allies they had by falsely spreading word of his demise? But Danika had proved persuasive.

"Three hundred men have already deserted," she'd said to him, never one to pull her punches, even scant hours after he'd regained consciousness. The despair must have shown on his face. "Do not look so grim. It was an easy way to weed out those who are loyal and those who are not."

"So loyal they'll stay to fight for a dead man?" Adrik had rasped from his bed as Nadya wept tears of relief into his chest.

Apparently, he'd been standing at the threshold of death's door. His heart had even stopped at the very moment a fresh supply of alkhemists — and the same poisoned blade that cut him — arrived to offer salvation. Only quick work by Danika and their new alkhemists had pulled him from the brink of death.

"Maksis will come for us whether or not we surrender now," Danika had said, relentless in her new scheme. "Papa will speak to the troops, rally them to the cause. Your army is mainly made up of Kotov. They were more interested in fighting *against* Maksis than fighting *for* you. And besides — your Impress still lives. I daresay they are as loyal to her as they ever were to Imperator Adrik Iosifvich Solov."

Nadya's hands clenched compulsively over his tunic. She raised her head and wiped the tears from her eyes. Her expression had gone vacant. Adrik tried to focus more on Danika's plan and less on Nadya's sorrow and said, "How would you do it? You'd tell the troops I'm dead and then in the middle of battle—"

"You will rise from death to join your men. Word of it will spread."

"As will word of our cause..." Adrik was slowly catching on. "And if I can return from the dead once—"

"It will make your surviving The Solov Slaughter all the more plausible."

He took a shuddering breath and tried to think like Avdotya. "Isn't it risky to build a reputation on an illusion?"

Danika grinned. "That is why you have me. No one is better at illusion than an alkhemist. Now, if you will excuse me, I have a shroud to prepare."

It had been mad, yes. But perhaps that was precisely why it worked.

Now, with Petrovia's stronghold secured, their next fight would come at Old Kirov — the capitol city where the Lunovnas had reigned ever since the birth of Sivka itself.

Famed as a hotbed of culture, art, and alkhemy, the city was the prime jewel in Maksis' crown. Old Kirov existed as Maksis' private municipality within the Taiga, just as New Kirov in Southreach had belonged to the Solovs back when they still reigned.

During Adrik's time there, New Kirov had merely been a gilded cage, a once modern and beautiful city gradually decaying from Maksis' neglect. Adrik hated to think of what the palace he'd lived in for the first six years of his life might look like now that it had been completely abandoned. A tomb instead of a prison.

Sensing his weariness, Nadya tucked in closer to his side. She ran a hand up his arm and offered him a reassuring smile. It warmed his heart, if little else.

"With Sivka's best alkhemists at their disposal... It could be half a year before Old Kirov runs out of food," said Avdotya.

"Not the *best* alchemists," said Adrik, tossing Danika a halfhearted wink. She flushed, looking much more like the doting girl he knew and less the seasoned warrior.

"We can scheme more tomorrow," Nadya said in a voice that reminded him eerily of her mama. "Our Imperator needs rest."

"Nadya—" Adrik growled, though he couldn't help but preen a little at her concern. Avdotya had been a lot of things as a caretaker, but maternal? Never. Like a starving man who suddenly found himself in a fully stocked kitchen, Adrik was a glutton for Nadya's tender mercies.

"Yulian, can you carry Adrik to bed? A room has been set aside for him upstairs."

In an instant, his delight with his wife evaporated. There was a limit to how much mothering a man could accept and still call himself Imperator. Even now, his troops wandered the halls, clearing rooms and checking for any traps Petrovia's men may have left behind. If even one of them were to see the Imperator being carried —

"Absolutely not! After all the work we've gone through to stage my resurrection, I won't have the men thinking I'm at death's door again."

"But—"

"No, Nadya. I won't be coddled. I'm not a child. I am an Imperator. And these discussions can't wait."

Her hand vanished from his shoulder, leaving a cold phantom in its absence. "Very well. I am going to bed. I will see you there — if you can make it up the stairs."

He watched her ascend the spiral staircase to the landing above the hall. When he did join her, there would be little warmth for him beneath those covers.

"We will have to destroy what stores Old Kirov possesses," Danika carried on as if there had been no interruption. "A small party could do it. Shura and I—"

Avdotya shook his head. "Sending a party into the city risks delivering a band of hostages to Maksis' door."

Danika's hands curled into fists. Adrik hid a grin. A sudden image sprang to mind of her as a child in the Kotov fighting ring, squaring up against boys twice her size. "I will go willingly," she said. "So will the others."

"A noble sacrifice, I'm sure," sneered Avdotya. "But your eagerness to die is unlikely to make your family care any less for your safe return."

"What do you suggest then?"

"We allow our plan to bear fruit. We allow word of Adrik's victory today — and his miraculous resurrection — to spread. Then we wait for Kliment to come calling."

Danika scoffed. "We *wait*?"

Rodin stepped between the pair, silencing Danika better than any rebuttal from Avdotya might have. "What is it your mad old alkhemist is always saying? About a watched cauldron?"

A smile tugged at the corner of Danika's mouth. "A watched brew never bubbles."

"Precisely. Avdotya's proposal is sound. We wait, and when more allies come—"

"Then we take Old Kirov," said Adrik, a surge of his own bloodlust finally warming his bones.

Kliment's letter arrived just as the blizzards of Whitewinter finally started to give way to the squalls of Windwinter.

"Read it aloud," Avdotya said to Yulian after he burst into the great hall, disturbing a scrumptious supper of roasted elk and glazed sugar beets. A thunderless storm pelted at the newly installed windows. It pleased Avdotya to know that they were dining in such warmth and splendor while Maksis and Petrovia's stomachs growled on barest rations in the Palace at Old Kirov.

Yulian scanned the letter and said, "He asks for an audience with 'The Imperator Reborn.'"

At the head of the table, Adrik barked a laugh. The little alkhemist and her sister looked equally smug. Rodin bore his usual expression of mild disapproval and the other sister — the one who'd been maimed in the Battle at the Sol, the skin of her face strangely rippled after the alkhemists had seen to her — was too focused on her candied beets to be bothered with anything so consequential as the future of the empire.

Avdotya gripped his fork and glared at Yulian. "Thank you for the summary but I prefer not to lose anything in the nuance. Read it aloud."

Yulian's summary had indeed hit the mark — Kliment was never one for subtlety. Avdotya's next task would be persuading Adrik not to answer personally.

"An Imperator Reborn does not have time to meet with a grand duke of a minor principality," Avdotya said. "It will undermine your authority if you meet with him in person. Allow me to go in your stead."

Adrik opened his mouth to argue, but then Nadya laid a hand on his arm and gave him a look full of meaning.

Avdotya had spies everywhere, including in the Impress's bed chamber, and they had reliably informed him that Nadya was more eager than ever to get with child. It wasn't a plan Avdotya had any interest in interfering with. Heirs would only be a boon to Adrik's claim on the throne, and the act of making them would keep the boy distracted from his alkhemist. Avdotya had half expected Nadya to abandon the effort once the farce of Adrik's demise had passed. He was relieved she seemed determined to stick to her promise.

As Avdotya boarded the sledge bound for the Steppe the next morning, he saw the Impress lean into her sister and whisper, "Fear not, Nika. I have had a vision — Kliment is no ally of ours."

How satisfactory, he thought. *Now I can prove them both wrong.*

Three days ride to the east, Kliment greeted Avdotya and Yulian from the gravel courtyard of his feeble sandstone palace. His estate blighted an otherwise dull landscape. It sat nestled on a patch of lush green lawn, vibrant even against the gray sky. Avdotya did the sums in his head on what it would cost to keep such a yard thriving in a desert during the winter seasons — it was no wonder his vassals spoke ill of him.

"Avdotya Rostislav — it's been too long." Kliment threw his arms wide and pulled Avdotya into a double-sided embrace. He endured it with gritted teeth disguised as a grin.

"You're looking fat and healthy," Avdotya replied.

Kliment guffawed. "And you're looking thin and old. War does not suit you."

"No, it doesn't. Which is why I'd rather it be ended sooner than later."

Kliment laughed again, though there was something forced in it. "We'll see what I can do to help on that front. Now, let me greet my nephew."

Yulian looked convincingly pleased to reunite with his slippery uncle — Avdotya had taught him well on that front — pressing a kiss to both of Kliment's cheeks and letting himself be perused at his uncle's leisure.

"You've grown up well, my boy," Kliment said finally. "I see Avdotya's taken good care of you in my stead."

There was little family resemblance between the pair — luckily for Avdotya. Yulian was the son of Petrovia's only daughter and took after her red hair and fair coloring. Kliment had the ill-mannered look of Petrovia's first husband — baggy eyes, receding hairline and jowls poorly hidden by a graying beard.

"Indeed he has, Uncle. I've learned much in the seven years since I left you." Yulian's voice dipped suggestively. Avdotya glared at him — an unspoken promise that Yulian would pay for his impudence later. Undoubtedly, that had been the point.

"Shall we go inside?" Avdotya was growing tired of pleasantries. It was time to seal Kliment's favor. "Those clouds bode more rain."

"Please! My hearths are lit and the vodka is poured. Let us talk of the resurrection of the Solov Empire!"

This time, the look Avdotya and Yulian shared was entirely without pretense. It was obvious to them and the legion of vassals lingering in the courtyard — Kliment was ready to pick a side.

"You were brilliant," Yulian mouthed the words into Avdotya's lips. "You had him wrapped around your little—"

"He's not the only one I have wrapped around my—" Yulian gave Avdotya's crotch an admonishing squeeze. Avdotya nipped Yulian's lips with a growl. "And it's not little."

"Are you sure? It's been some time since I checked." Yulian fell gracefully to his knees. He shoved Avdotya's hips back against the door. He let his head fall back, conscious of the noise they were making. But Kliment cared little for his nephew's welfare and even less what Avdotya did with it. "You're right," Yulian said, after he made quick work of the laces. "It isn't little at all. It's perfectly adequate."

Avdotya yanked at Yulian's curls. "That mouth of yours could find more useful employment."

After, they sprawled naked in the vast bed of Kliment's finest guest room. Avdotya had one leg thrown over Yulian, staring up at the orange silk canopy. Yulian thumbed the bare skin at Avdotya's hip. He'd always been fascinated by the contrast of light and dark, freckled and scarred pressed together.

"It's been awhile since we did this in a real bed," Yulian murmured with his usual post-coital softness. On the heels of such an overwhelming political victory, Avdotya was disinclined to curb it.

"I'm sure we've given the servants a ration of gossip to report back."

"Kliment will overlook anything now that you've promised him the Taiga."

"True."

Yulian's hand crawled up from Avdotya's hip to his waist. "A part of me hates to see him so happy."

"Hm." Avdotya turned to look at the boy — man — in his bed. Yulian had been a man grown for many years, but Avdotya remembered the sullen and shy thirteen-year-old he'd taken on as a ward. A child still reeling from the shock of his mama's untimely passing, unwanted by the uncle who probably killed her. "Do you ever imagine what would've happened if I hadn't taken you in?"

Yulian grinned. "You mean, would you and I have met?"

Avdotya scoffed. "No. I mean that *you* could have been the next in line for the Taiga. Petrovia never liked Kliment."

Which was precisely why Yulian's mother had taken so suddenly and inexplicably ill.

Yulian sprang up, preening. "Think of it — me, a Grand Duke of the Taiga, answering to no one but the Imperator. Giving *you* orders."

Avdotya licked his lips. "You've never been one for giving orders. Taking them, on the other hand..."

Yulian sighed, slumping back against the headboard. "You're right. I never would have made it that far, anyway. Kliment would've seen to me long before I became a threat. Giving me to you was the kindest thing he could have done."

Avdotya's breath caught. *Kind?* That was one word he'd never heard ascribed to himself. And that Yulian, of all people, thought to use it now... Something dangerously close to fondness swelled in his chest. He brushed a thumb over one of Yulian's ginger eyebrows. "You are a strange man."

Yulian caught his hand. "From you, Dunya, that is practically a declaration."

"Be quiet and kiss me."

It was difficult to celebrate Avdotya's victory, though apparently Danika was the only one who thought so.

Petrovia's great hall was packed to bursting with Kotov soldiers and Polvian scientists. It amused her to see them mingling together, deep in their cups, the brains and the brawn feasting and toasting and laughing together. The only group not in attendance were the alkhemists, who had just yesterday been sent to Kliment's estate to help ready his troops for war.

"You are only sour because his strategy worked," Lukin teased over the rim of his goblet. He was on his second cup — a rare indulgence.

Lukin did not drink much as a rule. He had admitted to her once during a dark night roaming the hills after training, that before his mother had left to take up with a man on the Vienper, her "dissatisfaction" had started with drink.

To hear Lukin tell it, the vodka had made his papa unsatisfying in his mama's eyes. Danika could not help but wonder if the dissatisfaction had led to the drink, rather than the other way around, but she never dared voice that suspicion to Lukin. He was just a boy who could see no wrong in his papa and hated anyone else who did.

Danika understood that impulse well. She understood resenting your mama as well.

"I am not sour," Danika said, and drank deep — *she* had no compunctions about alcohol. He raised his eyebrows, clearly unconvinced. "I am not! I am merely aware that my strategy would have worked better. With this plan, it will be Spring before we are prepared for battle."

"Raiding Old Kirov would have gotten you killed. And starving them out would have taken even longer."

"I do not want to talk about this any more."

"Very well."

There was amusement in his voice, and when she lifted her gaze from the depths of her cup, she found him grinning in that special way of his — that half-scowl, half-smile. It made her feel young and hopeful. It made her want to laugh. She might have been about to, when—

"Nika!" A warm hand fell onto her shoulder and she turned to stare into Adrik's fully smiling face. "Come and lead a toast to Avdotya. After all, when one of us succeeds, we all do."

Only Adrik's mischievous wink could have compelled her to honor such a request. She left Lukin to his goblet and made her way to the head of Petrovia's table, where Avdotya sat smugly to the right of Adrik's empty chair. Nadya sat on the left, a hand laid convincingly over her stomach — that was a problem for another day.

Adrik took up position behind his pseudo-throne. Ever since regaining his ability to stay upright for longer than an hour, he had taken full advantage, sitting only when he had no other choice.

Even now, his weakness lingered. He leaned surreptitiously against the back of the chair — a gesture so small, Danika suspected she was the only one who noticed, prone as she was to also prefer standing while she still could. He cleared his throat and raised his cup high.

"Attention! My most trusted advisor Danika Bodanson wishes to speak."

A little thrill shot up her spine, even as her mouth went dry. Public speaking was not among her skills.... The Kotov never demanded such blatant displays of boasting and she had dreaded the occasions when they came at Izumgray.

"She has a toast for Avdotya Rostislav — my other most trusted advisor."

As quickly as it had come, the thrill vanished.

Adrik grinned wickedly. Beside him, Avdotya flourished his hand in a 'by all means' gesture, and Danika bit the inside of her cheek.

She took a deep breath and began, "To Avdotya Rostislav—"

A scream pierced the air.

Every head in the hall turned. The enormous doors that had been left open to the courtyard as revelers drifted in and out from the encampment went still and vacant. The night sky glittered brightly outside — a serene spectacle as more cries and wails shattered the festive atmosphere. The musicians ceased playing just as a Kotov wardmaster clamored into the hall. "Imperator," he said. "Come quick."

The party flooded outside, pushing its way through the crowd gathered on the river bank. Floating on a barge down the Sol was the strangest sight Danika had ever seen. As it drew closer, it quickly became the most sickening.

At first glance, it appeared to be a staging of stuffed strawmen. Seven figures posed in various states of agony.

A man and a woman knelt at the front — the man with his arms stretched out in supplication; the woman clinging to a red gash at her throat, blood dripping between her fingers. Two young men slumped against the mast, their chests gaping and scarlet. A young lady leaned forward on a spear shot through her stomach and a toddler, a little girl, spread splayed and flattened on the barge floor.

The last figure — a boy with reddish-gold curls — was bowed over his knees, face hidden, clinging to a bloody head wound with a four-fingered hand.

It was the Solov Slaughter.

Imperator Iosif and Impress Mariya. Imperix Kolya and younger brother Kiril, the eldest daughter Tasya, baby Amaliya, and Adrik.

But as the eerie pantomime drifted slowly closer, one thing became abundantly clear — the figures were not made of straw. Stuffed canvas satchels formed the heads, but the torsos and limbs — the arms and legs, even the scalps, were frighteningly familiar.

A fresh scream. Shura shoved past Danika and raced into the water toward that which she, also, recognized. Shura — one of only a handful of alkhemists who had stayed behind while the others went on to Kliment. She stumbled onto the barge, clawing at the pieces...

A finger bearing a familiar ring. An ear with a birthmark. A pale head of hair. A leg with patches in the trousers.

They were familiar to Danika too.

Flora Rusinovna's ring — a gift from the Impress on her thirteenth birthday. Wilifred Ciskarvich's birthmark — she spotted it when he had been pecking at her neck in that corridor. Ulovi Drikovich's distinctive white-blonde hair — Flora had mocked him once for appearing nearly bald. Antonia Scarborough's frayed skirt — carefully maintained with embroidered flowers on the patches, doused to dance in an imaginary wind. She said it reminded her of home.

Apparently Danika had known them better than she realized.

She could not bring herself to join Shura, to rip apart the display as no doubt Maksis' soldiers had ripped apart their alkhemists — piece by bloody piece. She swallowed compulsively as the message from Maksis deteriorated, until it was nothing but bags of straw, a few unclaimed limbs, and the child-Adrik clutching his head.

Soon the few remaining alkhemists converged on Danika, shoving feet and hands into her own arms, begging and enraged.

"Chopped to pieces like slabs of meat!"

"How could this have happened?"

"Perhaps some are still alive! The right tincture or potion—"

Danika shook her head. She uttered the words through gummy lips. "It is too late. Maksis would not have let them live. I am sorry."

The pain was too sharp. To dwell in it would be to dwell in madness. She needed to think like Avdotya. In profits and losses. In next steps. But that offered little comfort. Their alkhemists were gone. What could she, Shura, and the five others that were left hope to accomplish on their own? The answer was too certain and final to utter aloud.

Maksis had slayed Adrik's advantage as fully as he had flayed her peers.

Danika extracted herself from the cloying hands, seeking the one person who could rally her — rally them all — from this nightmare. But their Imperator was nowhere to be found. Adrik had fled.

She looked back to the Adrik on the barge, to the boy who had made the man, as if he could provide the answers she sought, and something sharp caught in her throat.

The missing finger was on the wrong hand. The straw-Adrik's severed limb was on the left. Adrik's missing finger was on the right.

15. THE TRUTH IN THE LIE

Adrik was not seen or heard from for three days. Any man or woman who dared try to enter the Imperator's quarters was sent fleeing, usually with a heavy goblet hurled behind them. Avdotya made the first attempt. He left white with fury, mustache askew. Yulian went next — he still had the lump on his head from where Adrik's aim struck true. Papa followed Yulian, and Danika was certain he would be the one to succeed. No one with any sense could turn away the calm and stoic demeanor of Rodin Bodanson.

But Adrik had taken leave of his senses.

Papa emerged from the room, at least without any crockery to follow, but shaking his head all the same. "He will not see reason. He is blinded by rage and grief. And drink."

"Perhaps Nadya?" Danika suggested. Her sister, for reasons only Nadya could understand, had refused to even attempt to console her husband. She just shook her head and said that when he was ready, Adrik would come to her.

Sometimes, Nadya could be as stubborn as their mama.

The room stank of unwashed man, wine, vodka, and food gone slightly to spoil. There was no light but for a flickering candle perched beside a small diary, which Adrik hunched over, scribbling frantically, a white-knuckled grip on his quill. Danika entered slowly and silently, and when she peered over his shoulder, she could make no sense of the scribblings. The ink looked more like the scratching of animal tracks than discernible language.

A flush of anger crept up her neck. What right did he have to stew in his own pity? He had not recognized Antonia's patched skirt, had not endured Flora's boasting, had not kissed Wilifred's thin lips. The alkhemists were nothing but tools to him. Barely people at all. A means to an end. The familiarity of such a role curdled in her gut like sour milk and when she spoke, her words tasted just as foul.

"So this is how the Imperator Reborn is felled? One twisted trick of Maksis' and all our hopes turn to ash?" Danika rounded the desk to stare down into Adrik's face. When he raised his eyes, they were nearly unrecognizable, gleaming red and vacant in the firelight. It stole her resolve for a moment. But only a moment. She would not let the alkhemists die in vain. She would not let his bruised ego tarnish all they had worked for. Everything they still had to accomplish.

"If the men and women do not see you soon, they will start to think your resurrection was a dream."

"Perhaps it should've been," he grumbled, hunching further over his journal.

Danika smacked the quill from his hand. He surged to his feet with a roar, crowding her against the stone wall. The rough brick bit at her shoulder blades and his hot breath grazed her cheekbones. She had never realized how broad he was. She schooled her face not to show her fear. "I took you for many things, Adrik Iosifvich. But not a coward."

"This isn't fear. This is anger."

"And there is no elixir without heat."

He growled, fists clenching. His gaze flickered down from her lips to her throat — as if he sought a worthier outlet for his rage. She stared steadily back at him.

"To me, anger is confronting your foe. To me, anger is facing down Maksis — not allowing him to get away with more murder. What you are doing, hiding away in here with your drink and your diary, turning away all those who care about you? To me, that looks very much like running."

"How would you know? You won't be running anywhere soon enough."

She flinched. The words were designed to hurt her. She knew that. She tried to cling to her rage, but furious or not, tears still threatened. It burned just behind her eyeballs, but she would not dare let him see her cry. She ducked under his arm to flee the room.

"Nika, wait—" He raced ahead to block her path. Gone was the red-eyed monster, returned was her Adrik, albeit more drawn and exhausted than he had looked even on death's door. "I'm sorry, Nika. I didn't mean it."

"Perhaps not. But you are not wrong. I have 186 days, Adrik. One hundred and eighty-six days to try and preserve what dignity I have left." The tears had shifted, burning at the back of her gums, coiling like an alkhemical flame low in her belly. "Do you know how I know that number so precisely? I have been starcharting, can you believe it? I finally did as Babbin bid me. And now I cannot seem to stop." Her own fists curled against a desperate compulsion to reach out, to cling. "I cannot stop counting the tennights, days, seconds, until life as I know it is over. And if I cannot stop my fate within those 186 days? Then I intend to die in the attempt."

Adrik's face contorted, angry once again. "Don't say such things—"

"Surely you realize what you have asked us to do? What danger you have placed me and my family in?" Danika swallowed, looking down at his bare feet, pale and strangely delicate on the stone floor. "You must see what danger *I* have placed them in by bringing you into our lives?"

"Nika—"

"Most of the alkhemists I have recruited are already dead. But that is my burden to bear. None of us are doing it only for you. We all have our own reasons. Me, Papa, Yulian, Avdotya. Even Nadya..."

Adrik froze, chin tucked slightly. She recognized the expression from their many hours over the athanor in her lab on the Von — it meant he was really listening.

"But none of our reasons, none of our lives, will mean anything without you to champion them." She grabbed him by the back of the neck and hauled him in close enough the tips of their noses brushed. "I will kill Maksis with or without you. But I would rather you were there to see it."

His four-fingered hand — *wrong* — cupped the nape of her neck. He bowed his head to hers and said, "I will be. I promise."

Adrik pulled away first, of course, bounding off with his usual relentless energy. Danika had to take her comfort in that — that she had succeeded where no one else could. And if she could not find her satisfaction in the way she desired, the least she could do was proclaim her success to Avdotya.

The sun had fallen when she emerged from the house, the last vestiges of a pink sky tickling at a pale blue horizon. Avdotya's tent sat a short way down from the front doors. She approached to find an orange stripe glowing between the tent flaps. Voices stopped her at the threshold.

"It was a perfect replica," said Avdotya in a voice so hoarse and panicked Danika scarcely recognized it. "How could it be so unless *you* told him?"

"I didn't. I swear it." The reply came from a woman's.

Danika shifted one eye over the gap in the tent flap and caught a glimpse of a middle-aged woman with raven hair and a sharp nose. She wore an armor of black hide with silver epaulets — the armor of the Lun-Protektorate. Avdotya passed close in front of her hiding place and Danika bit back a gasp.

"Only two people living know what really happened that night and both of them are in this tent," he said.

Danika pulled away from the gap, trying to steady her breathing as she pictured the scene — Avdotya's penetrating stare, how the woman would have to force herself to stand firm, to not quail beneath it. But then, this woman was Lun-Protektorate. She had likely stood before men much greater and more intimidating than Avdotya Rostislav. Imperator Maksis, for one. Which begged the question — why was she here in Adrik's camp?

Avdotya spoke again. "There's only one way Maksis could know that the real Adrik is dead."

The world went perfectly blank. White, like the sudden descent of a Whitewinter snow squall. The ringing in her ears matched the storm, fuzzy and furious. Black spots encroached at the corners as the encampment tried to pierce the blizzard and come back into focus.

She could not have heard correctly. She must have misunderstood.

Or it was some scheme....

Yes, that was it. Another of Avdotya's schemes. She gave her arm a sharp pinch and more of the white haze succumbed to sharp reality. The golden glow at the tent flap shivered at the edges. The whole world, Danika included, seemed to tremble in the moment of uncertainty, waiting between breaths for an inevitable blow or swift salvation.

"I didn't betray you. Not then. Not now," said the woman.

"And the real Adrik?"

"I buried his body in a field twenty miles outside New Kirov. Just as you bid me."

"Did you tell Maksis that we snuck a servant boy from the palace that night? A boy of the same height and age?"

"No."

"Then he doesn't suspect an impostor?" Avdotya was ruthless in his interrogation. Relentless in his pursuit of truth. But this — nothing about this could be true. Could it? "Adrik assumes the scene on the barge was a threat. Was that all it was? Or does Maksis know the truth? Does he know we've built our entire cause around a lie?"

There was a clinking then — coin weighed between Avdotya's fingers — measured in what must be unimaginable quantities.

"That I couldn't say."

The clinking stopped. "I beg your pardon?"

"It's a big lie to keep, Avdotya Rostislav. Surely more than just you or I can have gleaned the truth in your years on the run."

There was a pause.

"It has been a long road," Avdotya admitted softly. "But I will not have it derailed this close to the end. Not by you. Not by Maksis. Not even by Adrik."

"And to which Adrik do you refer?"

"The only one that matters." There was a whoosh and a clamor as Avdotya tossed the bag of silver and the woman caught it. "Ensure it remains that way. Go now. And pray I think of another use for you."

Danika scrambled back, slunk into a shadowy gap between two tents, pulse pounding louder than any drum beat she had yet heard on the field of battle. The woman emerged into the cold night. She flung a brown cloak over her telltale armor and slunk off toward the exit. Danika followed. She did not yet know why. She lurked behind the woman as her mind ground over the words like they were the recipe to the Philosopher's Stone.

There is only one way Maksis could know that the real Adrik is dead.

I buried his body in a field twenty miles outside New Kirov. Just as you bid me.

It's a big lie to keep, Avdotya Rostislav.

Adrik was dead. And not the false death contrived by Danika's potions and tinctures and clever notions. And not Danika's Adrik — the one she had devoted herself to so completely. The *real* Adrik. Which meant that her Adrik, her golden-haired beacon of hope, the one who had promised her as much as he had denied, was nothing but a servant boy. A child Avdotya had snuck from the palace and raised as a false heir to the throne. But why? To what end?

Only one thing was certain. This woman knew a secret that would end the man Danika knew. The one she had poured so much of her faith into. His destruction would be the end of all of them — of Nadya, of Papa and Mama, Elin, Zin, and Mikhail. Even Papanik. His unveiling would be the end of their revolution, the end of Danika's quest for the Philosopher's Stone.

The question was — did Adrik know? Did he know that he was an imposter? That his entire campaign — his entire identity — had been built on a lie?

The answer — and whether it was a certainty or a hope, she could not be sure — came to her immediately.

No.

He could not know. Adrik was skilled in many arts, but lying was the least of them. And he would have to be an exceptional one to pull off such a ruse. Which meant that he — her charming prince and salvation rolled into one — had been as conned as any of them.

Avdotya had shanghaied a servant boy into the role of a lifetime. Had raised him up and molded him on a diet of lies and a foundation of betrayal. A part of her had always suspected Avdotya's motives — but to take it this far, to raise a vassal to Imperator and rally a country to his cause? Not even Danika could have fathomed something so dastardly...

Understanding the why of it would come later. Now, there was only the next step. The immediate problem — the woman had exited the encampment. She had moved into the tall grasses beyond the beach. There was little time to decide. It was only fifty miles to Old Kirov. To Maksis.

Time, for once, was on Danika's side. Night had fallen, and they were both dressed in black.

Was Avdotya really going to let this mercenary walk away with a truth that could destroy them all? A truth that labeled Adrik a fraud, and Nadya culpable by extension? A truth that, if revealed, would not only cause every ally — Sivkan and Kotov alike — to flee from their side, but would lead their own brethren to turn them into Maksis' executioner?

There was no choice.

Danika sprang on the woman in a sea of grassland, securing her hand over her mouth and dragging her to the ground. They tussled beneath the sway of the reeds like a pair of wild lynx. Danika reached for the dagger on her waistbelt. The woman's gray eyes had time only to recognize the glint of steel before Danika plunged it into the soft spot beneath her ribs.

She let out a guttural moan. Danika fell back onto her haunches and watched the woman's chest hitch once, twice, three times, and then still — mouth gaping, silver eyes shining like a double moon.

Danika let out a loud, ugly gasp. She clamped a hand over her mouth, afraid Maksis could hear it even from here. She panted against her sweaty palm. Her blade tumbled into the grass. She did not dare retrieve it. She bowed over her knees, heaving in and out.

This was not honorable death on the field of battle. This was murder. And she had committed it.

Her next moan reverberated against her hand. She hunched more, forehead pressed hard into the earth as she tried to regain control. Murder. *Murder*. Punishable by death on the Kotov Isles, exile in Sivka. Babbin would say it made her unfit to practice alkhemy.

Danika rolled up and retched off to the side. She sat up and her gaze fell on the body and she vomited again. She heaved and gagged until there was nothing left but the spasm in her throat, and eventually even that settled.

It was done. There was no going back now. She had to face it. Like any alkhemical process — one step after another.

She took a deep breath in through her nose, gagged on the strange commingling of earth and metal, blood and sick, then picked up her short blade and slid it back in its sheath on her waistbelt. There it would be for the rest of her life — the blade that had killed for Adrik.

Whoever that was.

She pawed the body for Avdotya's coin, tied that to her belt as well, and took the woman's cloak. Let Maksis' scouts find her and think her a deserter.

As Danika reentered camp, her body sought to betray her. She shook violently despite the warmth imbued in her coat. She tried to force her mind away from the physical, away from the rhythm of her pulse beating into clenched fists and the sharpness of bile on the back of her throat, and focus instead on the recipe. The next step.

Adrik.

Adrik must know the truth.

Danika had brought this lie into their lives, had invited Adrik into her home and into her family. Marrying her favorite sister to an Imperator on the run was bad enough, but to have married her to an Imperator who had no true claim at all?

Nadya must know the truth.

She floated numbly through Petrovia's halls. She climbed the spiraling stair and crossed the landing to the Imperator's quarters. She felt the bruising touch of Adrik's four fingers on the wrong hand at the nape of her neck, his breath against her cheek.

What did it matter if he was not a true Solov? He believed he was. Was that not enough? And did she even believe in some divine providence granted to true-born Solovs and Lunovnas? If she did, then she had no right to be rebelling against Maksis. And more importantly, did she really want to be the one to break an identity so many years in the forging — even if it was the truth?

To think that earlier today, her biggest concern had been Adrik's sulking. The pride that she alone had pulled Adrik back from the brink of self-destruction now felt hollow and pointless. The world had shifted irreversibly on its axis and Danika did not know who to turn to first to set it right.

Adrik or Nadya?

She still had not decided by the time she reached the Imperator's quarters. The room sat cold and empty. The candle on the table by Adrik's diary had gone out. His tortured visage appeared before her as clearly as if it were still there, hunched over his diary. How could it be that Avdotya had instilled in Adrik a grief so deep, he mourned a family that was not even his?

Adrik or Nadya?

She turned from Adrik's door to seek out her sister's room.

They were together, of course. The door stood ajar. Any servant that walked past could have seen them. But this was a tableau painted specifically for Danika — designed to torment or resolve her.

Adrik knelt at Nadya's feet. His arms wound tightly around her lower back. His ear pressed firm against her belly. Nadya smiled down at him, hands carding through his golden curls. She spoke to him so softly, Danika could not make out the words. His eyes drifted closed. He smiled and turned his face into Nadya's stomach, squeezing her tighter.

"Oh."

The noise was so small, so against her own will, that Danika did not realize she was the one to utter it. For the second time that night, she covered her mouth with her hands and ran. Ran down the hall, ran down the stairs, ran into the yard. She reached the sanctuary of her own tent just in time.

She had committed murder. She had gasped and heaved and wretched and struggled to remember how to put one breath after another. But not a single tear had fallen. Not until now. Now, the tears burst past her restraint, heedless, hard and fast and wet. As if her body was finally letting her in on some great secret. The obvious truth she had denied for so long.

You thought you could hide from this? it said. *You thought you could play the calculating advisor and the devoted sister and rise above it? Or perhaps you thought if you waited long enough, if you were patient enough, it would go away...*

Maybe — just maybe — you hoped it would all work out in your favor.

That Nadya would give you her blessing.

It was laughable. Danika's sob turned into a hiccup, a giggle.

In truth, this secret meant nothing to Danika. Adrik's name had never been what mattered. She had been drawn to him like an alkhemist to the Flame from the first moment, from the first time he had looked at her silver veins in awe and called himself Adrien. Solov or servant mattered little. Not even the promise of the Philosopher's Stone mattered. If anyone else had made the same promise, would she have believed it? Or had she only risked it all, put her life and family in his hands, because it was *him* that asked? Because it was those golden eyes, that rakish grin, that honeyed voice that asked the question?

You fool. You fool.

Only love could make such a fool.

There was nothing to do but let her body finish its work. To let it exhaust itself, drain every last bit of envy and sorrow and self-pity through her tears and bile. Then carry on. Bear it like a war wound. This was Danika's burden now. And she would wear it for him — for both of them. She would bury it when she could, let it out when she was alone. And if she wept over her charts each night, at least only the stars would know it.

16. THE BATTLE THAT NEVER WAS

Nadya dreamt of the forest. She knew in the dream that she was home, on the Von. Though she knew also that the Von had no forests such as these, with high evergreens as thick as the grass of the Steppe. Still, she waded, barefoot through the sand and earth, unperturbed by the strange amalgamation of lakeshore and woods.

Eventually, she came to the place where she and Adrik had wed. But instead of an inlet, it was a pond, surrounded by trees she had only ever seen in paintings. Their long stems floated to the ground, swaying in a still wind. Beneath their delicate leaves nestled two fawns, curled tightly around one another. They slept soundly in their cocoon, paying no mind as Nadya knelt beside them.

One was a beautiful tawny color with a white blaze between its eyes, like the star of Lunovna herself. The other, equally fair, bore cream spots along its back. Its tail twitched mischievously in its sleep.

She stretched out a hand to skim the blazing star with her fingertips. The fur was soft to the touch. The fawn did not so much as twitch.

Nadya reached next for the spotted creature, but before she could make contact, its eyes popped open. They were red. She yanked her hand away just as the creature let out a keening, unearthly wail.

It screamed at her for help, but Nadya could not move. She was frozen with fear — though she desired nothing more than to help the creature. To save it from what ailed it. The fawn screamed and screamed until its red eyes ran with blood, the corners of its mouth dribbled with it, its ears turned black and rotted. Its tail gave a final twitch. It was dead.

The other slept on.

Nadya woke to a kiss on her lips. When she opened her eyes, Adrik hovered over her, and he was dressed for battle.

Without the alkhemists to aid their steps, Kliment's army arrived later than promised. Avdotya crowed that any delay was for the best — the longer Maksis had to stew behind his walls at Old Kirov, the more eager he would be to surrender.

In the waiting, it occurred to Danika how much easier it would be to flee with her secret than stand and face it in a lie. To avoid the temptation, she kept herself busy. Busy brewing, busy starcharting and conferring, busy avoiding Adrik and Nadya at every turn.

It reminded her of the early days of their preparation on the Isles, when she had turned out potion after elixir after tincture, knowing that the difference between a solider's life and death could lay in the strength of her stamina alone. Then there was that brief shining moment of a full army of alkhemists before the attack on Petrovia's Estate. It seemed little more than a dream, now; though their mangled bodies on the barge had become a frequent nightmare.

At least she still had Shura — a thought that would never have crossed Danika's mind a year ago. Shura and Isma, Ilka, Tytus, Dominik, and Leena. They were not enough. Not nearly enough. But they would have to do for now.

Restlessness in the camp was at a high when the tawny uniforms of the Steppe's soldiers finally appeared on the horizon. Danika did not think the Kotov would have lasted much longer, idle and useless. Only the promise of imminent revenge for the alkhemists had stayed their fight. Only the habit of long years stayed Danika's.

Kliment seemed just Avdotya's type — smarmy, scheming, and disdainful. But even Danika could not argue with the sight of ten thousand men marching on the gates of Old Kirov.

She rode in the rear this time, Lukin trotting grudgingly beside her. He looked as ill-suited to horseback as a fish riding a duck. Whether he was or not, Adrik took to his steed like a true Imperator. She looked away as the thought occurred. *Do not think about that now.*

The outer walls of the city of Old Kirov soared high and long. Their timbers were broken and splintered — held back from ruin by the work of some skilled Artisanal Alkhemist. As expected, there was no army there to greet them, only a barred door. Maksis clearly intended to defend his city from the palace, to maintain the siege indefinitely. It was a task easily done. He had twenty times as many alkhemists locked up in the city with him as Danika had in the field. But as surely as the sun rose in the east, the Suncycle would come. And when it did, the tinctures of sustenance and bottles of warmth would be useless, and the alkhemists that brewed them nothing but more mouths to feed.

Of course, Danika would be useless by then too.

They both had reasons to break the stalemate.

The massive gates opened a fraction and a figure on horseback emerged. Danika expected it to be a regiment general in Taigan green, a member of the Lun-Protektorate, or even some political advisor like Avdotya — a slithery old man gilded in fine silver robes. The last thing Danika expected to emerge from the gates was a little girl.

The child had flaming red hair that fell in kinky curls down her back. She wore a lacy black dress fitted at the sleeves and poofed at the shoulders. A wide ruffled collar encircled her neck like a fan. She perched high atop a gray horse too big for her and, as she approached at a slow trot, Danika found herself bizarrely concerned that the girl would topple off.

The child stopped short. "Greetings," she said. Freckles spotted her pale face and there was an ugly scar where her right ear should have been. But her voice, when she spoke, was clear and authoritative for all that it was childish. "I am Tatya Aleksandrovna Lunovna, second child and eldest daughter of Imperator Maksis Lunovna. I've been sent to plead for your mercy. My poor papa asks that you allow him and his family to depart for New Kirov unscathed."

Adrik's horse chuffed as its master tightened his grip on the reigns. "Of course Maksis sends a child to plead for him," he spat.

"More likely he didn't want to risk his son and heir," muttered Avdotya.

"He is not a complete fool then," Adrik growled.

Avdotya cleared his throat. "Why would we permit your papa to leave this city unharmed when he has already shown us the extent of *his* mercy? He slaughtered some fifty of our alkhemists."

The girl, at least, did not deny this. "You'll still have Old Kirov and a victory if you let us go."

"I'm sure." Avdotya pursed his lips. "But why should we take a victory in battle when we can end the war here and now?"

"A battle is always a risk. Even more so when we have so many alkhemists and you have so few. My papa hopes that you take his offer." Tatya paused to smooth her black skirts, then carried on in the same pleasant tone. "He regrets to inform you that if you do not, he has a messenger laying in wait in the Hermen Mountains — one who is prepared to contact the Jinmen Empire if they fail to hear from my papa in three days."

"The Jinmen Empire?" Avdotya scoffed. "Maksis truly believes the Jinmen will come to his aid?"

"No, sir. He intends to inform them that the Kotov Isles are undefended. That the bulk of its army sits on his doorstep at Old Kirov, and if they strike quickly, they may claim the Isles for themselves."

It was as if Tatya's horse had kicked Danika in the chest. Beside her, Lukin's own steed stomped. Papa had gone very still. Danika was glad then that they were the only Kotov in the party and that the rest were some hundred yards back, well out of hearing range of such an intolerable threat.

"He would dare set a foreign enemy on his own people?" Adrik seethed.

For the first time in two tennights, Danika looked at him directly. One of his hands had strayed from his reigns to his pommel. His jaw clenched so tight she feared his teeth would crack. She wondered what Nadya would have her do if it came to a choice between Adrik and the innocent child who had wandered so helplessly into their midst.

Tatya looked almost embarrassed to utter her next words. "As the Kotov are always so proud to proclaim — they are not Sivkan."

"Leave us to confer," said Avdotya, grabbing Adrik's horse by the bridle to stop its forward surge. Tatya nodded serenely and trotted back to the gate, though she did not go back inside the safety of the timber walls. Adrik watched her with a blood-hungry gleam in his eyes.

"It was foolish of us to leave the Isles so undefended," said Lukin. Danika stared. She had never heard Lukin speak so bluntly in any council. But after the display on the barge, there was little doubt how far Maksis would go — and all for a man who was not even a true Solov.

Do not think about that now.

"We left some of the Host behind," said Papa. "But we did not expect an attack from the south."

"We can't simply allow Maksis and his family to flee." Adrik's gaze had not moved from Tatya. "Show him mercy he says?" His hand clenched again over the sunburst pommel. "*Mercy*?"

Poised on Adrik's other side, Yulian gripped his friend's shoulder. Danika doubted that would be enough to soothe Adrik's temper. She wondered where he got his hot-headedness from. Avdotya had called him "a servant boy from the palace." That could mean all sorts of things. Was he a dishwasher or a cook's apprentice? A delivery boy? Perhaps he had cleaned the chamber pots...

Do not think about that now.

"This is but one battle..." said Papa.

"But it could be the war!" Adrik shouted.

"A war you could not have even begun without us!" Lukin growled, kicking his horse forward in a half-hearted charge at Adrik. "And now you would leave your wife's own people to be slaughtered?"

Perhaps it was the use of the word "slaughter" that struck a painful chord, but Yulian was forced to haul Adrik back by the back of his neckplate to keep him from leaping at Lukin.

"Cease this at once!" Avdotya wedged his horse between Lukin and Adrik. "We're being watched."

Adrik seemed to remember himself. He drew his shoulders back, lifted his chin in a gross approximation of an Imperator. *Such an unquenchable thirst for revenge, born from nothing but a grim bedtime story....*

Danika chuckled darkly.

Lukin shot her an annoyed look.

"Is there time to warn the Kotov?" Avdotya said.

"What good would that do? They will only foresee their end. They will be no better able to stave it off." Papa sounded defeated. It was this that frightened Danika more than anything else. Perhaps he pictured Mama and Papanik making some kind of last stand against the Jinmen — Mama with her burnt frying pan and Papanik with his old whip, poised beneath the wattle-gate — and knew how futile it would be.

"It would take a tennight at best speed to send enough men to defend the Isles," said Avdotya. "And with Maksis' messenger already waiting—"

"But how long would it take the Jinmen to ready for battle?" said Adrik. "Surely—"

"The Jinmen are always ready for battle," said Papa.

"I don't suppose we could find Maksis' messenger?" Yulian's suggestion did not dignify a response. They puzzled in silence, keenly aware of the eyes on them from all sides of the battle line.

What was the old saying? When you cannot kill the man, kill the message? Would they do the same to Danika if she told the truth about Adrik? Or would she be rewarded for her candor? Thanked for saving thousands of lives that would have been lost in a war built on a lie?

Lost in morbid contemplation, it was several moments before she realized that all eyes had turned to her.

"Nika," said Adrik, voice cutting through her fog like a blade. "What do you think?"

"Tatya is right," said Danika, mouth gluey from disuse, but answer ready on her tongue. "It will be a victory for you no matter what. With the power of Old Kirov at our disposal, we stand a much better chance of meeting Maksis as equals after he flees New Kirov." She swallowed. "And I will not risk our home."

Not for any man — Adrik or Adrien, Solov or servant, lover or liar.

Adrik's lip curled as if he had swallowed something particularly sour. "Very well. Someone else relay the message. If I get within reach of the brat, she'll never make it back to her *poor papa*."

As Adrik steered his horse through the muddy streets of Old Kirov, he couldn't help but think how easy it would be to burn it all down.

It was a city built entirely of timber. Log buildings fanned out incomprehensibly in a maze of winding, narrow roadways. It reeked of Maksis' overconfidence; his wooden city was impervious now, infused with flame-proof tinctures — but come the Suncycle, there would be no protection.

Adrik tried to imagine the place in winter — streets snowpacked, bustling with horse-drawn sledges, the sweet tang of sugared nuts lingering in the icy air and little children bundled in furs, tossing snowballs at passersby. It was a nice picture. But now, at the end of a dull Wetwinter, Old Kirov had the same eerie, deserted quality he remembered as a boy in New Kirov.

Unsurprisingly, Maksis had left much of the mundane population behind as he fled for safety. The alkhemists he'd squirreled into his caravans, rattling past Adrik and Kliment's watchful soldiers as quickly as they could manage. Those who remained in Old Kirov had holed up in their homes, shutters closed tight, smoking chimneys the only evidence that anyone lurked behind the barred doors.

They were waiting. All of them waiting to see if Adrik would be a benevolent ruler, or take his desire for vengeance out on the nearest target.

He was still deciding that himself.

In the meantime, Rodin and Kliment deployed forces throughout the city, distributing food and medical aid to those who could be convinced to come out from behind their barricades. There was no harm in garnering some good will — whether or not Adrik decided to betray it later.

He led the caravan further into the city, to the twenty acres of carefully manicured woodland that surrounded The Palace at Old Kirov. The palace itself sat perched high on a grassy hill, allowing the afternoon light to turn the lumber facade a shining gold. A large tower with an onion-like domed roof formed the epicenter of the building. Dozens of dormers, stairways, and covered porches sprawled off the east and west wings, additions made over the centuries under different Impresses and Imperators — illustrative of Sivka's long and ever-evolving history. A history of which Adrik was now an integral part.

A covered staircase at the base of the hill led up to the small entry tower. As Adrik climbed its steps, he gripped the smooth bannister, wondering how many times Maksis had made the same climb, touched the same worn railing — all without sparing a thought for the missing boy in the tomb at New Kirov.

Inside the palace, he tried not to appear overawed at the ornate raftered ceilings, parquet floors and wainscoted walls. Alkhemically-lit sconces illuminated the rich carved furnishings layered in furs and velvet. It felt lived-in, ancient, warm. Too comfortable a place for Adrik's greatest enemy.

As they stumbled upon the Imperator's quarters, Avdotya took a more optimistic view. He scanned the hexagonal room with a clinical eye and said, "This is all yours now."

Adrik looked around. Wooden screens with cutouts in the phases of the moon covered the wall-to-wall windows, creating a soft, ethereal glow. Silver silks draped the four-poster bed and balls of alkhemical light danced across the ceiling like shooting stars in the night sky.

Avdotya was right — once they changed the sheets to a more appropriate Solov gold, Adrik quite liked the idea of sleeping in Maksis' bed.

His council met that evening in the library — a room no less miraculous than the rest of the palace. Bookshelves lined the high walls on either side of the narrow space, disappearing into a domed ceiling obscured by alkhemical cloud and constellation. Several bridges crisscrossed overhead, granting access from one side of the tall stacks to the other.

"We should send reinforcements to the Isles immediately," said Adrik, pacing in front of a pair of windowed doors at the far end of the room that led to a balcony overlooking the city. "We can't give Maksis that advantage again."

"Who shall lead the party?" said Avdotya. "It seems a job fit for a Kotov." He offered Rodin an obsequious bow. Avdotya was bearing the Kotov alliance with less and less grace the more new allies joined their cause. Now with Kliment at their side, Dunya was clearly all too eager to be rid of the Kotov Host. Maksis' threat offered the perfect excuse.

"They are my men," Rodin acknowledged. He leaned against the desk nearest the windows, arms crossed over his broad chest. "It is my duty."

"No," said Adrik. "I need you here. Without you, those who remain won't have much reason to stay."

"I will go," said Danika.

She lingered at the back of the group, as she often did lately. Adrik wondered at it. Her sudden coolness toward him seemed to begin shortly after Maksis' trick with the barge. Could it be that — despite what she said to him that night — she blamed Adrik for the slaughter of her alkhemists? Or maybe she blamed herself. Either way, he was reluctant to lose her counsel. She had been the mind behind so much of their strategy up to this point. She could see new avenues where Adrik and Avdotya couldn't. And he never quite trusted a potion unless it was brewed by her hand.

"What about Lukin?" Adrik proposed. "Couldn't he manage it just as well?"

Danika shook her head. "Lukin carries little authority," she said, not quite meeting his eye. "But as the Prime Chieftain's daughter — "

"They are more likely to listen to her," Rodin agreed.

Danika offered a thin smile. "And with the loss of our alkhemists, it would help me to pay a visit to Babbin. She may be able to replenish our stock, even if she herself will not join us. Meanwhile, Shura and the scientists can begin setting up a lab in the west tower. You do not need me here. Not now."

Avdotya vibrated with anticipation beside Adrik, undoubtedly biting back his vociferous agreement. Adrik sighed. "Alright. You can go. But be quick about it. I can't be without my alkhemist for too long."

"You never will be." The words were reassuring, but the emptiness of her gaze was decidedly not.

"I wish you were not leaving," said Nadya.

A small company gathered in the entry tower to see Danika and Lukin off. Danika had never been less eager for fond farewells. It had taken far too long to settle into the Palace at Old Kirov and make ready the Host to leave. She feared the longer she lingered in this place with her mind so unsettled, the sooner someone would discover her secret — Adrik's secret.

"I feel my own sense of duty," she said to Nadya. "The Host would not be here if I had not brought Adrik's cause before them."

Papa approached from behind and squeezed her shoulder. "Do not think so highly of yourself, Little Nika. The Kotov make their own choices. You did not cast the final stone."

But what Papa did not know was that the Kotov had cast their stones for an imposter. She swallowed back those dangerous words and said, "I will be back before Spring," instead.

She had almost crossed the threshold down to the long covered stairway, left the burden of these people and her choices behind, when Nadya caught her by the arm.

"I will miss you." She spoke with such desperation that, despite her desire to leave, Danika felt a pang of regret. She drew her sister into a fierce embrace.

They clung to each other for a long moment. "I hope when you return," Nadya whispered, "you do so as yourself."

Danika did not know what to say to that. She lingered in Nadya's arms a moment longer, and when she pulled away, tried to release the guilt as well.

"Will you do me one favor?" Nadya asked.

"Anything."

"Will you bring Mama back with you?"

"Mama?" said Danika blackly. A long journey across the Steppe and the Taiga with Mama by her side? If ever there was a prospect to make her stay away forever, that would be it. "I doubt you, let alone I, could persuade Mama to abandon her hearth."

"Tell her that I am with child."

For the second time in recent memory, the bottom seemed to fall out of Danika's stomach. It was not an appropriate reaction for such joyous news. Not when Nadya's face shone with some new, internal light. She blinked rapidly at Danika, equal parts elated and nervous. As the pit inside Danika yawned wider, a sticky, poisonous guilt rushed in to fill the hole.

"But how do you know? It has only been a tennight since your last test— You could not possibly be sure, even with the most effective tincture—"

"I saw it in a dream."

As quickly as the dread had born down on her, it froze — still and tentative. Waiting for either the thaw of spring or a late frost that would solidify into a second winter. "A dream?"

"I know what you think of my visions, but trust me in this, Danika." Nadya's gaze blazed with such conviction that Danika found it hard to argue. If Nadya was right and she *was* with child, it would indeed be a moment in need of Mama's guidance.

And if she were wrong... Perhaps Mama could help then too.

"Very well, Nadya. I will bring you your mama."

But as she and Lukin led the Host through the tunnel of trees and out of the city of Old Kirov, Danika could not help but wonder just how many more sacrifices for Nadya's happiness she was willing to make.

17. THE TRAPPINGS OF POWER

The first few days after Danika's departure, Nadya found herself at a loss for things to do. In a palace with twice as many vassals as residents, there were no chores to manage, no turnips to peel or clothes to mend. Instead she had taken to wandering the halls, memorizing the patterns of the walls. The curve of the painted ceilings. The cut of the parquet floors. It was a beautiful place, beyond her wildest imaginings. But still, it felt too big for her.

Nadya was discovering that her days racing from encampment to encampment with Adrik and his troops, bolstering forces and spurring a coup, had given her very little understanding of what it would mean to be an actual ruling Impress of Sivka. There was much to learn about her new country, its customs, its people, and what would be expected of her should Adrik emerge as sole Imperator.

Perhaps sensing this disquiet, Avdotya put her to work forming a household. To Nadya, the term "household" had only ever encompassed her mama and papa, her sisters and brother. And now, Adrik.

Avdotya had a very different definition.

"An Impress must have a full staff at all times," he explained as he, Nadya and Adrik took their evening meal around a small table in the Imperator's quarters. Nadya had yet to work herself up to ordering a full dinner in the grand dining hall. The prospect of filling those three dozen chairs frightened her more than she could say.

Maksis had left behind his staff — his vassals — in his flight from the palace. Avdotya swore he had ensured their loyalty by offering an actual, hefty wage for the first time in their working lives. Even still, an alkhemist tested every item before it left the kitchen — just in case one of the servants was an agent of Maksis' in disguise. Whatever their loyalties, they had not let the cooking suffer for it. Even the supper laid before them in the bedroom, which Nadya had requested be "simple and light" overwhelmed her with its ostentatiousness. Ginger-crusted chicken cutlets and veal with cream. Savory shallot pancakes with a side of borscht and black bread. Wine and vodka and lavender-infused water in tiny crystal glasses.

She shuddered to imagine what a true royal banquet might entail.

"Titles and gossip — it is the only way to keep the Sivkan nobility happy. And we will need them happy if we are to have support for Adrik's reforms once Maksis is defeated," Avdotya declared. "Give them some menial task. Private secretaries, valets, gentlemen and maids of the bedchamber, an almoner, chamberlain, cupbearer, doorward, Keeper of the Seal. Ladies-in-waiting, of course."

"And what would we do with all these people?" Nadya asked, heart racing even at the prospect.

"Let them follow you and care for you. Let them simper and curtsey. Provide plenty of vodka and opportunities to dance and gamble.... Turn a deaf ear to the whispers and backstabbing, and all will be well in your royal household."

Nadya looked to Adrik, who only smiled and took a large bite of veal.

"Do you have suggestions for who might fill these roles?" She skimmed the surface of her borscht with her spoon. Her appetite had vanished rather suddenly and she laid her other hand low over her belly, hoping there was some culprit besides anxiety to blame.

"I have a few in mind," said Avdotya. "The distribution should be evenly alkhemist and mundane. Maksis couldn't take all the alkhemists with him, despite his best efforts, and those are the ones we will need to get on side first. The mundane nobility, few though there are, will be all too happy to support a Solov Imperator."

"Even though I am an alkhemist?"

Avdotya smiled thinly. "It is why you two make the perfect pairing. Something for everyone. Start with Eugenia Godfrydovna. Her father is Godfryd Ciachowski — Master of the Sivkan Ballet. Then there is the Duchesses Delia and Michela Evanoff, and the Baronesses Nina Michalski and Iga Weworski..."

"I feel I should write this down..."

Avdotya's lip curled. "If you think it necessary."

"And what about a Kotov representative?"

"I beg your pardon?"

"You have spoken of alkhemists and mundanes, but I am first and foremost a Kotov. Should there not be a Kotov lady in my court?"

"Is there such a thing as a Kotov lady, Impress?" Avdotya said, sipping his water delicately.

Nadya flushed and refolded her napkin. "I am sure one can be found. My sister—"

"If you refer to the little alkhemist, I am afraid she is already much occupied waging a war. The other one is too brutish, and the last too...silent."

"Avdotya..." Adrik warned, laying down his fork with a pointed look in his eye.

"Apologies, Imperator." Avdotya bowed his head. "While the Impress' family is no doubt an asset to our cause... They are not best suited for this role. The point is to use these titles to invite new allies into our house."

And so Nadya found herself surrounded by Sivkan strangers just a few days later, in a rather vulnerable state of undress, as they argued about what she should wear for the upcoming Aadan's Day parade.

"The style of Sivka is set by the Impress," declared Eugenia Godfrydovna Ciachowski as she lay a bulbous black gown across the gold satin sheets of the Imperator's four-poster bed.

Avdotya assured Nadya that there were few people with more influence on the fashion and art of the country than Eugenia. Her father and his coterie of ballerinas were some of the only citizens in Sivka that Maksis allowed to travel outside the country's borders. Thus, their performances were renowned the world over and both Master Godfryd and, by extension, Eugenia, were said to have a more worldly viewpoint than most Sivkan nobles.

Danika had told Nadya of a performance of the Sivkan Ballet she attended in her first year at Izumgray, and the feats of the alkhemically-enhanced dancers sounded like something out of a dream. It had been one of the few times Nadya could remember being jealous of her sister's travels. Still, she detected a curling of Eugenia's lip anytime Nadya said something deemed "un-Sivkan."

"If you are to be one of us, you must follow in Impress Aleksandra's footsteps," said Eugenia, withdrawing another frilly gown from a chest at the end of the bed. Nadya shivered in her thin robe, watching helplessly as Eugenia pulled more clothes from the trunk. She stared at the gowns laid out before her in plumes of brown and black and white silk, and could not begin to imagine herself strapped into such behemoths. The bodices were tight, the shoulders enormous, the skirts pinched at the waist. It felt a little like grave robbing — and none of it reminded her of home. "At least you are an alkhemist. For some, that will make you easier to tolerate than your husband."

Nadya had rarely heard Impress Aleksandra's name in all of Adrik's talk of revenge. All she knew of Maksis' wife was that she wore a striking black eyepatch and was a devout Cyclican. Even so, Nadya could not help but feel a kinship for the only person in all of Sivka who could possibly understand her plight better even than she did herself.

"I would like to be one of you," Nadya said. "But I do not know that any of these dresses are *me* either...."

The other four Sivkan ladies tittered behind their hands as Eugenia drew up, looking more akin to a Kotov training master in a curly red wig than a Taigan noble. Delia, Michela, Nina and Iga all wore dark gowns donned in lace, precise copies of the rounded silhouettes laid on the bed. Nadya had a true collection of ladies-in-waiting now.

Her gaze slid to her Kotov page, Davin, who, she was pleased to see, eyed the dresses with equal displeasure. He was a slight figure of fifteen years with dark skin, shorn black hair, and a clumsy gait, but he could put a wardrobe together better even than Mama.

"I agree with you, Impress." Davin swept forward to caress the fine fabric. Davin could not technically be called a lady-in-waiting — Sivkans were very rigid in their gender roles. But he had a gleam of inspiration in his eye that reminded Nadya of Danika. "I do not think you have to follow in Aleksandra's footsteps. Adrik is a new Imperator with a new vision of equality. You are a new Impress. It only makes sense that we should impose your will on Sivka, rather than the other way around."

Nadya flushed. "I am not sure I wish to *impose—*"

But Davin waved her off, scooping the gowns off the bed and into his arms. "Do not worry. I will find you just the thing. The perfect marriage of alkhemist and mundane, Sivkan and Kotov."

He flashed a pointed grin at the other ladies, who glared at him baldly. Eugenia's wig looked ready to topple off in her indignation.

"Do not go to too much trouble," Nadya pleaded. "Supplies are limited and I would not like to be seen as frivolous."

"I will work only from what materials are readily available. Trust me — restrained, but inspiring — that will be the mission!"

They traveled with alkhemy instead of horses. Not only because it was swifter to race across the plains on feet that rarely tired, but because the two thousand Kotov warriors that ran with them would not be returning and they could not afford to lose the mounts.

Wetwinter in all its tumult had arrived with a swiftness that took Danika's breath away. Time was slipping away like distillate, eating at the edges of her awareness right alongside the corrosive nature of Adrik's secret. Before Danika had left Old Kirov, she had searched the palace futilely for any sign of the Philosopher's Stone. But that too turned out be another one of Maksis' broken promises.

Cold, damp air lingered over the frosted landscape of Steppe. Even in the warmest times of year, the nights on the grassland could be frigid. In Wetwinter, the cold would bite off a man's toe in minutes. The weather might have been a more potent threat than the whole of Maksis' army, if their blankets and clothes were not infused to protect them against such elements.

They made camp in a relatively shallow snowbank — only two feet high — stomping it down with their boots to make a clearing for their bedrolls. Danika lay atop the cocoon in perfect comfort thanks to a warming tincture applied to the blankets. Thanks to Kliment, Adrik's numbers had tripled even with so many Kotov out of the equation. Now, with two fortresses in the Taiga in hand, Danika imagined their numbers would swell even more by the time she returned. It should have been cause for celebration. A more victorious homecoming to the Kotov Isles she could not imagine. It was certainly better than her last one, when she had still been raw and wounded by her expulsion from Izumgray.

But as Danika listened to the rustle of ice and mice in the snow beneath her, staring up at a swath of stars that would not relent for any cloud, sleep was elusive.

By the next Aadan's Day in Spring, the snow would have melted, but the cold would still be biting. She could not help but imagine taking this same path to the Kotov Isles as a vassal — without any alkhemical weapons in her pockets. Like Mikhail's Mama, fleeing her masters without a silvnik in her pocket and a baby strapped to her chest. But that was before. Before Maksis had undone Aadan's Day and the biannual relief of letting vassals pay out their debt and seek asylum as Kotov citizens.

Her mind spun over and over the different futures an Imperator could incite with the simplest of decisions. Before too long, Danika gave up on sleep entirely and removed her journal from her pack.

The quill was difficult to manage with her thick gloves, but nothing would stop her in her quest. She would have plenty to show Babbin when she returned. The exercise she had once disdained had now become her obsession. When there was nothing left to calm her mind, Danika always had this. She could always chart the stars, day by day, one by one, until her time came.

"You are thinking too much." Lukin's voice carried loudly in the still night.

"What makes you think so?" she looked over her shoulder at his sharp profile. His bedroll was laid out next to hers and cold blue moonlight washed his face.

"I can see it on your face. You have the same look you had when we were seven and your papa would not let you join him on raid."

"I still dispute I was not old enough."

"I know you do."

Her hand continued to sketch over the page mindlessly. She drew a line between *Kantical Major* and *The Father's Sword*. She did not even need the moonlight to see by to know she had traced the correct path. She went on for so long in silence that she assumed Lukin had fallen to sleep, but—

"That is all you wish to say?"

She sighed. He was clearly in one of those rare moods where he wrenched Danika's thoughts from her mind with sheer stubbornness. This hypocrisy by her usually silent and sullen friend was not lost on Danika.

"I was surprised that you volunteered to return to the Isles," he said. "You seemed so... fixated on the cause."

"I still am."

"Then why—"

"It is *for* the cause that I felt I needed to go. Just for awhile." She expected more questions but none came. He did know her well — knew when to push and when to wait. "I need a new perspective. To be sure I'm making the right choice. I can become...obsessed by things."

He stared pointedly at her in the dark, at her quill and papers, at the way she had not stopped in her scribbling even now. "You do not surprise me."

She smacked his chest. He let out an exaggerated "*oof*." When he settled, she tried to explain. "If I had stayed, I would have lost myself in it."

"In him?" There was a hard edge to the question.

Danika did not answer. And that was answer enough. "I must focus. I must remember the true purpose of all this."

"Defeating Maksis?"

"Amongst other things."

She finished her last mark with a flourish. The planet Mercia. She always ended with Mercia. She packed the book carefully back in the bag and shifted down into her bedroll.

"Tell me again why we are doing this?"

Adrik turned from the mirror, where he'd been adjusting the belt on his velvet beshmet, to stare at his wife.

Nadya stood before her own full-length mirror, resplendent in a loosely fitted red gown with scarlet bodice and cape. A gold sunburst fastener nestled at the base of her throat. The neckline was scandalously low-cut — a choice Adrik could thank Davin for, apparently. It thrilled him to see her looking so regal.

"Because—" he said, crossing the room to snake his arms around her waist. He stared at their reflection in the mirror and wondered if Maksis would have any supporters left after the people of Old Kirov got a look at them, "—we need to announce our presence in Old Kirov. And Avdotya wants me to tell the people that I intend to restore Aadan's Day once Maksis is gone."

"Why wait? You have already declared yourself Imperator."

Adrik thought quickly. It was one of the many things he loved about his wife — she forced him to use his mind. "It wouldn't be safe to travel now. Not while

Maksis' troops are still loyal. This parade is a promise to the people. A glimpse of what's to come."

His hand drifted down from Nadya's waist to rest on her belly. So far as he knew, she still wasn't with child, despite their very best efforts. Adrik wasn't overly troubled by it. He was happy to keep trying and he knew the moment her belly swelled, they would have to stop.

He pressed a kiss to the delicate flesh on her neck, wondering just how difficult it'd be to get past all those skirts — when her hand stilled him. She wound her fingers through his, as she had so many times before, but this time, her thumb caressed the nub on his right hand where his pointer finger should have been.

"You never told me how you lost it."

He tried to pull away, but she held him fast. He sighed and said, "It's not a very heroic story. I don't like telling it."

"I do not need a hero. Merely a husband."

A different kind of warmth pooled in his belly then and, as always, he relented to her request. "I was nine. Studying in the library at the Wylburg Palace in Polvia. My tutor was Maester Zachert. The book was Sivkan history, of course. Avdotya tells me I learned other skills, but I don't remember them." Nadya laughed softly and he was encouraged to continue. "Avdotya came into the room and he was offering me an encouraging word for once. Blast it, I think he was even about to hug me—"

He broke off. Nadya squeezed his hand. "And then?"

"And then that pestilential bird swooped down off his shoulder and bit me!"

Her lips parted in surprise. For a moment, she looked as if she wanted to smile, but then it transformed into a frown. "Hard enough for this?" Her fingertips danced delicately over the scar.

"Apparently so. It bled terribly. The doctor — that's what they call healers in Polvia — he said the finger had to go to stave off infection. They don't use alkhemy there, even in the Luncycle. So off it went."

"That is why you hate Renata so much?"

"One of many reasons, yes."

Nadya twisted in his arms to face him. She cradled his cheeks between her palms and pressed a gentle kiss to his lips. He closed his eyes, savoring the caress of it, the chasteness. Nadya was the only person who'd ever kissed him without wanting more. He was surprised how much he enjoyed it. "My brave boy."

He grimaced. "Hardly. Dunya was furious that I wouldn't stop crying, even after the doctor numbed me. If Yulian had been with us at that point, his hide would have been black and blue."

Her thumb skimmed the ridge of his brow. "There is no weakness in crying, Adrik. Not then, not now."

The notion made him uncomfortable. The conversation had taken a less than ideal turn. He was about to face his people for the first time as Imperator. He couldn't be thinking about crying when he did it.... He pulled out of her arms, took her hand in his and led her to the doorway. "Come," he said. "Avdotya will be waiting."

A thick mist hovered over the Swansea, clouds too thin to offer true rainfall. There was little wind, but the fog offered poor visibility and a dampness that set deep into Danika's bones. An icy raindrop lashed against her cheek. They had gathered a fleet at Norgay and set sail for the Kotov Isles with haste, shaving off their expected arrival time by more than two days. For all Danika had longed for the scent of salt and sea air, she now ached even more the comforting warmth of the turfhouse's fire. She hoped they would make it before evening meal. Her stomach grumbled with the anticipation of seasoned mussels and sautéed whitefish.

"Do you suppose Mama will have turnips at the ready?" she asked Lukin as he manned the tiller.

"Unlikely." He flashed her a grim look. "She does not know that you are coming, remember?"

If she was not to expect a warm welcome from Mama, she could at least be sure of one from Papanik, Zin, and Mikhail.

"Perhaps we can persuade Babbin and your papa to return with us," said Danika. "Now that we have brought so many men back."

Lukin's nose wrinkled. "Papa may be persuaded. But Babbin—"

He broke off, staring past her shoulder at the horizon. The peak of Mount Ironwood had pierced the haze, its familiar emerald ridgeline a boon to Danika's spirits. Or it would have been, had she not looked closer.

A fine gray plume was rising off the cliff, so similar to the mist that permeated the air that if Danika had not taken alkhemical drops to her eyes several years ago, she might not have been able to discern it.

Smoke.

And, as they drifted ever closer...fire.

The Kotov Isles were burning.

18. SMOKE ON THE SHORE

Avdotya stood on a plinth at the east end of Old Kirov Square, wedged between a Mother Celebrant and a Father Celebrant, trying desperately to avoid Yulian's gaze.

The Mother Celebrant wore floor-length robes of purest white, the Father in matching gold. Each bore a hermaphroditic Thoth stitched upon a drape over their chests. The Mother Celebrant's Thoth was embedded atop a full moon, and the Father's atop a sun. Even their faces were much the same — gray and blank with pale eyes that never seemed to fix in one place for long.

Avdotya held little belief in the Cyclican religion and its teachings, but some irrational part of him still worried the combined power of the two Celebrants on either side could discern every dirty thought that had ever crossed his mind. Then again, as Adrik and Nadya trundled into view, perched high on the back of a three-horsed carriage, Avdotya supposed he had worse sins to atone for than Yulian.

The crowd that had gathered for the parade was meager. Fortunately, those in attendance made up for their numbers with enthusiasm. Adrik and Nadya struck a much more inspiring image than Masksis and Aleksandra had ever done — even in their prime. If Avdotya could only parade Adrik and Nadya in front of the rest of the country, the war would already be won.

Two golden-haired beauties, they beamed beneficently down at their adoring subjects — mainly vassals. It didn't hurt that Avdotya had given the accompanying honor guard silvniks to drop discretely in the gutter ahead of the couple. Avdotya would need to commission an artisanal alkhemist to paint the scene. The work could be replicated to hang in every village hall and noble ballroom in Sivka. And for a few extra coins, the artist would ensure the small crowd and gray weather was nothing but a faulty memory.

When the carriage reached the plinth and jolted to a halt, the celebrants welcomed "Adrik, son of Iosif" to Old Kirov — never once using the word "Imperator" to describe him. This had been a point of contention in the negotiations, but Avdotya had finally agreed so long as the words "Maksis" or "Lunovna" were never mentioned either.

Adrik gave a rousing speech about the promise of the future dawning under a new sun and vowed to restore Aadan's Day to the vassals just as soon as it was safe to do so. Avdotya smiled grimly, pleased to see Adrik taking some initiative in policy-making. Perhaps Rodin's daughters were good for something after all. Little did they or Adrik know that Avdotya had much bigger schemes in mind than simply restoring the two tennights a year when the door to the vassals' cage was left ajar. No, Avdotya intended to break the slaves' chains altogether.

The task was so enormous that it could never have been trusted to a true born son of an Imperator. Only another vassal could achieve the seemingly impossible feat of abolishing slavery in Sivka— whether Adrik knew it or not.

After the speechmaking, they retired gratefully to a reception in the foyer of the ballet center hosted by Master Godfryd Ciachowski himself.

A vast, white-haired figure of middling age, Godfryd wore the most elaborate uniform Avdotya had ever seen on a man. A black satin and crepe coat with poofed shoulders lay atop matching breeches and waistcoat, but the remarkable part was the hundreds of tiny golden ballerinas dancing to and fro across his broad belly, up his muscled calves and around his wide shoulders. Alkhemical excess if Avdotya had ever seen it.

"As Above," Godfryd said on approach — he even had twinkling gold stars adorning his traditional Sivkan beard.

"So Below," said Avdotya with a bow of his head.

Unlike many of the alkhemists in Maksis' court, Godfryd Ciachowski had never earned himself a noble title. It was for this reason, perhaps, that Maksis had left the ballet master behind. But Avdotya knew better than most that a lack of title didn't mean a lack of power, and he was grateful for Maksis' oversight and the entry it had granted Adrik into Sivkan society.

"Is this a sneak peak of what's to come?" Avdotya waved a hand at Godfryd's attire. The reception was to be followed by a special performance of the ballet, though how much of it would pierce the drunken stupor of the attendees remained to be seen. Barely halfway through the reception, and already the noble masses were toppling over with drink.

"It is indeed, Master Dunya," said Godfryd, taking a deep swig from his own pail. Avdotya wrinkled his nose — he wasn't fond of the familiar title Godfryd had bestowed upon him, but knew better than to argue with such a gracious host. "I hope our new Imperator won't be disappointed."

"Certainly not. I'm afraid arts and culture weren't high on our list of priorities as we hid from Maksis' Protektorate. And while Polvia has many qualities, alkhemical dancers isn't one of them."

It was Godfryd's turn to wrinkle his nose. "Polvia," he spat. "I don't know how you could tolerate such cultureless heathens for so long."

"A struggle indeed. But they've proven faithful allies against Maksis. Much as you yourself have, Master Godfryd."

Godfryd patted his belly in a self-satisfied sort of way. "I'll admit the risk has given me pause. It's one thing to tolerate your presence in our city, but to install my daughter in your Impress' household... Maksis will never forgive such action. I hope I don't come to regret my choice."

"I will personally see to it that you don't. I know Eugenia has already made herself the leader of their little faction. It seems only right that she have a title to go with such an honor."

Godfryd's eyes gleamed. "A title you say? You know that despite my family's many contributions to Sivka, we've never breeched that great divide between niceties and nobility."

"Bloodlines matter little to Imperator Adrik," Avdotya said, smirking at his own joke. "When he sees value, he'll reward it. A Barony seems the least we can do."

"A landed Barony?"

"Hm. How about a Parcel in the country? I know you're often in the city, but might it inspire your muses to get a taste of nature?"

"I daresay it will!" Godfryd chuffed, patting his belly again. "A seat on the Assembly! And think of the vassals that will come with it! That income alone will make an excellent dowry for Eugenia..."

Avdotya's lip curled. He had offered land, not men. But in Sivka, they were one and the same. He couldn't retract the offer so soon after it'd been made. It would have to be undone with time, just as all the rest.

"And who knows?" Avdotya said, pretending to sip his wine. "After the war, when we have done away with all those who don't support a true and just Imperator, perhaps a Duchy will open up..."

"Ho ho!" Godfryd's face went round and red and he smacked Avdotya hard on the shoulder — a sure sign of burgeoning friendship. "This is glad news indeed, Master Dunya! I'll see to it that both my titled and untitled friends hear of the possibilities that await under Imperator Adrik."

"See that you do."

Godfryd shuffled off, as graceless as his dancers were graceful. Yulian swiftly replaced him. "Making friends wherever you go?" he said.

"It *is* part of my job description."

"Have you attempted to breech that duo yet?" Yulian jerked his head toward the Celebrants, who watched the festivities empty-handed and vacant-eyed.

A long line of wealthy merchants and nobility had gathered in front of the Mother Celebrant to receive her blessing. Only a few waited for the Father Celebrant — yet another result of Maksis' influence.

"We are in a tentative and indefinite truce," Avdotya said, narrowing his eyes on the pair.

"Want to lay odds on how often those two have seen each other's nethers?" Yulian waggled his eyebrows.

"They're supposed to be celibate."

"Yes, and I was supposed to be Adrik's whipping boy."

"Leave my side if you insist on talking nonsense."

Yulian leaned in close, lips brushing Avdotya's ear. "I thought you liked it when I talked nonsense?"

Avdotya's grip tightened on his cup. The Celebrants, of course, chose that moment to approach.

"As Above," they said in perfect synchronicity.

Avdotya took satisfaction in Yulian's startled jump as he replied, "So Below."

The Cyclicans and accompanying Celebrants were a rather toothless bear, but still not one Avdotya was eager to poke. Unlike other countries riddled with organized religion, Sivka was fortunate enough to enjoy a comparatively hands-off approach. There weren't any great houses of worship or mandated altars for Cyclicans, no tithes or flagellations. Instead, Celebrants traveled the country, spreading word of "the great oneness of the Above and Below," and The Mother and The Father who had birthed Sivka into a fledgling world. When Celebrants came to visit, a Sivkan could choose devoutness, or not, as they saw fit.

In this way, their neutrality made easier entry for a coup, even if almost every household in Sivka still kept an Oratorium to honor the idols of The Mother and The Father. After all, religion might have been thin on the ground in Sivka, but tradition was not.

"Avdotya Rostislav, we've noticed that you haven't yet come for our blessing," said the woman in a soft, vapid voice.

"My apologies, Mother Celebrant. I'm afraid it's been a long time since I was last in Sivka and given the opportunity." Avdotya kept his tone even, though he could feel Yulian's tension beside him. Unlike the Kotov, Sivka did not permit marriage between same sex couples. Though they had no problem turning a blind eye to affairs in any combination. Relations outside the marriage bed were practically encouraged.

"Perhaps you've forgotten how a blessing works?" said the female Celebrant. "Allow me to enlighten you. You may seek my counsel as the voice of The Mother for questions of alkhemy, thought and imagination, physical growth, fertility, and interpersonal conflict." Her wide eyes flickered over Avdotya and Yulian.

The Father spoke next, voice as slow and calm as his partner. "I, on the other hand, may be of help to you in making a decision, advising on matters of the mundane or physical. I can even help with problems of personal willpower."

Again, the pointed look.

"Fascinating," said Avdotya. "Let me think on just who I should trouble for which ailment and get back to you. Shall I also sort my concerns into categories of 'good thoughts' and 'bad thoughts?'"

Yulian twitched with stifled laughter.

"Don't trouble yourself with 'good' or 'evil,' Avdotya Rostislav," said the woman. "Such things do not exist in the realm of Above or Below. Think only of the purification of your soul so that you may achieve enlightenment."

"I hear that you are mundane?" The Father asked baldly.

Avdotya grit his teeth. "I am."

"Don't be ashamed," he said, mistaking Avdotya's aggravation. "Some believe alkhemists are closer to The Mother and Thoth for it is the Flame in Her that gave life to Sivka and She is the fountain of heat and Fire. But even the blood in your body runs blue. And when it breaks the skin and turns to red, it represents the quenching of the Alkhemical Flame. You have as much power in your veins as any alkhemist."

Perhaps the vodka had breached Avdotya's lips after all, because the Celebrant was starting to make sense.

For all that Maksis and his alkhemists worshipped at the feet of The Mother, there was no reason Adrik couldn't usher in a newfound appreciation for The Father. After all, what nobler calling could there be than extinguishing the Alkhemical Flame once and for all?

The fires grew. Every shift and crack in the landscape came into sharper relief as they drifted closer to home. Where once floated five emerald isles against a gray sea now stood jagged pieces of molten rock.

No one came to greet them, which meant that no one was watching the shore. There were no Jinmen vessels lingering in the coves — the fight had been and gone. The question that remained was who had survived.

They reached Von Village first — a burnt husk of its former self. The stench of smoke hung thick in the air. Lukin took off up the hill — Danika knew he was headed for the forge.

In the village, the homes and shops made of ancient stone fared the best. Those buried into the earth survived with a mere singeing across the turfroof, like a man who had burnt the tips of his hair. She did not want to go any further, to see if her home had faced the same comical firing, or if, like Taito, there was nothing to find but ash and bone.

In truth, Danika had not realized that Taito was among the men and women to return to the Isles with them, though it made perfect sense in hindsight. A person could only stand by and watch Nadya and Adrik be gloriously happy for so long. Danika understood that better than most.

Taito dragged the bodies out of the ruin that was Bodan's Brews and into the street, chest heaving, eyes blackened with a rage she had only ever seen in Adrik when he spoke of The Slaughter. He lined the four charred corpses in a neat row — two adults and two children.

One of the children had a blackened hand curled around a shortsword. Manet — the little girl who had so ferociously held the same blade to Adrik's heart on a crisp Autumn afternoon in the dooryard. She would not have gone down without a fight.

There was no one to save, no one to aid, so Danika made the slow climb home. Her feet guided her along the familiar path as if she was in some dark dream and unseen forces pushed her inescapably forward. Only when the turfhouse finally came into view did she stop to see what she had wrought.

The gate into the dooryard that she and Papanik had built when she was a child was gone. Nothing but two stone posts remained to mark its purpose. The grass over the turfhouse, which should have been teeming with fragrant white blossoms, was blackened and singed.

Her lab was nothing more than a charred spot on the earth. It would have taken powerful alkhemists indeed to undo Danika's protective tinctures. She wondered if they had sought out her sanctuary intentionally, looking for Adrik's secrets. If they had, the perpetrators would have been disappointed. She had taken everything of real value with her.

Danika toed through the scorched grass where the hut Papa had built especially for her once stood, where she had trained a mundane boy in the ways of alkhemy and started this cauldron boiling. It served to delay the inevitable.

It was too quiet. If anyone was left in the house, they would have come to greet her by now.

The front door of the turfhouse had been smashed in. Danika ducked through the gaping entryway inside — the structure itself seemed sound, but the wooden loft where she, Nadya, and Zin slept had collapsed into Mama's oratorium. Beams skewered the small room, blocking access to the latrine. Inside the main hall, more trusses had collapsed, shattering many of the bedclosets. The long dining table, the epicenter of so much laughter and fury, was cleaved in two. All of the fineries — the tapestries, the furs, the plates and pottery — were gone.

A raid, then. In true Jinmen style.

But there was one hiding place they might have missed....

Danika drug a bench from the hall over to the place where their bed loft once perched. She climbed atop it and had to stretch to reach the loose rock in the wall. It gave way after a bit of prying. When she saw what was in side, she let out a wet laugh.

Zin's hoard of treasures remained untouched. Cousin Shelia's hairbrush, Elin's favorite ladle, a bit of cloth torn from Nadya's wedding dress, Avdotya's sunburst pin, the fire-shaped rock Mikhail had gifted Danika on her return from Izumgray.

She could bundle the tokens up and take them with her, but Zin had successfully hidden her stash from the Jinmen — it would not do to pillage it now. Danika replaced the stone and walked back out into the dooryard.

Where were the bodies?

The dream resumed and her feet carried her on. In what seemed like mere moments, she found herself at Lukin's door. Or what was left of it.

She had always thought it foolish for the smithy, a place nearly as full of fire and chemicals as an alkhemist's lab, to be entirely made of wood. When Danika offered to infuse the building, Dondar had replied with his usual, "A blacksmith is not an alkhemist. I will stick to my horseshoes." Lukin, in turn, had said that his papa was too skilled to ever catch fire to his own roof.

Lukin was right. But the Jinmen had applied no skill here.

Danika stepped carefully through the rubble and smoking coals. If she did not know the property so well, she would not have been able to tell where the forge once ended and the house began, but the two stone chimneys stood as anchors among the massive pile of charred wood. She could see no sign of Lukin, which meant either that he had left — perhaps in search of bodies of his own — or he was within the ruin.

Danika slipped between rafters and beneath gaps in the direction where she knew the kitchen to be and found him there in front of the only bit of house still standing — the hearth. The hearth where she had taken so many meals after a hard day's training. She and Lukin would regale Dondar with tales of the other children's antics and Lukin would sing Danika's praises, telling his papa how she had bested Egon — the biggest boy of their year.

The chairs they had sat in were gone along with everything else. Instead Lukin knelt amongst the ashes, his papa's body strewn across his lap.

Dondar was unrecognizable save for the ax dangling from the melted remains of his belt. She remembered Manet's shortsword and took comfort in the fact that no amount of destruction could melt away Dondar's hard work. She sank to her knees beside the body, the image burnt into into her mind as deeply as the burns blackened Dondar's once jolly face. Tears streamed down Lukin's cheeks, though his voice remained deep and steady. "Your family?"

"Missing. I thought...perhaps a mass grave, but—" She looked down at Dondar again.

"What about Babbin?" Pale tracks cut through the black soot marring his face.

"I do not know." She felt ashamed for having forgotten her old teacher. "I came here first."

"Let us find her then."

Lukin lifted his papa off his lap and laid him gently — ever so gently — across the stones of the hearth. He departed without looking back.

Danika was not so strong. She pressed a kiss to her fingertips and put them to Dondar's forehead, trying to ignore the crinkle of his skin beneath her caress. She removed the ax from his belt — he would want Lukin to have it, when he was ready. Lastly, she leaned close and whispered, "I will look after him."

She caught up with Lukin halfway down the path. His grief had melted into a quiet rage, one she knew better than to try to soothe with small words of consolation. She slipped the ax into a hook inside her coat and walked silently by his side.

What sun that could breach the cloud and smoke had set by the time Babbin's stone hut came into view. The gray smog surrounding them was unrelenting, lightening the night sky, blocking out the stars and clogging the lungs like a gaseous poison. But Babbin's house, of all things, sat unblemished.

"She must have fortified it before the raid."

"Or even the Jinmen were too frightened to tread here," said Lukin and Danika knew instantly that he was correct.

They were still fifty feet from the hut when the front door flew open and Zin raced out.

Danika bolted forward and caught the girl in her arms, lifting her up off the ground and squeezing her tight. Zin's grip was painful around her neck, saying all the things she could not manage in words. Danika set her back on her feet and captured her face in her hands, turning it this way and that, looking for damage. Save a scrape or two, she looked whole. Frightened, but whole.

"What happened? Are you here alone? What about—"

More figures spilled from the doorway — Mama and Shelia and Papanik. Danika ran toward Papanik, eager perhaps for his embrace more than she had ever been for anyone's. But as she got close enough to see his full form, she stopped short.

There was a stub at his shoulder where his arm should have been.

Her shock must have been plain, for he scowled at her. "I can hug my Little Nika just as well with one arm as with two," he growled and Danika fell forward. She buried her face into his chest and did not pull away until she was certain her eyes were dry.

She turned to Mama next, who watched her impassively. Even now, there was no expectation for a warm embrace from either of them. Like Zin, she appeared mostly whole. Scratched and bruised and perhaps a little pale. But her elegance had not faded and she stood without a hair out of place or a thread loose at her hem.

"Where is Mikhail?" said Danika.

"Sleeping below," said Mama.

Zin and Lukin approached, Zin's hand held fast in Lukin's. Some of the fury had left his face, as though he could not contain both it and Zin at once.

"He has a head wound," Mama said. "It was only Babbin's intervention that saved him."

Danika looked to the doorway and found her mad old alkhemist, still wearing her crown of twigs and leaves. Babbin threw out both hands at Mama's words, shaking her head. "Pah! It is you who saved him, my dear. By bringing him here. She wasted no time," she said to Danika.

"I see."

Mama became suddenly incapable of meeting Danika's eyes. "Zin and Mikhail were playing by the shore when the Jinmen arrived. One struck him over the head, but Zin managed to carry him away and run up to the house to warn me. I decided then that we all must leave. He was bleeding badly and I knew of no one else—"

The defensiveness in Mama's voice was unmistakable. Babbin laid a steadying hand on her shoulder. "You did the right thing."

As quickly as it came, Mama shook off her moment of weakness. "I ordered everyone to leave for Babbin's at once, but—"

Her gaze slid reproachfully to Papanik, who stared back unabashed. "It has been my home for longer than you have been alive, Marisha. I would not abandon it."

Mama chose not to argue the point. "I have never seen the Jinmen strike so hard and fast, nor leave so quickly."

"That is Maksis' doing," said Danika, and the full weight of it roiled up in her stomach like a sour meal.

"Maksis?" Mama gasped. Danika could understand. Despite their differences, Mama had likely never imagined that the Imperator would set a foreign enemy on his own people, his own sister.

"Trust me, Mama. Your brother will pay for his crimes."

When Adrik heard of what happened here, that he let Maksis go free for nothing... Servant boy or Solov — no power in Sivka would stop him.

19. FESTERINGS AND RECKONINGS

Danika wrote to inform the Imperator their journey would be extended. There was much work to do before she could leave the Kotov Isles again in good conscience.

Ironically, they were forced to set fire to the debris that remained. The smoldering beams, broken chairs and tables, and charred animal bones were piled into five massive bonfires on each Isle and lit together at dayfade. From the peak of the Von, Danika and Lukin watched all five fires burning bright and white — fueled by alkoal made from Danika's own blood.

The Jinmen fires had been fueled by her too, in a way. Fueled by her many thoughtless choices. If she had not killed the nameless guard, if she had revealed the truth of Adrik's identity, would her home be whole and safe now? Would Papanik be unmaimed? Would Manet be alive? Would Dondar?

They laid Lukin's papa to rest at the top of Mount Ironside beneath the bowed, but never broken, acacia tree. Lukin scattered the ashes at the head of the Dianara River and if he spoke any words of peace or faith, he kept them to himself.

All six of them — Danika, Mama, Zin, Mikhail, Papanik, Babbin and Lukin — took up residence in Babbin's tiny hut as work continued on the turfhouse. Mama insisted they not be separated or move back in until the residence was restored to its former glory. This would be a long time coming. Even with regular shipments from Polvia and Old Kirov, timber was difficult to transport this far out to sea.

"It is good for us," Papanik groaned as he crouched on the cold brick floor to eat his evening meal. At least Babbin's cooking was an improvement over Mama's. He balanced his bowl on one knee as he spooned carpstew into his mouth with his only hand. "Do you think Bodan had such luxuries as chairs and tables?"

"Pah, pah," Babbin answered.

"Precisely," said Papanik. "If it is good enough for Bodan, it is good enough for me."

"Adrik will want an assessment of the state of the other Isles," Danika said to Lukin, voice careful as she stared hard into the depths of her own stew. "I thought I would go to the Vienper tomorrow. See what they might be in need of. Will you join me?"

Lukin froze, spoon hovering at his lips. Danika held her breath, worried she was about to be caught in her scheme, but then he grunted an affirmative and kept eating.

Danika *did* inventory the Vienper, though there was not much to say beyond, *'It is gone.'* The Folktan had survived the incursion, but the price to keep it was high. Papa's friend Tangier explained that the whole of the isle had abandoned their homes to defend the sacred building and lost everything else in the process. Fortunately, the Vienper were hardy folk. Danika did not hear one word of complaint as they passed between tents and makeshift shelters, asking the people what they were most in need of. The answers were much the same as the Von — more places to sit and more mouths to feed.

As they passed through the spot where the gate out of the village once stood, Danika hesitated. Lukin stared back at her.

"Your mama is isolated on the moor. We should make sure she has all she needs."

Lukin's eyes darkened, though there was less betrayal in them than she had expected. Perhaps he had seen through her thin veneer after all. He kicked his boot into the packed earth and stared off at the distant horizon. It was the first clear day since their arrival, and the Swansea stretched out in an endless swath of chill blue. "Yes," he said finally. "Let us see her."

As they made their way east, Danika prayed they would not stumble on another tomb. She did not want to be responsible for making Lukin an orphan.

When they found a single white tent where Tanith Chaska's one-room house used to be, she let out a sigh of relief. Danika had not visited this place since she was a child, shortly before she left for Izumgray. The reason behind the trip she could not remember, all she recalled was that Lukin had stomped out midway through lunch and when she had gone to find him, he had swiped furiously at his face, trying to hide his tears.

Now, Tanith crouched over an open fire, searing a massive cod. She stared blankly up at them through the smoke for several long moments before recognition dawned and her shock passed. She stood, fire tongs still in hand and said simply, "Lukin."

Lukin's shoulders drew up around his ears. He nodded curtly. "Tanith."

Danika thought this a rather cold greeting — even by her standards — but Tanith paid no mind.

She was not a particularly attractive woman. Her broad features were better suited to a man and Lukin had inherited much of them, including her hard build. Her hair was almost the same muddy blonde as Danika's, slightly greasy and shorn close to the shoulders. A large scar crossed from her right brow to her bottom lip, but Danika could not recall if it was old or new. Her pale green eyes shifted to Danika. She seemed to be searching her memory. "Danika Bodanson? You have grown much since I last saw you."

"That is what happens after seven years," said Lukin. "Things change."

Danika tried to elbow him discretely in the ribs, but that was more easily done in the furs of Whitewinter. Tanith blanched and set the tongs by the fire. "I heard about your papa. I am very sorry. He was a good man."

Danika braced herself for another cutting remark, but none came. She looked to Lukin and saw his throat bob as he swallowed. "I see your house did not fare well," Danika said.

Tanith waved a dismissive hand. "It was hardly the Palace at Old Kirov. There were more important things to contend with that night." Danika did not doubt it. "I have heard much of your exploits though, the pair of you." Tanith waved a hand at the ground. "I would offer you a chair, but..."

"No matter." Danika sat crosslegged in the grass. Tanith claimed a spot on the other side of the fire, but Lukin had not budged. "Come, Lukin. Take a seat." Danika tugged hard on his pant leg and he slowly sank beside her.

Tanith grinned at this and started cutting into the cod. The flaky whiteness and rich smell made Danika's mouth water. Babbin had been making a lot of stews and they never quite seemed to fill the belly. Fortunately, Tanith had plenty to share.

As they ate, Lukin's mama peppered them with questions about their adventures, which mostly Danika answered, interrupted by the occasional one-word response from Lukin.

"You would be most welcome to join us on our return to Old Kirov," Danika said, and it was Lukin's turn to elbow her. "We have brought two thousand men and women back to protect the Isles." Though Danika doubted very much the Jinmen would strike again — not when there was nothing left to pillage. "It would be a welcome relief to return with a few new faces."

Tanith looked to Lukin, who stared hard into the fire. "I think not. I have a house to rebuild and I have seen enough of fighting."

Lukin's shoulders relaxed. Though whether it was because of Tanith's promise not to accompany them, or her promise not to fight, Danika did not know.

They made their excuses shortly after. Danika shuffled off first, hoping to give Lukin and Tanith a moment alone. She waited in the next field, pretending to pick wild blooms, but secretly watching as Tanith gripped Lukin by the shoulders. It was not quite a hug, but it seemed to be the most Lukin could tolerate and Danika was pleased to see he did not pull away.

They did not speak of it until the dock was in sight.

"Thank you, Danika," he said so quietly she could barely hear him over the creaking gangplank bobbing in the waves. When he faced her, she could see more of Tanith in him than she ever had before. "I am glad you brought me here. It is good to know—" His throat worked as he struggled to find the right words. "It will never be easy between us. But it is good to know that I am not alone."

She took his hand in hers, squeezed it tight and uttered the same words she had said to Adrik. "You never will be."

Nadya found Adrik a mile deep in the forest at the Palace at Old Kirov. Hunting, of all things.

He had to explain the practice to her more than once. It sounded like a combination of Jinmen raid and fishing excursion, only for pleasure instead of necessity. What fun there was to be found in the pursuit and murder of a defenseless animal, Nadya could not fathom, but Adrik assured her that all the noblemen of Sivka participated in such hunts and it would not do for the Imperator to be the exception. So when Danika's letter arrived, Nadya shook off her ladies — save for Davin, she could never shake Davin and rarely wished to — and made for the woods.

The day dawned crisp and cold, and was colder still under the shadow of the treetops. If she had not been in such a hurry, Nadya would have liked to linger under the snow-laden branches, dripping with the promise of Spring, listening to the music of the birds and the wind. She could close her eyes and pretend she was back at home on the shore of the Von. But the crack of gunfire fractured the peace, souring Nadya's temper further and assuring her she was getting closer to her prey. Adrik had promised they would not use the new weapons in the hunt.

It seemed to Nadya what little sport could be found in this exercise evaporated entirely with the unfair advantage of guns.

She spotted Kliment through the trees first. His canary yellow tunic and trousers were impossible to miss through the foliage. He stood chatting with Avdotya, leaning heavily on his rifle, and mopping his bald head with one hand while drinking deeply with the other.

Just what this circumstance needed — alcohol.

As Nadya closed in, Adrik came into view. He wore more practical outdoor attire, leathers and boots — but still cut with a flare that would never distinguish him as anything less than an Imperator. He hoisted his own rifle onto his shoulder and was taking aim just a few degrees to Nadya's left.

"Adrik — wait!"

He did not hear her. He clicked back the stock. Nadya looked to Davin, whose eyes went wide. The young Kotov raced toward the hunters and cried out, "Stop!"

Adrik let out a startled "Ho!" and pulled his weapon up toward the sky. Nadya and Davin raced into the clearing and Adrik's face contorted in anger. "Nadya! What are you doing out here? I nearly shot you!"

"Shot me with a weapon you swore not to use?" she demanded.

"Adrik is right," said Papa, taking her face between his hands, turning it side to side. "You should not sneak up on a hunting party, Nedeshda. Especially not so...camouflaged."

She looked down at her dress and saw that she was indeed wearing a fine emerald velvet.

Adrik whirled on Davin. "You! Why did you let her come out here?"

Davin bit his lip, his dark skin turning red at the forehead. Nadya pulled out of Papa's arms to turn on Adrik. "Davin does not control where I go! And perhaps if you did not engage in such reckless hobbies, I would not have to be so careful."

Adrik grit his teeth and glanced over at the rest of the party, which included Yulian and Elin, who were passing a flask back and forth between themselves like spectators at a sparring match.

"We'll talk about this later," said Adrik. "Now — what could possibly have sent you out here with such urgency?"

Nadya swallowed back her own arguments — they would indeed talk about this later — and pulled a note from her dress pocket. She held it out to him. "A letter from Danika."

Adrik skimmed the parchment. "Did she make it home safely?"

"The Kotov Isles were attacked. Maksis broke his promise."

Exclamations of shock echoed through the clearing. Elin shoved her flask into Yulian's chest and lurched forward. "Mama and Papanik? Zin and Mikhail?"

"Safe now," said Nadya. "But Mikhail suffered some kind of head injury and Papanik..."

Her gaze returned uncertainly to Papa, whose mouth formed a grim line. "Say it."

"Papanik lost an arm."

"Whoresons!" Elin shouted. "We must go back! We must attack!"

"Attack who, dear Elin?" said Avdotya coolly. He stepped up to take his usual place at Adrik's right-hand side. "Would you turn your saber on Maksis or the Jinmen? We already plan to do the former and the latter would be foolhardy at best."

"Do not call me a fool!" Elin stomped her boot, face now redder than Davin's. "The Jinmen should pay for this!"

"Which is exactly what Maksis hopes you'll do — be so distracted fighting a foreign enemy that you've no resources left to expend on him."

Avdotya's words settled like a rock in Nadya's stomach — not that she was overly concerned with revenge. Jinmen raids were a way of life among the Kotov, though they had not experienced one so devastating since Nadya was younger than Mikhail. Still, something had to be done. "I would like to go back," said Nadya. "See how I may help."

"Go back?" Adrik's golden eyes blazed. He shoved Danika's letter off on Avdotya, who merely gave it a snide glance and passed it on to Kliment. "What can you possibly hope to do? The battle has come and gone."

"My people need me there!"

"Your people are here!" The finality of his words rang louder than any gunshot. It was a long while before Adrik dared to break the ringing silence. "We should write to Danika and tell her to gather what remains of the Kotov and bring them here. It was foolish to think we could defend both the Isles and wage a war on Sivka simultaneously. We should abandon the Kotov Isles until Maksis is dead."

"Whoreson!" Elin shouted again and lunged at Adrik, hands balled into fists. Papa caught her around the waist, but it was a loose hold. He looked as likely to let her go as take a swing at Adrik himself.

"How can you say that?" said Nadya. "The Kotov Isles are our home. Your home too, now."

Adrik could not meet her eye. "They'll be safer here."

She edged closer to Adrik, though the gulf between them had never been wider. "The Eletskis are dead. Pierko and Noemi, Mindi and Manet are dead. Dondar is dead. Do these names mean anything to you or do you need more? Manet is the little girl you played with in the dooryard — the very day I began to think of you as more than an empty-headed brute. Pierko, Noemi and Mindi are Taito's Mama and Papa and little brother. Have you not taken enough from him that you must take his home too? And Dondar. He is Lukin's papa. You may fail to see it, but Lukin has been one of your staunchest warriors. Though I know perfectly well he does not do any of it for you. You would betray all of these people by giving in? By giving away their ancestral home to the man you despise more than any other?" She inched forward until they were breathing the same crisp forest air. "If you do this, you will be no husband of mine."

His grip tightened on the barrel of his gun. "I have to do something."

"Send supplies. Send more men if you must. But do not take from a people who have nothing left."

A short jerk of his head was all the acquiescence Nadya could hope for. When she stepped back, she saw Avdotya and Kliment watching her shrewdly.

Adrik was breathing hard — his frustration, his helplessness palpable. Nadya understood better than most. A squeaking sound from the undergrowth caught her attention. Just beyond the timberline, a red chipmunk trampled lightly through the forest. It had a white snout and an acorn between its paws.

Adrik took three short steps forward and shot it between the eyes.

It was the second tennight of Spring when Babbin approached. Danika was straddling a large wooden truss in the yard outside Babbin's hut, imbuing the new timbers that had arrived from Old Kirov with the *Wet Wood* tincture. "At least they will be protected in the next Luncycle," Danika said to Babbin.

The old alkhemist crouched down beside her in the wide field. "You are beginning to think in the long way," she said approvingly.

The Isles had made much progress in the last few tennights — most of the structures were now whole and sound, if not the people. Even the turfhouse was nearing completion. They had laid the new floor and replaced the dining table thanks to a special delivery from the Imperator. Mama was clearly eager to have her own space and her own kitchen to violate once more. For her part, Danika was all too happy to delay the reconstruction efforts a little longer. She did not feel ready to return to Old Kirov.

"You must leave soon," Babbin said, as ever sensing the direction of Danika's thoughts. "You have more important work to do than building houses."

Danika's lips pinched. "I thought you did not approve of Adrik's war."

"The boy's war, no. But yours... I still have faith in you, Little Nika." Danika's stomach squirmed. It never seemed to settle these days. "Do not stray from your mission now. Do what good you can with what time you have." Babbin's pale eyes met hers, but Danika could not read them. Whatever Babbin knew or did not know about the man calling himself Adrik Solov, her words were true. The path was set. Danika could not turn from it now.

She announced their imminent departure the next day. Cousin Shelia was present, pouring cups of cold cider into tin pails as they ate a lunch of pickled cucumbers and salted watermelon in the yard outside the turfhouse.

Shelia's presence was a constant these days, ever nipping at the heels of a sullen Lukin, perking up like an eager pup every time he deigned to look her way. Danika hoped she herself did not behave so desperately around Adrik.

As they finished their meal and the party broke up, Lukin took Shelia by the hand and pulled her around the back of the house and out of sight. Danika stared at the spot where they had disappeared, then gave herself a shake and resolved to make her long-dreaded approach to Mama.

It was easier than expected. Danika had not even needed to mention the hypothetical child. She only had to say, "Nadya has asked for you," and Mama began packing.

Shelia emerged from behind the turfhouse a short time later. She looked mussed, but not in the way Danika had expected. Her eyes were puffy and red, and tears splattered down her cheeks. Lukin appeared a moment later, utterly stone-faced.

The night before their departure, Danika could find no rest. She lay in the newly constructed bed loft, aching for Nadya, even as Zin panted at her other side. She thought of all that had transpired in the last two seasons. Even Danika could admit that she had been hiding here on the Kotov Isles. Hiding from all she had wrought and all she feared was still to come. She had half-convinced herself that this was just another holiday from Izumgray, untouched by the true problems of the wider world. But Danika's burdens had followed her across the Swansea and no doubt they would do so again if she did not address them soon.

She slipped from the bed, taking a fur to drape over her shoulders to ward against the ever-present chill that had lingered well into Spring. It was unusually dark in the house. Mama's oratorium had been rebuilt, but the relics from her old life — the idols and the fine copy of the Velvet Book — were turned to ash.

A dim glow emanated from the doorway into the main hall. Danika followed it and found Mama sitting at the table, features distorted by the light of a single taper. The open fires at either end of the long room sat cold and empty — no one had the nerve to reignite them, despite the bite in the air.

Danika dropped onto the bench across from Mama as if this were a pre-arranged meeting. And perhaps it was. A meeting that had been put off for far too long.

"Shelia has agreed to come here to live," said Mama, staring down at her pale hands, clasped tightly together atop the table. "She will look after Papanik and Zin and Mikhail while I am away."

Danika said nothing, though she was surprised at Shelia's generosity. She pulled the fur tighter over her shoulders and waited for Mama to work up the courage to say what was truly on her mind.

"I cannot look at you, Danika."

Danika licked her dry lips. Her voice cracked when she answered, "I know."

"It is not for the reasons you think. It is not dislike I feel when I look at you, but my own shame." A lump pressed painfully against Danika's throat. Mama's eyes were black over the candle flame. "Does it mean anything to you that I have learned my lesson?"

"Have you?" Danika's tone was sharper, more accusing than she intended. Or perhaps she had intended it. There was so much anger banging at the doors of her teeth, begging to be set free.

"I took Mikhail to Babbin right away."

"And I am grateful for that."

She was, truly. She only wished Mama had reached the same conclusion as swiftly for her.

The symptoms had shown early — though it was only in hindsight that they realized it.

The day after Danika had gone for a swim alone in the lagoon, she tried to sneak a gingersnap from the kitchen and been caught out by a gasp of pain in her arm — sharp like the lick of hot flame. Danika, only 10 years old at the time, thought nothing of it, far too concerned with Mama's scolding.

Papa and Papanik were away on raid. She missed them both terribly, felt like a criminal just for walking about her own house without them there. Mama always seemed to be angry at her for something — ever since Danika had discovered her Fire the season before.

When her first blood came in and she had seen the evidence before her, she had stolen Papa's knife, went behind the shed, and cut her palm in the shape of a star. Then she lit it. Danika held the silver flame in her palm, feeling like Thoth themself had reached down and blessed her.

Then she caught fire to the barn and had to run to Papa to put it out. He beat her bottom raw — she had never seen him so angry — but it was worth it to be an alkhemist.

Mama had not seemed to think so. Was her anger because Danika's Fire was silver and Nadya's was only blue? Danika had thought her Mama would be proud of the gift.

The night after her own body betrayed her for stealing a cookie, Danika lay awake with a pounding pressure in her head. By morning, she was alternately sweating and shivering. She climbed slowly out of bed and collapsed halfway down the ladder.

As she sank into fever's delirium, there were vague memories of Mama covering her torso with dew-laden peach leaves, Nadya tying sliced onions to the soles of her feet.

The fever broke, though her body still ached for days — nothing worse than the sharp pain that radiated up her arms and legs. She asked — once — to go to Babbin, but Mama refused her with a simple, "We do not require alkhemist tricks for growing pains."

Instead, Mama knelt at the oratorium and prayed.

Then, one morning, as Danika stumbled into the kitchen, her right leg dropped to to the floor — hard — and against her will.

Mama, Nadya and Elin stopped to stare. Danika's foot had begun to curl in on itself. Mama knelt with whispered words to The Father for another two days.

By that point, the fever returned, and she could hear Nadya's pleas from where Danika writhed in a bedcloset in the hall. She could no longer make the climb up the ladder to the loft.

She did not know what day it was when Mama finally succumbed and carried her down the hill to the Mad Old Alkhemist. She only knew that it was too late.

"Pah, pah," Babbin said as she circled Danika's quivering body. She had not stood up in days, but Babbin insisted it was necessary for the examination. "You should have come sooner."

Mama said nothing to that. "What is it?"

Babbin stopped circling to peer into Danika's face. At that time, they had nearly been the same height. "Tuck your chin to your chest."

Danika tried, but it was no use.

"Leave her here. We must keep her separate from the other children."

"What *is* it?" Mama said again, arms crossed, teeth gnashed.

"The Swimming Sickness. It is too late for this one. Her legs will be gone by tomorrow, but the others may be spared if you take this to them right away."

Babbin shoved several small vials into Mama's hands. Danika stared down at her feet. Her legs would be gone? They would just...disappear?

In the end, her legs did not disappear, but they may as well have for all the use they did her. Mama came to visit each night. For a little while. On one of the nights, Babbin told her, "I am working on a medicine. It will be done in a tennight."

"It will cure her?"

"No. But, if she takes it regularly, it will give her use of her legs. Until—"

"Until the Suncycle."

"Yes."

By the fifth day, her fever broke for good. All that was left was to wait for Babbin's medicine. But when night fell and Mama had still not visited, Danika began to weep. She asked Babbin if she was still dangerous, if she would ever be able to go home again. Babbin said, "Pah, pah," tossed back a purple vial, and carried Danika home.

As they passed through the gate, violet flames sprang into view. An enormous bonfire burned on the front lawn. Mama threw a familiar bundle of blankets onto the fire, followed by Danika's pillow, then her favorite doll — the one Papa had brought back to her from Norgay. Danika stared, transfixed. She had never seen her mother use alkhemical Fire.

"Pah, pah," Babbin said, and turned back down the path they came. "She will come for you tomorrow. You will see."

But Mama did not return. Danika laid in Babbin's hut another five days. And after she drank her potion, she walked back home alone.

Nine years later, Danika stared out of the hall into the darkened entry room — to the oratorium where Mama had knelt, futilely, for so many crucial days.

"You must know I regret it," Mama said.

"Must I?"

"It is because of my regret that I cannot— That we will never—"

"That you can never love me the way you do Nadya."

Mama said nothing. Danika swallowed. It was not a resolution, but it was some kind of peace to understand why it would never change between them. It was also one less burden to carry back to Old Kirov.

20. A DANCE WITH DESTINY

Adrik breathed deep the scent of timber and woodsmoke as the carriage rattled up the long gravel drive. The whole of Adrik's new court had gathered to meet the newcomers at the base of the stairs leading into the Palace at Old Kirov. It was a chill Spring day, the skies were clear, and Adrik didn't know whether he was more eager to see his alkhemist, or for his wife to see her sister.

Nadya had been in a foul temper ever since Danika's departure, a mood that only worsened when they received the unwelcome news of the attack on the Kotov Isles. Adrik had, eventually, come round to Nadya's way of thinking. To give up the Isles would be to admit defeat to Maksis and Adrik could never do that.

The carriage shuddered to a halt and Marisha, Danika, and Lukin tumbled out, looking dusty, travel worn, and utterly exhausted of each other's company. Apparently, Marisha couldn't be persuaded to take the journey on foot no matter how many tinctures her daughter offered. As a result, they'd had to make do with horse and carriage. Of course, no potion could make a horse trot any faster, but certain elixirs did make the carriage lighter and swifter.

Adrik pulled Danika off her feet with the force of his embrace. She squirmed stiffly in his arms, which only amused him further. He ruffled her hair as he set her down, noting that it was nearly as long as Nadya's now.

Rodin, meanwhile, greeted his wife with a passion Adrik only hoped he and Nadya still possessed at that age. When Rodin finally released Marisha, she took one look up at the Palace at Old Kirov and said, "It is smaller than I remember."

Her children shared awed looks and Adrik remembered abruptly that, until she had been shipped off to the Kotov Isles at age 17 to marry Rodin, this palace had been Marisha's home.

Nadya pulled her mama close. "Thank you for coming."

Marisha pressed a kiss to Nadya's temple. "My darling." She stepped back to examine her eldest with an appraising eye. The Impress was radiant as ever, but Adrik knew Marisha was not assessing Nadya so much as Adrik and how well he was taking care of her.

"You look well," Marisha said finally and Adrik's shoulders relaxed. "Better than I expected."

Nadya beamed. "I have much to tell you. You too, Nika."

But Danika didn't seem overeager for her sister's company. "Soon," she said. "I must give Adrik a full report of our time on the Isles."

"And we should start planning our final strike against Maksis," said Adrik, who was far more interested in that future than rehashing the failures of the past.

"Indeed!" cried a sanctimonious voice from the line of courtly onlookers. "My men are eager for their next victory!"

Kliment sashayed forward. He was a man whose presence was often too easy to forget. Perhaps that was why he chose to wear such vibrantly colored uniforms. Today it was lime green silks with a violet feathered hat. "My darling Aunt Marisha," he said, bowing deeply before Nadya's mama. "How wonderful it is to meet you at last."

Marisha blinked at him and Adrik threw a panicked look to Avdotya, who rolled his eyes to the Above. He cleared his throat and dramatically pronounced, "Marisha Bodanson. Allow me to introduce Grand Duke Kliment. It's to him that we owe our success at Old Kirov."

Adrik bristled at that descriptor. Similarly, Danika's expression turned sour. But Adrik knew better than to argue the point in front of Kliment, especially given that his forces now outnumbered the Kotov two-to-one — even if they were an army who hadn't so much as wet their blades.

Marisha ducked into a seasoned curtsy. "Nephew. I am grateful to you for all you've done to help my family."

It was an odd exchange of pleasantries given that Kliment was several years Marisha's senior and looked even older than that, despite being her nephew. Marisha was one of Maksis' two half-siblings, born much later and to a stepmother he'd roundly despised. Rumor persisted that for that reason alone, the Lunovna Imperator bore no love for his youngest brother and sister.

Kliment pressed a sloppy kiss to Marisha's hand. Rodin was scowling now too, though his wife bore a perfect mask of politeness. A true Sivkan.

"Now that we've all got reacquainted, the Imperator has some exciting news." Avdotya clapped his hands together and looked to Adrik as if offering him a great gift instead of a great distraction.

Adrik heaved a sigh and said between gritted teeth, "Avdotya has decided we should hold a ball to close the Aadan's Day celebrations."

"We went on parade shortly after your departure and it was a great success," Avdotya said, overstating things more than a little. "Now that word has spread of Adrik's presence in the city, a ball should draw an even bigger crowd."

"But Aadan's Day has not yet been reinstated?" Danika said with a raised eyebrow.

Avdotya's lips pursed. "Why let such trivialities get in the way of good politics? It will be an excellent chance to make new allies before we take the fight to Maksis in New Kirov."

This was the point Avdotya had used to convince Adrik of the plan. Maksis was safely ensconced in New Kirov with Grand Duchess Petrovia's Taigan army, and now Grand Duke Pytor's Southreach forces, at his disposal. If they were to mount a successful strike, they would need more than a handful of Kotov and the warriors of the Steppe to do it.

"Pardon me, sirs. But I've an urgent letter for you."

Adrik turned to find a small servant boy in vassal's rags cowering at his elbow. He held a letter out to Avdotya, pale face blanched in terror. The folded note trembled in his small grasp. An inexplicable wave of fondness — and pity — washed over Adrik. "Well, Dunya? Take the note and let the boy get on with his day." He flashed the child a grin and the boy smiled back, hand steadied slightly.

"Who's it for?" Dunya sneered down at the paper.

The boy looked at the note face where a name was scrawled on the front. "I—I don't know, sir. I can't read it."

Dunya scowled deeper and Adrik sighed, grabbing the note himself. The child jumped about a foot — obviously, he'd been told not to touch the Imperator. "Honestly, this is why educational reform is at the top of my agenda once Maksis is dead. Kliment — the letter is for you."

Adrik held the parchment out to the Grand Duke, who quickly unfolded the missive. His eyes widened with every line read. At the end, he stared up at them all, expression lodged somewhere between nausea and glee. "My mama is dead," he said to resounding gasps from the courtiers still lining either side of the palace stair. "Apparently, Grand Duchess Petrovia Lunovna took ill on the road to New Kirov. Not even Maksis' best alkhemists were able to save her."

The exclamations of shock behind Adrik had turned to whispers. It set his teeth on edge. Usually, Sivkans waited until they were behind closed doors to start their scheming. But to the people of Old Kirov, the death of the Grand Duchess of the Taiga would come second in importance only to the fall of Maksis himself.

"I'm sorry for your loss, Kliment," said Adrik. "She lived a long life. Take solace in that."

"I will, Imperator. If you'll excuse me, I think I will retire to my quarters while I absorb this tragic news."

"Of course."

Kliment bounced off, barely able to conceal the skip in his step. Adrik looked around at the rest of the gathered crowd. Like Kliment, they seemed torn between shock and the kind of giddy elation that only came from ill news.

"You're all dismissed," he said.

The group quickly scattered. Nadya took her Mama's hand and led her up the stairway. Marisha, at least, seemed no worse off for the news of the death of her half-sister. Danika made to follow, but Adrik called out, "Nika — wait."

She paused with a foot on the bottom step. "Yes?"

"Meet me in the library. I'd like to hear your recounting of the attack on the Isles." He stepped closer and pitched his voice low. "And with this news, there will be a power vacuum in the Taiga — I'd like your advice on how to fill it."

For all that Nadya had taken after their Mama in looks, Danika had clearly inherited Marisha's talent for inscrutability. She simply said, "Yes, Imperator," and started up the stairs.

"She's too young for the burden you've placed on her," said Avdotya — clearly eavesdropping.

A wave of indignation rolled over him. "Did you ever think perhaps I'm too young for the one you've placed on me?"

Avdotya offered no rebuttal.

Danika refused Nadya's invitation to dress for the ball together. She would explain later that she had been consumed by her fires — it would not be the first time, and it would not be a lie. The last few tennights, she had employed every excuse in her arsenal to keep distance between herself and her sister. As ever, her greatest tool in this quest was alkhemy. Danika's latest attempt at the Philosopher's Stone had resulted in nothing more than a smoking crater at the bottom of her cauldron. She had to bathe three times to rid the acrid smell from her hair.

When she emerged from the bath, Danika found a gown waiting for her on the bed. She approached it with trepidation. Rumor was that Nadya and the Kotov boy, Davin, had taken it upon themselves to invent a new style for Adrik's reign. And as a member of the Imperator's council, Danika was expected to don the uniform.

As she picked up the softly shimmering velvet garment, Danika was reminded never to doubt her sister in matters of fashion. It was as different as it was possible to be from the overwrought, overstuffed styles she had seen on the ladies of Old Kirov so far. The navy dress cut narrowly on Danika's hips. It had tight-fitting long sleeves and a high neck. All along the gown, exquisite silver beading shifted and spiraled in patterns that mimicked the moon and stars.

There were even knee-high velvet boots to wear beneath it. If Danika could find a complaint, it was that there was nowhere to store her vials or blades. But it seemed Davin had even thought of that — as she buttoned the boots along her calves, she discovered a half dozen narrow pockets waiting to be armed.

The dancing had already begun by the time she entered the ballroom.

It was not a room Danika had much occasion to enter — not since that first day when they had been clearing the halls of Adrik's enemies. Though it had changed little in structure since then, it was transformed now by the hundreds of attendees, dressed in their finest furs and silks, gliding across the parquet as the orchestra played an upbeat tune from the balcony.

The mingled aroma of salt beef and mulled wine set Danika's mouth watering. Those who were not dancing had cups in hand, conversing loudly at the perimeter. Nadya had draped the walls in blue velvet, and the silver light from the chandeliers hung unsuspended overhead — thanks no doubt to a skilled artisanal alkhemist.

But it was the windows at the far wall that drew Danika's eye. They soared some five storeys high, offering a breathtaking view of the softly falling snow and the twilit city below.

It was a late storm — even for Old Kirov. But it provided such a picturesque backdrop to the festivities that she doubted there would be many complaints.

A familiar shoulder collided with Danika's side. Elin had stumbled across the dance floor, careening between two couples without the slightest concern for decorum. She clearly had been at the drink, as she proclaimed, "Mulled wine, Nika — it is better than vodka, I swear it."

"It is a good thing then that your dress is red," Danika said, eyeing her sister's mussed braid and melted face. "Better to hide the stains."

"I will give you a stain if you do not—"

"I hardly recognized you in blue," a familiar, unwelcome voice whispered in Danika's ear. She spun. It could not be — but it was.

"Earnest." It was a hollow greeting. Her old teacher smiled — he had lost none of his swagger since betraying them to Maksis' Lun-Protektorate. He wore his finest silks — the ones she had only ever seen on high holidays at Izumgray. It was unfathomable to her now that she had ever found this man, with his graying auburn hair and weak chin, attractive. "What are you doing here?"

Elin, always a little slower on the uptake, was squinting at Earnest as if trying to place him. When she finally did, she grabbed for a whip that was absent from her belt. "You should be in the dungeons!"

Earnest bowed simperingly. "Fortunately for me, this Imperator is much more forgiving than the last. He's granted amnesty to all who wish to hear his vision for a new a world. Especially those from Izumgray."

Danika stepped close. Elin may not have had her weapons, but Danika's boot was full of tinctures that would make Earnest rue the day he turned his back on her. "I gave you that chance. You betrayed it."

"A fact I'm sorry for now. Please, Nika. We're old friends. Surely, that merits me a little forgiveness?"

Danika kicked up her heel, ready to show Earnest just how much he had earned, when she was interrupted yet again— "Pardon me, but are you Nedeshda Bodanson? Marisha's eldest?"

An older man had approached. He had a strong bearing and a full brown beard dusted with gray. His white kaftan bore a prominent silver sash and his epaulets spoke of some rank Danika could not decipher. When she continued to stare at him blankly, he gave a short bow at the neck. It allowed Danika a moment to inspect his full head of hair. Impressive at his age. Earnest was likely twenty years younger and more receding.

"I am Gavril Voyavich Lunovna. Your mama is my sister."

Danika gaped. This was the Grand Duke of the Tundra — he was also the only full-blood sibling Mama possessed.

"Uncle Gavril," she said, pushing her anger with Earnest to one side at the same moment that Elin literally shoved him off into the crowd. A hotheaded sister did have its uses. Danika offered her hand. "I am not Nedeshda, though I am flattered you think me dressed well enough for an Impress. I am Danika — Marisha's second daughter."

Gavril's brown eyes widened, then he smiled ruefully. "Of course — the alkhemist. I see it now in your gown. Exquisite by the way. I'm afraid my dress is a little inappropriate for the occasion. Should one wear the battle uniform of one Imperator to the party of another? But alas, it was the only bit of finery I had that was not eaten by mothballs. In the Tundra, we're more interested in warmth than fashion."

Danika laughed, finding herself instantly charmed by the gentleman — and not solely because he had confused her for Nadya. He reminded her greatly of Papa. "You do yourself proud, Uncle. I too am unused to the finer things. This has been an adjustment for us all. Are you enjoying the party?"

"I am. I must say I'm surprised at the number of Grand Dukes you have managed to gather here — especially to celebrate a usurper." Gavril flashed her a wink. "Five principalities in Sivka and Adrik has managed to bring three of them to bear tonight. Myself from the Tundra, Kliment from the Steppe, and Ostrov from the Mountains."

Gavril nodded to the dance floor where a handsome man of middling age twirled a young lady in a pale blue dress. Like Gavril, Ostrov wore his military uniform, though his was the color of gray rock instead of white snow.

"Of course, Pytor would never abandon Maksis or Southreach, and Petrovia is much too dead to be attending parties. So given all that, you've quite the turnout."

Danika laughed again. "Unfortunately, dancing with someone is not the same as going to battle with them. Perhaps you and I could—"

A tinkling of silverware on glass cut through the music and the attendees turned as one toward the windows, where Adrik and Nadya stood, shining in their dual magnificence.

Davin had dressed the couple to match. They each wore navy velvet — Adrik with a floor-length overcoat, broad in the shoulders and fitted at the waist. Gold beading in sunburst patterns trimmed his lapel. His mirror in every way, Nadya's own gown was unadorned, an elegant off-the-shoulder cut with tight sleeves and a flowing skirt. But it was her cape that was the true star. Fixed at her collarbone by an ornate gold necklace and sapphire jewels, the cape swept behind her in an open back, trimmed with golden comets. The simple iron crowns from their wedding day sat atop their heads and the snow falling behind them could not have set off their image more perfectly.

Danika leaned in to Gavril. "That is Nedeshda. You see now why I laughed at your mistake."

But Gavril shook his head. "I see Marisha in you both."

Danika hid her blush as Adrik raised his glass.

"Nadya and I wish to thank all of you for coming," he said. "This place was once a beacon of art and music, alkhemy and science, partnership and justice. Under Maksis' reign, that legacy turned sour. But it's here, now, this very night, that we will begin anew and restore Old Kirov to its magnificence — not just within Sivka, but the world over."

Adrik's words were met with an uneasy round of applause. As a rule, Sivkans did not trust foreigners, but Avdotya and Kliment stood in the wings on either side of Adrik and Nadya, leading the adulations. Kliment was dressed rather less ostentatiously than usual in dark green — perhaps Davin had persuaded him to conform to the new style.

"We still have far to go on our journey," Adrik continued. "And I won't stop until I see all of Sivka rid of Maksis' stranglehold. But until that time comes, I wish to share some blessed news with our friends, family, and allies."

Adrik smiled down at Nadya, who beamed back at him. A shard of ice began to freeze just below Danika's ribcage. She knew the words he would speak before they were uttered. But still, when they came, they knocked her backwards.

"My wife is with child. The next Imperator—"

"Or Impress—" Nadya interjected.

"Yes, of course, or Impress," Adrik conceded, inciting a riot of laughter, "will be with us soon. The Solov dynasty has been reborn."

"Cheers to the child," Avdotya called, raising his glass high. Even across the sea of revelers, his black eyes seemed to fix on Danika.

"Cheers to the child," the crowd echoed back.

The music started again. Coattails and skirts swirled around Danika in a joyous tidal wave.

"Are you quite well, Niece?" said Gavril, catching her elbow. "Do you need to sit down?"

"No. I am fine, thank you. I just— I think I must be going—"

But then a deep voice reverberated in her ear: "Dance with me."

She turned to find Lukin. His gaze radiated understanding. He knew what had left her frozen, paralyzed as the dancers tried futilely to skip around her. She noted a few hostile looks and caught snatches—

"That's the *alkhemist*."

"The Impress' sister. Can you believe it?"

Danika nodded numbly and Lukin swept her into motion. It was a lively song, which was fortunate. Much like in battle, keeping pace forced her to focus on one step after the next and not the rhythmic tune in her head, singing, *"Cheers to the child! Cheers to the child!"*

Soon enough the song switched from a group dance to a partnered waltz. Lukin made the transition easily. She followed his lead, not merely because it was the done thing, but because she could think of no other option. There was comfort in dancing with Lukin, the rhythm of it, the distance, and then the welcome return — his hands were as familiar as her own, his movements predictable and sure.

"May I cut in?"

Adrik's smile cut through all of it.

He cast an imposing figure on the dance floor in his navy and gold coat. He was meant to be an Imperator, after all, and tonight he sparkled like one. He swept her away without waiting for Lukin's response. "You've been avoiding me, Nika. Nedeshda, too."

Danika focused her gaze on the golden sunburst on his lapel. "I do not think so."

"I do. Even now, you won't meet my eye."

Defiantly, Danika looked up. His eyes were as startling as ever, glimmering in the precise shade as his trim. Even knowing what she knew now, knowing that he was no closer to Solov than any vassal off the road, it blinded her.

"That's better." He grinned. "I'd hate to think anything could come between us, Nika. I need your counsel and your expertise."

Expertise that in a mere seventy days would be as dull and worthless as the blood in her veins, as the life in her legs.

"There are few I trust more than you."

Danika smothered an inappropriate, humorless laugh. Trust. Where exactly did Adrik's faith in her stem from? He had no idea how false it was. No idea that it too would turn to ash if he ever discovered the secrets — the lies — she kept from him. Did it make her any better than Avdotya? Did it make her a traitor to her people? A traitor who, if she had only revealed the truth, might have saved her homeland?

"I see the thoughts whirling behind your eyes, but I know you won't share them with me."

"You could not handle it if I did."

His laughter rumbled warmly against her breast. "Probably true."

They took a wide turn around the north end of the room. A buffet had been set out. The dance floor emptied as the attendees began to gather around the food. She looked for Kliment at the head of the line, but either he had left the ballroom or his green silks camouflaged him better than she realized.

"Nika," Adrik said, a serious note in his voice that drew her attention. "You've made sacrifices for our cause — my cause — I know that. Please understand that I would never have gotten this far without you." She swallowed around the knot in her throat. "So whatever it is that troubles you... make peace with it. We're going to need you at your best when we defeat Maksis."

There was no arguing with that steely glint in his eye or Babbin's words ringing in her ears. *Do not stray from your mission now*, she had said. And how could she? If not for his sake, then at least for her own.

Seventy days...

A long table had been erected in front of the high windows for the Imperator and his closest advisors. Nadya sipped her wine, wondering what she had done for good or ill to deserve a seating next to Avdotya.

"Ostrov should be our next target. As Grand Duke of the Mountains, he sits on the outskirts of Sivka. He's far removed from Maksis in the family tree and his army is significant given that he must man the border between Sivka and the Jinmen Empire."

Avdotya had been scheming through the entire first course into the second and it was not talk that aided Nadya's digestion. Adrik, meanwhile, should have had Kliment at his right — clearly the worse bargain of the two — but the Grand Duke had not turned up for his meal yet, and so Adrik and Danika were chatting amicably over his empty chair.

Mama sat on Avdotya's other side, engaging him politely while Nadya long ago gave up feigning interest. "What of Gavril? After me, he is Maksis' least favorite sibling and to have survived the Tundra so long shows significant strength."

Avdotya waved a dismissive hand, displaying just how little weight he placed on Mama and her complex family ties. "What can Gavril offer us but chunks of ice and somewhere to stash our prisoners?"

"Might I interrupt?"

All three of them looked up from their plates into the face of Ostrov himself.

Nadya had not seen Ostrov since she was a girl — some four years old. He lived up to her memory of the handsome foreign stranger that had come to stay while Papa was off on raid. More silver in the hair perhaps, but that suited him too. He wore that hair short and slicked back in the Sivkan style. He had neither beard, nor was he clean shaven, but sported a dusting of stubble along the sharp line of his jaw. He did not have Papa's bulk or roughness, but unlike another Grand Duke of Nadya's acquaintance, he had not let his privilege eat away at his physique. He wore a silk amber kaftan that tapered nicely at his waist and a matching cape trimmed in fur.

"Impress," he said, bowing deep to Nadya. She offered him her hand and he kissed the back of it lightly. That he was already calling her by her title seemed a promising start. He straightened to greet her with a more casual smile. "Who would have thought that the next time I'd meet little Nedeshda it would be here, in these circumstances?"

"Certainly not I," said Nadya with a laugh.

Slowly, inevitably, Ostrov turned to Mama.

Davin had fit the entire family well for the occasion, but Mama looked particularly radiant in her emerald gown with her black hair trailing elegantly down her shoulders. "Ostrov," she said. "It is good to see you again."

"Marisha," he whispered, then mimicked the same bow and kiss he had bestowed on Nadya. "Or should I call you Dowager Impress?"

Mama's lips twisted. "You may call me that, but do not expect me to know to answer."

He smiled softly, gray eyes scanning her face. "Twenty some years... you haven't changed."

"You have never been a liar, Ostrov. Do not tell me it is *you* who has changed."

"Far too little, I fear."

They shared a look so full of meaning that Nadya found herself casting about for Papa. What met her instead was a pale and sweaty-faced Davin.

"Pardon me, Impress. But I am hearing reports throughout the city. I am afraid—" Davin's eyes shifted to the empty chair between Danika and Adrik. His panicked tone caught the pair's attention. As all eyes fell upon Davin, his hands began to shake. "I have heard that Grand Duke Kliment's soldiers are attempting to seize the city."

Adrik lurched out of his chair. "What? What do you mean?"

If possible, Davin went paler. "They are saying that Maksis has offered Kliment his mother's seat in exchange for— in exchange for—"

"For what, Davin?" snapped Danika. "Speak quickly!"

"The murder of you and your family."

21. SHIFTING SEASONS

"You must flee, Imperator," Davin said. "You must run now before they take the palace."

Nadya's hand fell automatically to her belly. She had faced the threat of Maksis wrath before, but that time the child in her womb had been nothing but a wish. Now, she could feel it pulsing inside her more and more with each passing day. The thought of losing it, of never seeing its face, watching it grow into adulthood, was an agony beyond reckoning.

"We must fight back," said Adrik. "Rally the Kotov! We won't abandon the city."

Nadya turned to Danika and saw the same concern reflected in her sister's eyes. There were barely any Kotov remaining to defend them. Kliment had twice their number in Old Kirov alone. Thoth only knew if he had more laying in wait....

As word began to spread, the music stopped. The voices in the ballroom turned from loud and boisterous to hushed and panicked. Nadya noticed for the first time the vacant posts at the doors. And then there was the empty seat at the table... There was no denying Kliment's betrayal.

Papa chose that moment to appear at Davin's side. His saber was gripped tight in his hand. Four Kotov warriors trailed behind him. "You have heard?"

Adrik seemed too numb to answer. A muscle ticked in his jaw and his hands were balled into fists. He scanned the ballroom as if searching for some miraculous solution, but Nadya knew what needed to be done. "We have," she said. "What is our best route for escape?"

"There are a number of paths out of the city through the woods, but Kliment may know them better than we do. We should break up. Flee in small parties and regroup elsewhere."

"The alkhemists," said Danika. Where Adrik had gone blind with fury, her stormy eyes were focused. "We cannot leave them or the scientists. Without them, we lose any advantage we have against Maksis." Her gaze shifted to Nadya and Mama just behind her. "The Imperator and Impress should go now. Lukin and I will try to gather the others."

"I will join you," said Papa.

"Rodin — no!" Mama's hands tightened on the back of her chair as she stared across the table at her husband.

"Nadya and Adrik will need someone to accompany them," Danika argued.

"I'll do it," said Ostrov. They all turned to stare at the unintended interloper in their conference. Ostrov had a sword at his hip and gripped the pommel as only a man who knew how to weild it could. He met Papa's eyes and said in the voice of a vow, "I'll get them to safety."

It was these words that seemed to snap Adrik out of his reverie — the words or the threat of the alternative. "Thank you for your assistance, Grand Duke. Between you, myself, and Yulian, we'll make a strong party. We'll gather as many others as we can on the way out."

"But keep the group small," Danika reminded him. "No more than ten."

"We should send someone to the armory," said Rodin. "Order them to retrieve what weapons they can and destroy the rest."

Adrik nodded tightly. "Yes. I don't want those guns falling into Maksis' hands."

"And what of the Kotov Host?" said Mama, looking between Adrik and Papa. Nadya was struck by the irony that she — the Sivkan — had asked the question that no one else could.

Papa and Adrik shared a grim look. In the end, it was Adrik who issued the order. "They will stay behind and cover our retreat. Tell them to meet us at the Broken Fork in Southreach. If they can."

Nadya gasped. "Adrik—"

"This is what soldiers are for, Nadya," Papa said, jaw set. "There is no victory without defeat."

Silence settled over them as true panic began to claim the hall. Partiers fled by the dozen. The sound of shattering glass echoed outside the doors. A tureen of mulled wine overturned and its contents spilled across the dance floor in a tide of scarlet.

"Go now," said Papa. "There is no more time to waste."

He caught Mama in a brief kiss over the table. Nadya squeezed Danika's hand before she was shuffled away. Nadya looked back to try to find her sister, but Danika was lost to the swarming crowd. Outside the high windows, snow continued to fall.

They could not save all the scientists. But Danika made sure to get every one of her six alkhemists out of the Palace at Old Kirov.

She would wonder, later, if she would have tried harder for those mundane men and women if they had the Fire in their blood. And she would know then, just as she suspected now, that she would have. Just as she would have fought harder for the scientists if Kliment's betrayal had come during the Suncycle instead of the Lun. As Papa had said, war was a game of numbers, and the living counted more than the dead.

Between Danika, Elin, Papa, Lukin and Gavril, who insisted on helping, they plucked Shura and three other alkhemists from the frightened crowd in the ballroom. The last two — Dominik and Leena — were found canoodling in the lab. As the pair broke up, Danika took the opportunity to gather her journals, starcharts and maps, she tucked them into the pockets of her white alkhemist coat, which hung off the back of a chair in front of the lab table with what remained of her last attempt at a Philosopher's Stone.

As their party set out into the woods — too large despite Danika's advice to Adrik — it occurred to Danika that none of them knew the terrain outside the city. They used her maps to navigate the forest to the Lun River, then followed it upstream, figuring it better to travel in the shadow of the mountains than to cross the open country of Southreach.

"Pytor will be looking for those fleeing the city," Gavril advised on the first night as they huddled by the riverbank to examine a map by dim moonlight. "I hope you have enough tricks in that coat to keep us hidden."

Fortunately, Danika did.

With a little help from Shura and the others, they chose potions brewed more for stealth than speed. So far as Danika knew, Adrik and Nadya had not taken any alkhemists in their party, which meant their reunion at the Broken Fork — if it came at all — would be a long ways off.

So they doused their coats in *Caden's Camouflage,* painted their faces and skin in *A Hint of Heat* to stave off the cold, and began their long march south.

The further south they drifted, the sparser the coniferous forest became, replaced by rock and then leafy trees the likes of which Danika had never seen before. Southreach was the one bit of Sivkan country Danika had never set foot on. The variety of its foliage and wildlife had her and the other alkhemists stopping a dozen times a day to forage for ingredients. With this much abundance to be found in the last dregs of Spring, her heart raced at the thought of what treasures Southreach might bloom in the Summer — the last season before the Suncycle dawned in the first week of Autumn.

Elin's patience snapped on the fifth day. "What is the point of these constant stops? It will all be useless soon enough!"

The force of six scathing looks silenced Elin so effectively that she did not utter another word for the rest of the day.

But Danika could not stop ruminating on Elin's words. They settled inside her like sand through an hourglass too wide at the mouth. Soon enough Danika would be buried beneath their weight.

On the seventh day, she, Papa and Gavril came upon a lush hillside still untouched by frost.

"I hope you accompanying us on this journey means you have joined our cause, Gavril," said Papa as he swung his saber through a bramble hedge in their path.

"I'm not sure how much good I would be to you. The Tundra's ranks are less than even the Kotov Host."

Papa's lips twisted. "The Host *has* shrunk considerably. And without Kliment..."

"Without Kliment, you don't stand a chance."

The finality of these words stopped both Danika and Papa in their tracks. Gavril winced. "I'm sorry to be so blunt, Rodin. But your forces have dwindled beyond hope of recovery. You won't even know the full strength of them until we reach The Broken Fork. Even then, I'm not optimistic. You can't hope to stage a coup against Maksis now, even if I were to join you. If you take my advice, you'll gather your family and flee to foreign shores. That's the only way you will escape Maksis' wrath."

They continued the rest of that day's trek in silence.

On the tenth day, they reached the shore. They planned to follow the coastline the rest of the two hundred miles to the Fork, but it was a dangerous road with few rocks or trees to cover their approach. Despite the chill in the air that seemed to grow colder every day, Danika suggested they replace *Hint of Heat* with a heady combination of her own design, which both quickened their pace and extended their endurance — *The Kotov Climb* — named after the ceremony every child undertook at the age of sixteen to join the Host. Under its power, they would only have to stop to rest one more night beneath the open sky.

That evening, after the brewing was done, Danika walked two miles from the camp to a rocky cove that hung over the sea. Its granite ledge provided the perfect perch to open her charts and stare up at the cloudless night sky. Izumgray was said to have the best view of the stars in all Sivka, but Danika thought that this place — somewhere at the country's edge, an endless ocean sprawled out beneath her dangling feet, so vast it made the Swansea seem nothing more than a pond — a close second.

"What are you doing all the way out here?" Lukin's voice did not shatter her solitude. It joined her in the sanctuary she had formed between the earth and the sea.

"Counting down the days."

"To what?"

The truth caught in her throat. She broke Lukin's gaze to stare down at her charts. "Until we are all reunited," she lied.

Lukin sighed. It was a melancholy sound, perfectly in harmony with the crush of the waves. He claimed the stony seat beside her, his hip a warm press against hers, and leaned forward to rest his elbows on his knees. "Until you are back with him."

Danika started. For once, her thoughts had been entirely elsewhere. "No. That is not— That is not what I—"

"I have decided I do not care for parties."

Danika blinked at Lukin, who stared out at the horizon, shoulders loose — looking for all the world as if he had not changed the subject to a time and place so many days, so many lives, away. She tried to join him there. To a ballroom where her biggest concern had been her own jealousy.

She forced a smile to her lips. "That is not true. You love parties. Remember when Shelia completed her Climb? I was sulking because Mama had me in the the kitchen peeling potatoes while everyone else was out celebrating. You snuck in with a bottle of vodka and we ate and drank every morsel before it ever made it out to the table."

She expected the memory to dredge up a grin from Lukin — or at least soften the dark set of his lips — but it did not.

"The two of us are not a party, Danika."

Something twisted painfully below her ribcage. "We are my favorite kind of party."

"You seemed to be enjoying yourself well enough, dancing with Adrik."

"Only because you had consoled me first."

"Yes. I did." The air between them turned scalding. "I was there first." He turned from the ocean to meet her eye and hold it. "I was here first, Nika." His voice was hushed. A shiver crawled up her spine. "And he is married."

The shiver turned to ice.

"I know that."

"To your sister."

"I know that, too. Do you think it could possibly have escaped me?"

"We cannot choose who we love, Danika. You do not to need to be wed to someone for it to be real. You do not even need them to feel the same."

"And I suppose you speak from experience?"

He could not have looked more hurt than if she had slapped him across the face. "Good night, Danika. I have had enough reminiscing for one night." He climbed to his feet and started back toward the beach.

She jumped up and caught him by the arm. "Wait. I am sorry. Please listen to me."

He turned in her grasp and she found herself clinging to him by his collar. Like the rest of them, he still wore his same clothes from the night of the ball. The difference was that he had dressed for that occasion just as he would have for any celebration on the Kotov Isles. The familiar softness of the doeskin beneath her fingers reminded her of home and she found herself desperate to pull it closer. She bowed her head so that it was pressed to the base of his throat, breathing deep the fur and ash and hint of metal that always lingered around Lukin even so far from the forge.

"I do not love him," she whispered fiercely, angrily.

"Nika—" His warm hands slipped beneath her alkhemist coat to settle on her hips.

"I do not. I do not."

She tilted her head up. He stared back at her, dark eyes swimming. She surged forward and caught his lips with hers.

He only hesitated a moment. One second of exquisite stillness.

Then he moved.

His lips, his hands, his feet. He put his whole body into the task. He returned her kiss with a passion Danika did not know he possessed for anything save the curve of an axe. His hands slipped up to her ribs, then shoved her coat off her shoulders. He pushed her back against the rock wall and pinned her there. She wrapped a leg around his hips, grateful that Davin had designed a dress so forgiving. She snaked a hand up his neck. He tried to pull away but she reigned him in by the fur on his collar. She started to push his own coat away and he finally broke free of her lips.

"Danika—"

"Hush now. Stop thinking so much."

His mouth opened. Then closed. Then returned to hers.

It was fitting in a way, that it happened between the stars and the sea. In the same liminal place where she had counted down the days until Adrik's great adventure would meet its ignoble end. There was no ignoring Adrik's presence between them here. In this way, they acknowledged it.

"Say my name," Lukin growled as she spread her legs and he slipped inside.

"Lukin," she said. "Lukin... Lukin..."

They sprawled together against the cliff-face for a long time afterward. The rocky outcrop pressed cold and hard against her bare shoulders, where Lukin's arm was soft and warm. His hair hung loose, brushing the hard line of his collarbone. The moonlight cast strange shadows over the plains of his torso, the bulge of his bicep, the sharpness of his jaw.

Tears sprang to her eyes and she looked away.

"Danika?" She turned her head further, but he shifted to lay over her, inescapable. "Danika?" He grabbed her chin with his thumb and forced her to look at him just as the first tear fell.

"You were right." He did not ask for clarification. He already knew. Still, she had to say it. For both their sakes. "We cannot choose who we love."

She closed her eyes and waited. It took him longer than she expected to release her. But, ever so slowly, his thumb fell from her chin, his fingertips broke from her arm. The warm blanket of his skin vanished. She listened to the sound of him gathering up his clothes, sliding into his boots, climbing down the ledge, and disappearing into the crashing of the waves.

There was no more time for starcharting after that.

They walked, and then climbed, another five days without rest. And when they finally came to the spot of the Broken Fork, where all three of its tributaries met in a low mountain clearing, there was no one else there waiting.

"They had no alkhemists," Papa reminded them. "They will be slower."

But as handfuls of the Kotov Host began to arrive the next day and the day after, and still there was no sign of Adrik or Nadya, Danika began to doubt.

"Their party was smaller than ours. Surely, even without alkhemy, they should be here by now," Danika whispered to Shura by the light of a silver fire on the sixth night.

Lukin sat several fires down, huddled with the hundred or so Kotov warriors who had arrived at dayfade. They had not spoken, nor so much as looked in each other's direction, since their night beneath the stars.

"Maybe they took a different path," said Shura. "Or got caught in a storm."

Her gaze lifted skyward, where indeed a torrential rain would have been dampening more than spirits were it not for *Rainy Day* — an elixir which sprouted an impenetrable bubble to shield beneath.

Danika approached Papa the next morning about sending out a search party, but he merely shook his head, casting a weary eye over the three-hundred Kotov warriors who had returned so far. "I will not sacrifice any more men for a hopeless cause."

When the rain stopped, restlessness drove Danika from the camp. She roamed the hillside, snipping seeds and blossoms from buckthorn, rowan trees, holly, and willow. She stumbled across a fox carcass and harvested the heart and liver.

If Adrik and Nadya did not come back...what then? Could they return to the Kotov Isles? Did Maksis know of the alkhemist that had sparked so much of Adrik's rebellion? And even if Maksis let Danika live, could she live with herself, going back to that place without her legs and without her sister?

She stopped at the northernmost fork in the river, watching as a flock of salmon swam upstream, their lithe pink bodies flailing against the tide.

Nadya and Adrik would return.

The tide would bring them in.

For once, her faith was not misplaced.

At suncrest the next day, the sentry cried out, "Man ho!" Danika raced to join him on his perch overlooking the valley and yelled, "Nadya!"

Danika sprinted down the hill, noting distantly that their party had grown from the one that set out from the ballroom so many nights ago. But she would do a headcount later, all that mattered now was squeezing Nadya's slight frame against hers — had she always been so brittle, so fragile? How could Danika ever have trusted anyone else to bring her to safety? She was angrier still with the way she had treated Nadya before the ball. Whatever her own selfishness, a child, especially Nadya's child, was to be celebrated. She did not think she had even offered her sister congratulations.... Tears stung Danika's eyes and she buried her face in Nadya's neck. Impossibly, she still detected a whiff of lavender beneath the sweat and dirt and...blood?

She pushed Nadya out of her arms and examined her with all the attention of a seasoned alkhemist. It took only a moment's appraisal to find it — a slight leaning to the left.

Danika lifted up Nadya's skirt, ignoring her sister's scandalized protests, and found her right calf poorly bandaged, a brown stain marring the white linen.

"What happened?" Danika demanded.

"Nothing. It was foolish. I slipped as we were crossing the river."

Danika's gaze rose to Nadya's belly. Nadya tracked the gesture and settled her hand over the slight swelling there.

"All is well. I am sure I would know if it was not."

Danika was not so sure. She grabbed Nadya's hand, intending to drag her into the camp's makeshift lab to see for herself, but Nadya was still talking, refusing to be moved.

"I was afraid to take any more brews until we arrived. I fear I delayed us by several days."

"Any *more* brews?" Danika said and, for the first time, looked around at the rest of the newcomers. "Who was supplying—"

"Nika, darling. How good to see you again." Earnest slithered out from behind Ostrov, smiling beatifically. "I saw the Imperator and the Impress racing through the halls and knew they must have intended to flee. I thought perhaps they could use someone with my skills on the road."

Danika's eyes narrowed. "You mean you saw a way to get out before Maksis caught you flirting with the enemy and you took it."

Earnest's dimples flashed. "An alkhemist should always think two steps ahead."

After tending to Nadya, Adrik's inner circle gathered by the fire in the fading dusk to debrief. Avdotya was as angry as Danika had ever seen him.

"Kliment will pay for this betrayal," he spat, pacing before the flames as the others shoveled spoonfuls of stew into their aching bellies. "He thinks Maksis' Taiga so much better than ours? Very well. We'll see how he enjoys life in the Tundra when we take the throne. And not as a Grand Duke — as an exile."

Adrik nodded, a fist pressed to his lips, eyes molten as he stared into the fire. But he was the only one to heed Avdotya's words. The others exchanged uneasy looks. Even Danika felt a hollow ache settle over her shoulders. She had Nadya back. What right did she have to ask for more?

"We should wait here another few days. See if more of the Host returns," said Papa. He stood behind Mama, who sat on a log, leaning back against his legs. Much like Danika and Nadya, the two had not parted since their reunion. "Then we should make for the sea. There I can find us a boat. Would Polvia still welcome you? Or perhaps Frexland? An ocean would be a good barrier to have between us and Maksis."

"Where exactly do you propose to go?" There was a steely edge to Adrik's voice, as sharp as any blade.

Papa's brow furrowed. "It will not do to linger here long. Pytor and Maksis will surely send search parties and our presence is not exactly subtle...."

"I'd offer you a home in the Tundra," said Gavril. "As I'm sure Ostrov would in the Mountains." The older man looked to Ostrov, who nodded curtly, gray eyes flicking to Mama. "But you're right — an ocean at least is needed to spare you."

"Spare us?" Adrik lurched toward Ostrov. "Spare us from *him?* I tell you now, there's no distance in this world that would spare Maksis from me. Not now, not ever."

Papa stepped between Adrik and Ostrov, a hand raised in Adrik's direction. "Look around you, my boy. You have a quarter of the weapons you once did. Seven alchemists. Five-hundred soldiers. *Five-hundred*. That is not an army. That is a death sentence."

Adrik's hands balled into fists. The firelight cast strange shadows across his face and his eyes sparked with the promise of fire. "I've faced a death sentence before. Twice. And lived."

"Then perhaps we should not test your luck a third time," said Papa.

Adrik launched forward, face twisted, fists raised. Papa was quicker. He knocked Adrik into the dirt with a swift hit across the jaw. Nadya surged to her feet, but Danika held her back. Adrik stared up at Papa from the dirt, hand pressed to the bruise already blooming across his chin.

"You have your life and your wife and a child on the way." For all his violence, Papa's voice was soft. "Let that be enough."

Avdotya stood between the pair in the silence that followed, still as a statue, and as Adrik scrambled up from the dirt, Avdotya made no move to help.

Adrik brushed the dust off his knees and glared at Papa. "You can flee if you choose. I'm done running." Then he turned his back on them and marched off down the hill.

Nadya made to follow, but Danika held her fast again, clinging tight to her hand. Nadya looked at her and Danika gave a small shake of her head. Nadya stared at the spot where Adrik disappeared and said quietly, "It is New Year's Eve. We should be together."

The party dispersed. Elin escorted Nadya and Mama to the nicest bed they could muster — a soft mound of grass and leaves. Gavril and Ostrov made plans to leave at first light. There was little left to fight for, and where Adrik was full of fury, Danika felt hollow. Sleep was elusive. She lay against the flat cold earth, staring up at the stars, Nadya's words drifted back to her in half a dream: *"It is New Year's Eve. We should be together."*

Thirty-five days remaining. Thirty-five days until life as Danika knew it ended.

Their dream of defeating Maksis and securing the Philosopher's Stone before the Suncycle now seemed like a fool's errand. She blinked at the twinkling planet of Mercia high above, letting its familiar arc follow her into sleep like an old friend....

Danika sat up.

She shoved off the alkhemist coat that she had draped over herself as a blanket and donned it instead. She gathered up her charts and maps and her journal and went to find a secluded knoll.

As she opened her chart in her lap, she could not help but recall the first night she had perched on the roof of her laboratory at Babbin's bidding — a laboratory and a roof that was now nothing but ash. It was there that she had begun her scribblings. As she traced her fingers over the elaborate lines and markings, she knew that she had not been as diligent as Babbin would have liked. But the task had been more therapy than assignment — a rhythmic shifting of hand over paper, a methodical counting away of time, a bitter reminder of how little she had left and all she still had to lose.

Danika dipped her quill into the ink and sketched out the guidelines by memory. She had tried every technique in her repertoire, every recipe she could get her hands on, and nothing had worked to bring the Philosopher's Stone into existence.

Some vile part of Danika knew that Babbin had the answer. Despite her idiosyncrasies, the old crone was still the most skilled alkhemist Danika had ever met, including her esteemed masters at Izumgray. But would her dear mentor really conceal the key to the only chance of making Danika whole?

She marked *Kantical Major* on the thirty-degree line and moved onto *The Father's Sword*.

Babbin did not believe Danika deserving of the answers, and perhaps she was not. But what did it matter? Maksis certainly was not deserving either and he and his ancestors had been hoarding the Stone for decades, dolling it out as rarely as their own favor.

Perhaps she needed to consider the phase of moon and the alignment of the stars in her brewing.... That was the Kotov way, after all. To them, alkhemy was but a communing with nature. And Babbin always claimed her best brews came at the right starlight.

Slowly, Danika began to flip back through her charts, one after another, after another.

There was something here. Something wrong.

Her heart hammered the further back she ventured. As she neared the night of the wedding that had precipitated all that followed, she flipped rapidly between the chart she had made under those stars and the one she had scrawled tonight.

"By Thoth."

Danika sprang to her feet, gathered her papers, and raced back to her makeshift lab. She tossed her chart onto the gravel and began to rummage through her other pile of books, searching for the previous year's diaries. She had brought everything she had ever written with her on the road. It was part alkhemist's habit, part vain hope that she would find some secret in a bit of old scribbling. And so she had.

She had discovered Babbin's secret, but it had nothing to do with the Philosopher's Stone.

When she found the old journals, she threw them onto the earth alongside the current year's chart, got onto her hands and knees before them, and began to compare.

It was only in the last year — at Babbin's suggestion — that Danika had begun religiously tracking the night sky, but keeping the occasional star chart had also been part of her curriculum at Izumgray. Through six years of diaries, Danika cobbled together some twenty other charts, tracking the incomprehensible progress of the stars overhead.

The slow lag which explained the unseasonable weather... The mosquitoes that had pestered and bit deep into Autumn, the frost that clung to the Steppe even in Wetwinter, the tides that did not quite reach the shore when they should, the snowstorm that had graced the Aadan's Day Ball in the middle of Spring...

Time was falling behind. Or rather, the calendar was.

And so Babbin had not been so callous and unfeeling after all. She had given Danika the answer. It just was not the one Danika expected.

The Sivkan calendar foretold that the Luncycle would end in precisely 35 days. But in truth, alkhemy would end 25 days sooner. And Maksis had no idea.

"Babbin — you little witch."

22. OF TIMEKEEPING AND TIME FADING

The sun had crept into the night by the time Adrik returned to camp the morning after his own father-in-law struck him across the face. A pale pink horizon heralded another chill morning and as he picked his way through sleeping Kotov, many with only a rock for a pillow, the snorts and shifting of deep sleep broke the silence. He passed by sentries kept on guard at all times, ever watchful for Maksis' approach, and climbed to the grassy knoll reserved for the Imperator and his council. No more comfortable, but slightly more private. He stopped short when he found not an untended fire, but a group of pale-faced, murmuring advisors, warming themselves by the silver flames.

"Adrik," said Danika, by far the most alert of the bunch. "We have been waiting for you."

There was a manic gleam in her eye. Faint hope began to kindle in his chest.

"What is it?" he asked, casting his gaze over Nadya, Avdotya, Rodin, Marisha, Ostrov and Gavril, but they looked as ignorant as he was.

"I know how to defeat Maksis," said Danika.

Her words were met with uneasy looks, but Adrik ignored them. He kept his gaze fixed where it mattered — on Danika. And he could see that she believed her words, even if no one else did.

Adrik had spent the entire night walking in circles as his mind did the same, trying to come up with a solution that didn't end in utter failure or at the end of a headman's axe; then trying to decide whether death in the pursuit of his birthright was the nobler end. No answers had come with the dawn. All he could do now was cling to the certainty that Danika had done what she always did — discovered the answer for him.

"Papa, will you please wake Earnest and bring him here? I will need him if I am to explain."

Rodin asked no questions, just brushed past Adrik on his way to the main encampment. He returned moments later with Earnest, who looked strangely pleased to be summoned at such an early hour. When he caught sight of Danika's expression, however, his smile slipped. "I suppose I should've known better than to think you'd send your Papa if it was reconciliation you had in mind."

In other circumstances, Adrik might have admired the man's gall. Now, he just hoped to avoid further bloodshed. As Danika glared and Rodin reached for his whip, Adrik laid a staying hand on his father-in-law's shoulder. Rodin cast him a sideways, almost approving look. Even as Adrik's jaw still throbbed, that gesture buoyed him.

"Come closer, Earnest. Take a look at these charts." Danika gestured to a makeshift table that had been erected with two logs and a piece of driftwood. Spread over its surface were dozens of papers and journals.

Earnest shuffled forward. Slowly, he began to pick through the papers.

"Care to explain to the others what they are?" Danika's voice was light, inscrutable. Adrik sensed a trap.

"They're starcharts, of course," Earnest said.

"And do you know what they reveal?" Danika laughed coldly. "Listen to me — of course you do not. If you did, we would not be in this position."

"I'm glad you are enjoying yourself, little alkhemist. But you are keeping us from our beds." Avdotya sidled over to the table and glared down at the papers.

"Would you please do us all the favor of skipping the dramatics and explaining what this is about?"

"The Luncycle will end in nine days."

Silence met her words. Rodin and Nadya stared at Danika as if concerned for her sanity. Marisha scoffed and Avdotya laughed. But Danika was not deterred.

"Care for an explanation? So would I." She stepped close to Earnest. "As you are so fond of telling everyone, *you* are the Imperator's Timekeeper. How precisely did this mistake occur? Was it intentional sabotage? Or merely incompetence?"

Earnest turned an unpleasant shade of green. When no protests or denials breached his lips, Adrik's heart began to race.

"You mean it's true? The calendar is wrong? How wrong?"

He tried to do the sums in his head, but Danika answered first.

"It is off by 25 days. Twenty-five crucial days. So I ask you again, my dear professor." Danika was within an inch of Earnest now, whispering in his ear like a lover or a torturer. "How did this happen?"

Earnest's smarmy face broke into a silent sob. When he spoke, his voice quavered, pleading forgiveness with every word. "I— I studied as an apprentice under the last Timekeeper. Master Breznik had calculated the last two cycles — the Suncycle in 3925 and the Luncycle in 3950. He was preparing me to take over for him before the next Suncycle, but he died so suddenly…." Earnest's eyes shifted again and, this time, Adrik caught a whiff of guilt. A whiff of poison. His tone turned petulant. "Do you have any idea how complicated it is to calculate the trajectory of a phenomenon we barely understand?"

"Danika managed to do it," said Adrik. Earnest blanched again.

"I admit, I was taken in by the status of the position. I suspected it might not be perfect, but in times of peace, such things rarely matter."

"It matters now," said Danika, staring down at her star charts. "Fortunately for you, this mistake falls in our favor."

Adrik stepped forward. "How so?"

"Maksis believes, as the whole of Sivka does, that the Luncycle will end in 34 days."

"What's the old saying?" Avdotya sneered. "The cycles are as regular and certain as a woman's blood?"

"Certain they may be. Regular they are not," said Danika. "This means that in nine days, all possibility of alkhemical warfare will cease. No more poison blades or caustic arrows. No impenetrable armor or alkhemical cures. Only the strongest army, with the greatest weapons, will win the day."

Adrik's breath caught as a surge of hope washed over him. "And Maksis doesn't have guns."

"We do not have many either," Rodin pointed out.

"We could send for more," said Avdotya. And nothing else could have confirmed this chance to Adrik more than the possibility brimming in Avdotya's eyes.

Danika nodded tightly. "We have no time to waste. For the moment, Maksis can combat our rifles with the alkhemical tools he has at his disposal. But take away alkhemy? What is he left with? Bows and arrows. Swords and shields. Against a bullet? Even you can do that math, Earnest."

Earnest sputtered. "But such a tactic would only work—"

"If we bring him to battle precisely when the Luncycle ends," said Danika.

"Can you do such a thing?" Earnest said in a whisper. He was staring at her with mingled jealousy and admiration.

"I believe I can."

"How?" said Marisha. "Even with this knowledge... We do not have the manpower to bring a fight."

"Do we not?" Danika turned her attention away from Earnest. Now Adrik understood why she'd included Gavril and Ostrov in their party. "Uncle Gavril, you said yourself you would offer what aid you could if Cousin Ostrov joined us. I have shown you both that there is a chance. If we commence battle at New Kirov, while the Luncycle still reigns, and then, in the midst of combat, the Suncycle takes over — all his alkhemical weapons will be useless."

"He will have no chance to recover and regroup," said Avdotya, finger circling his mustache.

"We merely have to hold him back until that point," said Adrik. He turned to the two men who now held their future in their hands.

Gavril was the first to yield.

"Maksis has hidden me up in the northern corner of the world for half my life — no doubt hoping I'd freeze there. He despises me as he does you, Marisha, for we had the audacity to be born of a different mother. If a Kotov bride had existed at the time, you can be sure he would have married me to her and been rid of us both in one fell swoop." Gavril scratched his gray beard, eyes distant. Then nodded curtly. "You will have my men. Whether or not it's enough."

All turned to Ostrov. If they were lucky, Gavril would bring two thousand to the fight.... But Ostrov — the Mountains had an army at least five thousand strong. But Ostrov had a loyalty to Pytor that might prove stronger.

Nadya had told him the story. Despite the Bodansons' inclination to refer to the Grand Duke of the Mountains as "Cousin," Ostrov was no true blood relation. He had been the ward of Maksis' loyal brother, Pytor.

Pytor was a fearsome fellow, balding with a bulbous chin, a mole on his cheek and bulging blue eyes. Apparently, his manner was as uncouth as his visage and somehow, even with his title as Grand Duke of Southreach, he'd never managed to secure a wife. No wife meant no children, hence Ostrov. Pytor had taken Ostrov in as his own when the boy was only seven, and had seen to it that he had the same advantage as any true-born niece or nephew of Maksis.

Across the fire, Ostrov's slate gray eyes found Marisha, of all people. "Pytor will never abandon Maksis."

Adrik's impatience surged. He refused to be thwarted now, when they were so close, by some illegitimate Grand Duke's misguided loyalty. "It's not Pytor I'm asking for help. Or do you still do his bidding?"

Ostrov's expression hardened, but he didn't rise to the jab. "I wouldn't even be a Grand Duke without Pytor. It would give anyone pause to betray their own father. You wouldn't hesitate if I asked you to overthrow Avdotya?"

The words impacted as keenly as Rodin's punch. Adrik and Avdotya had skirted around any titles so familiar as "papa," or even "uncle," but that didn't change the aptness of the comparison. He ducked his head and swallowed against his own revulsion. "Yes. Yes, of course. I'm sorry."

Ostrov stared at Adrik a moment. "Already you show your strength where Maksis has only weakness. I've never heard that man admit that he's wrong. About anything." His eyes flicked to Marisha again. "It will be a bloody fight — don't doubt it. Maksis still has 50,000 men at his disposal, more alkhemists than we could hope to best, and the terrain around New Kirov is not welcoming to outsiders. But then," his lips quirked, "you're no outsider, are you?"

"No," Adrik said. "I'm not. And I'm only too happy to rip Maksis from my home."

It was no easy feat to summon men from across Sivka in nine days. It could never have been managed in the Suncycle, but Avdotya made full use of what alkhemical advantage they still possessed and employed an administrative deftness that impressed even himself.

Polvia had refused to send men on such a vague promise of success — it was paramount to keep the secret of the Suncycle even from them — but their allies to the east had offered weapons and ships to ferry the Sivkan forces across the Swansea. The trader Antonia had proved a valuable asset, for no one knew the quickest and safest routes across Sivka better than she. More Kotov had arrived as well, following their trail from Old Kirov to the Broken Fork and finally to the mouth of the Kirov River near the border of Polvia, where they made their next and final camp at the Kirov River Fortress.

The fortress had been erected over five-hundred years ago, after Impress Lizabeta Lunovna broke with Polvia and all other nations to keep tight control over imports, exports, and the Philosopher's Stones. The men who manned the fortress were trained to look for enemies to the east, not from within. So Adrik had easily taken the fort from the west by cover of darkness and with the five-hundred Kotov left at his disposal.

The warriors hacked and slashed through Maksis' men with a fury that could only be born from righteous vengeance. It'd taken an entire day to clear out the bodies, pile them in a mass grave and ignite them by a silver flame.

Maksis would certainly see them coming now. But that was the point, wasn't it?

They stationed guards in every direction, ready to sound the alarm if there was any hint of Maksis deciding to strike first. But evidently, he'd decided it better to defend from the city of New Kirov than drift too close to the Polvian border.

Their greatest boon came two days after they secured the Kirov River.

When the sentries sounded the alert of an approaching hoard, everyone scrambled to battle stations. Avdotya took up position on a high tower, pulse racing, and squinted into the distance.

But the approaching forces did not look ready for a fight. For all their numbers — some two thousand by quick glance — they bore no weapons or armor. Their clothes were tattered and feeble. They hoisted pitchforks and shovels rather than sword or spear....

Avdotya ordered the gates open and Josef and his eldest son, formerly of Petrovia's holding in the Taiga, led the wave of vassals into the fortress.

"You came," Avdotya said, blinking rapidly. "You said you wouldn't. You said we had no chance—"

"I said to come back when you *had* a chance," Josef corrected. "You didn't, so we've come to you." He smiled weakly at his boy. He had a thick mop of dark hair and looked to be near in age to Adrik and Yulian. Avdotya vaguely recalled the young man tending to the bedside of a sick sibling when Avdotya, Yulian, and Nadya had paid their visit. Avdotya wondered briefly at the fate of that child and felt sure he'd rather not know. As if reading his thoughts, Josef's expression sobered. "We've come to fight for the Imperator Reborn. We're tired of being slaves."

Thanks to Josef, their army was now nine thousand strong. Still a paltry number compared to the fifty thousand Maksis, Pytor and Kliment likely had stashed in and around New Kirov. But armored with rifles and canon, there was a chance they could hold the line until the Suncycle dawned.

Avdotya had more than a few reservations about trusting the little alkhemist's calculations. Their victory or defeat hinged on her ability to map the skies. Needless to say, it wasn't a position Avdotya thought to be in when he and Adrik set out on this quest. All the same, Avdotya was glad when the moon rose in the sky the night before the last day of the Luncycle. It meant Maksis would meet them on their terms.

The knock at his door, when it came, was expected. What Avdotya did not expect was to find the little alkhemist on the other side of the door instead of Yulian. She stood in his entryway, silhouetted by the flame of the camp fires in the yard, arms crossed tightly over her feeble chest.

"Come to ask for sage advice on the eve of battle?" Avdotya sniped.

"Yes, as a matter of fact." She pushed open the door and shouldered past him into the barren bunkroom. Without the ring of fire around her, she looked less self-important and more like a little girl. A snide girl with ideas above her station, but still, a girl. "I need you to tell me how to sneak into the Palace at New Kirov."

Avdotya slammed the door in his shock, then schooled his face as quickly as he could manage. He didn't know what game she was playing, and he didn't particularly care, but with Yulian set to arrive any moment, he'd need to get to the bottom of it, and quickly.

"What makes you think I have any idea how to sneak into the palace?"

"Because you snuck Adrik out of it. Or rather, you snuck a servant boy out of it, seventeen years ago."

Only many years as a practiced liar could have kept Avdotya's expression neutral. He used every one of those skills now and pinned her with his most withering stare. "What in The Father's name are you implying, little alkhemist?"

"I know the truth. I know that the real Adrik is dead. That you snuck out a servant boy who witnessed The Slaughter and raised him up to take Adrik's place. I know that you did this by paying off a member of Maksis' Lun-Protektorate—" Avdotya had a thousand excuses ready on his tongue, but she carried on before he could get a word out. "I know this because I heard it from your own mouth. I heard you discussing it with the guard at Petrovia's estate—"

Avdotya had many lies prepared, but nothing for this. He thought back to that conversation, recalled it in damning clarity. There was little he could say to deny it, so perhaps he ought to stop thinking of what to say and start thinking of what to *do.*

"—I followed the guard out of the tent. I did what you could not and I eliminated the threat." She paused long enough to take in a shaky breath. "I killed her," she said, then shocked him still further by reaching into her pocket and tossing a familiar bag of silver onto his nightstand. It landed with a finality that rattled him to his bones. "I have kept the secret. Adrik's secret. Your secret."

Avdotya stared at the bag of silvniks, proof positive of her words and the situation he now found himself in. A part of him was grateful Protektorate Kaleva no longer posed a liability. For all that she'd proven herself a loyal and useful servant of the cause, the alkhemist was much less so. Neither useful, nor loyal. Not to him, in any case. But to Adrik...

He let out a long, dry laugh.

"What is so funny?" she growled. It pleased him to put her back on the defensive, where she belonged.

"I'm simply in awe of the lengths a girl will go for love."

Her mouth opened, but no words came out. Her jaw clicked shut. It seemed she had at least enough self-respect not to try and deny it.

"So why are you here now? Do you plan to reveal my secret to Adrik? To oust me as his most trusted advisor moments before he claims victory over Maksis? Do you hope that somehow such a gesture will win his heart? Because I assure you, all the truth will do at this point is break it."

"I know that. If I had planned to tell him the truth, I would have gone to him. Not you."

"Yes. I suppose that's true." He ran a finger over his lips, trying to glean her purpose and found himself at a complete loss. "Then what is it you want from me, little alkhemist?"

"I told you — I wish to sneak into the palace."

"Why?"

"Because Maksis has a Philosopher's Stone."

Avdotya dropped his finger from his lips. "And what do you plan to do with it?"

"I want it. My reasons are no concern of yours. And it is a weapon in his hands. He can use it to sustain himself and his power, even through the Suncycle. You will never truly defeat him while it is in his possession."

"I see. So you mean to lead a contingent into the palace?"

"No. I will go alone. I will not risk anyone else for— for this." Her eyes shone. "Will you help me or not?"

It seemed the little alkhemist had solved Avdotya's problem for him. Suicide was neater than any plan he could muster. She would scurry into the palace in a futile search for Maksis and the Stone, be killed in the attempt, and his new liability would be gone with the last. Avdotya's secret would die with the alkhemist.

"Very well. Write this down."

23. BATTLE AT NEW KIROV

Much as it pained Danika to admit, calculating time by the stars was no easy feat, and far less precise than she would have preferred. All she knew for certain was that the Luncycle would end today — likely sometime in the afternoon. Therefore, the safest option was to attack New Kirov at suncrest and hope they could hold the line until the world changed.

As far as anyone else knew, Danika was staying behind in the encampment with Avdotya. For this task, he was the one person Danika did not have to worry would give her away. She had assured Nadya that she would go to the medical tent if anything unexpected — or expected — should happen. Ever the trusting soul, Nadya had not doubted her. Danika thought she caught a lingering look from Adrik, but if he doubted her intentions, he did not say so. Lukin she avoided altogether — he would have read her in an instant.

She left the camp before the troops were even awake. New Kirov was as unlike Old Kirov as it was possible to be. There were no high walls to fortify its protections — there was no need when the natural buffer of the river served better. Built some three hundred years after Old Kirov, and left largely unattended since the Solovs imprisonment, New Kirov operated as a capitol under Maksis' sole domain within the province of Southreach. Grand Duke Pytor kept a house some fifty miles away on the southern coast. But Danika imagined the city was bustling now as it had not done since before The Slaughter. Maksis, Pytor and Kliment had moved their forces and remaining allies into the city, taking up the homes and apartments left abandoned for so many decades. Where everything in Old Kirov had been built on timber and tradition, New Kirov stood on limestone and decay.

A solid mask of white filled the sky and the damp chill here sank deeper than the dry cold of Old Kirov. Stray raindrops pierced the air like bullets, never quite making it to the ground. They were in true Spring now — though no one but the upper echelon of Adrik's command knew it. To them, it was Summer and this was yet another late storm. It amazed Danika that she had not seen what was so obvious before — flowers still in bloom past their prime, sweaty Autumn nights in the bedloft, snowpacked winters that drifted too long into Spring. And to think she called herself an alkhemist. Not for much longer.

She wore a gray vassal's cloak over her alkhemist coat, hoping to blend in as she approached the first bridge over the many tributaries into the city. Fortunately, Avdotya had a number of spies to aid her crossing. After all, New Kirov had been the home of the Solovs for far longer than it belonged to Maksis. All Danika had to do to gain entry was offer a heavy bag of silver to the right guard and she was behind the lines, hiding in plain sight.

The cobblestone streets spread out in a sensical grid, precisely as Avdotya said they would. Lined on either side by neat, unbroken stone facades some four storeys high. The grocer's shop was nearly indistinguishable from the bakery or the bakery from the private residence next door. There was a certain beauty to its uniformity, a modernity that Danika could have appreciated more if the walls were not also crumbling, the streets rutted, and the storefronts empty.

The palace lay at the center of this tidy arrangement, approachable from a number of entry points. But Avdotya had directed her to the most discreet — in the back of a butchery. He assured her the place was abandoned, but she passed through the darkened shop on high alert. It stank of stale blood and rotting meat and, as quickly as she could, she exited out the back to a small gravel courtyard. In one corner sat a wooden hatch — her way into the palace.

She climbed down the ladder, closing the hatch behind her and descending by the precious light of the alkhemy still in her veins. When her feet touched solid earth, she clicked her flint rings to ignite a silver flame in her palm and trotted quickly down the low, sloping dirt passage. This must have been the same route Adrik and Avdotya had escaped by so many years ago. She tried to imagine it — first as a protector saving a young prince from unimaginable violence; then as a scheming advisor, forcing a servant boy to witness mass murder. Neither scenario warmed the blood.

Eventually, the path began to climb. It ended in three steps leading up to a door. Danika's heart thudded loudly in her ears. There was no knowing what awaited her on the other side of that door. Avdotya was hardly a friend, and this could be his attempt to rid himself of her once and for all. But, then again, she had chosen to go on this foolhardy journey. She had resigned herself to a one-way mission. She had failed in her quest to make the Philosopher's Stone and, try though she might, Danika could not stop the cycles. In fact, all she had managed to do was speed them up. This was her only way forward.

The door stuck.

She threw her body into it once, twice, three times, before she remembered that the Suncycle had not struck yet and she was still an alkhemist with a tincture in her pocket. She reached into her coat for the appropriate vial. The cork had a pipette at the end which allowed her to place three precise drops into the keyhole. A fizzing sound and a puff of smoke told her the deed was done.

She emerged into a barren stone hall, lined on either side by empty sconces and many identical doors. Avdotya had bid her to turn left, so left she turned. A dozen or so paces down the hall, she took the fifth door on her right. Another identical corridor stretched out before her. It was a zig-zagging maze and one that she hoped she would remember in reverse if she emerged from her mission alive. Eventually, she passed through a door that fell out into a courtyard.

The courtyard.

It had the same stale, forgotten feeling as the butchery, but with more blood. The pale pea-stone gravel could only absorb so much and the bodies sprawled out before her had clearly spilled everything.

Her stomach rolled to see the faces that no doubt haunted Adrik's dreams. To maintain this macabre display, preservation tinctures would need to have been applied regularly. Had Maksis sent his minions down here every season, arms weighted with preserving liquid that they would brush on, like artists on canvas, trying not to the gag through their scarves? Or did Maksis make the trip to do the deed himself? Reveling in each brush stroke?

Danika had to hunt for a family resemblance in the siblings, as the bodies that undoubtedly belonged to the Imperator and Impress lacked heads thanks to Maksis' heinous wedding gift. But the two heads were not the only pieces missing from the picture. The oldest sister had lost an ear. The younger brother had no hand. Who knew what other amputations were hidden beneath clothes and boots?

Danika forced herself to look at what was there instead of what was not. She thought she saw a similarity to Adrik in the sister's brow, the brother's curls, the father's arms...before she remembered.

This was not Adrik's family.

Danika whispered a prayer she did not believe, but Mama would approve of, and took the next door out.

As she emerged into the upper hall, the sounds of battle raged outside. Her heart lurched at the boom of canon fire, the caustic screech of alkhemy in flight. How many of her own people would die waiting on the promise of her calculations? How long could they hold out if she was wrong? How many could she have saved if she had only stayed in the fight? But it was too late. There was no calling off the battle now. No more time left to freeze. Danika focused her attention on the present, on her mission. The time left to save herself was dwindling fast.

Danika had reached the occupied section of the palace — the sconces were lit, drapes hung from the windows, chairs lined a wide corridor — but even this place was eerily quiet. Avdotya had told her to avoid the inner chamber where the women and children would be held under guard — old Sivkan notions of propriety and femininity — but that Maksis would be in the study, waiting for word from the front.

There were no guards outside the chamber. The door gave way without so much as a squeak of the hinges. The arrogance was breathtaking.

Maksis stood alone, with his back to the door, at the end of a long room with high windows. Just like the library in Old Kirov, the view looked out over the city, the battlefield, where Maksis could watch men die like a vulture on a perch, deciding which corpse to feast over.

He did not turn to greet her. "Who is it?"

She thought for a moment how best to answer, then settled on — "Your niece."

He spun slowly to face her. Danika did not know what she expected. A beast, certainly. A ragged, milky creature, soured by the weight of his sins. But she was startled to find that he was just a man, no different from any other she had encountered before. She could detect surprisingly little alkhemical vanity in his person or attire. He had a magnificent head of hair that curled around his shoulders, though time had faded the auburn to gray. His beard was even more impressive, full and wide, brushing his collarbone in shocks of silver. He wore a black kaftan with a silver chain and the Sky-Crown on his head.

Danika had seen the Sky-Crown depicted often enough in paintings and statues. An intricate blending of silver and gold, it was actually two crowns melted into one. Back when the Lunovnas and Solovs ruled together, they each had their own headpiece to don. But once the families agreed to rule alternately, there could be only one symbol of power to pass from one Cycle to the next.

The blended metal band weaved around itself in a crown of roses. In alkhemy, the golden rose represented the successful marriage of opposites. The centerpiece of the bed of roses was a golden sunburst married with a silver moon. It was doused with a lightening elixir to make it easier to bear. If Danika had her way, by the end of the day, it would be on Adrik's head. And it would be a heavy weight indeed.

"I don't know you," said Maksis, looking her over blankly.

"We have never met. I am Marisha's daughter."

"The traitor," he said, voice as blank as his face. "She sent a child to do her bidding?"

"You yourself once sent a child out to treatise with us. Your own daughter, if I recall correctly?"

Maksis shrugged. "I didn't say I disapproved. Children are useful tools. Why else would we have so many?"

He reached out to straighten one of a dozen glass jars lining his desktop. The jars were filled with the cloudy liquid of a preservation solution. Floating within were body parts. An eye, an ear, a toe, a hand. A finger. Danika swallowed past her revulsion, forced her attention back on the monster before her.

"This child has come to rid you of the last weapon at your disposal."

"And what is that?"

"The Philosopher's Stone."

Maksis watched her. He did not smile, but his eyes glimmered in some strange amusement. The eyes were old, she noted. Pale. Watery and tired. "The boy doesn't think he can kill me outright?"

"You are difficult to kill locked in a tower."

"You made it here."

"I am not leading a battle."

"No. You are wiser than him, I daresay. The smartest ones lead from behind." Maksis rounded the desk. He moved like an old man, but unlike most, an old man with no fear of his own mortality. He sank onto the edge of a daybed that was tucked into an alcove in the wall.

"You think the Stone keeps me alive? Or do you seek it for some other purpose?" She did not answer. He grinned. It hollowed out his features, contorting them into a whisper of the monster that lurked inside. "Ah — I see. You're not so noble as you look. You want it for yourself." The terrifying smile dropped and his eyes narrowed. "I remember now. Marisha came to me years ago — begging for her crippled child. It's you, I presume?"

Danika staggered against the desk. Mama had come to him? But how? When? Why had she never said? She thought back to the haze of memory and pain from that time.

The five days of isolation in Babbin's hut... No word, no visitors... Certain she had been abandoned by the very person who had failed to protect her.

"She came to you?" Danika whispered. "And you refused?"

He muttered an affirmative, rolling to lay flat on his back and place his hands over his heart to stare up at the canopied ceiling. Like a pantomime of a body on a burial shroud. "If it's any consolation, even if she had not been some half-breed relation, I wouldn't have given it to her."

It was not a consolation. Danika needed her resentment. It had taken her this far. To contemplate forgiveness now was to rethink everything she had done up to this point. She shoved the thought from her mind. *Focus.*

"It does not matter what happened then." She held out a hand, the other tightened on her saber. "Give me the Stone."

"And then what? You'll let me live?"

"I will kill you quickly. I assure you, Adrik will not."

"No." He sighed mildly. "I don't suppose he will. The bloody deaths are much more satisfying. He'll learn that soon enough."

She fought a burst of anger. "Adrik is not like you."

"That is true. I, for one, am actually royal."

She could not take his bait. She grit her teeth. "Where is the Stone?"

He waved a hand toward the desk. "The upper left drawer. In the green bag."

Danika raced to the desk, keeping the saber pointed at Maksis, though he did not seem at all threatened by it. Her heart raced in her throat, her legs tingled in anticipation, as if they sensed salvation was near. She pulled the drawer open, removed the green silk bag and tipped it over.

A cut gem as blue and clear as the Swansea itself, fell out onto the desk.

"You see why we had to ration. It would not have sustained me for much longer, but it should suit for your purposes. Light a flame beneath it and catch the condensation with your tongue. You can light an alkhemical flame?"

Danika glared at him. "Yes."

"Pardon me for asking. Marisha is only half Lunovna. And she married that mundane Kotov — I'm surprised any of you carry the Fire."

"I was trained at Izumgray," said Danika, unable to ignore the insult. "I bear the Celestial Fire."

"Indeed? Not that you need the Alkhemical Fire to use the Stone. But perhaps I would have spared a drop or two for you after all. I don't suppose I could persuade you to join me in exchange for the rock?"

She glared again. "No."

"Too bad. Still, it won't make much difference. From the sounds outside, I'd say the battle is reaching its end. Your boy will be dead soon and then I will have to kill you for a traitor — cripple or not."

For the first time since entering the room, Danika noticed the roar of the battle, the sound of the gunfire rattling the windows, the haze of smoke blanketing the city outside, making it impossible to see Adrik, firing down from high atop his white steed.

But perhaps he was already dead. Perhaps they were all dead.

"Why attack now?" Maksis queried. "I grant you the value of the element of surprise — I had assumed he would wait until Cycle's end to strike—"

"The Cycle will end by dayfade."

It did not occur to her until the words were spoken what a risk they posed. Maksis could still call a retreat, redouble his forces, wipe them out before the Suncycle struck. But she had wanted to wipe that bland look off his face. She had wanted to shock him.

And shock him she did. For the first time, Maksis looked away from the ceiling to stare at her with intent. "You know this for certain?"

"I calculated it myself."

"A pity indeed to have missed out on such a clever niece. Very well..." He heaved in another sigh and clapped his hands down at his sides as if to ready himself for the pyre. "Get on with it. When the cycle ends, I'd rather Adrik not find me still breathing. And given what you've just told me, you know that you cannot leave me alive."

He was right. She had not considered that in her surge of pridefulness. In telling him their plan, she had given herself no other choice.

Danika pocketed the Stone, its weight heavy at her hip. She paced slowly over to Maksis and leveled her saber to a point just beneath his chin. In her other hand, she unsheathed her favorite short blade from her waistbelt. The same dagger that had killed the last person to threaten Adrik. Would Maksis Voyavich Lunovna, Imperator of Sivka, really give up without a fight?

Then he played his final card.

"You know you fight for an imposter? That boy out there is not Adrik Solov."

The words would have devastated her — perhaps even stayed her hand. If she had not already known the truth. If she had not already decided that what he *was* did not matter, only *who*.

"I know," she said, and slit his throat.

A familiar face met Danika in the hall.

It was Tatya — the redheaded child who had delivered Maksis' truce at Old Kirov. But staring into her hard gray eyes, it was clear she was no more a child than Danika. A useful tool indeed.

"Is he dead?" she said, as blunt as her father.

"Yes."

"Did you kill him?"

Danika hesitated. "Yes."

The girl's hand clenched over the pommel of a sword. It was small and short — fit for a warrior her size. Her gaze turned to the red rock in Danika's hand. "He gave you that?"

Danika nodded. She could feel the stone beating triumphantly against her palm, as if it too had a pulse and sensed victory near at hand. Danika had come into this palace expecting to die — but now that she had made it this far, and with the Stone in her grasp, she found that she had never wanted to live so much, never had so much to live for. She would not let this child stand in her way.

"He was a bad man. He did...many things. Things The Mother would despise."

Danika's gaze drifted to the scar where Tatya's ear should be, thought back to the portrait of Impress Aleksandra with her striking eyepatch. It seemed wrong to argue, even worse to agree.

"If you let me go, no harm will come to you. Adrik will let the women and children live. I swear it."

"What of Stepan?"

An image flashed in her mind of Maksis' heir — strong and healthy, wearing armor that cost more than a thousand vassals. He, like Adrik, was leading from the front.

"That I cannot promise."

The girl's grip wavered as she considered. The sword clattered when it fell. "Go."

Danika did not need telling twice.

It took her a long time to find the front. With Maksis' blood sticky on her cheeks, she weaved through the bodies until she had no choice but to step on them, climb over them. How could anyone be left to fight?

Adrik's army had moved so close to the palace entrance as to be knocking on the door. It was a sight to behold — Kotov, Sivkan, and vassal crawling over New Kirov like ants on a hill. She cast her gaze to the sky. The sun had past its crest. It would have to happen soon...

Danika emerged just behind Maksis' defensive line. She cut her palm with her nail, then sparked the flint between the rings on her thumb and forefinger and watched the silver flames leap from her palm. Panting as if she had run a mile, Danika held the little Stone over the flame and waited.

A thin mist began to bubble over its cerulean surface.

She held her breath until that mist turned to liquid and a translucent droplet dangled from one broken end. She raised the stone to her mouth and let the drop fall on her tongue.

There was no taste except freedom.

She threw off her gray cloak and dove into the fray. A pistol bounced alongside the saber at her hip, waiting for the moment her potions became useless. But until then, she would savor every last second of alkhemy at her fingertips.

A Burning Sickness had one Southreach corporal vomiting acid onto his compatriot.

Sharp Steps transformed the cobblestones beneath a charging horde of Taigans into razors.

An unnamed potion of Danika's own creation loosed the bricks on the nearest building and turned them into projectiles.

It was life and power, synthesis and distillation, Above and Below... all dancing to the tune of her song. It would hurt to lose it, but it would be worse to have never had it at all.

Then the puff of pink smoke from Shura's *Waking Nightmares* went flat. The bricks dropped out of the sky. An arrow pierced a set of armor that should have been impenetrable.

Danika pulled the pistol from her hip as her attacker set forward, a manic gleam in his eye. She aimed for his head and pulled the trigger. The weapon let out an earsplitting crack, her attacker's head ricocheted back in a splatter of red — not unlike Maksis throat — and her legs went out from under her.

She landed flat on her back, the wind swept from her lungs, head spinning. Had she been knocked down? Had she tripped? Had a potion shook the earth, breaking her stance?

But no, there were no more potions. No more tinctures or elixirs or vapors.

Danika stared up at the dusky stars above the smoke as realization set in. She turned her head to stare at her left hand, still clenched into a fist around the Philosopher's Stone — or what she had thought was the Philosopher's Stone. She uncurled her fingers and stared at a plain brown rock.

Her legs could not move.

She did not try to move anything else.

She lay there a long time. Those still in the fight mistook her for a corpse. Danika stared at the sky and listened as the momentum of the battle shifted. Gunfire overwhelming the clatter of sword. Shouts of surprise and fear. Green and gold and blue armored men racing past her in retreat. Soon, even that faded and only the cries of surrender remained.

Then, a new sound pierced the cacophony.

"Danika? *Danika?* What are you—?" Lukin pulled her into his lap. He pawed at her, looking for the injury. "Danika — speak to me. Are you hurt?"

"No." Her voice was like a door that had been rusted shut.

"Then what—" She felt his hands skim over her ribs, down to her hips, then felt nothing at all.

His chest pressed warm and solid against her arm as he heaved in a deep breath. He scooped her up and climbed to his feet. He carried her just as Adrik had carried Nadya out of the Swansea on their wedding day.

"I have you," he said. "The tide will bring us in."

She let the rock fall from her fingers.

24. A New Dawn

The stone, of course, was a fake. Whether the real one yet existed remained a mystery. All that was certain was that, even in death, Maksis had two more limbs to add to his collection.

Lukin carried her to a small bedroom on the ground floor of the palace after the battle. There had been an examination by Shura, who could not meet her eye, and seemed as bereft without her potions as Danika without her legs. She told Shura to leave, that it was hopeless, and had not spoken again since.

Danika did not know if Adrik was angry with her for stealing his revenge. She did not know if Nadya felt betrayed by Danika's lie. She did not even know if Lukin had forgiven her. The only person she would let see her was Mama. Mama did not try to goad Danika into conversation or even attempt to comfort her with empty platitudes. Mostly, she knitted. And left Danika to her thoughts.

Three thousand men had died fending off Maksis' soldiers while they waited for the Suncycle to come. It was an incalculable loss and one which she would have gladly tolerated if the Stone had worked.

She did not like herself for this thought. But she did not like herself much at all these days. Over and over, she uttered the alkhemist's oath in her mind — the one she never got to take, thanks to her untimely expulsion.

"Will you with me tomorrow be content,
Faithfully to receive the blessed Fire,
Upon this Oath that I shall here you give,
For neither Gold nor Silver as long as you live,
Neither for love you bear towards your kin,
Nor yet to no great man's pleasure
Will you disclose the secret that I shall teach,
Neither by writing nor by swift speech;
But only to him which you be sure
Hath ever searched after the secrets of Nature?
To him you may reveal the secrets of this Art,
Under the Covering of Philosophers before this world yet depart."

Perhaps this was her punishment for giving into a great man's pleasure, for teaching a mundane the secret of alkhemy.

One day, she did not know which, Mama broke the agreed upon silence. "Adrik has asked to see you. I think he wants to convince you to attend the coronation."

Danika said nothing.

Mama threw down her knitting. "Speak to me, Danika — you are lame, not deaf."

Only such cruelty could have forced her lips to unstick. "I am not in the mood for parties."

"A coronation is not a party." Mama stood. She stared down at Danika. It was an odd sensation. Danika had outgrown Mama many years ago. But she supposed she would have to get used to people looking down on her. "I have indulged your self-pity long enough. It is time to rejoin the world."

"Self pity? Self—" She was speechless with rage. When she finally found her words, they could only be vile. "*You* did this to me!"

"Fate did this to you, my girl. I only failed to stop it."

As quickly as the fight had risen in her, it went out. Mama watched her in silence, then sank to the edge of the bed with a sigh.

"I am not a strong as you, Danika. Not as smart, nor as brave. I could not stop fate, even when it was in my ability to do so. But you — you manipulated time itself. You killed my vile brother. You put a Solov on the throne. You have changed the fate of all Sivka. And you did it with your mind — not with your alkhemy, not with your legs."

Danika considered that. Mulled over each word like a sour candy turned sweet at the last.

If even Mama could believe in her...

Slowly, Danika pushed herself up on her pillows. It was a painstaking task and she was breathless by the end of it. "Are you just going to sit there or are you going to get me a wheelchair?"

Adrik had never seen Avdotya weep. But weep he did as the Sky Crown was placed on Adrik's head.

They held the coronation in New Kirov, on the bones of his mama and papa, sisters and brothers. Adrik was determined that the Solov empire be reborn in the place it had died. Then, as soon as the task was done, he would never return here again. He wanted to begin his new life in Old Kirov. He wanted to live with Nadya and their unborn child in a palace not haunted by the memory of fear and the stench of blood. To make no mention of the fact that he still liked the idea of sleeping in Maksis' bed.

There was much to be done in this new world — already, the after-effects of the Suncycle were being felt. Alkhemically-imbued buildings had collapsed, the number of sick and injured were rising, food supplies dwindled. Then there was the Lunovna loyalists to exile and the traitorous Grand Dukes to behead.

But, as Avdotya reminded him, none of that could be solved in the span of a coronation. So, for now, Adrik chose to revel in all he'd accomplished, all he'd earned.

He looked to Nadya sat on his left, no less magnificent than The Mother herself.

They both wore cream silks beaded in gold suns and moons and stars, bedecked in the most ornate jewels that could be found in Maksis' coffers. Precious jewels each — though none the jewel he knew Danika longed for.

For this occasion, Nadya had forgone her usual simple silhouette and wore a ballgown with a shimmering cape. Her belly bulged beautifully, full of the promise of their reign. Her crown, slightly smaller than Adrik's but no less significant, fit her like an Impress.

The two Celebrants from Old Kirov had made the long journey to conduct the ceremony. Adrik gave the Father Celebrant a starring role. As The Mother held the Sky Crown over his head, The Father uttered his prayer:

"Voice of The Father and The Mother, Imperator of all Sivka, this visible and tangible adornment of your head is an eloquent symbol that you, as the head of the whole Sivkan people, are invisibly crowned by The Mother of The Mother, The Father of The Father, and that they bestow upon you the entire authority over their people."

Then Adrik recited his own vow.

"Father of The Father, Mother of The Mother, they who created all things by their word, and by their wisdom has made the Above and Below — has made man so that he should walk uprightly and rule righteously over their world. They have chosen me as Imperator and judge over their people. I acknowledge their purpose towards me, and bow in thankfulness before them. Through the grace and mercy of The Mother, who once bled for us, and The Father, who led us to our home, I will possess all the honor and glory unto ages of ages. As Above, so Below."

Adrik didn't see Danika until it was over. He sought her in the crowd, half afraid of what he'd find. Nadya had tried a dozen times to gain entry into Danika's room over the last few tennights, beside herself as her Mama turned her away again and again. Adrik had felt only relief at being denied. But it wasn't an ignorance he could live in forever, and as Marisha steered Danika's wheeled chair toward him after the ceremony, he was forced to face it.

She looked exactly like herself. Proud, stubborn, slightly superior. Only because of his closeness with her over the last year could he see the bruises under her eyes, the tense line of her jaw, her fingers white-knuckled on the arms of her chair. And, of course, she was sitting. Other than at the dinner table, he could count on one hand the number of times she'd sat in his presence. It was only now that he realized why.

"You look well," he said in a hearty voice that sounded false even to him.

Danika bowed her head. "Thank you, Imperator."

"Don't go getting all formal on me now just because the Sky Crown is on my head."

Her lips twitched. "It is amazing they could make it fit — bloated as it is."

Adrik laughed. It was a true laugh, though he cut it short. With the pleasantries dispensed, there was nowhere to hide. She'd stolen from him a revenge that was rightfully his. But by the same token, she'd given him everything he desired. Not just his rightful inheritance, but her sister — his wife, his Nadya. There was no question which weighed more in the balance.

"I'm pleased to see you out and about. Now that you're recovered, we have much work to do."

She stared at him, shock plain. "We? I thought I would return to the Kotov Isles."

He pretended to misunderstand her. "No time for that. Avdotya already has enough schemes to fill a dozen tomes. I need a Vice Minister to reign him in."

"Vice Minister of the Sivkan Council? Me?"

"Who else would I choose, Danika? Your value isn't any less because you now sit in a chair instead of at a cauldron." She ducked her head. He did her the courtesy of looking away as she gathered herself. "I can't do this without you."

"You will never have to, Imperator," she said, like a vow, and he was pleased to see some of the old fire behind her eyes.

They would leave for Old Kirov tomorrow. The entire family had journeyed to New Kirov to see the coronation — Zin, Mikhail, even Papanik. Though Danika suspected Papanik did not come so much for Adrik as for her.

Zin and Mikhail had been frightened to approach her at first. Danika tried to hide her disappointment as they raced toward her with open arms, then stopped short upon seeing her wheelchair.

But then Papanik had blundered forward on his peg leg and scooped her up, holding her fast to his chest, supporting her with his one remaining arm where her own legs could not. She breathed deep the scent of him, the goat fur and tobacco, and pretended, just for a moment, that she was still an alkhemist.

"It evens the odds, Little Nika," he said, deep voice reverberating against her ribs. "What most people need four limbs for, we can do with two."

Danika laughed wetly. Though she could not help but think Papanik's disability so much nobler than her own. He had given his arm in the heat of battle, defending his home. Danika's paralysis was nothing but a childhood illness she had not been smart enough to cure.

Papanik set her back in her chair and Zin and Mikhail, seeing the proof that she would not break under their affection, clambered into her lap.

Later, Danika returned to her room to pack her meager possessions for the journey east, wondering who in their household would make the Palace at Old Kirov their final destination.

Papa and Papanik were Kotov — they belonged nowhere else but the Isles. Mama had no desire to dwell under the roof of her childhood home again and she would not be parted from Papa, which meant Zin and Mikhail would stay with her. Elin, like their patriarchs, would not find much to entertain her in Old Kirov now that the fighting was done. Suddenly, the prospect of Vice Minister of the Sivkan Council seemed exceedingly lonely.

There was only one person left unaccounted for.

She sent a note, asking Lukin to come to her room. When he entered, a heavy silence hung between them, broken only by the lashing of snow against the window above her bed. A brittle chill had seeped into the limestone walls. It would be a long, cold journey across Sivka without alkhemy to sustain them.

“All packed?” she asked him.

“What little I had.” He paused. “I offered to escort your family back to the Isles.”

A hollow pit formed in her stomach. “You are not coming back to Old Kirov?”

“Do you want me to?”

She found she had no answer. So instead, she asked a favor.

“I need you to do something for me.”

“Anything.”

The immediacy of his answer stole her breath for a moment. “I need you to find someone. A young man. He came to camp before the battle at Petrovia’s Estate, looking for Adrik. His name was Kiren. He insisted on seeing Adrik, even though I told him he was dead.”

Her mind drifted back to that blustery night almost a year ago, so full of fear and uncertainty. She had been distracted over her plan to resurrect Adrik, her promise to give Nadya a child. Those worries seemed as distant as Petrovia’s Estate now, but for so many of the nights she had spent locked up in this room, seeing and speaking to no one but Mama, Kiren’s freckled face had haunted her dreams.

“He knew,” she said, mostly to herself.

“What did he know?”

That Adrik was not who he claimed to be.

“I cannot answer that. I am sorry, but I cannot. I can only ask you to trust me.”

She could see the malice, the temptation, simmering behind Lukin’s eyes. There was no man in Sivka she trusted more than him, and no man in Sivka who should have trusted her less. Despite all of it, he said, “I do trust you. Tell me what you need.”

Her shoulders slumped. There was still much to reason between them, but at least she had not ruined this. "I need you to find Kiren and bring him back to the Isles. Keep him safe there. Keep him quiet."

It was this last order that was the most important. Lukin nodded. "I will write to you when it is done."

"Thank you, Lukin."

His lips twisted. The silence fell again. He stepped forward and touched his fingertips to her forearm. When she did not pull away, he crouched down and encircled her wrist in his grasp. "Danika—"

She reared back, pushing the left wheel of her chair hard with her free hand. He released her immediately. She grasped her burning wrist. Her heart hammered in her ears. "I need you to find Kiren," she said, order as sharp as any Kotov battlemaster.

"I will."

She chanced a glance at him. He was staring down at his feet, blinking rapidly. "I am sorry, Lukin. I just—"

"Goodbye, Danika." He spun on his heel and pushed out the door.

She stared at the spot where he had vanished. It was for the best. She was not enough for him now, if she ever had been. He deserved someone who would make him whole and happy. Someone who would never hurt him. Someone like Shelia.

Besides, Danika had an empire to build, an Imperator to protect. And that mission started with Kiren.

Her visit to the courtyard in the Palace at New Kirov had confirmed something. Maksis' twisted diorama with Solovs trapped like specimens in amber had been missing a key figure. The rumors were true. One Solov child did escape. The real Adrik was out there somewhere.

And his name was Kiren.

ACKNOWLEDGEMENTS

Writing a book is one thing, getting it to publication is another beast entirely. The Inksters helped me tackle that monster with flare (and a bit of fun).

The Inksters was inspired by the Inklings group founded by J.R.R. Tolkien and C.S. Lewis — but no two people are more inspiring to me than my co-founders, Hannah and Jenna. Other than myself, no one has read more drafts and iterations of this book than them. Every plot hole, grammatical error, and timeline problem was solved thanks to their tender attention. Every piece of marketing material from the back cover blurb to the promotional stickers went through them for critique and cheerleading. They built an online platform and created content to fill it almost entirely to support me and this book. They asked smart questions that uncovered new subplots, rooted for their favorite ships, and debated endlessly with me about the conundrum that was Part III (may she rest in peace until her resurrection).

Much like Frodo bringing the ring to Mordor, I could not have achieved this dream without my fellowship. You truly are my Ink-sisters. Thank you.

(Also, Tom). The unofficial Inkster, whose friendship, support, and business acumen was just as valuable to me as his first read-through. You were my litmus test for whether this story would hit with a readership. You truly made me believe in it in a way I hadn't before. As you always remind me — be brave, and mighty forces will come to your aid. Also, how dare you?

Emma and Morgan — you have strengthened The Inksters and this story immeasurably with your unique perspectives and devoted friendship. I deeply appreciate every moment you provided a patient listening ear as I ranted about the latest step in this process. Morgan, you also achieved the impossible and took not just one, but multiple author photos that I actually adore. You made a very nerve-wracking process fun and I am so grateful to you for that.

Audiobook narrator Scott LaBree brought my world to life in ways I never imagined. *The Spark & the Star* wouldn't have an audiobook if it wasn't for you. I will never forget the full-body chills I got the first time I heard your interpretation of the prologue. Thank you for bringing all your substantial passion and skill to this project (and for inadvertently helping me with the copyedit).

Brittany — my Scorpi — you are one talented lady. When I considered the idea of putting together a book trailer, I knew there was only one person for the job. Thank you for going down another wormhole with me.

My gratitude to Clint English for the beautiful and eye-catching cover and Jamie Whyte for the utterly inspired map of Sivka.

Thanks to James and Rachel at Dreamscape Coffee Co. in Woodstock for providing the fuel — coffee, pastries, advice, and good chat — to push this book over the finish line.

Finally, Mom and Dad — this book simply wouldn't be possible without you. Not only because of your generous support, but because you made me into a person who believed she could do this in the first place. Turns out the obsessive rewatching of *Anastasia* was good for something. Mom, thank you for instilling the love of all things fantasy, sci-fi and royal history in me at an impressionable age. Dad, thank you for having the audacity to ask me, "Why don't you try writing a book?"

ABOUT THE AUTHOR

Tess Hunter has lived in every timezone of the continental United States, and even on the coast of England. She currently resides in small-town Vermont. She has a B.A. in Film with a specialization in screenwriting, and a Master's in Professional Writing. She has worked in independent film and television, as a game writer, a journalist, and a barista. But her most important role is as a dog-mom to a high-maintenance chiweenie.

ABOUT THE INKSTERS

Founded during the pandemic so that three friends could talk about writing while wearing silly hats, The Inksters has grown from a virtual club to an online community and, now, a small publishing company. Join the journey by following us on TikTok and Instagram @theinksterswriting and signing up for our newsletter at theinksters.com.

www.ingramcontent.com/pod-product-compliance
Ingram Content Group UK Ltd.
Pitfield, Milton Keynes, MK11 3LW, UK
UKHW041632190726
13854UKWH00006B/2440

9 798994 973523